GAME ON

15 Stories of Wins, Losses, and Everything in Between

Edited by Laura Silverman

VIKING

VIKING

An imprint of Penguin Random House LLC, New York

First published in the United States of America by Viking Books,
an imprint of Penguin Random House LLC, 2022

This book is a work of fiction. Any references to historical events, real people, or real
places are used fictitiously. Other names, characters, places, and events are products of
the authors' imaginations, and any resemblance to actual events or places or persons,
living or dead, is entirely coincidental.

The publisher does not have any control over and does not assume any responsibility
for authors or third-party websites or their content.

For Competitive Hearts

Content Warnings for the following stories:

"One of the Good Ones"—*depictions of racism,
police brutality, and parental death*

"The Girl with the Teeth"—*self-harm
(biting, blood, and depersonalization)*

"The Plum Girls"—*death, violence, and alcoholism*

"Weeping Angels"—*drowning*

CONTENTS

GAME ON

LET IT SPIN

Sona Charaipotra

As I stare out the grimy New Jersey Transit window, the Raritan River glitters with snow, surprisingly beautiful as it follows the sun down into the city.

But it's so crowded I can barely breathe. God, just let me fall asleep.

The train roars toward the tunnel as I'm drifting off. But I am acutely aware of someone watching me. You know, the kind of staring that you can actually feel. I open my eyes.

Jason. Should have known.

I've been seeing him on the train the past couple of weeks. I heard he's at NYU, at Tisch, studying animation or production or something. Makes sense, considering. He's always had that penetrating way of looking at you, so you can't escape his gaze, familiar and ironclad.

It's just like Saachi's, that definitive take, done deal. The way she locks moments into place from her own perspective, sealing them up tight so there's no room for you to share your version of history. Believe me, I've tried.

I know he recognizes me, catching my eye, waiting for me to make the first move. Well, why should I? Why can't I be the one who's pursued for a change? But that's the way it goes with him. With everyone lately. And I'm over it.

At least it'll give me something to tell Saachi. I can't help the smirk settling on my face, unbidden.

So not worth it. I hear her voice in my head, clear and sharp, like it's been there all along. Like it's been there forever. It's been months since I've seen her. Probably my fault. But I can't help my grudge. Never could. Now dread roils in my stomach like bile, making me want to turn right back around on the next train to Jersey.

But there are some moments in life that we don't get to skip. Usually the ones that leave scars.

Saachi was sixteen when she stopped talking to me. Not literally talking, but you know. Having those deep, intimate conversations you have with someone who's loved you since you were six. I didn't even know why.

But I could feel it, deep down, in my fumbling to fix things. In the echoes of that dark, disturbing nightmare, the one that struck every so often, the one I tried to push down and away. Always the big, grand backyard I spent endless childhood hours in, the swing set abandoned, the ground frostbit. A black-and-white sky, pale flowers spilled out over the milky picket fence. A moment I've lived a million times in my head.

I still can't quite unravel what it means. Saachi's long dark pigtails flying—cheeks still chubby, eyes pale and bright—as she coasts by on that rusted red tricycle. The vivid crimson a warning, a reminder, stark against the muted dreamworld hues. Then the fall, the wheels spinning endlessly, vicious and cruel like the circle of life and death. And blood on the concrete, shocking but familiar as yesterday.

Somewhere in the distance, I hear it, the call of moments past, lost. The Bollywood beats muted in the background, that comforting clink of glass bangles and ice in crystal glasses. The roars of lions long since tamed, smoke filling the room as the men shed fatherhood and other responsibilities to cackle endlessly at jokes I still don't quite understand.

It's always that familiar, strange laughter that wakes me up in a cold sweat, clammy hands still grasping, helpless and unsure. It echoes in my ears, loud and rough, spilling secrets once forgotten.

When we first met, I was barely a person. More my big sister Raina's shadow, really, following her around as she led me by the hand, nearly disappearing in the presence of strangers. But Saachi saw me, claimed me, like no one else had—at least not at six—and it was like the first time I took a bath in the big tub, the bubbles enthralling and dangerous as it filled up and over, the delicious, looming threat of being swallowed whole.

That's exactly what happened. We'd barely moved into the little chocolate chip house on Library Place when Saachi's family—four doors down—invaded ours. Mama would spend endless hours whispering with Madhu Auntie over chai and pakore, reminiscing over lazy Delhi summers and complaining about day jobs. Our fathers split lawn work, Saachi's brother, Veer, bearing the brunt of it really, as Subhash and Mohan bonded over stock trades, cricket scores, and the riots and injustices happening thousands of miles away, across oceans and continents. They became a united front, an army of two, basically the same person. Maybe not physically, but the same spirit. The same broken, often comical English, the same urgency, the same happy, whiskey-soaked slur as they laughed late night over endless hands of blackjack and samosas.

It was only natural, then, for Raina and I to adopt Saachi, to make her the other sister.

While Raina developed an instant crush on Veer, who alternately tortured or ignored us, Saachi became our American ambassador, tasked with explaining everything from Halloween ("dress up, but make it scary") to boy bands and school politics.

Raina always wanted to be the boss of me, but Saachi was mine to lead—if just for a moment—before I became the one to follow. And she was lovely. How could I not adore her? Long, silky black hair, skin pale as moonlight, and she looked just like her father—the same fat, pink lips, melted chocolate

4

eyes, that small nose, and no jawline at all. Not a pretty little girl by any standard, yet entirely feminine. Delicate, like a doll.

A walking, talking, breathing doll that followed me around and hung on my every word. Being someone's sun is fun, at least for a little while. Though I knew I was hardly worthy of worship, with my little-boy looks, my hair cut close like Daddy's, and those awful toy guns, I let her believe in the awesome powers she thought I possessed, all the while ignoring her own. I wanted to be just like her. Even though I pretended the opposite.

It got to the point where it was Saachi-and-Raina-and-Ruby instead of Saachi and Raina-and-Ruby.

Not that we minded. Or at least I didn't.

Except when it came to boys.

Nearly sweet sixteen, and never been kissed. This was it. My chance. If I'd just take it.

For as long as I could remember, I'd had my heart set on Jason. Citrus and cinnamon, golden hair and ocean eyes. He wanted to be a lawyer and was on the debate team with Saachi, but also helped with the sets for drama, doing woodwork and painting. I'd volunteered to do makeup, so we hadn't quite connected. Yet.

That fall, the start of sophomore year, he volunteered to be in my chem lab group. And I knew. That he liked me back. Or could, possibly, if nudged. Maybe for once, I could actually be the one who made someone's heart beat just a little faster.

The way his eyes twinkled, the hiccupy way he laughed at my jokes in chem class, the pink climbing up and settling into his pale cheeks as he leaned close, our hands touching as we passed beakers and poured out the hydrogen peroxide and sulfur. Just this once, someone could actually like me back.

But Saachi was forever the third wheel, shushing us and scrawling in her notebook as Mrs. Greco droned, reminding us to measure carefully. Saachi was so focused on stimulus and reaction, talking about science the way I talked about movies or makeup. Smitten. And it totally distracted Jason from my inept attempts at flirting, foiling my every move.

That day—like every day—I'd missed the point of the experiment, of course, fixated instead on the roses our chem lab teacher handed out as she continued her lecture. "Careful to avoid the thorns," Greco warned as Jason and I worked to tape the flowers into the cups. Saachi focused on measuring out the sulfur, her eyes eager and faraway. They lit up with heat as she struck the match, a little cloud bursting forth. The petals drained of color, instant and shocking, as the smoldering scent of flowers burning filled my nose and mind.

"Quick," Saachi ordered, snapping me back to attention. "Dip them in the hydrogen peroxide. Now!"

Jason blushed as he watched her soak the pale roses in the liquid, their color reviving. Like bringing the dead back to life.

"Magic," he'd whispered then.

He didn't hear me when I agreed.

That night, I paced, worried. It was now or never. I had to make my move.

And I officially had nothing to wear. Wendy's party started in an hour, and I was nowhere near ready. In times like these, I'd wished more than ever that Raina and I could be like real sisters, the kind who shared clothes and shoes along with secrets. But I'd outgrown her—in every department except for boobs, of course—long ago, and it burned in me like a hardly secret shame.

I avoided full-length mirrors—didn't even keep one in my room. They revealed curves in all the wrong places. Pretty face, yup. And I knew how to work it, accentuate and highlight, to make myself stand out. But the rest of me? Sigh. Lately, I was all about oversize T-shirts or long, flowy dresses. Made me stick out like a sore thumb at school. Then again, so did everything else.

I rifled through the options on the bed, tossing aside dresses and rompers. Nothing was quite right. I had to be perfect. I was still pondering options when Raina knocked, pushing the door open before I could say "Come in." The way she always did.

"I thought you might look pretty in this."

Raina was holding up an embroidered blue kurti—one she'd bought in Agra when we visited the Taj Mahal last summer. She'd gone all swoony at the Taj, telling everyone and anyone that tragic-but-timeless love story of Shah Jahan and his wife Mumtaz Mahal, reputedly the most beautiful woman in the world. "Can you imagine?" she'd said over and over. "The whole thing cost more than thirty-two million rupees—and it took more than twenty thousand men to finish the job. If only someone loved me that much."

I rolled my eyes. Somebody, of course, meant Veer, even though she'd never said it aloud. Boring. I preferred my love stories straight out of Bollywood films—complete with song and dance. Though neither of us had any experience in that department ourselves. Tonight, that could change. *Would* change. I could feel it.

Raina held the shirt up to my chest. "The blue really pops against your skin," she said, nodding to herself in approval. "And I can do your nails. Gunmetal?"

I wished then that she would come with us to the party— even though she was a junior and Fridays meant SAT prep. Raina had never been one for parties and painting faces. She was too busy with college applications and the school paper. I opened my mouth to ask her again, but she shook her head, holding up the polish with a grin.

Half an hour later, I was ready. Half-tucked cobalt kurti and a too-short denim skirt Papa would hate, a paisley scarf belted through the loops. My hair cascaded in dark waves down my back, and I'd finally pulled off that deep kohl cat's eye I'd been practicing for weeks. My lips shined with a rosy gloss, lush and kissable.

Sitting on the edge of the bed, I wiggled my toes as Raina finished the last one, and they sparkled up at me, shimmering and perfect.

It was already cold for September, but to show off Raina's efforts, I'd have to wear those strappy silver chappal. I couldn't hide this art. Plus, they'd go well with the kurti.

"There." Raina grinned, satisfied. "You look beautiful."

I grimaced. Not really. But Raina always said so anyway.

"Are you excited?" she asked, a hint of longing in her voice.

My stomach rumbled. "I could go," I said, hopeful, "or I could stay. We could make popcorn and watch a movie."

Raina almost gave me an out. But then the doorbell rang. "That's Saachi," she announced, standing. "You better move."

Ever the chaperone, Saachi frowned, an eyebrow arched as I walked up the driveway. "You look, uh, nice," she said, taking in my strappy chappal and the bright blue of the kurti.

She was wearing too-crisp jeans and a black button-down top she might have borrowed from Madhu Auntie, along with the same black leather loafers she wore to the endless debate meets she made us sit through. A mini-adult, dressed for the office. I didn't say a word. It was the first time I'd managed to convince her to come with me, and her company was the only reason Papa had said I could go at all. "Come on, we're late."

The sun was settling in as the two of us walked to Wendy's house, the sky blazing orange and pink, with undertones of purple taking over. Raina's absence rattled like forgotten keys, making me want to run back and call the whole thing off. But we were there before I could hesitate. A deep bass thrummed low and heavy, beckoning us toward the house, fairy lights crisscrossing the dusk like stars as we headed toward the backyard, lured by the scent of meat and chlorine.

Saachi paused, turning to face me, her mouth firm and serious. Another proclamation, I could hear it coming. She'd been looking at me like that since we were six, like she was my mom about to warn me not to cause a scene, and not the actual baby of our little trio. "I think we should make a pact," she said, determined. "If either of us feels uncomfortable, we leave."

It was just a party. A big party. Maybe a life-changing one. If we ever actually made it inside. I sighed and nodded. But it wasn't enough.

"Pinky swear," Saachi said, smiling, and for a minute, I saw a flash of that big, gap-tooth grin that made me love her in the first place.

I lifted my little finger, a streak of silver glinting at its tip. "Pinky swear," I promised.

Wendy's house was huge. The party spilled out from the cavernous living room into an endless yard, benches circling firepits, and what seemed like fifty kids gathered in bunches, roasting marshmallows and making s'mores. Saachi stuck close as I made my way through the crowd, sucking her teeth as I chatted up cheerleaders, frowning at the artsy crew, and bolting when I found my people, the theater kids. But she always stayed in my sightlines, chaperoning even as she settled in for a long chat with Marie from the debate team, their animated arm-waving pausing occasionally so she could eye-spy me as I blew through an overdone burger and dipped into the obviously spiked fruit punch. I'd had wine coolers before, and so had she, courtesy of our dads, to be honest. But this was different, heady and thick, pungent at first, but then it went down too easy, maybe. I had one, two, three, to Saachi's zero, her frown getting deeper and deeper as she took notes in her head.

I was lost for a minute or ten, talking about the rumored Broadway revival of *Rent* with some of the theater kids, when I felt it. The electricity of his presence sent gooseflesh up my arms, a flutter of hope down into my belly. Jason, laughing, near the barbecue, that familiar hiccupy chuckle, like something had truly delighted him.

And I knew before I saw them that it would be Saachi standing there, a bit too close, eyes bright as she looked at him grinning down, the little rose in his hand. An offering. She smiled up at him, those endless lashes fluttering demure and seductive—in a way I couldn't ever be, no matter how I rehearsed it. He leaned down, whispered something into her hair, and she faltered a moment, her eyes searching, then laughed. Seeing them standing there together locked everything into place, made her version of the story the truth, no matter what I had to say about it. The way it always was. The way it would always be.

I didn't stay to see whether she took the rose.

I needed to get lost. As the air cooled and the crowd thinned, birthday girl Wendy—already stealing scenes as the Nurse in the fall production of *Romeo and Juliet* as a sophomore, and therefore my idol—wolf whistled to get everyone's attention.

She held up a green glass bottle labeled s. PELLEGRINO. Fancy water. But it was empty. "All right, kiddies," she said, a smug smirk spreading across her face. "It's time for fun and games."

Maybe that's what I needed. Wendy shuffled the pack into the house, the music turned down low, the bass still vibrating beneath. There were maybe twenty of us squished into the living room, and for a moment I panicked, learning to swim without a floaty, as the crowd gathered in a circle. I was pushed forward, so I took a seat on the floor with the rest of them, my eyes searching for Saachi.

She stood frozen in the doorway, her face wary, her eyes hunting for me. She frowned when they found me, motioning for me to come back outside. Then Jason plopped down next to me, his hand landing close to mine on the floor, the rose crushed in his palm, apparently rejected. But all I could smell was sulfur. I tried not to flinch as he touched my pinky, the silver glint of polish streaked over it. "Neat."

I pulled my hand away, the heat climbing up from my chest to my throat to my cheeks. This was it, the moment I'd plotted for days, weeks, months. The moment I'd imagined a thousand times in my head. But it was inside out, lopsided. Not how I imagined it would be, floating and incandescent.

It was too loud, too crowded, too forced. I looked back toward the doorway, hoping to bolt, but Saachi was gone. Somehow, though, I could still feel her eyes on me. There were snickers as she settled into a small space across the circle, the grimace giving her away as she stared me down. She wasn't the only one. She was flanked by Andrea Wood and Lia Chao, Jason's ex, who rolled her eyes in irritation. She wasn't done with him yet, clearly. Saachi flashed me a tight smile, and my stomach roiled with bile, butterflies plotting an escape.

I looked down at the center of the space between us, where Wendy placed the glass bottle. "Birthday girl goes first," she sing-songed, already drunk and happy. "Round and round it goes, where it stops, nobody knows."

I couldn't take my eyes off the green of the bottle as it swirled, dizzying, spinning the earth in its orbit, deciding fates.

It stopped on Matt Kwon, to hoots and hollers from the crowd. Wendy leaned into the center and kissed him, a painless peck, no big deal, like she did it all the time. Matt spun next, a doofy grin on his face. A game, easy, effortless, meaningless.

The butterflies surged and swarmed. Maybe I was the only one freaking out. Maybe it was the alcohol. Maybe it was Jason. Maybe it was Saachi, watching, her eyes blinking hard and fast, the creases in her forehead betraying her nerves. I'd made her come. And she stayed for me. The panic on her face was clear, the beads of sweat dripping down her cheeks like tears.

I could hear her heart racing, despite the music, the crowd, the distance. Mine echoed its frantic beat, I knew from experience. And still the bottle spun, ready to claim its next victim. If it landed on Saachi, she'd never forgive me.

But it didn't. It landed on Lia, who gave Matt a quick kiss, her eyes more focused on Jason, indifferent, than Matt's smirk as their lips met. Lia spun next, careful and deliberate, her pout a prayer as the bottle began its whirl, the glass clinking on the dark bamboo floors, the glint of green mesmerizing and seductive. Maybe she was owed a miracle, because I couldn't believe it when it stopped on Jason.

It was like Lia planned it, the way the slow grin spread across her face like a strawberry-glossed stain. But Jason's stance was firm and unyielding as he offered a cheek, cold as she caught him straight on the mouth. Wendy turned up the music as Andrea and a few others whooped, enjoying the show.

Then it was Jason's turn to spin. He whirled the bottle in the center of the floor and it seemed to go forever, round and round and round.

I prayed that it would stop on me. And prayed that it wouldn't. It didn't.

It stopped between Andrea and Saachi, who looked about

ready to throw up. Andrea, vicious as always, preyed on Saachi's unease by picking up the bottle and facing it right at her. "Your turn, Saachi," she said, her nasal tones squawking upward with glee and contempt.

I should have stepped in, said something, defused it or whatever. This was not Saachi's scene at all. She'd only come because I made her. But it was happening again. I watched Jason, sitting next to me, his hand on the floor still just inches from mine, his eyes all lit and hopeful as he stared at the girl I called my best friend.

In that moment, I knew without a doubt exactly how wrong I'd been. All those times I thought he might like me, cracking jokes and making faces behind Greco's back, they hadn't been for me at all. They had been for her. She wasn't the one intruding. I was.

Saachi stood abruptly, annoyed, her eyes on me as she announced, "I'm not playing."

She looked across the circle, at Jason, then at me, her eyes expectant, waiting for an endless moment. But I couldn't fall in line, give in to her version of the story. Not this time. This time, I had to make it my own.

So I didn't move, even though every cell in my body wanted to. Even though I pinky swore.

Saachi's face fell a moment, then she nodded, disappearing quickly into the crowd without another word.

Jason looked slightly crushed—the way I felt, those

butterflies smothered in sunlight—but just for a second. Then he smiled, eyes hopeful, and said, "Guess I'll just spin again."

I knew I had to get up. To find Saachi, like I'd promised, and head straight home. To put it all behind me. Behind us.

But I couldn't. Jason was going to kiss someone that night. I willed it to be me.

I watched the bottle spin, spin, spin. And when it stopped, finally, it sealed my fate. Landing halfway between me and Jason. Allowing us to meet in the middle.

"Are you in, or are you out?" Wendy asked, already bored. In her mind, Saachi and I were the same, a matched set, like all the brown kids.

Jason closed his eyes and leaned in toward me and so I did the same. I could smell whatever spicy cologne he'd borrowed from his brother, and somewhere underneath it, that familiar clean lemoniness of his soap. Up close, he was all freckles peeking through the fade of a summer tan and the cherry burn on his ears, forever a giveaway. But then there were his lips, soft and salty as they brushed mine. The kiss was over before I even had time to absorb it. I opened my eyes and a million people were staring and maybe whispering or snickering or even laughing. But in that moment, I didn't care. Because I'd just had my first kiss. With Jason McIntyre.

The game was a blur after that, but thankfully, the bottle didn't stop on me or Jason again. I spent the rest of it looking down, and when he disappeared halfway through to go get a soda, I was glad. Even though my hands crushed the rose he'd left behind.

I'd kissed him, finally. But now I didn't know what to do with myself. Eventually, I got up, too, knowing I should go hunt for Saachi. Hoping Jason hadn't found her first.

I looked in the kitchen and in the backyard and in the living room again. Then I accepted what I already knew. Saachi was gone. And I, Ruby Arora, had broken my pinky promise. And I hated myself, because I knew, deep down, that it had been worth it.

It took me more than a year to work up the courage to tell Saachi about kissing Jason the night of the party. I still had the rose, pressed between the pages in my journal, sulfur-scented and rancid. When I finally confessed, she shrugged. Like it wasn't anything at all. Like it just didn't matter.

But it did. It wasn't really about the kiss. It wasn't really about Jason.

It was bigger than that, the damage done.

Because that's when *forever* ended, and I don't know how to get it back.

That September night, that's when the spiral started. Even though I pretended it was just the same. That nothing could really change it. Us.

It had already been forever since we'd shared one of those nights—countless as kids—when the three of us would lay tucked all in a row the wrong way across Saachi's droopy queen bed, sharing secrets. My hot-pink toes would hang off one end, while Raina's little legs were still inches from the edge. Saachi always insisted on being in the middle, even though the mattress sagged and both of us would roll in onto her. "Stop squishing me," she'd squeal, husky tones softening. But we knew she loved it, being at the center of our little universe. Being there with the sisters she was never meant to have.

I missed the seconds before sleep when our whispers would turn to books (which I hated) or boys (which Saachi hated) or where we'd be when we were eighteen or twenty or thirty-two. When the gleaming future infinitely promised that, no matter what happened, we'd face it all together. Because that's what sisters do.

Until they don't.

Saachi was sixteen when she stopped talking to me. And it was all my fault.

For the longest time, I pretended I didn't know why. But of course I did, somewhere in my head, because how could I not? I claimed not to notice. The slow unwinding, the way fates are decided.

First, I blamed it on distance. An unexpected move. Saachi changing schools. The space between us growing too big to close. Then there were missed calls, texts left unanswered. It started as small silences and little dismissals—casual *yup*s, *uh-huh*s, and *see you later*s. Slowly, slowly, until she disappeared completely, like she never existed at all.

Which, of course, wasn't true. I'd hear her and Raina on the phone, whispering late into the night, my sister's voice hushed and urgent, her bedroom door closing as I walked past.

I could never bring myself to ask. About what happened. Because deep down, I knew why. But I didn't know how to explain myself. I gave her no reason to forgive me.

I know what I did, the damage it caused. And she never said a word. Not to me. Not to Raina. She kept that hurt a secret. Our secret.

But secrets have a way of spinning, of unwinding everything, picking up momentum until there's nothing you can do stop them. Secrets have a way of taking up space, leaving gaping wounds too big to ever really heal.

The train pulls out of the darkness and lurches to a stop, shaking me out of memory.

"Final stop, Penn Station, New York."

I look up, and Jason's still staring. Thinking back, it doesn't make much sense. She didn't even want him. She never wanted anybody. But there was that small moment, when he tried to hand her the rose. I wonder if it could have been different. If it weren't for me.

When I stand, he's already by my side, taller now, his hair darker, his eyes bluer. He smiles down at me, too familiar and friendly, as he walks me out into the chaos of the city. But I'll leave him here with smiles and small talk.

I have to. Can't risk it again.

Or maybe I can. I'm already the villain in this story, after all.

"Guess who I ran into today," I'll say to her. "You'll never believe."

She'll cut me off. "Listen, sweetie, can I call you back?" she'll say in that too-bright way that makes me feel like I'm a spoiled six-year-old. "I'm kind of busy."

"Um, okay. Maybe we can get dinner tonight or something?"

"Maybe," she'll say, like it's the most ridiculous thing she's ever heard. "I'll call you later."

She won't.

Half an hour later, as my cab pulls up to the innocuous-looking redbrick building, all I can think of is the way she used to look with those long braids, long gone. I pretend to know her well. But it took all my strength to come here today. I give the cabbie twelve bucks, gather my coat, bag, and courage, slam the door shut behind me. Up the escalator, and then to the elevator. As the door opens onto the seventh floor, the medicinal odor of sick people fills my nostrils.

A man in a smock and socks walks up and down the halls, his IV following him around on a trolley. "Working out," he says to me, grinning and lifting an arm to show off his dilapidated muscles. I try not to stare.

Saachi's mother rescues me at reception.

"Throat cancer, serious," Madhu Auntie tells me, and my parents know. Raina does, too. Always knew, apparently, although she didn't tell me until this week. Until it was too late. "They keep saying he's terminal," Auntie says. "I think they're right." She babbles on about treatments and medications, timelines and schedules.

"Can I see him?" I ask, stunning her into silence. Like she'd forgotten I'm here. She ponders my request for a long moment, and I'm afraid she might say no. And afraid she might say yes. I can't afford to be shunned from this moment. I can't afford to be shut out of Saachi's life again.

"One thing before we go," Madhu Auntie says, standing. "I need you to be positive." She looks at me, her eyes filling for the first time since I got there. "It's just—it's bad."

Room 717. Saachi's father, Mohan Uncle, lies in a hospital bed, the front part elevated to simulate sitting, half a dozen machines and IVs and tubes weaving in and out of his body. A catheter cuts into his throat, as if it, not cancer, might kill him. He's surprised by my sudden presence, clearly, but tries to hide it.

I barely recognize him. His head is swollen with fluid from the IVs and infection. He can no longer open his eyes. His arms are bruised black and blue from needles. The skin hangs loose from his bones. Machines monitor every breath and heartbeat. His big, fat mouth—Saachi's mouth—is deflated. So is his spirit.

He knows I'm there, and I know he doesn't want me there. No father wants their child to see them like that.

"Ruby," he announces, pleased with the recognition, his

voice shaky and shattered by the catheter. "Aaja, beta. Come give me a hug. How are you doing?"

I walk over to the bed, aware of Auntie's eyes on me. I lean down, tentative, careful not to crush him. "I'm good." My voice a whisper. "How—I. Will you be okay?" Blood races through me, throbbing and loud, like I might explode. Or at least have a heart attack. Thank god I'm already in the hospital. "I didn't know," I add, shaken. "I'm so sorry."

I don't mean to cry, but it's inevitable. Mohan Uncle flashes me a version of that mischievous smile—the one I remember from all those hazy summer days, when Papa and Uncle would plot secret water balloon fights or taunt us about arranging marriages. The grin shoots all the way up to his eyes, crinkled with age and faded sunshine. "Don't you worry, acha? I'm in good hands here."

Madhu Auntie nods, as if this is the story and they're sticking to it.

Saachi's not there. "She hadn't eaten all day, so I sent her to the McDonald's," her mother tells me, exhaustion wearing her thin, hollowing her cheeks as if the cancer is eating her, too. "She'll be happy to see you."

I'm not so sure.

As I walk the block from the hospital to McDonald's, the sun beats down as cheerfully as it did when I was six. It seems disrespectful.

For a long while, I watch her through the window, a muted

version of herself. When I walk through the door, she will be surprised to see me after so long—forever really—then turn on that too-bright smile.

"The doctors say he'll be out by Monday," she'll say cheerfully, sanitizing her life for me, the way you do for strangers. "They've taken him off the chemo, but they might put him back on after six weeks."

She'll tell me that it's okay that she's missed so much school, she was ahead anyway. "Maybe by next semester I'll transfer to Yale . . ."

She'll talk about the sun glaring down as if it isn't January.

I walk into McDonald's, order a Coke, watch her through the corner of my eye. Her hair has grown out, longer than I remember, and her pale skin shows signs of stress.

Her eyes glisten when they finally meet mine, unsurprised. Like she knew I would come. Like she's been waiting all along.

"Ruby," she whispers, walking over and collapsing into my arms.

And for once I don't bother her with words.

HELL WEEK

Amanda Joy

YOU'D THINK COACH CASTILLO IS ABOUT TO ANNOUNCE A SUR-prise team trip to Paris from the way she's beaming. But I—and every other returning member of varsity—know better. Today is the first day of our final week of cheer camp, which can only mean one thing.

Coach claps—not a gentle slapping of hands, but a cheer clap: hands cupped so the sound echoes around the Fieldhouse like low-grade thunder—and the scattered conversation comes to a grinding halt.

We sit arranged in a semicircle. The few girls who are still stretching all pop their heads up at Coach's clap. They tuck their legs underneath them, listening dutifully. We've already done warm-ups outside—on Mondays we do drills running up and down the bleachers—and no one wants to risk being sent back into the August sun.

A twinkle of delight shines in her eyes. Coach Castillo is like a combination of Ms. Frizzle and Beyoncé. Her long, straightened dark brown hair is shot through with copper highlights. She's by far the most glamorous teacher I know, with her matching gold link jewelry and daily full face of makeup. On the other hand, the rhinestoned football earrings dangling to her chin are more camp than glam. Every day she wears a different red-and-gold outfit; today it's an Adidas tracksuit with what must be custom gold stripes.

She launches into a speech I could probably give myself by now. "Most of the upperclassmen know what I am about to announce, but I hope none of you have spoiled the surprise for those new to varsity. Today is your first day of Hell Week." Coach pauses for dramatic effect. I swear she thrives on our fear. "I know you've been working hard all month, but this last week of camp will undoubtedly be the hardest. As it should be, right, seniors?"

Dutifully, me and nine other seniors shout, "Right, Coach."

"Right." Her smile deepens, and those bejeweled footballs bounce with the movement. "Welcome to Hell Week."

My eyes slide past Coach to where Angel sits. Her narrow face is turned up, listening like I should be. Instead I take the opportunity to watch her. My ex-friend (ex-ish? Can you call someone an ex when you ghosted them? Does ghosting an ex make?) and teammate, Angel Arceneaux. Her long arms rest atop her knees; even folded in on herself, she manages to look lanky. Silver bracelets, a smart watch, and half a dozen hair ties cover her wrists.

Before I can pull myself away, her eyes flick to me. Angel's eyes are big and that perfect honeyed-brown shade you can see right through. Luckily the weight of her gaze is somewhat diminished by the distance. Still I'm stuck staring openmouthed for a beat too long, cataloging the details: the high cheekbones, the ever-present dimple at the corner of her mouth, and the soft divot in her chin.

So long that she arches an eyebrow, mouth twisting into a frown. I duck my head and focus again on Coach's words.

"Last week we finalized stunt groups for the season," she says, scanning our faces.

I can't help but scoff at that. *We* didn't finalize anything. Coach rebuffed my requests to switch stunt groups all summer. I even said I would work with the few freshmen and sophomores on the squad and get them up to speed. All of which she ignored and put me right back into my group from last year. With Angel. It's completely unreasonable.

Coach continues, "Each stunt group will have the privilege of performing their skills for a panel of outgoing seniors, who will help me choose the center group. Today is day one. On the odd days of the week, you will practice a different skill. On the even days, you'll perform. Now, I want to see showmanship. Try your best to make your performance as safe and as entertaining as possible. Emphasis on safe, folks. I don't want to see any injuries before our season even begins. At the end of the week, on Saturday, I'll tally your scores and announce the winners. There's one new aspect to this competition."

At this, we all lean forward. I made it onto varsity sophomore year once I finally mastered my back tuck—the standing, no-hands backflip required to make this team—and
in my first two years, Hell Week has always been the same.
In the mornings, Coach works us to the bone, making sure
our jumps are high and our cheers are crisp. In the after-
noons, we stunt until our legs are noodles and we're ready
to collapse.

"You've all been wondering when I will choose this year's
captain." No one speaks, but I can feel our collective interest
surge. That's about the only thing everyone has been talking
about since camp began three weeks ago. Most years Coach
would've announced the captain on the first day of cheer camp,
so they could help her run our conditioning sessions. But there
hasn't been a word about it, and we're all too chickenshit to
ask. Up until regionals last year, I was certain either Angel
or I would become captain, but apparently neither of us was
impressive enough to earn the spot.

Which, if I'm being honest, is kind of a relief. Last year,
I wanted that recognition, simply for the accomplishment.
Our team is competitive—we've won state two years in a row
and went down to Orlando for nationals—and being captain
would look great to all the cheer programs I'm looking at for
college. But when I think about being saddled with the innu-
merable responsibilities of football season while I'm worried
about my applications and keeping my A average, it doesn't

sound pleasant. But I know from the look on Angel's face as she stares up at Coach she still wants it.

"This competition isn't just about your spot on the mat. Our top group will be your measuring stick and guides; as our top flyer will help me coach the rest of the flyers, our bases and our backspots will do the same. But more importantly, I'll be choosing one of them for captain."

Murmurs begin to surge through the team. I turn to Cyerra, another member of my stunt group and my closest friend on the team, who smiles and bumps my shoulder with hers. Cyerra and I could be sisters; we have the same brown skin, upturned dark brown eyes, and dense curls, though Cy's ends are bleached copper now. "Don't look so terrified," she says. "We would've gotten the top spot last year if we were seniors."

"I'm not afraid. I'm . . . excited," I whisper, trying to match her positive vibes with my own and failing. The thought of working with Angel all week is anxiety inducing. If my gawking earlier is any indication, I'll reach unforeseen heights of embarrassment by the end of the day.

Cy peers at me, a question in her eyes. Luckily Coach isn't quite done.

"Questions? No?" Coach Castillo claps again, her slicked-back ponytail bobbing with the effort. "Great. Get those mats down and stretch for jumps. Afterward, we'll warm up your preps and extensions."

She retrieves her clipboard and neon-yellow Nalgene (plastered with vinyl stickers of our mascot, Victory Viking, who's basically a Lady Thor cosplay gone slightly askew), and we are dismissed. I wish Coach had let that speech go on another ten minutes, because I can already feel dread creeping in.

Hell Week is nothing new. This week is most stressful for flyers like me, since we have to put our literal lives in the rest of our stunt groups' hands, but I've been cheering since I was seven. Flying since ten. Being tossed into the air a couple hundred times this week doesn't scare me—in fact, I long for that breathless, weightless feeling—but when there's any discord in a stunt group, things get messy. I won't forgive myself if my issues with Angel ruin this week for us.

I turn, intending to confess part of this to Cyerra, and realize she's already up. I'm the only one still sitting on the floor. Everyone else has already made it to the other end of the Fieldhouse where the rolled-up mats are stored.

Damn it.

The Fieldhouse is ours alone today, since freshman and JV are practicing outside. It's huge, half as long as the football field, with locker rooms, an unused (and some say haunted) sauna, and several coaching offices attached. The mats hug the wall, like giant Fruit Roll-Ups.

I climb to my feet and jog over to find Cyerra and Kristina trying to shove one of the mats onto its side. Angel stands apart, tapping the touchscreen of her watch. Typical Angel, always texting someone. She's one of those people who will never let anyone catch a glimpse of the home screen. It drove me crazy last year. It took me way too long to realize I was just jealous of whoever was receiving those texts.

I stop at her side. Of course she pretends not to notice me. We've exchanged maybe . . . twenty words all camp, and I'm pretty sure all twenty were when she unkindly corrected my jump form in front of everyone. (Angel is the team perfectionist when it comes to her specialties—jumps and tumbling—but it's not particularly soothing knowing she would've said the same to anyone else.)

We're all wearing the same warm-ups—a pair of red-and-gold shorts and matching, lightly bedazzled tank tops—and even though my weird staring earlier should've been enough, it's hard not to look at Angel. I can admit that at least. The shorts are slung low on her hips. She always orders a size up, so they don't ride up unbecomingly like on the rest of us. She shifts and I catch a glimpse of what appears to be a tattoo on her rib cage—expressly against the rules unless completely concealed in uniform—and remember she turned eighteen a few weeks ago. Her long black hair is wound up in her usual two French braids, but a good three inches at the back of her head has been shaved, which is new. And the only makeup she's wearing is a long swipe of black eyeliner and strawberry Carmex that I can smell from here. She's nearly ten inches taller than me, so I can't exactly hide my appraisal with my chin in the air. Still, Angel doesn't acknowledge my presence, which is not new.

It still stings though, and at this point, I have to admit I want her attention. That must be what prompts me to say, "I doubt Coach will make you captain if you're texting all week."

A pause. Her dark brows draw together, and her mouth opens and falls shut. Not a single word. Not that I think aggression is going to soothe the tension between us, but still, I expected something.

"You could help them, you know," I say finally. That has to be neutral enough.

"Or *you* could help them, you know, Ariana," Angel parrots, without looking up from the screen.

Here's the thing: Angel almost never calls me that. She says my name doesn't suit me, whatever that means. Usually she uses my last name, Simmons, or Ari, like everyone else. So I know she said it to provoke me.

Don't take the bait. Don't take the bait. Do not take—

"Oh, so you were waiting for me? So we can both help?" I ask, in this fake sugary-sweet tone designed specifically to grate on Angel's nerves. I wipe my wet palms on my shorts, suddenly glad my annoyance is masking my nerves.

Finally—*finally*—she looks up and with a humorless smirk says, "Yeah. I was waiting for you, Ariana." Like I'm the last person who she'd ever be waiting on.

Which is fair, because I spent the last four months ignoring her texts without any explanation. And since I'm not prepared to do any explaining today, I trudge up to Cy and Kristina and help them roll the mat onto its side. It takes a minute, but eventually Angel follows.

"So what's up with you and Angel?" Cyerra asks a few hours later during our lunch break. She passes the bag of fries back to me. Her cloud of coils is pulled up into a high pony that reaches the car's ceiling.

I stop mid-bite and scan the parking lot. We're sitting in her ten-year-old Prius named Dorothy, sharing the two-burger special from Pop's. I dig into the greasy bag and shove a few fries into my mouth. Not exactly the best fuel for three more hours of cheer camp, but these fries are one of the ten wonders of our Chicago suburb. They're impossible to resist when Pop's is just a two-minute drive from campus. "Not sure what you're talking about," I lie.

"Listen, Ari," Cy says. "We've got exactly fifteen more minutes of lunch. Just long enough for you to spill."

I decide there's no use in keeping it to myself at this point. Maybe Cy can help. "So you know how I've always had a thing—"

"For Angel? That's old news, keep going."

I roll my eyes. Cyerra knows I'm bi. She's one of the few people I told last year. I'm not exactly shocked that I've been so transparent, but it's not the best feeling, realizing what you thought was covert pining is actually hella obvious. "Well, last year we sort of . . . stopped hanging out. I may have ignored her texts all summer. Possibly."

"Really, Ari?" Cyerra groans. This is yet another entry into the file marked ARIANA SABOTAGES HERSELF. I don't know why she's even surprised. *I'm* not. "Did you at least have a good reason?"

"Uh, is my mom taking special notice of my crush on Angel good enough?"

She hadn't just noticed. My mom started setting up family gatherings whenever I had plans to hang out with Angel. She asked pointed questions about Angel's parents and who was supervising us at her house—like two-seventeen-year-olds need a chaperone—and I'm pretty sure she checked my text messages.

My parents aren't usually strict, but suddenly last year when Angel and I kept hanging out long after the season ended, I was given a curfew. One they only seemed to care about when I was with Angel. It didn't take too long to realize what my mom was afraid of. Ever since I got caught kissing Felicia Downey in fifth grade, it's been this way. As soon as I get close to a girl who isn't obviously straight—or, god forbid, who's an out lesbian like Angel—my mom finds a way to drive a wedge between us. Like if she just keeps me away from every queer person on earth, I'll be free of temptation. Free to be the perfect preacher's kid they've raised me to be.

It's all so ridiculous and silly, but my parents aren't about to accept anything else. I try not to think about it too much. I'll be free to date whoever I want next year at college. That way I've got at least a good four years before I have to tell them anything. Maybe by then I won't be so attached to their image of me, and I'll be okay with disappointing them. Until then, I'm half in hiding. My friends know—I even told Angel last year—but that's about it. Sometimes I feel sick about the fact that I can hide so easily, like it means that I'm actually straight and just pretending. That's what you learn in church. The wide spectrum of sexuality is just sin confusing you because there's only one right way to be. I know that isn't true, but it's hard to completely clear those ideas from your head.

Cyerra shifts in her seat and passes me the fries again. The low afternoon sun makes her bronze skin gleam. Even after a few hours of doing jumps, each hair on her head is still in place, her edges coaxed into patterns like breaking waves. "I think that's a perfectly good excuse . . . but you should tell Angel."

"Umm, I don't think so. Why tell her my parents hate her? That'll just make her uncomfortable. I'll find some other way to make it up to her." My favorite thing about Angel is that she's fearless; she tumbles like she fully expects to take off in flight. And she'll confront anyone over her friends. Most insults roll right off her, but I refuse to let my parents' shitty opinions hurt her.

"Are you sure you want to do that?" Cy asks, her nose wrinkled in disapproval. "Another lie told is another secret to keep up with. And if you really do like Angel—"

"Cy, do you really want me disturbing our fragile peace over a crush? We have to see each other almost every day. Angel's probably talking to someone anyway." And she deserves someone who isn't afraid to show their parents who they really are. "You must've noticed her checking her texts between each stunt this morning."

"Actually I didn't. And what peace? You and Angel spent half the morning glaring at each other. And you do realize you're a terrible liar, right? She's going to find out eventually."

"Yeah, well, eventually could be a month from now." My hair is up, like Cy's, but much more haphazard. I tug at one of the rogue curls that has slipped from my ponytail.

"Or it could be tomorrow. If we get through today without any trouble, you can keep your secrets. If not, find some way to fix this." She crumples the now empty bag from Pop's and tosses it behind her into the fast food graveyard that is Cyerra's backseat. "Angel's not the only one of us who wants to be captain."

So Cy had noticed Angel during Coach's speech, too. At this point, it looks like I'm the only one who doesn't want to compete for captain. If I let my feelings for Angel ruin this for them, Cyerra might forgive me, but I doubt she'll forget it. I can't let my mess get in the way. Before we return to the

Fieldhouse, I promise Cyerra to stop picking fights. For now, it's the best I can do.

After lunch, we finally start practicing our stunts. We start off with a few preps—where the bases hold me up at chest level—and try out our extension. It's nearly as smooth as it was last season. Cyerra, bless her, does most of the communicating, and I try not to fixate on Angel's warm fingers on my waist.

Our first dustup begins after Coach comes over to warn us off trying difficult stunts too soon.

As soon as she's out of earshot, Angel rounds on us. "So let's come up with a plan. We shouldn't have any problem showing them up." She points a thumb over her left shoulder, at the nearby group. Their flyer, Jayde, is a freshman who hasn't even started high school yet, but I know her from the gym where I used to do gymnastics. She's tiny, doll-like, with perfect dark brown skin and her hair in hundreds of micro-braids. She's beaming like this is her first football game, but their stunt is wobbly.

I open my mouth, about to call out the obvious problem. But Cyerra beats me to it, shouting at the two bases to stand closer together.

"But," Angel continues, eyes sliding to the right, "those overachievers? That'll be tough." The other senior flyer, Elena Blume, is already up in a one-leg stunt. Her thick, dark hair hangs down her back in a rope-like braid; unlike Jayde, Elena's dark blue eyes are tight and focused. We aren't even practicing liberties until Wednesday. Showboat.

Angel goes on, "We need something fairly simple, but strong enough for Coach to remember it. And it has to be solid. If we drop our stunt tomorrow, that's it."

"We just need an interesting transition. And to throw it perfectly," Cyerra adds, practical as always.

"Roundoff into extension, cradle down," I suggest, throwing out a variation of a stunt we did last year. Then we'd done back handsprings into the stunt. It had taken us a while to learn, but once we had it, it was solid.

It's a perfectly reasonable suggestion, but Angel turns to me the moment the words are out of my mouth and asks, "You think you can manage that? Out of shape and everything? It's not like it was easy last year."

Seriously? Out of shape?

Uh, yes, I worked at Zarlengo's over the summer and developed a nightly craving for their blend of soft serve and blue raspberry Italian ice, but I also run five mornings a week for Kristina, Cyerra, and Angel's benefit. I'm not like Jayde, or even Elena, who are both lithe and elegant. By comparison, I'm curvier. Still petite enough to fly for now, but my frame just isn't small enough to continue flying in college. I refuse to chase a body type that's not meant for me, and Coach hasn't replaced me with someone smaller because I'm *good*.

And I'm good because I love it. I love flying because it's a leap of faith every single time. I love flying because it's difficult and it makes me feel brave. And I love that you can't say we're not badasses when you see a basket toss. Whatever you think of cheer, no one can deny we're athletes when you see a stunt go up with perfect precision and grace.

"Number one, I'm not out of shape, or whatever that means," I say, taking a step toward Angel. "And please, correct me if I'm wrong, but I wasn't the one who took two weeks to get the counts right on that stunt last year. That was someone else. Are you sure *you* can manage it, Angel?"

Angel practically bares her teeth. When she takes a half step toward me, I catch the smell of her strawberry lip balm. It hits me like the slap of cold water on my face. For a split second it's hard to remember what we're even arguing about.

Apparently my dazed expression throws her, because her anger quickly turns to irritation. "Whatever, Simmons," she says. "As we're all so in shape, you should have your full down ready for tomorrow, right?"

A full down is just one twist in the air after the pop. Which I can do in my sleep. (Okay, okay, not in my sleep.) But like everything else, I have barely practiced in months. Kristina and Cyerra fall silent, watching the two of us. Cyerra's hands are curled into fists, and only at the sight of them do I remember my promise. Even though I didn't start this, I can end it. So I just shrug. "Whatever you need, *Captain.*"

Angel just stares at me hard. She looks disappointed, like she wanted the fight to go on. Or like she wanted to be the one who ended it. Cyerra finally breaks the silence. "We're settled on a plan then. Less bickering, and more practicing please."

Angel and I don't speak for the rest of the day, but I still catch her giving me that same hard stare a few times. I wish I was brave enough to meet it, but instead I keep my eyes to the floor.

The next afternoon, we're all gathered to present our first stunt. A long table has been set up in the middle of the Fieldhouse. Coach Castillo sits in the center, with Coach Sherri at her right and Melissa Didion, our choreographer, at her left.

Our dynamic has only marginally improved since yesterday. Angel and I have barely spoken today, but at least we haven't argued. Cyerra begged me to talk to Angel during lunch, but once I pointed out the possibility of my apology turning into another fight, she let up.

I put on my most confident smile as we rise to replace the second stunt group. The underclassmen had gone first, and since both groups simply presented a cheer with their stunt incorporated, I'm not worried about being shown up. We're offering something competition worthy.

I recognize the two former teammates, Elise and Mara,

who will be judging us; both are going on to cheer in college this fall. The rest of the stunt groups, along with the JV and freshman squads, sit cross-legged on the floor to our right. In total, there's just under seventy-five of us gathered—our squad of thirty, along with the twenty students on JV and another twenty from the freshman squad. They beat on the ground as Cyerra approaches Coach Castillo, seated at the center of the table.

"What is your group presenting?" Coach asks once the beating quiets down.

"We're showing a roundoff into an extension with a full down, Coach," Cyerra says.

There are some whoops from our small audience, but Coach just nods and asks Jacob Meyer—one of three guys on the team—to act as our front spot.

My heart hammers in my chest as I step forward. I give my brightest game-worthy smile, which soothes my nerves somewhat. We're not at a game. This is practice, and though there's pressure to perform, it's nothing like a competition or field show.

Cyerra, Kris, and Angel start in their usual positions. I'm standing fifteen feet away, facing them. Cy and Kris crouch with their knees slightly bent, hands waiting to catch me. And Angel stands behind them, her eyes on me. She looks determined, but not quite as confident as usual. It sends a pang of longing through me. Last year our stunt group's bond felt shatterproof. Our unshakeable confidence in each other was how we got through the season with no injuries. But now a tremor rolls through me, because that bond? I'm the one who broke it.

Angel starts the count. "One, two, three, four . . ."

I listen hard, the familiar rhythm washing over me, and let my body take over. I take off, running full tilt for them. When I'm close enough to see the sweat beading on Cyerra's forehead—nerves, I wonder?—I pitch forward until my hands hit the mat. I flip over and into their arms. Kristina and Cyerra cradle me and we dip once. With their help, I get my feet under me and into their hands. I hover there for a breath, feeling weightless from the momentum of the flip. Again we dip.

As soon as it begins, I know I'm going to fall. Our timing is off. When Cyerra is still sinking into a squat, Kris has already begun to rise.

I try to listen for Angel's counts, but her voice falters. She notices our pace is off. Still, her hands on my ankles tighten almost painfully as they hoist me up. I straighten to my full height, squeezing every muscle in my body.

"Lock *out*, Ari!" Angel yells, a thread of panic in her voice. I'm canting to the left now, but Angel's firm grip on my ankles keeps me aloft.

I try, squeezing my core, hands fisted at my sides. But it's not enough. My feet are uneven, one of my toes tilting down, and worst of all, my heart is in my throat. Coach always says, "You can't fly scared."

She's right, because the moment the fear takes over, all I want are my feet planted firmly on the ground. Just as I'm about to tip forward, I see Jacob below me.

I reach for his hands, and we drop our first stunt in front of the judges. Everyone claps politely as my face burns. I can feel Cyerra's and Angel's frustration.

Once everyone is assured none of us have been hurt, Melissa says, "You get points for ambition, but . . ."

Not one to mince words, Coach Castillo grabs the mic from Melissa. "But you would've gotten more if you'd actually executed. Next!"

We leave the mats and join the rest of the audience, while the second group of seniors runs onto the mats. They announce their stunt, and my stomach turns—back handspring to extension with a full down. Our stunt, but with a degree more difficulty. Brilliant.

I don't watch them throw it, but I know from the shouting rising around us that it goes well. I can feel Angel's eyes on my face, but I refuse to look at her. If she expects an apology for how that went down, she's going to be waiting awhile.

The next morning, I get a text from Cyerra telling me we're all meeting early at the Fieldhouse to talk about yesterday's failure. I'm about to decline—seriously, a dropped extension is not that big of a deal—when I realize if I don't go, Angel will be free to blame the whole thing on me. Which is completely unfair. None of us were in sync.

My mom drops me off on the way to work, and though Angel is the only one standing outside, when I open the car door she says, "Have a great day, honey. Tell Cyerra she's welcome for dinner tonight."

Anger flashes through me, but true to form, I smother it. I flee, hefting my duffel bag over my shoulder and jogging across the parking lot toward the Fieldhouse. I pass Angel, who's on the phone arguing with someone. I wonder why she isn't inside with Kris and Cyerra. I slow as I near her, but soon as Angel sees me, she glares and I decide I'll be better off finding the others.

Only when I get to the doors, they're locked. I try peeking through the glass, but I can't see anyone inside. When I turn back to Angel, she's still glaring down at her phone.

I pull out mine and scroll back through my text thread with Cyerra, making sure I didn't miss anything. Maybe she wants to meet on the turf? Cy's never late, but there's a first for everything. I'm about to call her when Angel says, "Don't bother. They're not coming."

"What? No way. Cy—"

Angel offers a humorless, lopsided smirk. "Apparently Cyerra thinks this is our fault."

"Oh." I rock back on my heels. "What did she say exactly?"

"We have to 'resolve our differences'?" Angel's sharp, dark eyebrows draw together as she frowns. "Whatever she means by that."

"It's pretty obvious what she means." The words rush out of me, gaining momentum as they go. "You're clearly pissed at me, and you have every right to be. I know I, like, ghosted you all summer, and I'm sorry, but it's not my fault we dropped that stunt yesterday and—"

"Wait, wait. Hold on, I'm the one who's upset? Whatever, you were busy over the summer. It's not like we were . . ." She shrugs and shakes her head, but can't quite meet my eyes. "You're the one who's been all hostile! You're always pouting or glaring at me—"

"I don't glare. And you are mad. We've been in camp for the last three weeks, and you barely spoke to me until Monday."

In the same instant we both become aware of the shrinking inches between us. Angel hops back a step, her honey-brown eyes bright with affront. "Sounds like you're projecting. Is that what's been happening? You think I'm going to be rude, so you have to get there first. I know you're competitive, Ariana, but damn, this is next level."

I open my mouth, grasping for a response. She sneers, folding her arms across her chest, and I realize why I'm angry. "Oh, my mistake. I should have known. You're too chill to care when your friends just disappear."

"Ari, you didn't just *disappear*. You stopped talking to me and only me." Finally her eyes meet mine, and the hurt in them is clear. "I checked with Cy to see if she'd heard from you. Apparently y'all had been hanging out. I figured you were going through something with your family and you would get around to telling me."

"Angel, I didn't mean—"

"But you didn't," Angel says. "Say anything to me. We've been here for weeks and up until a few days ago, you avoided me."

I let out a breath, and it's like all the anger and fear flow out with it. "Well . . . I suck."

I swear Angel's fighting laughter. "I think we've established that pretty well at this point."

I snort. "Right, thanks."

"So what was it? Did I double text too often?"

A dozen lies instantly materialize in my head. Everything in me is screaming to *hide*. Days ago . . . hours ago I would've literally fled from this conversation. But Angel admitting she checked up on me makes me feel like I'm flying, mid-leap and breathless.

Brave.

I knit my fingers together and squeeze, the slight pain distracting me from the deeper discomfort of vulnerability. "MymomfoundoutIlikeyouandkeptsendingmetoyouth-group."

"English please, Simmons?" Angel says, staring down at me with those copper-flecked brown eyes.

Because I am a child and I have the sneaking suspicion

that I'll turn to a column of flame if I admit this to Angel's face, I turn around and say, "My mom found out I like you and kept sending me to youth group."

It's the single most embarrassing sentence I've ever uttered. My eyes are shut and I am afraid to even peek until I hear Angel's laughter. I whirl around to find her with a hand over her mouth, attempting to smother her laughter. I turn on my heel, prepared to run all the way back to my house and never emerge again.

"Wait, wait," Angel says, grabbing my arm. It seems to take no effort whatsoever for her to spin me around.

"I know I've been terrible, but you could at least not laugh!" I growl, folding my arms across my chest.

"I'm sorry, I shouldn't laugh, it's so . . . Why not just invite me to youth group? Ari, I promise I don't care if your mom thinks I'm trying to seduce you. Those Saturday fish fries at your church are worth the suspicion even if we have to sit through two hours of testimonies." She lets out another peal of laughter—I'm talking actual giggles—that I can't help but join in. The only time I brought her to youth group last year, we tried sneaking out and got caught by one of the deacon's wives. Ms. Debra gave us each a handful of peppermints and made us sit in on the rest of the service and adult Bible study.

I notice she's ignoring my confession and try not to let disappointment show on my face. My throat tightens, and I wonder how quickly I can leave this conversation, because this terrible queasiness in my stomach will go away once I've cried. "Ha. Ha. More like I didn't want you to know my mom's kind of a jerk."

"Simmons, I don't care if your mom hates me. She's not the first, she won't be the last." My face is so hot I bet steam is rising from my forehead like in anime. But even Angel's light brown cheeks are tinged red when she says, "And I should say, I am flattered that you—"

Oh god. She's *flattered*. That's nice person for *Sorry, never gonna happen*. I cut her off. "Sure, uh, thanks, Angel. Since we have this extra time, should we figure out our next stunt?"

Her brows draw together in confusion, and for a second I think she's going to continue letting me down easy, but she shakes it off and grins. "Well, I'm thinking half up to a liberty, tick tock to scorpion, full down cradle? How's that sound?"

"Seriously, Angel?" I shove her shoulder with mine and bite my cheek hard until the impending tears are long gone. "Is your plan to kill me and get a replacement flyer?"

Angel wraps an arm around my shoulder. "Please, Simmons, I would never get rid of you."

I'm saved from spontaneous combustion by the arrival of Coach Castillo and the rest of the coaching staff. "Early start, ladies?"

"Just a little team building," I say, my voice a touch too high as we follow them inside.

I try to remind myself that this is what needed to happen.

I told Angel the truth and we'll have a great practice today. I remind myself that even if Angel returned my feelings, I'd still have my parents to deal with, and since I'm not ready to come out to them, this is for the best. But it doesn't feel that way. It feels like there's a hand in my chest, squeezing tighter and tighter, and soon my heart's going to break.

Saturday morning, after we've all changed in the locker rooms at the Fieldhouse, Coach asks us to meet on the football field. Someone has tied red, white, and gold balloons to the trees that line the path to the turf. There are even a few of those little gold-and-red footballs we toss out during games stuffed between branches. Since we got our uniforms last night (and felt all the feels watching the freshmen get theirs for the first time, while realizing this was our last), Coach told us to dress game ready.

Angel removed the silver stud in her nose, and her crescent moon tattoo is hidden neatly beneath her shell. Coach had chewed her out over the undercut, but Angel promised it would be grown out by competition season. ("I'm shaving it all off the moment we win state," she'd sworn when Coach had moved on.) I'm sure between then and now she'll have even more uniform violations to conceal.

We let Kris, tamer of curls, and Cyerra, master of paint, pretty us to their satisfaction. Angel's long dark hair is up in a braided bun, complete with a glittery bow, and her makeup is the same as usual, except with a liberal coating of pink-gold lip gloss. Had this been a real competition, Cyerra would probably have us rubbing Vaseline on our teeth.

Even so the air is charged outside, and it fills me with that buzzy, light game-day feeling. I'm ready to earn our spot today.

The week went smoothly after I talked with Angel on Wednesday. Even though I still have to hide my hurt feelings, things between us shifted completely. We're nowhere near our old closeness, but after practice that day, we talked about her plans for college. Like me, she's shooting for the coast, east or west.

On Thursday things went as well as possible for our group. When we threw our one-leg stunt—scorpion full down—and it went up so smoothly, it seemed like even our breathing was in sync. The other seniors tried another stunt that combined tumbling, but Elena went up lopsided and fell. She fought to stay up for a while, unlike when I'd abandoned our stunt early on Tuesday.

Either way, we both have one fall.

The other two stunt groups haven't dropped any stunts, but none of theirs have measured up to ours in difficulty. So even though everyone will be presenting a basket toss today, the competition to pick the top spot—and captain—is between the two senior groups. Just as I knew it would be from the beginning.

The thing about basket tosses: they run on trust. Let one

person throw too hard, and you could be launched up at an angle and come down not in your friends' arms, but on their heads. Or if the flyer hesitates while they're in the air, they could come down mid-twist or toe touch.

The same long table from the Fieldhouse has been brought outside, and instead of the six judges from the week, there's just Coach Castillo, her clipboard, water bottle, and a microphone.

The first senior group is up first, with Jayde's group spotting. Instead of the single extra spotters we've had for the last few days, each senior group has been paired with the younger ones to help spotting. It seems like they've learned the same lesson we have, because they set up without any fuss. The two bases take each other's wrists and make a basket with their hands. Elena jumps on top of their locked hands, her face serious and her eyes fixed on the horizon, and they all dip as one before flinging her skyward. Elena goes up graceful as an arrow, toes perfectly pointed. As soon as she reaches her zenith, she does a toe touch, her legs jutting wide. Her back spot, Arnelle, watches her trajectory as she comes down, stepping back so they're right under her when she lands.

It goes perfectly. They haven't made any mistakes, but we have an edge on them because our toss is harder. We'll have to be better than perfect, and actually look like we're having fun while doing it. I pray Coach takes off points for Elena's dour look.

I barely pay attention to the next two groups, except when

we spot one of them. Cyerra stopped them mid-stunt and adjusted the bases' posture and handgrips, saving them from a bad toss and hopefully gaining us some points in Coach's mind. After that, it's our turn. Instead of butterflies, my stomach seems to be filled with giant winged horses. Fire-breathing pegasi with talons.

Coach lifts the mic to her lips. "Ariana, what can I expect from your group?"

This time, I approach the table and announce, "Full with a toe touch, Coach." Exactly as we've practiced.

"Ah, another high-level stunt, ladies. I hope you all can execute this time."

That's all the encouragement we need. I turn around to face my group and catch sight of Angel's smile and that dimple right by her mouth and her bright eyes that look gold in the sun. My heart thumps in my chest. I wonder when, if ever, she'll stop having that effect on me.

I join my group and we set the stunt. Kris stands on my left and Cyerra on my right, with Angel behind me. Cy and Kris lock arms, and I place a hand on each of their shoulders and set one foot on their wrists.

I smile as wide as possible, and Angel starts the count. "One, two."

We dip, my other foot joining the first. "Three, four."

Kris and Cyerra explode into motion, their joined hands heading straight for the sky. And just like that I'm airborne.

In the ascent I feel weightless, like I could keep on flying right to the sun, and utterly at the mercy of my body's motion. In the few seconds before gravity catches me, I'm balanced on a knife's edge between joy and terror.

It's absolute bliss.

I hold my body tight while I twist, and once completed, I can feel myself sink. I fling my legs wide, going into a deep toe touch. My legs snap back together. My thighs sting, but a second later, that pain is chased away by Angel's, Cyerra's, and Kris's arms, which I know will leave bruises. But that's typical, such a familiar pain that I don't even notice it.

Before they can put me down, Angel murmurs into my ear, "Fucking killed it, Simmons."

I pray Cyerra and Kris can't feel the shiver of pleasure that goes through me.

They let me down. Unlike the other groups, who all walked off calmly, Cyerra steps in front of me and launches into our old favorite chant, "V-I-C-T-O-R-Y, LADY VICTORY, THAT'S OUR CRY." We cheer and whoop and kick and do wild facials. The crowd joins the chant, and I understand exactly why Cyerra wanted us to do this.

Coach Castillo eventually quiets us down. "All right now, go join the others. This should only take a moment."

Beside me, Angel smothers laughter as Coach pulls an old calculator from her pocket. What I wouldn't give to see how she rated us! In the end though, it must not be too hard, because five minutes later, she's ready to announce the winners.

"When I started Hell Week, I had my eyes on a few of you for captain. I'm surprised to say I didn't have this person on my radar, but I'm so pleased with how they've led their own group, and helped others throughout the week. Our captain should be concerned with more than just their group, right?"

"Yes, Coach," we say in unison, but the words are rushed. Everyone's getting impatient now.

"Exactly. That said, I'm so happy to announce Cyerra Lyons, your new captain." Coach continues to speak, but the rest of her words are drowned out by Kristina's and Angel's shouting. We all climb to our feet, but Cy just sits there, looking so deeply pleased and proud of herself. As she should. Considering how she handled my drama this week, it's well deserved.

She allows us to pull her to her feet, and everyone on the team stands to cheer for Cyerra. We're all pressed close, jumping and yelling her name. In the madness, I find myself standing in front of Angel. She grins and pulls me into a hug. She pulls back, but keeps her hands on my shoulders. Heat rises in my cheeks.

Just a friendly hug, Ariana. Nothing more, nothing less.

Despite the fact that all of our teammates are around us, it feels like we're alone. I ignore my instinct to put space between us and look up at her. "Are you disappointed at all?"

"Nah. Not really. She's the girl for the job." Angel reaches for my hand. Her fingers curl around mine, warm and sure in their grip.

And as good as it feels, I pull my hand from hers and step back. "I know we're friends again, but full disclosure: my feelings haven't changed, which makes this"—I wave my hand at the less than ten inches between us—"hard."

Angel takes a half step back, but with everyone packed around us, there's not much room to maneuver. "Well, what about my feelings?"

My eyebrows raised, I blurt, "Huh? What's that got to—"

Then Angel Arceneaux leans down, places both hands on my cheeks, and kisses me. Her lips are unreasonably soft. I gasp, stretching up on my toes to deepen the kiss. I can still taste a faint hint of strawberry beneath the glide of her gloss. I don't notice that I've grabbed her shell to pull myself up until Angel breaks the kiss.

Distantly I hear that cheering has started up again, but I'm too afraid to peek out and see every single eye on us. Then I hear Cyerra shout, "You're welcome."

A beat later, Kris adds, "Finally!"

I glare over my shoulder to find Cyerra and Kris standing next to Coach, their heads bent together. Coach actually starts to laugh at something Cy says.

I grab Angel's wrist, and she allows me to drag her to the opposite end of the football field. The freshly painted turf crunches beneath our feet.

"Quick question," Angel says. "Is there any way you could skip one week of Saturday-night youth group and hang out with me instead?"

"I . . ." The smile on my face falters. Because as much as I want to say yes, my mind instantly goes to my parents and how *they* will feel. And especially, what effect their disappointment will have on me. I wonder, if I'm still not ready to tell them, can I choose Angel—or better yet, myself?

I take a deep breath and stare up into her eyes, summoning the bravery I felt during our stunt. "I can manage that, but I might need Cyerra to run point."

"What would we do without Cy?" Angel says wistfully. "Thank goodness Coach picked her."

I lace my fingers with Angel's and tow her back down the field to congratulate our friend again. Soon my mom will pull up to drive me home, and maybe I will have to sneak out tonight, but for now, I won't let go of Angel's hand.

THE LIBERTY HOMES

Katie Cotugno

THE SUMMER THE LIBERTY HOMES STARTED DISAPPEARING WAS the first summer Theo's little brother, Henry, was officially old enough to play Manhunt.

This was before the panic, you understand; this was before the news vans and the government vehicles and the scientists in their Neil Armstrong hazmat suits crouched on our dry, dead lawns taking soil samples. This was before everyone had heard of us, before the cover stories and the YouTube videos and the conspiracy theorists on social media arguing over whether or not we were a hoax.

Also, and probably more to the point: this was before it started to spread.

"Hurry up," Theo told Henry as they ambled up Van Buren on that first blue night of summer. He could smell his deodorant working, feel his T-shirt sticking to his back. We were three days into a heat wave, the temperatures hovering in the nineties long after the sun had begun to set. "And don't be embarrassing, okay?"

"I *am* hurrying," Henry protested, trotting along behind him past the tidy rows of faux-colonial houses—their front doors painted cheerful shades of blue and green and yellow, their shutters stamped with cutouts of candles and crescent moons. "And if anybody's embarrassing, it's you." He made a face, his coppery freckles connecting across the pale bridge of his nose. "Are you wearing *cologne?*"

Theo ignored him, running his thumb over the warm metal curve of the whistle in his pocket as they rounded the corner onto Adams, where the rest of us were already clustered outside the Coopers' house: stretched out on the porch and slouched cross-legged on the glider, tucked into the forked, gnarled trunk of the juniper tree. Grace and Maddie perched on the steps like a pair of birds identical in their brightness, freshly pierced belly buttons smarting under their tank tops. Alex sprawled dreamily on the lawn. Jenna stood off to the side wearing denim shorts and a watchful expression, her hair in a long, dark braid down her back.

Theo climbed the steps of the porch like he was ascending to a pulpit. A sprinkler hissed on the lawn next door. The cicadas hummed up in the trees that lined the wide, even sidewalks of the development—or they should have been humming, anyway. One or two of us had already started to wonder, even way back then at the beginning of the summer, if they hadn't seemed weirdly quiet this year.

Theo hadn't noticed. "Henry's playing," he announced, the set of his shoulders daring anyone to complain about it. None of us did. Most of us were thirteen and fourteen that summer; Henry was ten but looked younger, with legs that bowed like a new deer's, and a slightly crooked haircut courtesy of a backyard chop with a pair of kitchen scissors. Their mom had done Theo's, too, dragging him out there every six weeks with a chair and a fraying bath towel, until the previous winter when he'd finally gotten fed up and ordered a pair of clippers online.

Now he took the whistle out of his pocket, twirling the blue nylon cord around his fingers. He'd inherited it from Reshmi George at the end of last summer; Reshmi had gotten it from Taylor Lazaro, but none of us were old enough to remember who'd had it before that. The legend was that it had been passed down through the neighborhood since the Liberty Homes were first built back in the nineties, the shrill, sharp call of it echoing through the quiet development every night at the start and the end of the game.

"Okay," Theo said now, the metal glinting in the yellow glow of the porch light. He lifted it to his lips. "One, two—"

"Theo," Jenna said, her voice ringing out in the darkness. Jenna was the kind of pretty that should have made her popular at school but hadn't, so far; she was too much of a human granola bar, crunchy and responsible. "Maybe you want to give us all a refresher on the rules?" Her sharp blue gaze cut to Henry, then back again. "You know, since it's been a while."

"Oh." Theo frowned, looking a little put out at having his big moment interrupted. "Uh, sure. The rules are simple," he said, then did a patently miserable job explaining them: the teams and the boundaries and the jail here on the Coopers' porch where he was standing, how to tag people in and out until finally one side successfully captured everyone on the other. By the time he was finished he'd managed to confuse even himself, sort of, but none of it really mattered: Liberty kids had been playing Manhunt forever, or at least as long as any of us had lived here. We'd grown up waiting for our turns to gambol off every night after dinner—to spend our summers wriggling into new and arcane hiding spots, working out complicated variations on the game. One year we used water balloons. One year we used Nerf guns. One year we used walkie-talkies, but the frequency of them made Mr. Leone's shih tzu bark his head off over on Eisenhower Crescent, and Manhunt was a game of stealth.

"So, that's it," Theo said finally, looking pointedly at Jenna as he lifted the whistle one more time. "Ready?"

He blew the whistle and we took off, all of us scattering in a dozen different directions: scuttling up into tree houses, crouching behind SUVs. The crawl space under the Chungs' back porch had been in high demand last summer, but then

Mrs. Chung saw a racoon under there and told us we weren't allowed to use it anymore until she called the county and had animal control come to take the creature away. "It wasn't bothering anyone," said Eleanor, who was our resident animal rights activist. "It was minding its own business until we came along."

Later, after everything happened—hot spots blooming all across the county, breaking news chyrons crawling in perpetuity across our television screens—we would think of that first night of the summer as the last time anything was normal. That night, Eleanor got bored and wandered home to play video games without telling anyone. Brady wiped out on the blacktop and got road burn all up and down his leg. Grace and Maddie had a fight over the lifeguard at the town pool, and which one of them he might have been looking at that afternoon in line at the snack bar, which is how Theo found them hiding together behind the garage at Jenna's house. "Ladies," he said grandly, gesturing in the direction of the jail.

The two of them sighed in noisy unison and shuffled behind him back to the Coopers', where Alex was staring off into space and eating an ice cream sandwich while he acted as prison guard. The Coopers had the biggest house in Liberty; their wide front porch was filled with geraniums and potted herbs, the smell of rosemary and basil sticking to our skin when we got into bed at the end of the night. "Two more," Theo reported, then took off one more time across the grass. "And pay attention, will you?"

Jenna listened to the familiar crunch of his footsteps—holding her breath as he ran right by her, so close she got a whiff of his shampoo. She'd scoped out her hiding spot weeks before school even ended, a hollowed-out log in the woods behind Theo's house that wasn't quite wide enough to shimmy into but was more than tall enough to crouch behind. Now Jenna leaned her head back against the cool, smooth bark, listening for the steady trickle of the creek at the back of the development and trying to ignore the creeping feeling that she was running out of time. She knew we were getting too old for this—that as far as the game went we probably only had this one summer, and maybe not even the whole thing. Theo had stopped talking to her in school sometime back in the winter; she'd seen him at the pool that afternoon, and she knew he'd seen her, too, but instead of saying hi or even waving he'd turned and followed Alex in the direction of the deep end, his face inscrutable behind a pair of plastic sunglasses. Still, three hours later, there he'd been at her back door just like always, standing in her kitchen, scratching at an infected mosquito bite while she frantically tried to change her tampon in the half bath next to the laundry room. "You playing tonight?" he'd asked when she emerged.

Jenna shifted her weight, uncomfortable. She hadn't gotten the angle right, in the end; she'd only started her period a couple months back. "Um, maybe," she said, trying not to let on that she'd been waiting for this, his explicit invitation. "Thinking about it."

"Okay." He shrugged, wiping a tiny smear of blood from the mosquito bite on the leg of his shorts. Then, looking up at her suddenly, he frowned. "Hey," he said, "what happened to your mailbox?"

Jenna blinked. "My what?" She wondered briefly if this was some kind of innuendo, if she was walking directly into a trap and was going to have to spend the remainder of the summer listening to him snicker about her with Brady and Alex, but Theo just looked curious.

"Your mailbox," he repeated. "It's not on the post anymore."

Jenna shook her head. "I don't know," she said. "Maybe somebody stole it."

Theo seemed to accept this answer, though Liberty was not exactly known for its criminal activity. "Maybe," he agreed. "Okay, well. See you out there, then."

Now Jenna waited until his footsteps receded in the distance, standing up and brushing leaves off the back of her shorts. She glanced over her shoulder one more time to make sure nobody was coming—she could creep through the Coopers' side yard, she thought, and tag Grace and Maddie out of jail—then turned back toward the creek and stopped short. Jenna stood frozen for a moment, staring at the water.

Or, rather, at the place where the water should have been.

The creek was narrow, only a few feet across at its widest. In the spring it rushed, the sound of it audible from the street as they waited for the bus in the mornings; in the fall it slowed to a trickle, but normally that wouldn't happen for another couple of months, and anyway the more she stared at the scarred-over patch of earth in the moonlight, the more sure Jenna felt that she wasn't seeing the normal ebb and flow of nature.

The creek wasn't dry, exactly.

The creek was just . . . not there.

She stared for a long time in the half dark, wondering if possibly she was imagining things. She'd heard Brady make jokes about girls getting crazy when they had their periods; Brady was an asshole, mostly, but still she wondered for a second if that was what was happening now. If she was hallucinating. If possibly she couldn't trust what was right in front of her face.

She was still standing there when she heard leaves crunching behind her, the heavy tread of footsteps. She turned just as Theo reached out and touched her gently on the arm.

"Gotcha," he said. "Dude. Were you even hiding?"

"I—" Jenna shook her head, the contact barely registering. "I—"

Theo frowned. "You what?"

Jenna looked behind her at where the creek used to be, then at Theo again, hesitating; there was a time when he'd been her best friend in the world. But then she remembered how he'd turned away from her at the pool that afternoon, the way the sun had caught the drops of water beading on his shoulders and back. "Nothing," she said finally, and shuffled off behind him toward the jail.

She didn't say anything to the rest of us, either. The ones of us who are left always think about that now: if we'd started talking to each other a little earlier—if we'd trusted each other enough to compare notes, been a little less worried about drawing attention to ourselves—if maybe things would have turned out differently. If maybe we'd all still be here.

If maybe we could have stopped the spread.

Instead Jenna went home once the game was over, letting herself into the cool, dark house and getting a glass of iced tea from the fridge. "Hey, Mom?" she said, pausing in the doorway of the living room. "I think the creek is gone."

"What?" Her mom was sitting on the couch, her face pale in the glow of the laptop. She was finishing her master's in social work that summer, her head bent over her case notes late into the night.

"The little creek in the woods behind Theo and Henry's house," Jenna explained, her voice sounding a lot calmer than she actually felt. "It's not there anymore."

Her mom glanced up, but only briefly. "It's summer, honey. It's dry."

Jenna frowned. They'd lived in Liberty since she was nine,

and she'd been playing this game in those woods for almost that long. "I don't mean it's dry, Mom. I mean it's gone."

"It's the heat, sweetheart." Jenna's mom tilted her head back against the couch, smiling tiredly. They'd lived in six different apartments when she was little, the two of them trundling from place to place as her mom worked her way up the ladder at a big-box chain. "One good rain, you'll see." She shut her laptop and set it on the coffee table, held her arms out in Jenna's direction.

Jenna sat next to her on the couch, closing her eyes and letting her mom twirl her ponytail around two fingers, giving in to the impulse to be soothed. Still, when she went upstairs a little while later, she looked out the window of her bedroom for a long time, craning her neck to try to see past Theo's. Maybe it *was* just dry—after all, there'd been a drought warning all across the county for months now, perky little PSAs about taking shorter showers playing during commercial breaks on the evening news.

Theo had been right, though, she noticed with a tiny pang of trepidation, her gaze landing on the empty post jutting up beside the driveway. The mailbox was missing, too.

She was just about to turn around when she caught sight of him through his bedroom window—Theo reaching back and pulling off his T-shirt, shuffling across the carpet toward the closet door. She could see the pleats of his spine right through his skin.

Jenna swallowed hard, her whole body warm and flustered, then yanked the curtains shut and scrambled under the covers. She didn't fall asleep for a long time.

We met again at dusk the next night.

"Is it hotter?" Maddie asked, sitting down on the curb and stretching her long legs out in front of her, folding herself in half until her forehead touched her freshly shaven knees. "It feels like it's hotter."

"It's the same as it's been," Grace said crabbily, though she wasn't really listening. She squinted, turning a slow circle on the dried-out grass as she scanned the Coopers' yard for the metallic yellow flicker of fireflies. Her little brother and sister had gone out with a mayonnaise jar the night before, only to trudge back inside an hour later empty-handed; it had suddenly occurred to Grace, as her mom told her the story this morning over waffles, that she hadn't seen a single firefly at all yet. "Light pollution," her dad had said, turning back to the news on his tablet, and maybe he was right. Still, the whole thing made Grace feel like there was a blister rubbing raw on the thin, sensitive skin of her Achilles tendon, even though her sneakers fit fine.

Theo blew the whistle. The rest of us ran.

• • •

That night Henry caught Maddie and Alex making out behind the Georges' sun porch. Eleanor fell asleep in the bed of the Lazaros' truck. Theo found Jenna in the same place he'd found her the night before, standing in the woods behind his house staring blankly at nothing: "Again?" he asked with a grin, tagging her gently on the soft skin of her shoulder. All at once he remembered the very first day she moved into Liberty—kicking a soccer ball around with Henry, watching her and her mom unload the van. There were rules in the neighborhood about what color your front door could be painted and how long your grass could get before you had to cut it; Theo's parents had sent him across the street with a pan of homemade brownies and the number of the lawn-care service everyone used.

He stepped back, watching her. "You gotta mix it up a little, dude."

Jenna didn't smile back. "Can I ask you something?" she said, still not quite looking at him. "Didn't there used to be a creek here?"

Theo shrugged, distracted; he thought he saw Brady running through the trees out of the corner of his eye. "Maybe?" he said, half remembering. "Yeah."

"Maybe?" Jenna whirled on him then, her voice rising. "Either there was or there wasn't, Theo."

Theo's eyes widened. "Take it easy," he said, holding his hands up in the darkness. "I said yes. What happened, it dried up?"

Jenna's shoulders dropped. "Forget it," she said, and stomped off in the direction of the jail at the Coopers'. Theo glanced over his shoulder one more time before he followed.

Henry, as it happened, was incredible at Manhunt.

That first week of the summer, he was the last person standing on three separate occasions, sneaking up behind the Coopers' and tagging his whole team free. He was small and quick and a brilliant hider, chameleoning himself into his surroundings while the rest of us dashed on by; Eleanor swore he must be scrabbling across the roofs of the development like a monkey, though she hadn't been able to prove it so far.

"Have you been practicing?" Jenna teased him as they walked home down Van Buren a few nights later, their footsteps echoing on the pavement in the still, hot air. Brady and Theo trailed along behind them, the whistle still dangling from Theo's hand. "Coming out here and scaling people's houses in the middle of the night?"

"Maybe," Henry said, smiling his wide, gap-toothed smile. He was preternaturally good-natured, Henry, always up for a snack or a round of crazy eights or a ride in the car. He used to like to follow the octogenarian mail carrier through the streets of Liberty, the two of them chatting like the oldest of friends. "Or maybe I'm just a natural."

They'd said their good nights and were almost to their

respective doors when Brady called out from down the sidewalk: "Shit," he said, jutting his chin at the house between his and Theo's, "what happened to the Hendersons'?"

Theo frowned, his thick, dark eyebrows creeping as he followed Brady's gaze. For as long as any of us could remember, Mrs. Henderson's garden had loomed larger than anyone else's in Liberty, big, marshmallowy clusters of blue and pink and yellow bursting into bloom every spring. Mrs. Henderson's fanaticism about its care and upkeep was the stuff of Liberty legend. Twice she'd chased Theo out of her yard with a broom.

Now though, the garden was gone: the browning front lawn ran straight and flat and crispy right up to the scalloped blue shingles of the house, almost like there'd never been any flowers there at all.

Theo shrugged, tucking the whistle back into his pocket; Henry had scooped a fraying tennis ball off the lawn and was tossing it in the air to himself, unconcerned. "Maybe she ripped it out?" Theo guessed.

Brady looked unconvinced, his face canny in the warm glow of the old-fashioned streetlights that studded the streets of Liberty. "Since this afternoon?"

Theo felt a surge of anger then, though he wasn't sure why or at who. "Dude, how should I know?" he demanded. He glanced across the street at Jenna, her glossy hair just catching the porch light as she disappeared inside her house.

• • •

The Fourth came and went, all our families gathered on Liberty Green to watch the fireworks. Afterward, Eleanor's parents had us over for a barbecue, the smell of grill smoke and chlorine thick in the air. We skipped the game that night in favor of ice cream sundaes on the dry, brittle grass, Theo and Alex cannonballing into the deep end of the swimming pool over and over. Henry rolled delightedly around on the ground with Eleanor's fuzzy goldendoodle, looking more like a puppy than the dog herself did. The thermometer read ninety-four degrees.

We picked up Manhunt again the following evening, the sound of the whistle slicing through the thick, unmoving air, and the soles of our sneakers slapping against the smooth black pavement. Theo was creeping along the fence line in Brady's backyard when he thought he heard footsteps crunching through the leaves that had already started to fall from the oak trees overhead. For half a second he found himself hoping it was Jenna, then immediately put the thought out of his mind.

They hadn't talked much since the start of the summer. Well, they hadn't talked much since a while before that, Theo guessed, but it was only lately that he'd started to notice it, to miss her constant familiar chatter in his ear. He thought of what she'd said about the creek behind his house, the way her shoulders had risen like a drawbridge; then again, Jenna was always getting worked up about something or other, gender equality or professional football or the lack of vegetarian offerings in the cafeteria at school. It was just the way she was.

Theo listened for another moment, but the air was still and quiet. He crossed from Brady's yard back into his own, headed for the edge of the woods.

Then, all at once, he stopped cold.

The woods were gone.

Instead of the thick line of trees that had buffeted the yard for as long as they'd lived there, the property ended abruptly at a tidy wooden fence. Theo looked over his shoulder, thinking maybe somehow he'd gotten confused about where he was, what direction he was moving—but no, this was his own backyard, there was the driveway, there was Alex prowling around unstealthily in front of Jenna's house across the street.

Everything was the same.

Except it wasn't.

He made his way over to the fence—slow and careful, a wild feeling in his chest like possibly the border was radioactive or a portal to another dimension entirely—and stood on his tiptoes to peer over it. The yard he saw was a mirror image of his own, only nicer: an aboveground pool and a playhouse, a trampoline with netting around it to keep you from flying off into the air. He could see into the window of the house that lay beyond, where they were watching the nightly news in the living room, an anchorwoman with a severe blond haircut yammering cheerfully away.

Theo put his hands on his head, staring blankly, confusion and panic thrumming deep inside his skull. He knew that yard; it belonged to the Porters, over on Grant Street. But he'd never been able to see it from here. Instead Theo had grown up in the thick swath of woods that lay between their respective houses, his dad pointing out the birds to him and Henry: how to distinguish a wren from a chickadee, a larkspur from a snow bunting. One winter they'd spent half an hour holding absolutely still while a cardinal roosted proudly in a tree high above them, a blood-red splash against the dense white sky. Theo felt the sweat dripping down his spine and longed for the cold, wet bite of that day, the feeling of the snow seeping through the seat of his pants.

He didn't wait for the game to be over. Instead he turned and marched through the yard and back into the house, where his dad was in the living room watching a military show on cable. "What woods?" he asked, when Theo announced what he'd seen.

Theo felt himself get very still. "Our woods, Dad," he said slowly. "Behind the house."

"There aren't any woods behind the house, bud," his dad said, one eye still on the television. "Our backyard touches the Porters'."

Later, Theo said he didn't know why he didn't argue. He

thought about it, he told us, just like he thought about running outside and yelling Jenna's name until she wriggled out from wherever she was, begging her to forgive him for everything he'd done—and everything he hadn't—for the better part of this year. Instead he went upstairs and dug out the Audubon guide his dad had gotten him for his birthday the year he was Henry's age, and looked at the drawing of the cardinal until the rest of us got tired of the game and drifted home.

Two days later, the Porters' yard was gone, too.

It started happening fast after that. By the beginning of August all of us had noticed, in one way or another: Eleanor swore there'd been a tree house at the Georges' before this summer. Alex was pretty sure the Lazaros used to have a shed. Grace started timing how long it took her to run to the edge of the development and back, her dark hair streaming behind her like a flag as she dashed past our tidy, well-kept houses.

"You're just getting faster," Maddie pointed out, clocking the seconds on her phone. They'd been together when they'd discovered the Liberty Green was missing, a wide patch of manicured grass where the library did auxiliary programming and senior citizens practiced tai chi.

"Maybe," Grace said—bending over and bracing her hands

on her knees, sucking in mouthfuls of thick, hot air. "Or maybe it's a shorter run than it used to be."

Still, we kept playing, assembling in front of the Coopers' house at sundown, the teams shifting every night. The weather still hadn't broken, the concrete burning hot beneath our feet; Mrs. Henderson had fainted in her empty yard on the way back from getting her mail that morning; Henry jumped up off the hammock and ran inside the house to get help. Theo, in panic and desperation, had sprayed her with the hose until she woke up. It was only then, as she excoriated him for getting her dress wet, that he realized she'd never said anything about her lawn.

Everyone kept telling us rain was coming. Everyone kept promising it was only a matter of time.

A few mornings before school started, Theo was brushing his teeth when Henry appeared in the doorway behind him, a too-small T-shirt stretched over his bony shoulders.

"Theo," he said. "Can I tell you something weird I saw last night while we were playing?"

Theo looked at him in the mirror for a long moment, his crooked haircut and plaid pajama pants. "No," he decided, and spat.

• • •

"They caught Henry," Jenna reported on the very last night of summer, dropping out of a dying apple tree as Theo darted by in the dark. "I just saw Brady bring him over to the Coopers'."

"Really?" Theo asked, surprise flickering across his face. "First time for everything, I guess." Then he smiled, shrugging with one careless shoulder and lifting his chin in the direction of the street. "We'll get him out."

Jenna nodded, tightening her ponytail in determination; Theo was turning toward the fence line when she took a deep breath and reached for his arm. "Theo," she said, quiet enough so that any of us who were hiding nearby wouldn't be able to hear her. "Are you scared?"

"Because they got Henry?" Theo joked. "I mean, I think he'll be okay."

Jenna didn't laugh. "No," she countered softly. "Because of everything else."

Theo opened his mouth, then shut it again. Opened it one more time. For a second Jenna was sure he was going to tell her he had no idea what she was talking about, but in the end he just barely shook his head, infinitesimal, the kind of movement she might not have noticed at all if she hadn't been watching him so carefully all these years. "Nah," he said, his sharp face only half visible in the pale glow of the backyard light. "I mean, we're together, right?"

Jenna's whole body flushed warm as August, heat blooming

from her cheeks to her toes. "Theo—" she started, feeling herself smile for the first time all summer.

That was when it started to rain.

It came with no warning: a thunderclap Jenna could feel in her molars, a flash of lightning cleaving the sky in two. All of us were drenched in seconds, our bones rattling inside our skin.

"Come on," Theo shouted—loud enough so that we all could hear him, taking Jenna's hand and nodding at the rest of us hovering nearby. "Let's go get him."

We took off—careening through the streets of Liberty, our sneakers sliding in backyards turned suddenly to mud pits as the downpour soaked through our shirts. Maddie slipped and took Grace down with her. Brady was laughing almost too hard to run. Just for a minute none of us were thinking about how weird and bad and unsettling everything had felt all summer. Just for a minute, all any of us were thinking about was the game. We splashed through puddles that were already creeping up past our ankles as we cut the corner onto Polk, dashing across the driveway into the Coopers' front yard— and then we stopped.

None of us said anything for a moment, squinting through the dense wall of water.

Theo was the one who spoke first. "Alex," he yelled, his voice barely audible over the rumble of thunder. "What are you doing?"

Alex frowned. "What do you mean what am I doing?" he

called back, looking at Theo like he was an utter bonehead. His blond hair was plastered to his skull. "I'm guarding the jail." He swept his arm grandly behind him, then froze halfway through the gesture, his hand dangling in midair like a bird shot clean out of the sky. "What the hell," was all he said.

Later, this moment would be what the whole world remembered. This moment, to everyone else, would be the start. The first tragedy, they'd call it, but the rest of us would know better. The rest of us would know that the tragedies had started a long time ago.

For now we stared past Alex without speaking, sodden and slack-jawed, everything we'd understood all summer but hadn't had the words for clicking neatly and horribly into place. The jail was gone. The porch was gone. The Coopers' entire house was gone, evaporated, the lot it had been sitting on nothing but silt. Behind him we could see the gate to the development, concrete eagles roosting on top of the tidy stone pillars; beyond that was the road that wound slowly into town.

"Guys," Jenna said, her gaze darting from Theo to the rest of us and back again. "Where's Henry?"

Theo didn't answer, fumbling clumsily at his pockets. Jenna started screaming Henry's name. The rest of us joined in even though we already knew it was useless, the sound of our voices lost in the roar of the rain hitting the concrete and the shriek of the whistle echoing over and over through the dark.

MYSTERY HUNT

Gloria Chao

I'M ABOUT TO EMBARK ON THE FAMOUS LINGUISTICS Department Annual Mystery Hunt. The one I've been look-ing forward to since I researched colleges in high school and put Cornmouth University at the top of my dream list despite my high school friends asking me why I wanted to go to a school "with such a weird name," "in the middle of nowhere," and "with a nerdy reputation." I want—*need*—to win. For my dad and me. Puzzles and games have always been our thing, our way to bond and communicate, and it's a big reason why I'm pursuing a career in linguistics. He and I have been talk-ing about the hunt for years, and he's already texted twice today.

My palms are sweating. Not just because I've been wait-ing for this forever, but also because of who I'm teaming up with today.

A moment later my partner arrives and my heart leaps into my throat. No idea why—he's only tall, dark, and handsome, his floppy dark brown hair always looking messy but like he spent time making it just so. Today is no exception.

"Hey, Speedy," he greets me, same as he always does, and even though I've heard that nickname many times in the two months I've known him, it still sends a flutter through me. His giant one-dimpled smile lights up his face, causing the corners of his eyes to crinkle.

"Hey, Pierce," I respond, as usual, no cute nickname because I'm shy. (Does it count that I call him Piercing Baby Blues in my head?)

"Are you ready? Do we need to rub ol' Carl for good luck?" he asks as he rests an elbow on the base of the bronze statue dedicated to the university's founders, Cornelius and Earl Cornmouth, or Carl for short. The going rumor is that the brothers were so unattractive they requested a statue of their hands mid-handshake instead of one of the usual obnoxious full-body statues found on other campuses. The structure consists of two giant hands overlapping and the thumbs sticking up in the air to form a diamond-shaped window with the index fingers.

Pierce reaches a hand toward Cornelius's pinky, aka the easiest-to-reach spot, which is now gold from being rubbed so many times before tests, dates, or sports games.

"Don't!" I grab his hand, then flush at the contact. My palm immediately floods with sweat, and I let go as if his hand burned me. I quickly try to explain, "I heard the frat guys like to pee on it since they know people rub it for luck."

Pierce cringes. "Exactly why I have zero interest in the

Greek system." Then he smirks. "Well, just that Greek system. I'm very interested in alpha, beta, gamma . . ."

I'm melting on the inside but can't seem to put into words how much I love his joke. Apparently, I'm extra quiet when it's just the two of us, which is a first today—we usually saw each other in study groups.

"Shall we?" He sticks his elbow out for me to loop my hand in, and I shyly press fingers to the inside of his bicep—his very muscular bicep, firmer than I would have guessed based on his lean frame. But then as we start moving, his arm droops a little, my fingers drop, and we walk to the library with our hands shoved into our pockets.

The Mystery Hunt kickoff is taking place in one of the library's seminar rooms. When we arrive, it's already packed and buzzing with excitement. The atmosphere is the epitome of one of my favorite Mandarin phrases, *rènào*, which I don't think has a worthy translation, not without several words. I consider sharing that with Pierce, but I refrain, worried it would sound nerdy even though, by all indications, he would love it. Like me, he's planning on majoring in linguistics. We met during orientation two months ago. In our first conversation, I'd told him that I was named Faye, a Westernized spelling of my Chinese name, Fei (菲), and he'd joked that I was destined to study linguistics since my name is a combination of two languages, of sorts. My feelings for him pretty much started then and only grew as he talked about how words first came to life for him during Latin class in high school. His love of etymology, of how words have a unique history and can bend and change over time—meeting him was like the phrase "two peas in a pod" coming to life for me. I'd never felt that with any other person before, and especially not someone who shared my passion for language.

Unfortunately, for someone who wants to study communication, I'm terrible at it. Not always, but with my crushes. With Pierce. Truth be told, I haven't had many crushes—just superficial ones that don't seem to count now that I've met Pierce. I wasn't always tongue-tied in his presence, but once he started calling me Speedy (after he saw how fast I solved our first exercise in Intro to Phonetics and Phonology), all my words seemed to disappear.

Pierce and I slip into seats at the back of the seminar room. The morning sunlight shining through the window catches his unruly hair. I look away in case my cheeks look as hot as they suddenly feel.

Most of the participants and usually the winners are traditionally juniors and seniors, and after a quick scan through the room, I'm pretty sure we're the only freshmen here. The few faces I recognize are in a vague maybe-we-sat-near-each-other-in-the-library way.

Pierce nudges me gently with an elbow. "We got this. You're our secret weapon, Speedy."

I try not to combust on the spot. And I also try to ignore all the doubts in my head telling me I'm not good enough, I'm too young, I'm a nobody.

Professor Margolis, head of the department, takes the stage, and everyone quiets. As she talks, volunteers pass through the room, handing out sealed envelopes, one per team.

"Welcome, everyone, to the thirty-third Linguistics Department Annual Mystery Hunt!" her voice booms. A pulse of energy surges through the audience. So rènào. "We are so proud that this tradition has become as big as it has, even attracting students from other departments"—a handful of whoops come from different parts of the room— "yes, yes, thank you for coming! I'm *very* excited about the puzzles this year. We use many different languages, and the faculty had a lot of fun putting this together. Now, teams of two—you should be registered online—the first team to find the hidden coin receives research assistant positions with faculty members of their choice! And any other teams who solve all the puzzles before midnight tomorrow will be invited to the fireside chat that will precede our closing ceremony!"

The room erupts in claps and hoots, including Pierce and me. He's mentioned to me how important the RA position is to him, and I'm also coveting the opportunity. Getting to do research our freshman year would mean we'd be hitting the ground sprinting toward future internships and job opportunities. I've even been making a mental list of faculty I'd love to work with, though overall, that's my secondary motivation. Not only would winning make my dad proud, but I have this weird belief that it would bring our relationship to the next level, like it's the biggest way I can show him how much he means to me—maybe the only way.

"Wait, wait, wait!" Professor Margolis shouts. The hubbub decreases. Then she smirks. Quickly, she yells, "Ready-one-two-three-go! Game on, mystery hunters!"

Shrieks and *oh my god*s and *hurry up*s fill the room. Groups spread out for privacy, and since the chairs immediately around us are empty, Pierce and I elect to stay put. He stretches out now that there's more legroom, his torso relaxing an inch toward me. I resist my temptation to lean toward him, too.

He rubs his hands together. "All right, Speedy. Let's do this."

I rip open the envelope, and out tumbles a Mystery Hunt notebook, some pens, a six-by-six piece of cardstock, and two sheets of paper—the first of which is puzzle #1, and the second of which is labeled FINAL SHEET, FOR AFTER YOU HAVE ALL 3 CLUES. Pierce picks up the cardstock and shows it to me.

HINT
If e'er you're stuck with nowhere to turn,
the answer is already in sight.
Past clues may offer new things to learn,
at times, if only viewed in new light.

I scan it and nod even though I barely register the words. The excitement is overwhelming. I grab the sheet of paper that contains our first puzzle.

"It's smaller than I expected," I joke, flipping the page

over to the blank back, then front again. A single sheet for something I've been looking forward to for *years*. It's . . . well, a little anticlimactic.

Pierce, on the other hand, doesn't seem let down at all. In fact, his voice is downright ecstatic as he gestures to the paper and exclaims, "It's pinyin!"

My eyes scan the puzzle quickly. He's right. I focus on the paper so his piercing baby blues and knowledge of Mandarin don't melt me on the spot. I know he's been taking Mandarin this semester, but it didn't hit me until this moment just how connected it makes me feel to him. But I should have realized sooner—isn't this why I love language so much in the first place?

The puzzle consists of the following:

Clue:
( ) zhōng – (♥) xīn = ?

————

Where to go next:
(#) bā + (#) yī = ?
+
(❄) xuě – (💧) yǔ = ? ↻
+
(#) chī – (#) yī = ? ↻ ↺

=

———— ———— ———— ————

At first glance, it appears to be a mix of emojis and the pinyin romanization of Mandarin words, with each emoji pairing with the pinyin word that follows. Those are then set into equations. Solving the first one should give us clue #1, and then combining the answers to the next three equations will tell us where to find puzzle #2.

Because the pinyin tells us the pronunciation of the target word and Mandarin consists of many homophones, my pen hovers over the paper, not sure which specific character corresponds to each sound.

"This is kind of like Phonetics and Phonology," I muse.

"Then it's your time to shine, Speedy."

With those words, my heartbeat speeds up, *Spee-dy Spee-dy Spee-dy*, my confidence rising with each accelerated beat. I refocus, and this time, the heart symbol in parentheses leaps out at me. That plus the sound *xīn* is suddenly so obvious: it has to refer to 心, the character for heart.

"*Xīn*, nice work!" Pierce says as I write 心 down. Even though he looks a little embarrassed, Pierce pronounces the word correctly with only the slightest accent. It thrills me to hear him speak the language I learned first.

Pierce points. "I thought *zhōng* might refer to *middle*, but that doesn't match the handshake symbol."

I snap my fingers. "*Zhōng* meaning *middle* is the answer! What comes after the equal sign! The handshake *zhōng* is this one, for *loyal*." Next to the handshake symbol, I write 忠.

"Oh my gosh, so if you quote-unquote subtract *xīn* from that . . ." Pierce trails off as I write it down: 忠 – 心 = 中.

"It's Chinese character math!" I exclaim.

It's not funny, but we laugh because we're so excited at already having the first clue of three. I write the answer in the space provided: 中.

Now that we know how it works, we quickly solve the third equation—*xǔe* means *snow*, matching the snowflake symbol, and *yǔ* is *rain*, yielding: 雪 – 雨 = Ǝ. After some deliberation, we figure out that the ⇅ symbol is instructing us to rotate the Ǝ 180 degrees, resulting in an *E*.

By this point, it's just us left in the entire room. Groups have been trickling out over time, and the hushed whispers have now melted into overwhelming silence. My palms grow slick, the worry rising. Have they all moved on to the next clue? If they have, and on a puzzle we have a clear advantage on, then we don't stand a chance.

Unfortunately, we don't pick up any speed because the remaining two equations are complicated. We deduce that the hashtag refers to numbers and that *bā*, *yī*, and *chī* refer to *8*, *1*, and *7*, but then we get a little lost.

"So eight plus one equals nine, and seven minus one equals six," I say out loud, confused.

Nine and *six*—in roman numerals or Chinese characters—do not go with the *E* we already have.

My pen taps in sync with Pierce's bouncing leg.

"So we're doing math with the Chinese characters," I think out loud, too into the puzzle to worry about whether or not I'm saying anything embarrassing. "Except it's not really math. With the snow equation, we treat the Chinese characters as pictures. We're not looking at the meaning. If we were to subtract rain from snow, we'd get, I don't know, cold temperatures? Doesn't matter." I'm talking fast now, too excited. "We need to do the same with the numbers, use the characters as pictures. Okay . . . so . . ."

As I fill in the Chinese characters for the last two equations, Pierce is staring at me in awe. I want to take a moment to enjoy it, but I'm too panicked about us being behind.

With trial and error, we settle on the following answers:

八 + 一 = π (with Pierce getting that one, proving that he indeed is a fan of Greek letters)

七 – 一 = a backward J, which, rotated 180 degrees and then flipped backward (↻ ↺) = r

I scribble the new answers out: π E r. "That's two languages."

Pierce points to the four blank spaces at the bottom of the puzzle. "And it's only three things for four spaces."

I scan the page. "It's supposed to tell us where to go next. Since the E and r are both English, it's probably the *pi* that needs to be—oh my god." I cross out π and replace it with *pi*.

"The pier," we whisper together excitedly.

"Let's go!" I shriek. I grab my things so fast that I drop everything and have to do it again.

The pier isn't really a pier. It's a shoddy wooden platform that extends over a pond. But since it's the only body of water—if it can even be called that—on campus, students have joked about its romantic significance over the years. The pier is constantly the center of a joke or prank, with students one year setting up a sad carnival ring toss near it, and another year a bonfire and s'mores. Since the Mystery Hunt traditionally features iconic campus locations, I'm embarrassed it took me as long as it did to figure out where we were supposed to go.

Pierce and I take the shortest route possible, through the Thru, aka the main corridor on campus. It was originally named the Thruway but over time became just *the Thru* to the Cornmouth community. As a linguistics student, I can't help but obsess over how words evolve and grow to mean something to some people, and nothing to others. Like how every day we say *p-set* for *problem set* and *prefrosh* for *prospective students* and *Carl* for the statue. To an outsider, it probably sounds strange. I write all of these in my purple polka-dot notebook, my glossary of Cornmouth's secret language; the list resides next to my collection of favorite phrases from other languages with no good translation, like *rènào*.

Long-legged Pierce shortens his steps as I lengthen mine so we can keep pace. We pass students huddled on benches and standing in groups. They could be part of the hunt, but since we're not wearing anything different, I can't be sure. I almost want to run up to them and see if they're holding hunt materials, but I obviously don't.

In the middle of the Thru, Pierce asks, "So what started your love of puzzles?"

Warmth fills my insides as I tell him, "It's because of my dad. He and my mom immigrated from Taiwan in their thirties, and because of the language and cultural differences, communication hasn't historically been the smoothest for us." *Hasn't historically been the smoothest? Who talks like that? Be more normal!* I chastise myself.

"I thought you spoke Mandarin fluently."

"I do, and I think in Chinese, if that makes any sense—"

"It totally does."

We share an in-smile born of understanding. I continue, "And my parents speak English, so we speak the same languages, but . . . there's still that divide. Like, you speak a lot of languages, right? But it's still different than if you grew up in that country, using that language as your primary one. There's just that extra . . . space. I don't know how else to describe it."

Pierce nods slowly, and beneath his baby blues, it looks like his mind is churning, as if he's trying to understand. "So, playing games is when you feel closest to your dad?"

I nod. "He uses game metaphors to tell me things he can't express otherwise. It's the only time he opens up."

Pierce nudges me. "He's not the only one."

89

I blush. But his words also inspire me to share more. "The first time it happened, I was in fourth grade. I studied really hard for this math test but still failed. I was embarrassed and scared my parents would be upset, so I didn't tell them. My dad must have gone through my backpack because later that night, we played Chinese chess, and when he won, he cleared his throat and said, 'It's okay that you lost. I'm proud that you worked so hard.' It was so subtle I just stared at him, not sure if he was saying more than that, but then he patted my hand and said, 'I struggle with some things, too. Like English. And communication.' That was when my fascination with language really took off, when he found a roundabout way to convey so much to me with so little.

"He's super excited about the hunt and has been texting me game metaphors all day," I finish, holding up my phone to show him the latest: Chess is won by patience, thinking ahead, and focusing on the board in front of you, not any other games around you.

"Well, we better win this." Pierce's voice is matter-of-fact, confident, and when my gaze meets his, he has a twinkle in his eyes.

My heart fills. Sharing, for me, is historically followed by regret, but in this moment, I'm bouncing off the walls. Somehow, even more than at the start of today, we feel like a unit. A team. Two peas in a pod.

"What about you?" I ask. "You seem pretty into games, too."

Pierce's gaze falls to the ground, and the shyness is endearing. "I had a hard time making friends. But cards and video games and charades were an easier way for me to be myself. I get so caught up in them that my brain's filter turns off."

"Me too."

We share a conspiratorial smile. How can it be that our connection feels this deep after only knowing each other a short amount of time? I want to reach out and touch his pinky just like he had reached for Cornelius's earlier, but we've arrived.

The pier has been decorated for the hunt. Streamers are strewn about and a photo of Professor Margolis cheering is sticking out of the ground, attached to a stick. In front of her is a box painted in Cornmouth's green and yellow (the colors of corn, of course). We struggle with the latch, and when we finally work the lid open, a loud bang echoes. We both jump back as a handful of green and yellow confetti rains over us.

"We must be the first ones here!" Pierce deduces. He's so excited he looks like he wants to hug me, but he holds back, maybe because I'm staring at him. I heard his words, but they haven't sunk in yet.

I examine the box and realize only one confetti popper had been rigged to explode.

"You're right," I say, though I'm still struggling to wrap my head around it. "I can't believe . . . This is so . . . Wow."

We actually have a shot at winning. I came into today assuming I'd be fighting to stay a part of the pack, and though

I wanted to win, I didn't really think it was possible until this moment. Now I'm imagining what it would be like to tell my dad we did it.

Pierce raises a palm for a high five. I wish I hadn't taken so long to catch up, missing the window for a hug. But I smack his hand and we dance around a bit, the excitement needing a way to exit our bodies.

I briefly worry that the only reason we're ahead is because we know Mandarin and our lead will disperse with the next puzzles. But I keep those doubts to myself.

Pierce grabs one of the envelopes inside the box and hands it to me.

I tear it open and for a second it feels like we're on *The Amazing Race*. What I wouldn't give to run across the globe together. He would be my top choice for a partner. We'd be able to communicate in so many different countries; we'd be unstoppable. Except for the fact that I get horrible motion sickness and would be knocked out from Dramamine half the time.

The paper is filled with symbols. Letters. But they all appear to be different languages. Again, the top puzzle is one of the three clues—another piece to go with 中 from puzzle #1—and the bottom tells us where to go next.

I focus on the first line for now and point to a few of the symbols as I guess their language: "Greek, American Sign Language, um, hieroglyphs, I think?"

"Wow." Pierce's eyebrows arch even more than they naturally do.

"I didn't say I know what they are. Just what languages they appear to be. Well, the Greek one I do know. Alpha."

I'm staring at the page gripped too tightly in my hands when Pierce's voice startles me. "Should we relocate? Maybe grab a bite? We might want a table so we can spread out, take notes, look stuff up, you know."

"Good idea. I know a great boba place nearby, and they have rice bowls, Chinese breads, Pocky—"

"You had me at boba," Pierce says with a wink.

After I get honey green tea with boba, Pierce orders an Okinawa boba milk tea in a way that suggests it's his usual. Once we receive our drinks, we settle side by side into a cozy corner booth next to blocky wall letters that read: ALL YOU NEED IS LOVE AND MORE TEA.

I take a sip and try not to groan. Meanwhile, Pierce happily laps up the liquid that has spilled through the straw hole onto the top of his cup. It's sloppy and puppy-like, and the fact that he's so comfortable with me makes me pull out the second puzzle so I can hide my giant grin behind it.

My eyes are only partly focused on the page, but then they catch on the text the way you catch a reflection of yourself in passing. Because the letters are familiar, in my bones, something I know backward and forward. These were the building blocks of my Chinese school education.

"It's Zhuyin Fuhao," I exclaim, tugging on Pierce's sleeve as I point with my free hand to the ㄚ and ㄜ symbols sitting side by side a few lines down. "Bopomofo. It's the Taiwanese phonetic system; our version of the ABCs, our version of pinyin." I point again, more frantic this time. "This is *ah* and *eh*. But . . . I don't know what it means; they don't combine to form a word."

"Let's start looking up some of these other symbols," he suggests.

By the time we're halfway through our drinks, we've managed to identify several of the symbols by guessing what language they are and googling.

"So far, a lot of them correspond to the letter *A*," I say, looking at the ASL symbol and the Hebrew aleph. "But I'm thrown by the *ah* and *eh*. *Ah, eh,*" I repeat. Then, slowly, I realize, "They're kind of the sounds that the letter *A* makes, right? Which I guess is the best you can do with Mandarin."

We look at each other.

Pierce's dimple appears. "These are representations of the letter *A* in different languages."

I google "hieroglyphics letter A," and the bird that's drawn on the page pops up on my phone.

We both take a moment to stare at the letters.

"It's so cool seeing the same sound represented in so many different ways," I think out loud. These symbols feel like a representation of the world and how we're all connected, a perfect summation of everything I love about language.

"That's exactly how I feel." Pierce's baby blues are shining, likely reflecting what my own eyes look like.

Even though we're in a race, we take a couple minutes to look up a few more symbols, which becomes easier now that we know what they sound like. After I identify the Hangul and Georgian ones, I make myself focus.

I write *A* as the answer to the second clue. "Okay, let's figure out where we're going next."

After that, there's just one more clue, and if we can figure out how to combine the three clues quickly, maybe I can make that winning phone call to my dad, the one that will indirectly say *I did this for you* and maybe even *I love you*.

In a reverent quiet, Pierce and I look up the rest of the symbols. It's perfect, this nerdy love letter to language, shared with Pierce over boba tea. I take a mental picture, not wanting to forget this sugary feeling enveloping me. As I'm capturing this moment in my memories, he looks up at me and I swear he's doing the same thing.

I feel as warm as my honey green tea.

• • •

As we suck up the last few wayward tapioca pearls, we complete the part of the puzzle that tells us where to go next. The word *thru* has been spelled out in multiple languages. Again, the Mystery Hunt loves to take advantage of Cornmouth culture, lore, and lingo, and the Thru is as iconic as anything. Even though figuring out the four-letter destination was easier for this puzzle than the first, we're left with a new challenge.

"Which part of the Thru?" I ask. "I didn't see any boxes or markings on our way here."

"Me neither."

We make our way to the south entrance and pause. No boxes in sight. Nothing out of the ordinary.

I shrug. "I guess we start walking?"

The Thru is so long that we travel it once at a normal pace because examining it inch by inch would take hours.

Nothing.

We pass countless students, and I can't tell who's part of the hunt and who's not. But I swear I see a few groups hustling toward the pier.

I'm getting so antsy I start jogging back toward the south entrance, but Pierce stays in place, deep in thought. I hustle back to him when he opens the hunt envelope to retrieve its contents.

"Think there's something in there?"

"I don't know. Maybe." He shoots me his one-dimple grin. "I like that you embody all meanings of your nickname, Speedy."

I blush. I'm already sweating, which makes my cheeks flush faster than normal.

Pierce flips through the first puzzle, then the second, and then he lands on the cardstock.

I read the hint aloud to refresh our memories: "'If e'er you're stuck with nowhere to turn, the answer is already in sight. Past clues may offer new things to learn, at times, if only viewed in new light.'"

Pierce opens our notebook to where we've written all our answers thus far: *thru*, *A*, *pier*, and 中.

"Zhōng!" he practically screams. Then he catches himself and returns to normal volume. "That's got to be it!"

I'm already nodding. "Zhōng, middle. We have to go to the middle of the Thru." I clap him on the shoulder. "Great detective work, Sleuthy!" I'm *mortified* as soon as the nickname comes out of my mouth, but Pierce is grinning so wide I forget my embarrassment.

"That was worth the wait," he says shyly.

Sleuthy sounded so silly a moment ago, but seeing how much he loves it changes my mind. It's not about what the words are or how they sound, it's about their meaning.

"Come on, Sleuthy," I say with confidence.

We're both smiling the entire way to the middle of the Thru.

Since we don't know for sure where the exact middle is, we take our time combing through the bulletin boards, doorways, and corners of a fairly broad area. And finally, we find a box that has been painted almost the same color as the wall so it's camouflaged, save for one yellow and one green stripe running down the center, which is what my eye caught.

"It seems to be getting progressively harder," Pierce muses. "No giant Professor Margolis cutout pointing this one out."

From the box, we grab a rolled-up piece of paper and unfurl it. I can't tell if we're first or not, but the box is pretty full. Why couldn't this one also have a confetti popper?

I suggest we make our way to Strolle Library, my favorite of the many libraries on campus. This one is a glass dome that's gorgeous day or night, sunshine or stars, and yes, I've had many fantasies of a romantic moment there.

My heart skipping in time with my quickened steps, I lead Pierce inside to my favorite desk farthest from the door for maximal privacy. We pass several groups with bilingual dictionaries, a few of the faces familiar from classes and a few, I believe, from the kickoff. I can't see the papers in front of them, but I swear I hear mentions of a dozen languages, including Spanish, which must refer to the puzzle in my hand. My palms fill with so much sweat I have to tuck the paper against my side so I don't make it gross.

At my favorite desk, I run my finger quickly over the familiar carving on it—two hands shaking, like Carl, with a heart above and two initials on either side—but there's no time to tell Pierce the backstory I made up about it even though, for once, I want to.

I smooth out the last puzzle before us.

Two ladders are drawn on the page, the left one labeled *English* and the right *Spanish*. The one on the left has English words sitting on each rung, with the word *voice* at the top. On the right, there's nothing, just three blank spaces per rung.

"Is this a translation exercise?" Pierce asks. "*Voz* is *voice* in Spanish."

I write *voz* on the first rung on the right, one letter per space.

The next English word is *sickle*, which we have to look up: *hoz*. As I write it below *voz*, a light bulb goes off. "*Hoz* is one letter different from *voz*. Maybe that's a pattern."

Two rungs later, we confirm my hunch.

From there, we hit a stride, working together—him googling the words we don't know and me writing. Some of the spaces have a box around them, perfectly encircling one letter in the Spanish answer. We decide to ignore them for now.

Once we finish, we both stare at it.

"The boxes next?" I ask. There are five in total, in seemingly random spots.

Pierce nods. "Well, the letters inside from top to bottom are *o, f, t, h, e*."

"Of the?"

I write it in the margin at the bottom of the ladder, next to where it says *Clue*, followed by three blank spaces. Those spaces are the last rung of the Spanish ladder, below *a él*, for *to him*.

"Del!" I blurt out, but remembering to keep my voice low because of the surrounding competition. "It's *of the* in Spanish, and it's one letter different from *a él*."

Pierce high-fives me. "So the third clue is *del*." He retrieves the final sheet of paper from the envelope, and on the provided blank lines at the top, he writes our three clue answers: 中 *a del*. "What the heck is that?"

Our eyes travel down to the words printed beneath, and we read the final hint to ourselves:

You're so close but not quite there.
Finish this ars magna, all,
for the coin's where if you dare.
Nothing's what it seems, big or small.

"Ars magna. That's Latin for *great art*," Pierce says, reading the translation off his phone.

But I'm focused on the last line, which jumped out at me. Since the 中 feels most out of place in "中 a del," my gut tells me that the 中 isn't what it seems.

"Wait," I say slowly, feeling the answer before I've pinpointed it. "The first puzzle was in Chinese and Greek. And English, since we translated *pi* to English letters. Maybe we need to also use all three of those languages now, to translate the *zhōng* clue into something workable."

"Hmm, okay," Pierce says, nodding. "How do we employ

Greek? In the puzzle, we had a Greek letter, *pi*. Maybe we need a Greek letter here somehow."

It hits me. "Look at this." I jab excitedly at the 中. "It also sort of looks like . . ." I rewrite it, rounding out the corners: φ.

"Phi," Pierce whispers. "A Greek letter."

As the final hint said, nothing's what it seems.

"And we could spell it out in English like we did with the *pi* in *pier*."

I rewrite the clues as *phi a del*.

"Phiadel. We've done it!" I joke.

Thank goodness we're tucked away in the corner, because after a pregnant pause, Pierce practically explodes, "Adelphi! Isn't that a place in London? The Adelphi theater? *Adelphi* is an anagram of the three clues. Just like if you take *ars magna* . . ." Pierce rearranges the letters in the two words and writes *anagrams*. "The *ars magna* in the poem was telling us to anagram the three clues to form *Adelphi*."

"Holy crap," I blurt out. We're silent for a moment. "This hunt is so freaking brilliant."

"It's the coolest, Speedy. The coolest."

The air between us feels electrified.

"So now what?" he asks. "We can't go to London."

"Maybe it's something to do with the meaning of the word?" I suggest.

He pulls out his phone. After a few seconds of typing and scrolling, he says, "The Adelphi district of London was so named because it was built by four brothers." He looks up from his screen. "Of course, it's from the Greek *adelphos* meaning 'brother,' or 'from the same womb.'"

I've never found him hotter. But I don't have time to dwell on it because it hits me. "Brothers!"

"Carl!" we whisper-yell at the same time.

We're off like bullets.

After we reach Carl, the excitement fizzles. There's no sign of the coin.

The sun is setting. I'm feeling panicked. We rushed out of the library so fast I didn't survey the progress of the other teams, and I have no idea where we currently stand. At least no one else is here.

But maybe the coin is already gone.

Pierce puts a hand on my shoulder. "Hey. Don't worry, the hunt is one more day. Maybe we should take a break."

I nod even though I'm thinking about how awful it would feel to call my dad and tell him we were this close but didn't win.

In the hesitation that follows, I think maybe Pierce is going to ask me to have dinner, but he just says, "Let's get some rest and regroup tomorrow. Thanks for such a fun day, Speedy."

For a second I wish he had offered to walk me home, but my dorm is mere steps away. I return to my room dejected.

Since my roommate is out, I spend most of the evening poring over the hunt to no avail, only stopping to make ramen with my plastic electric kettle.

Then my dad texts. It's part metaphor, part something else. Something new.

> Sometimes the end goal isn't the same as when you start. No matter what happens with the hunt, know I'm already proud of you. Don't forget to have fun.

It's so straightforward I almost don't know what to do with it. I consider telling him that I'm close to finishing, but he's right. That's not what's important.

I came into this wanting a lot but not expecting much out of myself, and at the end of today, I'm expecting a lot, in a good way, from myself, the girl who reached the pier clue box first. That girl doesn't need metaphors, not anymore.

I text my dad back.

> I love you.

Almost immediately, he responds: I love you too.

No game metaphor could make me feel what those four words do.

My dad is a hundred percent right. The end goal is no longer the same as when I started.

That night, I dream of letters, confetti poppers, and piercing baby blues.

• • •

The next morning I become Faye Fierce, sister of Sasha Fierce, Beyoncé's alter ego. As I slept, I finished my metamorphosis and emerged in the morning light, Kafkaesque, as a different person (but still human). More confident. More myself. (And how perfect is it that *Fierce* is Pierce's and my version of *Carl*, aka our supercouple name?)

I've asked Pierce to meet me at Carl. My palms are sweating even more than yesterday. Because today, it's about more than just the Mystery Hunt.

"We got this," I whisper to my bud Carl.

I recognize his languid walk before I can see his face. "Hey, Sleuthy."

Pierce beams. "Morning, Speedy."

I hand him an Okinawa boba tea and polish off my honey green.

"Wow, thank you. You've been a busy bee." He has *no* idea. He takes a sip and groans. "Okay, I'm ready. Any sign of other hunters?"

"I saw a group looking around earlier," I tell him. "But they've since wandered off after not finding anything." I hold back how their presence made me so antsy I worried I'd pee myself.

"Well, we can get it before they come back," he says confidently. Then he peers at me curiously. "How long have you been here?"

I shrug, then distract him by handing him the envelope. It works; he begins brainstorming out loud.

"So I've been wondering if we should focus on the cardstock hint. Because we're definitely stuck with nowhere to turn, and it feels like the answer should already be in sight."

I nod, encouraging him to continue.

"So maybe we need to look at our past clues in a new light. Either the *a, del, phi*—or *zhōng*—or maybe where we've been? The pier and the Thru? Or some combination of everything?"

"I feel like we've looked at *a, del,* and *phi* in so many different lights already," I point out. "Let's start with the pier and the Thru."

"Okay," Pierce agrees, nodding. "The pier and the Thru." He puts his drink down, takes out the notebook, and writes the words down, side by side. "In a new light," he murmurs to himself. Then he starts tapping the page urgently. "That's it. Pier Thru. In a new light." Below, he writes *peer through.*

"The diamond gap!" I say as Pierce points to Carl and yells, "The window made by their thumbs!"

Pierce climbs onto the statue, then leans down and holds his hand out, pulling me up. There isn't much space on Carl's base, and we have to press our bodies against each other and the statue to keep from falling. Our faces are so close . . . if I just leaned up . . . *Not yet*, I tell myself.

"You do the honors," he offers, nodding toward the gap.

I rise on tiptoe to "pier thru."

"It's a whole bunch of nothing, just the path leading to

the science buildings." I lower back down to my heels. "That can't be it, right?"

We gingerly dismount and repeat our climb on the other side so we can peer through the opposite way.

On the other side, I'm safely snuggled between Pierce's arms and the statue. Even though Carl's metal is cold enough to be felt through my layers, I could stay here forever. Reluctantly, I gesture upward. "Your turn."

I can feel his breath on top of my hair as he leans forward to center his face in the window. "Aha!" he exclaims, the triumphant declaration of a treasure hunter finding the X. "Look!"

I carefully maneuver myself to peek through the hole, and there it is: a standing birdhouse centered perfectly in the view through the gap.

"Come on," he says eagerly before jumping off the base and turning to offer me a hand.

I don't take it and jump off after him. Then I start sprinting toward the birdhouse. I can't wait.

Once I reach it, I pause. Coming up behind me, Pierce pants, "What are you waiting for? Grab that coin!"

I stand aside. Somehow, I manage to keep the smile off my face. "I want you to do the honors."

"What? No, this hunt was all you! You earned it!"

I shake my head, but Pierce also stands his ground. "Together?" I relent. He nods.

We slide our hands into the birdhouse. I keep mine higher than his so he'll be the one to grab what's inside.

Pierce's eager smile falters. "It's not a coin." He pulls out a piece of paper and unfolds it. "Oh. It's another puzzle."

Only six pictures are on the page. He points to them, trying to work them out. They are, in order: a signed testament; a female sheep; a board game with black and white circular pieces; an umpire with a clenched fist; a box with a line measuring it side to side; and lastly, a turtle.

It takes him a few minutes, but he eventually sounds out the pictures to form a question: "Will . . . ewe . . . go . . . out . . . width . . ." he trails off.

"Speedy," I supply. "Will you go out with Speedy?"

His mouth drops open. He looks from the paper to me, then back. Like he can't believe what's happening. Then his eyes glisten and my heart fills. He answers, "Wǒ yào. Quiero. Yes, in all languages."

I place the coin in his hand. The one I retrieved from the birdhouse earlier this morning. His fingers interlace with mine, the coin trapped between our palms. Somehow, it's all come together today. We won the hunt, the RA positions, and I'm going to tell my dad that he helped me achieve this, but the sweetest cherry on top of the Okinawa milk tea is: I found my voice and went for the pea in my pod.

When Pierce and I kiss, no words in any language can capture how it feels.

SHE COULD BE A FARMER

Nina Moreno

Critter's Hollow, Summer, Year 1

Hi Camila,
You forgot to tend the cows but I still left you a glowing light ring
in your chest!
ur neighbor,
Lily

Hey Lily,
It was your turn, I got the chickens
and THANK U, I was so sick of running home in the dark, you're
the best
-Cam

Fall, Year 1

Yo Camila and Lily,

I can't figure out this game.

how do I get into my inventory chest or down into the mines?

also do either of you have last night's homework???

all best,

Ernesto

Dearest Ernesto,

there is no school or homework in Critter's Hollow!!!!

Sixth grade is the worst, pls don't bring that energy here

p.s. you have to build a chest first, my dude. go chop down

some trees for wood. just not the ones by my cottage.

they're too pretty to die

-Cam

Dear Camila,

I'm so happy you like the oak trees I planted for you!

I figured you'd love the leaves when they change colors

also, welcome, Ernesto! Also yes, I have the hw

ur study buddy,

Lily

Spring, Year 2

Cam,

I had the weirdest dream about you last night. We went to the

movies but not in real life, instead it was here. it was like we

were really living here in critter's hollow.

They should add a movie theater in the next update, just saying
love,
Lily

Lily,
Will they ever update this game??? It's been a year!
that's MY dream
which movie? was it fun??
-Cam

Cam,
I don't remember the movie, but we had cherry cokes and a
jumbo popcorn.
It was super fun.
love,
Lily

Winter, Year 3

Dearest Camila,
winter is coming, please stop stealing my wool
is anyone going to the dance?
forever cold,
Ernesto

Ernesto the best-o,

STOP TALKING ABOUT SCHOOL HERE
And ugh, never. The 8th grade dance is a joke
also Lily knitted me a bunch of sweaters!
(with your wool)
-Cam

Dear Ernesto,
I thought it might be cool . . . the dance and sweaters
(there's more wool in the barn!)
xo,
Lily

Summer, Year 4

Yo Cam,
Where is Lily? Haven't seen her at her cottage in a while
there's a bunch of weeds, really giving me haunted house vibes
you should look into that because . . . spooky
all best,
Ernesto

Ernesto,
She's at summer camp and then she's going to visit her
abuelos.
She should be home soon . . . I can't wait.
-Cam

Three (IRL) years later . . .

Every Saturday night, Camila Reyes went to the corner store with her best friend, Ernesto Flores. They walked all the aisles even though they already knew they would buy a party size bag of Takis, two slushies, and pressed Cuban sandwiches from the deli, extra pickles for Camila.

Camila enjoyed a routine, and that the familiar shop around the corner from her house was never busy. But this particular Saturday, it was packed.

"What is this? Who are all these people?" Camila groused as she perfectly poured layer after layer of wild cherry and piña colada into her jumbo cup.

"They are our classmates," Ernesto replied distractedly as he went full throttle with blue raspberry.

Camila took it personally whenever something derailed her routine. She liked knowing what to expect and loved the simple joy of picking up their usual orders before heading back to her house to hang out for the night.

Realizing her popular classmates had discovered her favorite corner store felt personal.

They were a black-tie swarm. A nuisance.

"Why are they all dressed up?" She popped her lid securely onto her drink and gestured with it toward the very glittery crowd. She'd thrown a hoodie over the shirt she slept in last night, but everyone else was decked out in sequins, slinky dresses, and suits.

Ernesto sighed patiently as they navigated past the group crowding in front of the freezer. "You know why. Tonight is homecoming. The dance?"

Camila pushed her round glasses up her nose as she craned her head back to meet his amused expression. He was ridiculously tall. "Homecoming is a weird thing to celebrate in high school. We're not *going* home, we're already here and haven't gone anywhere else yet."

He blinked as a pensive look pulled his dark brows together. "I think it started as a college ritual. A nostalgic weekend for alumni to return to their old stomping grounds and remember the good ol' days."

Ernesto enjoyed taking her hypothetical grumblings seriously, but Camila would have plugged her ears if her hands hadn't been full. She did not want to talk about college or next year or the mountains of essays she still had to write for her college applications. Life was ramping up, pushing them all to some proverbial cliff, and she just wanted it all to stop. For a moment. For a deep, full breath.

Two boys in suits bumped into them. Camila recognized the taller one from the boys' soccer team—because of that time she accidentally ended up at one of their matches. It was a long story.

"Watch it, will you?" she complained as she sidestepped their mumbled apology.

Ernesto tossed an amused, wide-eyed smirk over his shoulder. "We need to feed you before you go on the attack like a—"

Camila rushed closer. "If you call me a hissy cat again, I swear, I will—"

Her best friend laughed loudly. Where someone else might have used a more colorful insult in the face of Camila's sour mood, Ernesto never did. His Filipino mother once hated for her young sons to curse. Understandable when you had a house of small, rowdy boys. She'd passed away when Ernesto was only nine. To this day, he had never uttered a curse word.

Camila snatched up the big bag of chips and quickly ducked away from a kissing couple nearly blocking the aisle. To Ernesto, she complained, "I'm supposed to have two days away from all of this."

"All of what?" Ernesto asked. "Love? Romance? Public displays of merriment?"

Camila knew of the first but had yet to experience the second. Surrounded by all this revelry, she felt a pinch in her chest. She looked forward to these ordinary tasks, but her weekend routine now felt small and silly. She stepped out of the aisle, almost crashing into two other girls.

"Sorry," she mumbled, but they just skipped past, unaware of her as they compared their energy drinks.

"A plague on both your houses," she hissed beneath her breath.

"Hissy cat," Ernesto sang.

When they finally reached the deli counter, it was only

to discover there was *also* a line there. "Bah," Camila said. "Homecoming."

"Tell me more, Uncle Scrooge."

"You know, technically it's also harvest time."

Ernesto spared her a quick, confused glance. "What?"

"Samhain," Camila explained, thinking about her late-night dive into witchy blogs. She had a weakness for cottage aesthetics and tea recipes. She was also considering getting into crystals. "Instead of celebrating returning to a place we never even left, we should be out collecting crops for the season."

Ernesto's dark eyebrow went up in that perfectly comical way she envied. He glanced at the chips and giant drink in her hand. "Are *those* your crops?"

She offered a short, sarcastic huff of laughter, but the joke snuck between her ribs and struck true. Why was tonight making her so moody? And nostalgic. Homecoming *was* a curse. Because now Camila was remembering a different October. One when she'd dreamed of a soft, wholesome life with her best friends on a cozy little farm. But that was just a game, and her naive imagination. This was real. Busy shops, fast food, the clattering sounds of the happiness of others over dances she would never go to.

She took a step forward in line and closed her eyes as anxiety tightened her chest. Camila filled her lungs on a deep, calming breath to ease the sudden knot. Her imagination may have been silly, but it was also stubborn. As she inhaled slowly, she couldn't help but wish for blue skies and crisp autumn air, but all she got was burnt popcorn and the cheap cologne all the boys had drowned themselves in. She coughed sharply.

Ernesto playfully tapped her nose. Camila's eyes flashed open.

"Daydreaming again, are we?" he asked innocently.

"It's called mindfulness," she deflected. "Every time you insist on bringing up college, I ground myself and try to imagine I'm in my happy place."

He cocked his head to the right as he sucked down a mouthful of super-sweetened blue ice. "Ooh, where's that? Am I there?"

"Of course you are." Anywhere she went, Ernesto did, too.

Their bond had been forged in elementary school, within the fog of a young boy's overwhelming grief. Ernesto had two younger brothers and a single dad who worked too hard, and so much of his home life was shaped by responsibility. Camila was his chosen sister and always offered him a safe place to fall apart or recharge.

When there was only one person ahead of them, Camila eyed all the food behind the glass case. "We should incorporate more vegetables into our life," she said thoughtfully. "Hearty ones you can put into a soup, you know? Like carrots and, uh . . ."

"Broccoli?" Ernesto offered after a drawn-out pause.

"Right, broccoli!"

"Oh my god, did you really just forget every other vegetable? And you're out here worried about an imaginary harvest?"

Camila ignored him and stepped up to the counter. To Mr. Romero, she ordered, "Dos sándwiches cubanos, por favor."

Ham, roasted pork, and melted Swiss cheese with mustard and pickles, served between grilled buttered bread. Heaven.

"Aw, you're a Cuban sandwich." Ernesto booped her nose again.

Camila batted his hand away. "Stop pressing my nose, it's not a button."

"It's a very cute button nose and you just need to accept it."

Camila touched her nose that her oldest brother had referred to on more than one occasion as a meatball and found comfort in Ernesto's sweeter interpretation. That was the magic of her best friend. He always found a silver lining.

"Order up!" Mr. Romero called, and Camila loved that he always did that. And how warm the sandwiches were in their paper bag. There was nothing wrong with appreciating the little things, she decided.

On their way outside, Camila pushed open the exit door just as the entrance opened beside her. The automatic bell sang out as cold night air swept over her, and she caught the gaze of Lily Ramirez, who was walking into the store.

Those three seconds were nothing more than a blink. But Camila felt each passing beat as her heart squeezed too tight and she fought to not stare at the girl in the blue, glittery dress, surrounded by her friends. Three breath-less, tortured seconds when Lily's soft, honey-brown curls bounced around her bare shoulders. Camila would have sworn that her lungs filled with the smell of Sun-Kissed Citrus, the cocoa butter and sugary lemon lotion and body spray Lily always wore.

Used to wear, Camila corrected herself silently. She didn't know what Lily wore now. They hadn't hung out since ninth grade.

The door closed, swallowing the noise of everyone else. Of another high school life filled with first love and romance that Camila never got. She sighed into the silence.

"Wow," Ernesto whispered into the quiet night, squeezing Camila's hand to steel her.

"Wow what?" she asked, nearly breathless.

"I have to catch my breath. I'm suddenly drowning in romantic tension."

Camila's face burned. "Stop it."

"I've been telling you for years, it's not just you." Ernesto and Lily were still friendly. A hey-remember-how-we-used-to-be-friends-in-middle-school level of friendly. "I see her also staring at you whenever you're not looking." He nois-ily finished his Slurpee. "Watching you two is unendingly frustrating."

Unfortunately, Ernesto was also a hopeless romantic. Lily never looked at Camila. Not like she wished she would. They became a trio after Lily was assigned to their reading group in fifth grade. Ernesto loved to read out loud for the whole class, saving both the shyer Lily and Camila, who'd already been an introverted grump. They'd balanced each other out in middle school, and it had been perfect.

Until Camila ruined it all in ninth grade by falling for her best friend.

Fall, Year 4

Cam,
What's going on with u and Lily?
I know, I know we don't talk about school here
But also stop playing, yes we do
all best,
Ernesto

Ernesto,
Idk, we're in high school now
She joined the soccer team, super busy
New friends, no time, old story
-Cam

Dearest Cam,
So you're just never gonna tell her?? ☹
Even after she knit you all those sweaters???

Best,
Ernesto

Ernesto,
Those were imaginary
This is real life.
It's probably time for us to stop playing anyway . . .
-Cam

Saturday night at the Reyes house was a warmly chaotic affair. Her oldest brother, Leo, was away at college this year, but that didn't make anything quieter. Bikes were strewn across their driveway as her youngest siblings hung out with their pack of friends in the front yard, all of them shrieking about something or another. Camila's abuela greeted her and Ernesto on the porch, where she was gossiping with their next-door neighbor, Mrs. Chavez, in rapid-fire Spanish.

They stepped inside and kicked off their shoes. Music was blasting from the kitchen. Saturday nights were her parents' "date nights," but they were also trying to save money, so instead of going out, everyone got takeout and a front-row seat to her mom and dad's loud music as they told the same stories and reminisced over a bottle (or two) of wine.

They were currently singing along to their Selena playlist. Her mother's short, dark curls bounced around as she danced in the middle of the kitchen, her hips swirling in a pair of ancient, faded jeans as she circled her husband, who was digging into their charcuterie board, waving away her efforts to get him to dance, too. He was still in his work shirt—REYES stitched over his heart—and looked tired, but happy to be home. The night was young, and her dad would be out of his seat by "Baila Esta Cumbia."

Thankfully they hadn't sunk yet to the dramatically slow turn of "No Me Queda Más."

They were adorable. Ridiculous, but adorable.

In socked feet, Ernesto and Camila slid past the kitchen and down the long hallway, until finally she was back in the haven of her bedroom. It was a cluttered space filled with books, throw pillows, and knitted blankets. Wood-wick candles that crackled and smelled like pumpkin pie or cashmere woods, whatever that meant. There were hanging plants beside the window and a reading nook beneath it.

"You're the only one who can be in here when my door's closed," Camila pointed out.

"Because your mom likes me," Ernesto said proudly as he dropped down onto the throw pillows on the floor.

She rolled her eyes. "My Latina mother is a sucker for boys."

"Unlike her daughter," he teased.

Camila poked Ernesto's nose before stepping over him to grab her remote. "I like you plenty." Her parents knew Camila's sexuality, and she was lucky how much they loved and supported her. She loved them, too. Enough to never go to karaoke with them.

They set out their spread of food on the floor, and Camila grabbed each of them a pair of fluffy socks. She had a collection and always had a pair on hand in Ernesto's larger size.

He smirked as he tugged them on. "You're so soft, Cam."

She offered an innocent shrug as she popped open the bag of Takis. It was true that Camila wished for a cozy life. When she learned what the word *hygge* meant, she'd finally found a way to explain her relentless pursuit of embracing comfort and also correctly pronouncing the Danish word with her Cuban American tongue.

Camila and Ernesto usually watched a movie, binged a season of *Schitt's Creek*, or caught up on YouTube channels, but tonight their favorite streamer promised a special livestream of a surprise video game.

"¡Qué lo que, mi gente!" Commander Bunny was a popular nonbinary Dominican American gamer. They mostly streamed different RPGs and indie games, and Ernesto and Camila loved their joyful bilingual energy and penchant for playing chill games that worked great as background noise when they were working on homework or their dreaded college applications.

"I've got a really exciting announcement, Team Fluffy!"

Ernesto glanced over and guessed, "Think it's a new game? What's a big title that's coming out soon?"

Camila took a bite of her sandwich and shrugged. Where she had once been permanently attached to her beloved Nintendo 3DS and still sometimes played mobile games—distracting episodic ones—she was too busy and broke to invest in recent releases on the new generation of consoles.

"I'm just here for the vibes and Commander Bunny." She popped a chip into her mouth.

"I've got a total exclusive!" With a gleeful grin, her favorite gamer held up a very familiar 3DS.

The next chip stopped halfway to Camila's mouth. She still vividly remembered shoving hers beneath her pillow whenever her mother checked to make sure she was asleep because it was *way* too late on a school night.

"Whoa, remember those?" Ernesto asked. "I traded mine in like an idiot. Only got like ten bucks for it."

"*What?*" Camila demanded, aghast.

Ernesto rolled his eyes and gestured around her cluttered room of mementos. "I know the idea of giving *anything* away offends you, but some of us prefer a more minimalist lifestyle."

"I can give things away," she argued.

"Okay, hoarder."

Commander Bunny flipped open their 3DS, and all the air left Camila's lungs in a rush.

"Tonight, I'm playing *Critter's Hollow!*"

Ernesto shrieked and shoved Camila's shoulder, but she was frozen in place.

"It's our old game!" Ernesto said happily.

The multiplayer farming sim had been their favorite game for years. Camila and Lily started playing it the summer before middle school, Ernesto joining them later. Those digital years had been as real and meaningful as the ones that marked her own calendar. They'd built a quiet, happy life where they celebrated festivals and birthdays, and Camila's heart squeezed at the familiar, brightly colored title screen. The leaves in the corner still fluttered just like she remembered. Her throat closed at the sound of the gentle instrumental music, plucked from her memories like a lost lullaby.

This was my happy place.

Ernesto liked the game well enough but hadn't been as obsessive about it as Lily and Camila. But still, he'd continued to log on for Camila after Lily stopped playing right before high school. Her real life had become too busy for pretend. With no new updates, Camila gave up soon after.

The years were long and a blink, because now Camila was two months away from college deadlines and had to make all these grand decisions about the rest of her life. And it was here, on the cusp of all this change, that a game's intro screen was enough to blast open that old, shuttered window in her mind as that soothing main menu theme song swept inside like a breeze, scattering memories and wishes.

"This indie game was developed by a single creator and was a huge cult favorite!" Commander Bunny explained.

Starland Farm, Camila silently chanted like a wish. *We named our farm Starland.*

"Unfortunately, the developer, the single person who created the entire game, infamous recluse Simon Yang, stepped away from game development after *Critter's Hollow* experienced a huge boom of popularity. Simon left us all with this one shooting star of perfection." Commander Bunny smiled brightly. "Until now."

"Wait, what did they say?" Camila latched on to Ernesto's arm, her pulse pounding too loud in her ears.

"Ouch!" Ernesto complained, tugging at her lethal grip.

"There's a new game?"

"Oh my god, Cam, hush so we can listen!"

She didn't know how she felt about a new game. She didn't want to go somewhere new and start over. She wanted to go *back*. Back to a time when all Camila had to do was click a few buttons to get online and then Lily was opening a door back into her life.

"But I am happy to report that *Critter's Hollow* is getting—" Commander Bunny paused for dramatic effect, and Camila was sure she was halfway to a heart attack. Beside her, Ernesto tried to untangle her claws from his arm. "An update!"

"An update?" both Ernesto and Camila shouted at the same time.

"Yes, an update!" Commander Bunny answered, as if directly to them. "We are not talking a sequel or new game, but a long-awaited update to *Critter's Hollow*! Our beloved town is being expanded with new neighbors, quests, and a bigger map that will include a brand-new seaside village!"

Ernesto and Camila screamed.

Camila's bedroom door flew open. Her wide-eyed parents raced into the room. Her dad's shirt was half-unbuttoned. "What happened? Who's hurt?" her dad demanded. Her mother's frantic gaze quickly searched every corner.

Camila jumped to her feet and in a deadly serious tone explained, "They're updating *Critter's Hollow*."

A beat passed. "Should I know what that means?" her dad asked before sliding a confused glance to his wife.

But Camila's mother was still scanning the room, her worry replaced by frustration. "Ay, Camila, look at all this stuff." Her parents respected their children's space and boundaries, but her mother would leap at the chance to have unfettered access to her room so she could dig through her daughter's belongings in the name of organization, aka snooping.

Ernesto and Camila spun back to face the TV. With one hand on her chest, the other gripped by an equally awed Ernesto, they watched as Commander Bunny started a new game.

"And for those of you who hold on to everything like me—"

Camila's mother laughed.

"If you log in tonight, you can download the update for free!"

Ernesto spun to her. "Do you still have it? Oh my god, what am I even saying, of course you still have it! Where is it?"

Camila spun in a circle. The save file for Starland Farm was on her 3DS. Because they were friends, whenever Camila got online, Ernesto and Lily could travel to it, but the only way to go back to everything they'd built was to find that 3DS. In a burst of motion, Camila dove for the closet. She whipped the door open, and behind her, Ernesto and her parents gasped.

"There's so much stuff!" Ernesto complained.

"I'm out," her dad said. "Dibs on the playlist, babe."

But Camila's curious mother stayed behind to take a closer (nosier) look.

Camila pulled out box after box. There were baskets and bins of keepsakes and souvenirs from trips. Concert T-shirts she planned to one day sew into pillowcases. Crafting supplies and more books. A pair of roller skates and every Halloween costume she'd ever worn. Camila wasn't necessarily anti-social despite evidence to the contrary. She loved dancing at concerts, disco night at the skating rink, and sitting in a dark theater with a Cherry Coke and jumbo-size popcorn in her lap.

She just didn't have fun doing those things with acquaintances she needed to impress. High school had demanded a level of socializing that stressed her out. A handful of really good friends was her sweet spot.

Ernesto dug into the box beside her. He pulled out a tall white hat with a red flower and black trim. "This is from that

year you and Lily went as Cher and Dionne from *Clueless*."
He put the hat on and checked his reflection in the nearby
mirror.

Eighth grade. She still vividly remembered Lily in that
yellow plaid blazer and skirt set.

It did not escape Camila that her mother was on her other
side doing her own digging. She kept sighing at the amount
of stuff, but her eyes were bright with excitement over being
allowed to stay. Her mother held up a sweater from their
school's soccer team. "This isn't yours."

Ernesto gave her a cheeky grin. "No, *that* was Lily's."

"Aw, Lily, I miss her." She cut a sharp glance at Camila.
"Did you steal this?"

The summer before freshman year, Lily went to soccer
camp and then to visit her abuelos. She was gone almost
the entire break, and Camila had missed her so much. She
spent that whole summer decorating Lily's house in *Critter's
Hollow* and listening to all of Lily's favorite songs on repeat.
The day she returned, Camila raced straight to Lily's real
house.

And after Lily's mother invited her inside, Camila stood
on the threshold, shocked to see that Lily already had friends
over. Soccer teammates filled the living room, and Camila
couldn't believe that after so many weeks apart, Lily had
invited them over before coming to see her.

And that she clearly hadn't missed Camila as much.

Lily greeted her kindly then introduced her to everyone. Camila's feelings felt too big for such a small space, and she left soon after.

When the soccer season ended, Lily asked to hang out, and Camila had been wildly hopeful. *Finally* they would get back to before; back to when it was just them and Ernesto.

But instead, Lily asked her to a party at some popular junior's house.

It was the last thing Camila expected her to say. So, she laughed. From the surprise and rush of fear. Camila never went to parties, especially not house parties at some jock junior's house.

For a beat, Lily had looked hurt before it flashed into anger.

What's so funny?

A house party? Really, Lily?!

They're fun and I want you to come with me.

But Camila didn't want to be dragged to some party as Lily's pity invite. Camila had all of these feelings, and no time to make sense of them, because Lily was pulling away from her. She didn't want to come back. Lily was blossoming, and high school was the worst, because it felt like everyone was waiting for Camila to outgrow her games and cozy routines. Growing up meant leaving it all behind.

I don't want to hang out with your friends, Lily.

You're so stubborn.

And you're suddenly so popular!

We can't just sit in your room and play Critter's Hollow *forever, Cam.*

Then leave! Go hang out with all your new friends!

Lily never came over again. And Camila never logged back in to *Critter's Hollow*.

The crushing memories of that last fight that ruined everything—even her favorite comfort game—grew worse the longer she looked at Lily's old sweater in her mother's hands.

"Maybe you should give it back." Her mother turned it around to read the label. "But wash it first."

"No!" Camila said too quickly, and snatched it back. For a while it had still smelled like warm citrus.

Her mom and Ernesto shared a knowing glance. "Lily absolutely left it on purpose," Ernesto said wearily. "Why does no one else see this?"

"I see it," Camila's mom agreed.

"Thank you!" he crowed.

Camila growled at them. "This is not a walk down memory lane, people, we have a mission here."

Ernesto gave her a thoughtful look. "But the mission *is* technically a walk down memory lane." He still wore the hat, and at some point, he'd squeezed into one of Camila's thrift store finds. A T-shirt that read DOG DAD.

"What exactly are we looking for?" Her mother was now wearing one of Camila's bright yellow headbands as she shuffled tarot cards.

"*You* are not looking for anything." Camila took the deck out of her hands.

"Her old Nintendo," Ernesto explained. He now wore a purple scarf, too.

"Stop putting my clothes on!" Camila dove toward him to take the scarf back.

"You can just buy a new game," he reasoned, batting her hand away from the scarf.

"I don't want a *new* one." Because it wouldn't have their old save file. It wouldn't have Starland Farm, where a version of Lily and Camila were still together, going to candlelit taverns, knitting sweaters, and raising ducks and cows together, happily ever after.

"Is this it?" her mother asked, and Camila nearly fell on top of Ernesto after being drawn into a wrestling match for control of the scarf. Their heads whipped toward her, and there in her mother's hands was her old 3DS.

Camila scrambled off Ernesto, and it was silly and sentimental, but having that piece of old, chunky technology in her hands again was like happening upon a time machine. A delighted laugh flew out of her before dying abruptly when she flipped it open and saw the black screen. Of *course*, it would be long dead.

"A charger," she called out, desperate. "I need a charger!"

They all returned to the boxes with renewed determination.

"Here it is!" Ernesto victoriously swung the cord above

his head. Camila grabbed it and plugged everything in, and when the screen lit up for the first time in years, they all let out a cheer.

Her mother sounded winded as she fell back against a box. The headband pushed her curls off her flushed face. "I'm not going to lie, I've had like two or three glasses of wine, but I am *incredibly* invested."

On her TV, Commander Bunny was setting up their first season of crops, and on Camila's tiny 3DS screen, she clicked on *Critter's Hollow.* The title screen popped up, and Camila had to swallow the delighted squeal that bubbled up in her throat.

Her finger tapped the button to go to the next screen.

The save file popped up. Starland Farm was safe.

Ernesto dropped his chin onto her shoulder and mumbled, "I do miss my 3DS. I mean, of course I have a Switch, but that's because I'm not an old lady buried beneath knitted blankets in her cozy depression hovel."

"Hey!" Camila's mom protested.

"Not you," Ernesto assured her as he pointed an accusing finger at Camila.

The game loaded, and it was like finding Atlantis. Narnia. Neverland. Her character woke up and stepped outside into a bright, blue autumn morning of the seventh year of this save file.

"Yikes," Ernesto said. "Those weeds really got away from us."

The place *was* overgrown, but it was still there. Orange and brown leaves fell from trees, a lazy cat napped in the garden, a sad jack-o'-lantern sat on her porch where she'd left it so many years ago.

The game had saved their place, patiently waiting for them to come back.

Camila's heart sank, because even as she was delighting in the digital magic of this time capsule, she couldn't help but wish that Lily would log on and virtually step out of her cottage to greet her like before.

"Look, you have mail," Ernesto said. He pointed at her mailbox. The flag was up.

"Do you want this?" her mother called out, now deep within her closet.

Camila ignored her and clicked on her mailbox.

There were unread letters. From Lily.

Winter, Year 4

Dear Cam,

I'm sorry about our fight. I didn't mean it. I mean, yes, you're stubborn, but of course I want to hang out and play this game with you. But I also want to take you to parties. And to see you at my soccer games. I want to go to movies and concerts together.

But I don't know how to ask you on a date. So, I'll try here.

I like you, Cam. So much.

I miss this imaginary life. And our real one. I miss you.

Maybe we could run away and start a farm when we're older?

Just an idea.

Let me know what you think, please.

Yours,

Lily

"Oh. My. *God*," Ernesto breathed at her ear. "I told you!"

Camila couldn't speak. All thought and words had crashed to a buffering stop.

Camila's mom stumbled over a box in her hurry out of the closet. "What happened?"

Fall, Year 5

Dear Cam,

I understand if you don't feel the same.

Miss you.

Forever yours,

Lily

"Oh my god, Cam!" Ernesto said again, as if she hadn't heard him the first time. He was still wearing her hat, sweater, and scarf, his eyes dancing. "Lily likes you!"

"She sent this forever ago," Camila reasoned, in a small,

strangled voice, her heart punching her ribs. Winter, year 4 in their game would have been . . . ninth grade. Right after their fight.

Fall, year 5 . . . was their sophomore year. Camila's head was spinning.

"Who cares when she sent it, she likes you! She wants to run away to a farm with you." Camila still hadn't moved, so Ernesto turned to her mother for an ally. "Mrs. Reyes, do you hear this?"

Camila's mother's eyes were bright. She clutched an armful of papers and tangled yarn to her chest. "You have to go to her," her mother said.

Camila was stuck in place, her head spinning.

Ernesto shook her. "Camila, *now*. You have to go to her right now!"

"What? No!" She tossed the 3DS onto her bed like it might reveal her current panicked state to Lily. She needed to think. "This doesn't mean . . ." Camila shook her head quickly. These letters weren't real. It was an imaginary farm and just another one of Camila's silly games. High school was too sharp to be this soft. To give space to her dreams. "She might not even . . . not like I do. You know?"

Camila's mom dropped everything and stepped up to her daughter. "Camila, be brave."

"I cannot crash the homecoming dance, Mom! She probably has a date!"

Her mother grabbed her shoulders and, leaning close, said, "Who cares what anyone says, the only thing that matters is your love."

Camila's confusion turned into a sudden frown. "Are you singing a Selena song to me right now?"

"I'm paraphrasing." She glanced at Ernesto and explained. " 'Amor Prohibido.' "

"Great choice," he told her sincerely.

Camila's heart was racing. But it didn't feel like the hot rush of anxiety she knew so well. It felt like . . . breathless anticipation.

"Exactly!" Ernesto said. "You've had a crush on her all through high school and you just found out she liked you back, and she's at a dance right now, of *course* you have to go!"

"Yes!" her mother agreed. She let go of her and spun around. "But shouldn't you wear something nicer?"

"Yes!" Ernesto said just as Camila shouted, "*No!*" She put a hand to her middle. "I'm going to throw up, I'm so nervous."

"Camila, listen to me." Ernesto grabbed her hand, and she watched the teasing light in his eyes turn fierce. "You've always been worthy of this love story. And right now, you just have to be brave enough to go after what you want."

Ernesto's certainty was infectious. Camila paced away before stopping in front of one of her wood-wick candles. It flickered, and the warm scent and soothing, crackling sound went a long way in luring her back into the safety of her cave.

But this new information cast the last four years into a whole new light. The possibility was thrilling and *terrifying* because she had to push herself out of her literal comfort zone to go and get it.

Camila made a wish and blew out the candle before turning to her mom. "Can I borrow the van?"

Her mother considered her before smiling hugely. "Only if I can finish cleaning your room."

"You're a terrible driver," Ernesto complained from the passenger seat. He cocked the tall hat aside. "You're so slow! This is the part where you race to get there! Come *on!*"

Camila ignored him, her hands on ten and two. "I'm a cautious driver." Who was very, very nervous as what she was about to do hit her. "What if she doesn't feel the same anymore? What if she didn't mean it like I *think* she means it? She might not even like girls."

"Yeah, because straight girls dream of running away to a farm together."

Their high school was all lit up, and people began to spill out from the gym doors.

"I'm late," Camila worried. "It's too late."

"No, it's not," Ernesto assured. "Look! She's right there!"

Camila slammed on the brakes, right in the middle of the parking lot, and jumped out of the van. Fueled by hope, a rediscovered lullaby, and a world of possibility she hadn't known to dream, she ran toward Lily. She stopped just in front of her. Even after a dance in a sweaty gym, Lily looked like a dream in her blue dress while Camila still had on her fuzzy socks.

Breathless, Camila stood too long in the silence.

Lily's expression turned into a frown.

Camila's hope died, and she jerked her hand up. "I have your sweater." She held the junior varsity soccer sweater out to her.

Even from here, she could hear Ernesto's groan of dismay.

"Thanks." Lily drew out the word as she took the offered sweater. Her friends were an intimidating wall of puzzled whispers and hushed laughter behind her.

Camila couldn't do it. She spun around and took two hurried steps back to the van but stopped as her gaze met Ernesto's. He stood in the wedge of the open door as he shot her a bright smile. He tapped his nose meaningfully, and Camila's heart did a wondrous thing. Because it wasn't small and silly at all. Her wild, vulnerable heart was big enough to be head over heels for the girl behind her, and to also love this boy who confidently believed that her nose was cute, and that she could do something as bold as this.

Camila turned back and called out, "I finally got your letters."

Lily stood in the same spot but had tugged the sweater on.

Camila scrambled to get her 3DS out of her pocket. She held it up. "I only just got them, and—" She held her breath and jumped. "Yes. I want to run away to a farm with you."

It was too much for Lily's friends. They broke out in confused, cackling laughter. "*What?* Who says that?"

"I did," Lily said with a stunned look. She stepped off the curb. "I thought . . . I thought you got them and never responded because you didn't feel the same way."

Camila shook her head fiercely then stopped with wide eyes. "No, wait! I mean, I do! And I did then, too, but I never played again after you left my house that day." Camila nervously ran her free hand through her hair before shoving the 3DS back into her jacket pocket. "I felt like I wasn't enough for you anymore. Like you'd outgrown me."

Lily shook her head slowly as her lips softened into a vulnerable smile. "My feelings for you just kept getting bigger, Cam."

That smile and confession made it all real. Real and right here, right now. Camila's heart raced wildly as Lily moved closer, her voice soft and low. "You made everywhere feel like home. I've missed disappearing into your cozy little cottage of a room."

Camila laughed, dizzy with wonder and a wild sense of happiness that felt bigger than anything she'd ever felt. "I got even more plants."

Lily laughed, too. "Of course you did."

Camila could have floated away, but she noticed Lily's friends, standing just beyond them. Her first instinct was to step back from Lily, hide all this joy and vulnerability. But

Camila noticed that their eyes had gone soft. One of the girls looked giddy as she waved at her. Camila sucked in a shoring breath and lifted her hand to return it.

To Lily, she admitted, "I shouldn't have been jealous of your friends, but I didn't understand then that I—"

"That you what, Cam?"

Camila's existence wasn't small. She loved her routines and rituals. She loved being present enough to find joy in simple comforts, games, and songs. And she was also brave enough to close the space between her and Lily and, after three torturously decadent seconds, kiss her. A warm, soft kiss that turned her ordinary Friday into something extraordinary.

Cheers broke out from Lily's friends and from the nearby minivan.

Lily leaned back with an incredulous laugh. She pressed her forehead to Camila's, and quietly, just between them, confessed, "I've wanted to do that forever."

"You still smell like Sun-Kissed Citrus," Camila returned, and with no intention of wasting another second, kissed her again.

And there on a cold October night, with bright autumn stars shining above them, huddled with her once best friend and first love—her other best friend noisily celebrating from her mother's minivan—Camila Reyes finally understood homecomings.

Winter, Year 7

Camila & Lily,
Hello, my dearest flower girls. Your new expanded place looks
great!
I barely snooped, I promise.
I did steal a few sweaters. I never forgot about the wool
You better bring me back a souvenir from the seaside village!
forever yours,
Ernesto

Ernesto FLORES,
Of course we brought you something! It's in your chest that I
finally made for you, slacker.
And you're a flower, too.
Forever your button-nose,
Cam

ONE OF THE GOOD ONES

Isaac Fitzsimons

*Content warning: depictions of racism, police brutality,
and parental death*

I'M THREE SECONDS AWAY FROM MAKING OUT WITH THE MOST
gorgeous guy I've ever seen when the door bursts open and my
older brother barges in. I say "older," but we're the same age:
seventeen. We're not twins, though. It's confusing, I know,
but not as confusing as him being here in the first place. West
Troyer parties aren't exactly Kyle's scene.

His eyes sweep the room. It's all pastel pinks and purples.
Probably belongs to the little sister of whoever is throwing
this party.

Kyle crosses his arms and says, "Come on, we're leaving."
He's giving me the same look that Dad gave me as a little kid
whenever my behavior chart dipped below green at school.

He's not mad about who I'm with or what I'm doing. This

isn't the first time he's walked in on me with a guy. He's mad about where I am.

Reluctantly I push myself up off the fluffy white rug. The gorgeous guy watches me, lips slightly parted, a blush visible under the light sprinkling of freckles dotting his light brown skin. I don't even know his name. We didn't spend much time on formalities before escaping upstairs.

"Logan. Now," warns Kyle. A part of me really hates my brother at this moment.

"I'm coming." I hand the boy my phone. "Give me your number. I'll text you later." Our fingers brush when he takes it. His fingers were what I noticed first, plunging into the kitchen sink, pulling out a beer, and shaking ice from the can.

He saw me waiting and tried to move out of the way. I moved, too, and we did a sort of clumsy waltz before giving each other an awkward smile. I reached around him and dipped in my own hand, grabbing a bottle of water. Yeah, water. I don't drink during game weeks.

"Wild night, huh?" His voice was lower than I expected.

I bit my lip to hide my smile before facing him again. "I have practice tomorrow."

"Me too." He raised his beer. "But that's not stopping me."

"What do you play?"

"I'm a pianist," he said, leaning close to my ear to speak over the pounding music blasting from the living room.

Clearly "practice" to him didn't mean grueling sprints and

crushing tackles. I figured as soon as I mentioned football, I'd lose him, so I played along. "Jazz? Classical?"

He popped open the can with his long fingers. Musician's fingers. "I don't limit myself to one genre." He took a sip, watching me intently.

"Me neither," I said. And we both knew we weren't just talking about music. A few minutes later, we were fumbling upstairs.

He gives me back my phone and I stand, leaving him sitting on the floor. I follow Kyle out the door, down the stairs, and through the living room, where the party still rages on. A few people look at Kyle like they've seen a ghost, which makes sense because he's probably the palest thing this side of the train tracks.

Outside, I shiver as the chill October air hits my bare arms. "Damn, I forgot my jacket." I start to head back, but Kyle grabs my arm.

"No time. We have to get going."

I shake free from his grasp. "I just want my jacket. What's the big deal?"

"I'll explain in the car. Trust me on this, okay?" His steady gaze catches mine, and for better or worse, I do trust him.

"Fine, but I'm driving," I say.

"Like hell you are. I saw the beer."

"That wasn't mine. It was . . ." Crap, I didn't get his name. I scroll through my contacts until I find his entry. Ezra!

But I'm too cold to argue with Kyle, so I climb into the

passenger seat. I blow on my hands while the car warms up. The smell of burnt leaves and tortilla chips billows out of the vents. It's an old car. Belonged to my dad. But it's mine and Kyle's most favored possession.

Kyle switches on the headlights and pulls away from the curb.

"How'd you find me?" I ask after a few seconds.

"You forgot to turn off your location," he says, rolling his eyes. "Again."

"Shit, does Mom know?" I don't know why I'm asking. It's not like she's in any state to care.

"Nah," he says. "But I was out at Rico's with Ellie, and Officer Miller stopped by on a break to grab something for dinner."

Hearing Officer Miller's name makes my chest tighten, but I don't say anything and Kyle doesn't notice.

"He said they're cracking down on high school parties tonight," he continues, "so I thought I'd pick you up before anything happens."

"The cops are coming?" I watch out the side-view mirror as the house retreats in the distance. As West Troyer parties go, this one was pretty tame. About two dozen or so kids. Yeah, there was some drinking, and the clothes I'm wearing are headed straight to the wash to get rid of the weed smell, but it was mostly just dancing. A midweek precursor to the homecoming parties this weekend.

I think of Ezra still at the party and fire off a quick warning text. It's the least I can do. "Maybe we should go back and offer him a ride."

"Not going to happen," says Kyle. "If you get caught, you can kiss playing in Friday's game goodbye."

He's right, of course. Almost on cue, two cop cars with the Troyer Police Department markings approach us and cruise down the street. I duck a little lower in my seat and try to look innocent, even though I haven't done anything.

"Got you out just in time," Kyle says with a satisfied smirk.

"Yeah, thanks," I say distractedly. Ezra hasn't texted me back. I hope he saw my warning.

The car rumbles over the train tracks, and just like that we're in East Troyer. The saying goes that East and West Troyer share two things: train tracks and a love of football. Just looking at the two of them, you'd think they were completely different worlds. But looks alone don't tell the full story.

Kyle turns onto our street. It's on the Historic Founder's Row, a particularly fancy part of Troyer, with redbrick sidewalks and huge houses with wraparound porches. He pulls into our driveway and parks the car. I go to unbuckle my seat belt.

"Mom might be up still. Take that off before we go inside," he says, pointing at my do-rag. "I told her you were studying with me and Ellie."

I give him the finger but take the cap off my head and

stick it in my pocket all the same. It's not something I usually wear unless it's under my helmet or I'm at a West Troyer party. I brush my hand over my cornrows. They'll need to be redone soon.

Kyle reaches for his own seat belt, then stops. "Logan, don't you ever get tired of . . ." He trails off.

"What?" I ask.

"Nothing." He unbuckles his seat belt and moves to open the door. He's chewing on his bottom lip like he does when he's thinking. Mom and our sister, Brynn, do that, too.

"You obviously have something to say, so say it."

Kyle sighs. "Don't you get tired of pretending to be someone you're not?"

That hits harder than any tackle I've ever received on the field. "Don't you ever get tired of being a condescending asshole?" I fire back. He shakes his head and leaves the car, slamming the door.

I watch him walk up the shrub-lined pathway to our house. The problem is, I don't know what I am. That's not true. I'm an athlete. I like to think of myself as a pretty good son and brother, most days at least. But sometimes I feel like my life is a quick-change act and I'm never sure which costume I'm supposed to be wearing.

First, there's Logan Comstock, grandson of Eli Comstock, Troyer's chief of police currently embroiled in several racist scandals.

Then there's Logan Comstock, the adopted Black kid you see in the Comstock Christmas photos.

There's the Logan Comstock who approaches guys at parties without fear and takes them upstairs.

Then there's just Logan. That's when I pull out the do-rag and take an Uber into West Troyer. There, nobody knows who my grandpa is. And since most of them go to West Troyer High School while I go to East, they don't know who I am, either. There, I can be just another Black boy.

The only time I feel like all the versions of myself merge together in a way that fits is when I'm on the field as number twenty-one, running back for East Troyer High School, currently leading the team with seven touchdowns this season.

But the rest of the time I'm in between. I don't expect Kyle to get it. He's the type of guy who towns like Troyer were made for. Starting quarterback with golden-blond hair and bright blue eyes, dating the head cheerleader. Midwest, corn-fed personified.

He's my brother, but he's also my best friend. And when he says stuff like that, I wonder which version of myself he sees me as, and whether he'd accept me if I chose a different one.

The first thing I do the next morning is check my phone for a text from Ezra. But there's nothing. I try to shake off the uneasy feeling by going downstairs and making a protein shake. Usually whoever is up first will make enough for two, but I'm still pissed at Kyle for what he said last night. I hesitate with the scoop then cave in, adding another one. We've never been good at holding grudges, Kyle and me, and I don't plan on starting now. Not with the homecoming game this Friday. We're tight as brothers, but we're even tighter as teammates. And I can't let anything affect our performance on the field.

I take a sip, and Kyle comes in all sweaty from his morning jog. He tosses a paper bag of bagels on the counter. "Where's Mom?" he asks.

"Still asleep." She gets up later and later these days. I pass him a glass. He takes it with a nod of thanks.

"The bagels are fresh," he says.

"Chompies?" I ask. Chompies has the best bagels in Troyer, but you have to cross the tracks to get to it.

"Why would I go to Chompies? They're from Uptown Deli. I got the Comstock discount." Being a Comstock in East Troyer comes with certain perks.

I grab an everything bagel and smother on some cream cheese.

"Apparently it went down in West Troyer last night," says Kyle.

My hand holding my bagel freezes inches away from my mouth. "What do you mean?"

"They were talking about it at the deli. Some kid ran into a cop car."

My mind immediately jumps to Ezra and the two patrol

cars slinking up to the party as we left. I picture everyone spilling out into the streets at the first sign of lights and sirens. "What do you mean 'ran into'? Are they okay?" I ask.

Kyle looks at me like I'm an idiot. "They hit a moving car. You can probably guess who came off worse."

Something feels off about what Kyle is saying. "Why do you keep saying they hit a car?" I ask.

"That's what they said in the deli. The kid was trying to run away and hit a car." Kyle takes a huge bite of his own bagel and chews noisily. But I'm still stuck on his words.

"If the car was moving, wouldn't the car have hit the kid?"

Kyle pauses to consider it, then waves his hand as if to say *tomato, tomahto*. "If they didn't have anything to hide, they wouldn't have run. Remember what Dad always said? If a police officer stops you, just do what he says. Simple as that."

I open my mouth to say something back. He must know it's not that simple for me, right? But we've just gotten over one argument and I don't want to start another. Not before the homecoming game. I leave him and go upstairs. Before jumping into the shower, I send Ezra another text asking if he got home okay. When I get out, there are still no new messages in my phone.

I don't hear anything from Ezra all day at school. It's last period and I'm checking my phone for the umpteenth time when Mrs. Watkins, my math teacher, slams her hand on my desk, making me jump.

"Put that away now, otherwise you're getting detention for the rest of the week." She must see my surprise. "Yes, even tomorrow," she says before I can protest.

There's this unspoken rule at East Troyer that football players are given some slack. Miss a homework assignment? No problem. Couldn't study for a test because of practice? Take it next week. If I get detention, I won't be able to play on Friday, which means our chances of beating West Troyer get cut in half.

I turn my phone off, put it in my backpack, and try to concentrate on solving the quadratic equation on the board when phone alerts go off all around the room.

Suddenly the "no cell phone" rule doesn't apply as everyone takes their phones out from where they were hiding them under their desks.

"Okay, class, settle down," says Mrs. Watkins. She reads aloud from her messages, " 'PUBLIC SAFETY ALERT— The town of Troyer is ordering a curfew from eight p.m. tonight until six a.m. Friday.' "

"This has got to be about the kid who got hit in West Troyer," says a girl to my left.

I think back to my unanswered messages and wish Ezra would just text me back. I'm used to being ghosted after hooking up with a guy. Sometimes they're not out and don't want a relationship. Sometimes they are out and don't like that I'm not. Sometimes I'm just not their type. I get that. But I want to know that Ezra's okay.

"Holy shit," says Mason, the guy sitting next to me.

"Mason, please don't use that language in my classroom," says Mrs. Watkins.

"There's a video," says Mason. There's a screech of chairs as everybody gets up and crowds around Mason's screen. I lean over to get a closer view. It's grainy, like it was shot on a potato, but the video shows a kid darting out into the street. He freezes and raises his arms as headlights approach. The car hits the kid and he rolls over the top of it and out of frame.

It plays on a loop.

"I think I'm going to be sick," says Mason.

I keep watching, squinting to make the footage clearer. I try to remember what Ezra was wearing last night. I was more focused on getting him out of his clothes than noticing what he had on. Then on the third viewing, I see it. My jacket. The one I couldn't go back for. I watch my jacket fly out of the kid's arms as he's hit.

It's my turn to feel sick. I lean back in my seat and take a few shaky breaths. That's Ezra in the video.

My actions after leaving the party last night flash through my head. I should've warned him earlier, or maybe later. I don't know. But I can't help feeling like it's my fault he was in the streets when he was. I know I only met him yesterday, but I need to be with him. I need to do something. I stand suddenly.

"Can I go to the bathroom?" I ask.

Mrs. Watkins has given up any attempt at classroom management and nods. She doesn't even say anything when I take my backpack with me.

I stride down the hallway and wait outside Kyle's English classroom. We have the same English teacher but different periods. I really like her. Whenever we read something with a dead parent, she lets me go to the library and pick out another book if I want.

I knock on the door. She looks over. I mouth *Kyle*, and she nods. A few seconds later, Kyle comes out.

"What is it?" he asks, mildly annoyed, as if missing ten minutes to talk to me will ruin his chances at valedictorian.

"It's Ezra," I say, sinking down to the floor and putting my head in my hands.

"Who's Ezra?"

"Ezra, the guy I was with yesterday. He's the one who got hurt."

Kyle's eyes widen in shock. "Shit, that sucks. But he was okay when we left."

"It's all my fault," I continue.

Kyle shakes his head. "No, it's not."

"If I had warned him earlier—"

"Logan, like I said, if he'd listened to the cops—"

"You're really an idiot, you know?" I say angrily.

Kyle puts his hands up defensively. "I'm just trying to help you out here."

"Do you think the cops would do that if it were an East Troyer party?" I ask.

Kyle's eyes narrow. "What's all this about? You're not going full ACAB on me, are you? What would Dad say?"

My entire body flinches at that low blow. I wipe my eyes. "I knew you wouldn't get it."

"Get what?" For the first time Kyle looks less like my brother and more like the other white kids at this school. The ones who call me "Oreo" while describing things as "lit."

A memory comes to mind. Something I've never told anybody. "Have you ever been stopped for no reason?" I ask.

"No, but neither have you," he scoffs.

I say nothing.

Kyle's forehead creases in concern. "Right? Logan?"

I take a deep breath and begin. "Officer Miller stopped me once while jogging." I liked jogging at night when it was cooler. I had an EDM running playlist blasting through my headphones and was concentrating on my footing in the dark, so I didn't notice the cop car until it pulled up right beside me.

"What happened?" Kyle's voice is softer now.

My pulse quickened, pounding in my throat at the memory. I mean, I sort of get why he stopped me; you don't see a lot of Black people in my neighborhood. But I can't think of anything less threatening than a guy in running tights.

"He pulled up beside me in his car and asked for ID. When I said I didn't have any, he turned off the engine and got out." What I don't tell Kyle is how when he approached me with his hand on his holster, all my blood pooled in my legs, making them heavy as lead.

"But then when he got closer, he recognized me."

"Did he say why he stopped you?" asked Kyle.

This was the part that played on repeat in my mind afterward. "He said he wanted to make sure I was one of the good ones."

"Tell Grandpa," says Kyle. His mouth is set in a firm line.

I shake my head. "Yeah, I'm not doing that." Officer Miller is a friend of the family. He was one of the officers who carried the casket at my dad's funeral. Dad was a cop, too. He died in an accident last year. And with everything going on—my mom barely making it out of bed in the morning, Grandpa with all the investigations around his police department—I don't want to add more stress by accusing one of Grandpa's officers of discrimination.

"Okay, well, what can I do?" asks Kyle.

I look at him. Sometimes it's painful because he has so much of Dad in him. "Give me the car keys."

"Why?"

"I have to go see Ezra. Make sure he's okay."

"Are you sure? They might not even let you in."

"I have to try."

Kyle looks like he can't decide what to do.

"Please, Kyle."

If there's one thing he can't resist, it's being the hero.

"Okay, but you're not driving. Not like this. Let me grab my stuff. Last period's almost over. I'll tell her you feel sick and I have to take you home."

Of course, Kyle's right. I can't get past the hospital reception desk. It doesn't help that I don't even know Ezra's last name. Even Kyle tries, flashing his most charming smile that gets him extra bacon at the monthly police pancake breakfast, but the intake nurse barely looks at him.

Kyle doesn't rub it in though as we sit in the parking lot of our favorite diner, a bag of fries between us on the dashboard.

I watch as a man puts plywood against the diner window, covering up the sign that says GO EAST TROYER TIGERS!

I lick salt off my fingers and sit back. "Do you ever think about how if things were different, we would be on opposite teams tomorrow?"

Kyle nods. "Yeah, it's weird. I can't imagine playing without you on my team."

"Because you know that if we were on opposite teams, I'd kick your ass," I joke.

He laughs before pulling out another fry. "One year."

"What?"

"One year we weren't on a team together. Remember?"

I nod. We'd both joined Pop Warner at six years old. Like any good son of Troyer, we were expected to live, eat, and breathe for the pigskin.

Kyle took to it like a duck to water, but what I really wanted was to take dance classes like our older sister, Brynn. Before the next season started, I screwed up all the courage I had in my little seven-year-old body and told Mom that I wanted to quit football and join dance. Mom and Dad had a tensely whispered conversation in their bedroom, but the next day I was allowed to go with Brynn to her dance class. I loved everything about it. Tap was my favorite, followed by acro. I loved the sound my feet made in tap shoes, and the shapes I could make with my body.

One day a casting director from a local theater came looking for kids to audition for the musical *Oliver!* I remember being psyched because as the only boy, I thought I'd have a good chance at getting to play Oliver. I was waiting backstage before my audition when the girl in front of me asked who I was auditioning for. When I told her, she wrinkled her nose and said, "Yeah, if they want a ghetto Oliver."

I didn't know what "ghetto" meant, but the way she said it and the look on her face didn't make it sound good. On the way home I asked my mom what it meant. She changed the subject.

I didn't get Oliver. It went to a girl who stuffed her long

blond hair in a newsboy cap before the show. After that year, I quit dance and rejoined Kyle at Pop Warner.

"I'm glad you came back," he says.

"Me too," I say. And I am, but I can't help thinking of that other Logan in an alternate universe and wonder what his life is like.

Kyle takes the bag of fries off the dashboard and offers me the last one. I shake my head, so he pops it in his mouth, crumples up the bag, and tosses it in the back seat. I check the time on the dashboard. "We should get back or we'll be late for practice."

"Yeah." He takes the keys out of his pocket and sticks them in the ignition but doesn't start the car. "Logan?" He turns my name into a question, but he's not looking at me. "Do things like that with Officer Miller happen a lot to you?"

It's an awkward conversation talking about racism with my very white brother. I shrug. "I mean, yeah." I dig around for an example. I don't usually have anybody to talk to about it, so I bury it deep. It's easier that way.

"You know how I go to Chompies to get bagels and not Uptown?"

"Yeah, because you have bad taste."

I punch him lightly. "No, because last time I went to Uptown and paid with a twenty, they said it was counterfeit and called the security guard."

I wait to see Kyle's reaction. "Well," he begins, drawing

out the word. "You don't know if they did that *because* you're Black, right?"

I shut down. Just when I think he's getting it, he goes and says something like that. "Forget it. Come on, let's go."

We rush into the locker room a few seconds late for practice.

Coach P glares at us. "Thank you, Comstocks, for deciding to join us," he says around the wad of chewing tobacco tucked between his right cheek and gum. Drug-free school zone, my ass.

"Sorry, Coach," we both say.

"Like I was saying," Coach P continues, "tomorrow's game will go ahead as planned. However, you should expect heightened security. Additionally, there's a strong chance that some of the West Troyer players will try to hijack the game and make a statement regarding everything going on." He rolls his eyes as if what happened to Ezra has inconvenienced him personally.

"I want to be clear. I expect all of you to remain on your feet for our national anthem and give it the respect it deserves. It's a big game. There will likely be news media. We need to show everyone that we stand behind our country and those who are fighting to protect our rights as Americans, including our men and women in blue. Is that understood?"

A low rumble of "Yes, Coach" goes around the room, but I don't say anything.

"Anybody on my team who attempts to pull a stunt at the game will be removed from the field immediately. There's a time and a place for all this. When you're on the field, you're on my time." His hard stare circles the room and lands on me. It stays a split second longer than it does on the other guys.

Here's the thing: I like Coach P, and he likes me. And he's never said or done anything outright racist, to me or any of the other handful of Black or Latino boys on the team. But sometimes I can't help but notice the way he talks about me compared with how he talks about Kyle. With Kyle it's all about his intelligence, his decision-making ability. With me, all I hear is what a beast I am on the field. It's like in his eyes I'm more animal than boy. I'm sure he doesn't even realize he's doing it, but I do.

Coach P's gaze moves on, and I try not to let it bother me too much as I pull on my Under Armour.

Out on the field, I let myself get swept up in practice. The cold air whistling through my helmet. The sting of the ball hitting my hands from Kyle's snap. The burn in my legs as I run up the field to score a touchdown. I feel so alive. I think that's why my mind suddenly jumps to Ezra. Alive and alert, according to the news reports, but in what condition? I remember his long fingers wrapped around my wrist last night. Can he still play piano?

How am I supposed to carry on like normal tomorrow

when Ezra is lying in a hospital bed and the cop who hit him is walking free? That thought runs through my head for the rest of practice and stays long after I hit the pillow that night.

"Logan!" Kyle's voice jerks me out of my stupor at breakfast the next morning.

"What?"

"Watch what you're doing."

I look down and see that I'm dangerously close to drowning my Cheerios in orange juice. I shake my head and put the orange juice away and take out milk instead. "Sorry, I didn't sleep well."

Kyle gets a couple glasses from the cupboard. "Worried about the game?"

I watch him carefully measure out protein powder for our shakes. I wonder what it would be like to only have the game to worry about. After our conversation yesterday, it's clear there's still so much he doesn't get. I try a different tack.

"What if it had been you?" I ask.

"What if what had been me?"

"Let's say you got hit by a car."

"Gee, thanks."

"I'm serious. The school would probably have a day of mourning. The team would wear black armbands. It would be this huge thing. And we're expected to play a game like usual. It doesn't seem right to me. To not acknowledge that something has happened."

"It's football. We're not denying anything happened, it's just not the place, like Coach P said." The blender whizzes to life, drowning out anything else I might say.

Where is the place to talk about it? I can't say anything at the dinner table because Mom will get upset and go to her room, and dinner is pretty much the only time I see her.

In school we learned that segregation ended in the sixties, but someone should tell that to Troyer. And it's really fucking hard to call someone out in the classroom when you're the only Black kid and even the teacher doesn't have your back.

And I tried yesterday with Kyle, but he made it clear he thought I was exaggerating. Sometimes it feels like my head is going to explode with all these feelings that I can't speak.

But maybe if I can't speak, I can act.

Kyle's back is to me, still blending our shakes.

I'm going to protest, I think to myself. Hearing those words, even just in my own head, builds my resolve.

As far as I can see, there's no "good time." I'm sure Ezra didn't think Wednesday night was a "good time" for him to get hit by a car.

Kyle revs the blender up even more.

"I'm going to stand up for Ezra," I say. Out loud this time.

Kyle switches off the blender and turns around. "Did you say something?"

I open my mouth then shut it. He takes a sip of his shake. White foam sticks to his upper lip. I play football, but Kyle, he lives it. I can't make him choose between me and the game. And I hate to even think it, but I don't know if this is something I can trust him with. What if he tells Coach P? I don't know if he'll understand.

"Nothing," I say.

This is something I have to do alone.

I chew on my rubber mouth guard as the team huddles in front of the banner before the game. Our collective breath hangs visibly in the chill air, like smoke billowing out of a dragon's nostrils.

The entrance song plays, and we move as one, bursting through the banner and onto the field where cheerleaders flash their pom-poms at us. I soak it all in, because after what I'm about to do, it may be the last time I get to play under these lights.

We line up for the national anthem. As the band plays the first note, some of the West Troyer players break from their line and take a knee. On the sidelines, Coach P spits his tobacco juice in the direction of the West Troyer players, and there's a smattering of boos from the stands, both of which strike me as more disrespectful than kneeling. I stay standing. I can't be kicked off the field. Not yet.

The final note plays, and the crowd breaks into applause. I take my position on the field, ready to play the game of my life.

The whistle blows. With Kyle as quarterback, we move down the field like an invading army, swatting away the West Troyer players like gnats. Every snap moves us closer to the end zone. The noise from our side of the stands fills my ears. They're shouting our last name. Whether it's for Kyle or me, I don't know. All I know is that they probably won't be yelling it for long.

At third and seven, Kyle sends me a perfect pass. It sails through the air and I jump to catch it, twisting away from a West Troyer player. I leap over outstretched arms and away to the end zone, ducking and weaving through the West Troyer defense. The roar from the stands grows louder in my ears.

I'm three yards from the end zone. Two yards. One yard. And just before I reach the end zone, I veer off the field.

At first, there's confusion. The players from the West Troyer defense stop short, not sure whether to tackle me or not.

Then I lift my jersey, and there are gasps as an image of me is displayed on the jumbotron with the words JUSTICE FOR EZRA written on my Under Armour in blue Sharpie.

After the gasps come the jeers. I take off my helmet and tuck it under my arm, then hand the ball to one of the West Troyer players. He pats me on the back, and I become aware of another sound: applause. I glance into the stands and see the West Troyer crowd on their feet. At the sidelines, Coach

P is practically foaming at the mouth. Kyle is standing frozen. I walk off the field, ignoring the shouts behind me.

I reach the locker room to grab my stuff when the door swings open and there's Kyle in the doorway.

"What the hell was that about?" he yells. I can't read his face through his helmet, but he sounds angrier than I've ever heard him before.

I don't know what to say.

Another figure comes behind him, and it's Coach P, huffing and puffing. His face is beet red.

"Kyle, get back out there!" yells Coach P. Kyle hesitates slightly. Through his face mask I can see his eyes darting between me and Coach P, and for a second I think he's going to talk back to Coach P, but he doesn't. He gives me this half-hearted shrug and leaves me there alone with him.

Coach P crosses the room in three steps, backing me up against the lockers. "What are you playing at?"

Some spit falls onto my cheek. I wipe it away.

"Get off of me," I snarl. I try to sound strong, but deep down I'm terrified.

Coach P puts both hands on either side of my face, pinning me where I am. "You are a disgrace to the Comstock name. Your poor dad is rolling in his grave."

White-hot anger flashes through me, and it takes all of my self-control not to punch him in his tobacco-stained mouth. Instead, I shove him out of my way. "Don't talk about my dad."

Coach P steps back. "You're off my team. You've got five minutes to get out of my locker room." He slams the door shut behind him.

I breathe deeply, still shaken by what just happened. What I did out on the field, what Coach P said about my dad, getting kicked off the team, and worst of all, Kyle abandoning me when I needed him most. My phone vibrates in my bag, dragging me back to the present. With trembling fingers, I pull out my phone and see a bunch of messages. But there's one that makes my heart stop. It's from Ezra. I open it.

Ezra: Sorry, I missed your text. I've been sort of busy . . .

Despite the adrenaline rushing through me, I feel a sense of relief knowing that he's okay.

Are you home? I text back.

Ezra: Yeah

Logan: Can I come see you?

Ezra: Now?

Logan: If that's ok.

I wait a few moments, then Ezra sends me his address. I get the car keys from Kyle's locker.

Ezra lives in a small house in West Troyer. I ring the doorbell, and a woman answers. She's darker skinned than Ezra but has his freckles. She looks tired but gives me a warm smile.

"Hi, I'm a friend of Ezra's," I say. I don't know what to do with my hands. I think maybe I should have brought him flowers or something.

"Of course, come right on in," she says.

She points me to a den with a piano pushed to one side, as most of the space is taken up by a pullout bed. Ezra's lying there. His arm is bandaged, and one of his legs is in a cast and propped up on a pillow. His face breaks into a smile when he sees me.

"Hey," I say from the door.

"Hey." His voice is raspy. Probably from being intubated in the hospital. A plastic band is still wrapped around his wrist.

He pulls himself up slightly on his pillows. "I have to say, I'm a little upset that you lied to me."

I freeze. "What do you mean?"

He shows me his phone, where there's a picture of me on the jumbotron. "Football? I was thinking you played trombone or something." He cracks a smile that melts my heart.

I take his smile as an invitation, and I grab a chair, pulling it close to his bed.

I gesture toward the piano. "Nice to see you weren't lying. Does she get lonely at night or something?"

"I don't usually sleep here," he says. "It's just easier than having to climb the stairs with my leg."

"How are you doing?"

He shrugs then winces like he wishes he hadn't. "I've been better."

"I'm sorry this happened to you," I say, knowing that my words can't change anything.

"Thanks for coming," he says. "I just wish that Wednesday night hadn't ended like this."

"How do you wish it had ended?" I ask, leaning closer.

Ezra blushes behind his freckles. "Well, as I recall, you were about to kiss me before that guy interrupted us."

"Yeah, sorry about my brother."

"Your brother?" he asks.

"Couldn't you see the resemblance?" I tease, automatically pulling one of the lines I keep in my back pocket for when I'm asked awkward questions about my family.

I watch as awareness dawns on his face. "You're a Comstock," he says. There's no trace of a smile now.

In East Troyer, being a Comstock is a badge of honor, but here, especially now, I wish I could scrub it off my birth certificate.

The light pink blush in Ezra's cheeks is replaced by red, angry blotches. "Is that how you got out in time? Did your grandpa tip off your brother?"

I recoil like I've been slapped. Partly because of how close to the truth it is.

I raise my hands defensively. "I swear, I didn't know when he picked me up."

Ezra looks like he's not sure he believes me. And why would he?

"I swear," I say again. "On my dad's grave."

"He was a cop, too," says Ezra.

I stiffen defensively. "Yeah, but he was . . ." I trail off. I was

168

about to say that he was one of the good ones, and it sounds weak even to me. When I was little I used to love when he'd pick us up after school and blare the siren in the parking lot. But now the sound of a cop car makes my heartbeat quicken. If that's how I feel, growing up in a police family, then I can't imagine how Ezra feels, especially now.

I need to make Ezra understand. I try again. "What happened to you was wrong, and I want to help fix it."

Ezra scoots back like he's trying to get as far away from me as possible, which is hard with his leg. His eyes roll up to the ceiling to avoid mine.

"Look, I appreciate you coming all the way here. But what makes you think you can fix anything?"

"I don't know. But I'm here now." Desperation creeps into my voice. That night at the party, I felt like things could be different with Ezra than with all my other hookups. I could see myself really liking this guy. And I thought maybe he'd feel the same way, until he found out my last name.

"Ezra, please, just look at me."

Ezra turns his head away. "I'm getting tired. I think you should go." The action shifts his neckline, and I catch sight of more bandages poking out underneath his shirt.

Instinctively, I reach out to take his unbandaged hand, but he pulls it back. "Now," he says.

His dismissal hurts more than being kicked off the team. I stand up and leave.

I stumble out of Ezra's house and crawl into my car. I slam the steering wheel, wishing for a bone-crushing tackle, the kind where your head reverberates in your helmet and leaves your knees weak. That would be better than the pain I'm in now.

Numbly, I turn on the ignition and steer onto the road. I'm near the tracks when I pull over. Where do I go? Not back to school where the game's still going. Not home. Not anywhere.

Then headlights shine through the windshield, dazzling me as another car approaches. It stops and someone gets out of the passenger side, but I can't make them out until there's a knock on my window and I jump, then almost faint, because first, I think it's my dad. My heart rate slows when I realize it's just Kyle. He's only in Under Armour and is still wearing his game pants.

I open the door. "What are you doing here? You should be at the game."

"Screw the game. I had to make sure you're okay." His eyebrows are knitted together with worry. He keeps his hand on my door as if he's afraid I'm going to shut it on him. "Wait here. Let me say bye to Ellie." He leaves for a second, and I watch him lean into the driver's window of the other car and kiss Ellie. She drives away.

He climbs into the passenger seat. "Turn on the heat. I'm freezing."

I start the car.

"How did you know where I was?" I ask, breaking the silence.

"Dude, if you don't want to be found, turn off your location."

I let out a chuckle, then pull away from the curb.

"Man, we are in so much trouble," he says after a few minutes. I glance at him, and he's wearing a slight grin.

I know he's right. I've probably cost the team the biggest game of the regular season—so school on Monday is going to be hell. But despite all that, I feel like a spark has been lit inside of me. The applause I got, the acknowledgment from the West Troyer stands, the backslap of solidarity from the West Troyer players, has ignited a fire. Now I owe it to them, and to Ezra, to be in this for the long haul.

"Good trouble," I say back.

"Logan," begins Kyle. He pauses, and I can practically hear the gears turning in his head as he tries to find the right words. "I just want you to know, I wasn't mad at what you did. I was mad at myself that you didn't feel like you could tell me. I know I don't always get everything, but I promise I'll do better."

Sitting there in our car that smells like tortilla chips, I realize that there's another version of me, too. It's one I don't even think about because it's so natural, the Logan when it's just Kyle and me.

We cross the tracks that separate West from East. Yes, West Troyer and East Troyer share train tracks and a love of football. But they also share me: the boy birthed by one, raised by the other, accepted by neither. I'll always be Black. I'll always be a Comstock. And that's the truth.

Ezra's right. My single act isn't going to fix everything. And I'm not arrogant enough to claim that I hold all the answers to healing this town, but maybe what I did tonight will bring us one step closer. And with Kyle on my side, at least I know I'm not alone.

Whatever happens, whatever position I play, I'll be ready for it.

JUST TELL THEM YOU PLAY SOCCER

Anna Meriano

ALL MY LIES COME CRASHING DOWN AROUND ME—IN THE MOST
ridiculous way possible—the Friday before Labor Day.

I attribute my downfall to carelessness, brought about
by the relief of turning in my first college exam and feeling
89 percent confident that I didn't bomb it. Environmental
science—which was the slacker science option in high school—
has definitely leveled up in college. But so have I.

But because I'm so happy with finishing my test, I don't
think about the tabs I have open on my laptop when I spin
it around triumphantly to face my suitemates, Xiumiao and
Clarisse, who are roommates in one of the bedrooms attached
to our four-person shared bathroom and common area. The
problem is, I was listening to a quidditch-themed podcast to
calm my test anxiety, and the tab that says QUIDDITCH ANALY-
SIS is fully on display directly above the line of text that says
TEST SUBMITTED: ROSAS, MADELAINE S0555892.

"Wait," Xiumiao says, reaching past my arm to tap the trackpad and bring up the podcast. I've been discovering over the past two weeks that my pre-med suitemate is not big on boundaries. "How do you know about quidditch?"

I've never exactly been good under pressure, so instead of playing it any amount of cool, I yelp and yank my laptop to my chest and ask, "How do *you* know about quidditch?" in a way that absolutely reveals how much I know about quidditch. Of course that's the moment that Olivia walks in, probably fresh from, like, a ten-mile run or something, and from the way she tilts her head and raises her eyebrows, it's clear that her elf ears heard exactly what I just said.

She looks, as usual, like a model in an athletic-wear commercial: muscled, effortlessly glamorous, and sweaty in an ethereal *glistening* way instead of a soggy gross way. I am a simple tall disaster bi; when I see a girl this beautiful, I fall for her. When I share a room with a girl this beautiful, I . . . well, I spend weeks constructing elaborate lies to impress her that fall apart in the most ridiculous way possible.

She looks at me, at Xiumiao, at my laptop (still open to the quidditch podcast, with a page designed to showcase how very clearly in-depth and in-group the analysis is), and a smug grin creeps onto her face as she wipes wisps of dark hair off her forehead. "Wait . . . I knew it! I knew you didn't play soccer!"

• • •

This all started before orientation week, when I had the brilliant idea to work out some of my pre-move-in anxiety at the campus gym.

I hadn't actually been to the University Rec Center since I got my acceptance letter (which explains why I do not have sexy athletic-wear-ad muscles; I go to quidditch practice a couple of times a week, but I never do any extra workouts on my own). I have been to the Rec before, of course, because I've lived on campus since I was in fifth grade. But there's an added element of novelty now that I'm going as an admitted student, not just a live-on-campus professor's kid.

It was always weird to be the kid who grew up at a college. My parents head one of the dorms ("residential colleges"— it's a whole thing) here at Rice, so I'm used to being the token child at the holiday party, the permanent kid sister— gangly, dorky Maddi running around babbling about worms or legumes and leaving streaks of dirt on everything—to hundreds of new faces every four years.

The best part of getting accepted (aside from the free tuition, which is also very much appreciated) was knowing that I'd finally be a real member of campus life, part of the cool kids' club, not a tagalong or afterthought.

It's not like Carolyn, the shuttle bus driver, ever made people provide student IDs before letting them ride around in a scenic circle of the campus, but it was exciting to think that if she did, I would be totally legitimate.

So when a hot girl got on the shuttle one stop after me and sat right across the aisle, sipping her water bottle and tying up her bouncy brown curls in what felt like cinematic slow motion, I smiled confidently and gave her my best (and only) line, delivered in my signature breathy squeak. "Hi, I like your shoes!"

(No, that has never worked for me, why do you ask?)

The hot girl (it was obviously Olivia, because my life is just determined to be ridiculous) replied by telling me how great the arch support of her sneakers was, and then continued (in what I would later learn was her signature easy, outgoing chitchat) to tell me that she was a freshman track and field runner and that it was her first day of summer training. And I, exhilarated by the fact that she was talking to me, squeaked that I was heading to the Rec, too (and I'm sure I daydreamed about the two of us walking in together and then giving her my number as violins played Tegan and Sara acoustic covers in the background).

"Oh, do you play a sport?" the hot stranger asked me, pointing at my gym bag full of cleats, a water bottle, and a (luckily out of sight) assortment of quidditch headbands.

And here's the thing . . .

I am a simple ginger Mexican American with an anxiety disorder, and when I meet a hot girl who looks cool and chats confidently and has sporty interests and whom I'm vehemently hoping is a Fellow Queer, the last thing I want to lead with is "I play quidditch."

Even though quidditch is very athletic! And very queer! It's more inclusive than basically any professional sport, and doesn't have the baggage of decades of policing out trans people and exploiting athletes of color. If you actually get into the community, quidditch has roller derby vibes with the added benefit of not being on freaking wheels.

But I didn't have time to explain all this or to answer the questions "How do you fly?" and "How does the snitch work?" or to explain that this all-gender, full-contact sport is in no way affiliated with the very public anti-trans figure who wrote the franchise it was based on. I had to get this girl to fall in love with me, or at least give me her number, in the next five minutes!

So I remembered an old quidditch adage passed down from self-conscious nerd-jock hybrids before me.

And I told her I played soccer.

My roommates are having a ball laughing at my misfortune.

"The cleats?" Olivia gasps. "What are the cleats for?" And I stammer until Xiumiao responds for me by holding up a (freaky fast) text from her high school quidditch friend confirming that you do use cleats in quidditch. "Oh my god," Olivia exclaims, "this is why you ran away when I asked about what soccer position you play! This is why you never wanted to talk about the US women's national team!"

Clarisse is giggling uncontrollably while Olivia pieces together more and more of my deceit. She's a giggler.

"This is . . . Can we all move on with our lives, please?" I would love to develop an invisibility superpower right now. I'm definitely doing my signature blush, which radiates out from my nose like I'm the freaking Rudolph of humiliation, and the biggest injustice in the universe is that I can't even go to my room and ugly cry in peace because Olivia would see and hear me and wonder why exactly my heart is crushed by this. "It's not a big deal."

"It wouldn't be, except why did you lie about it?" Olivia asks. She's pulled up the Rice quidditch team's social media, which means it's only a matter of time before she finds the pictures of sophomore-in-high-school me at my first practice, braces and weirdly-growing-out hair from my bob phase and all.

God, ancestors, santos—someone out there, please end my suffering.

"Like, this was the *one* thing I knew about you," Olivia says. She's tilting her head and squinting in a way that makes me want to hide under a rock like the spineless creature I am. It's by design that she doesn't know about all my weirdness. "That's what really throws me."

Clarisse nods, eyes suddenly wide and giggles vanished. "That's true, actually. Do your parents even live on campus? Or was that a lie, too?"

"Clarisse, you've been to my parents' house."

"Or have I?"

I look to Xiumiao for help, but she's predictably glued to her phone and insensitive to my distress, and Olivia just shakes her head at me.

"Sorry, but you don't get to act like we're unfairly impugning your honor. This impugning is totally justified."

And yes, even in the midst of my humiliation, when a hot girl uses the word *impugning* in everyday conversation, I swoon.

"I've been living with you for almost a month," Olivia continues, "and we've barely had a real conversation. You're just this looming mysterious presence except for this one clue that you play—I thought you played—soccer."

Hold on a second. Olivia thinks I'm mysterious? Olivia thinks I'm *looming*? What exactly have I done to loom other than be tall and exist in space? It's not my fault that I don't know how to make friends outside of quidditch practice and end up hanging out in our room alone all the time!

There was that one time when Olivia got on the phone with her parents and mentioned something about me in Spanish and I spoke up to let her know I wasn't the monolingual gringa she assumed I was, which was a pretty big moment of character growth for me because I really *wanted* to hear what she was going to say. I guess that sort of freaked her out. But that was me trying NOT to be creepy! I have in fact worked extra hard not to loom or creep or try to fish for information about her sexuality, or generally give Olivia any unwanted attention related to my desperate infatuation.

I guess it's possible that I went too far and ended up giving her no attention of any kind. But really, she should be grateful for that.

Olivia sighs. "I mean, here I was thinking that you must consider yourself too cool for us, but now I know for a fact that *that* can't be it."

I'm starting to feel really attacked right now. "What is that supposed to mean?"

Olivia just blinks at me. Behind us, Xiumiao helpfully explains (without looking up from her phone), "Because quidditch is not a cool activity."

Wow. "Wow." I feel irrationally offended, even though that was more or less the reason I lied about playing quidditch in the first place. How dare they try to shame me based on a part of my life I was ashamed of! "Maybe you're the one who considers yourself too cool for everyone!" I huff at Olivia.

It's not a great comeback. I've always been terrible about spitting out random angry-sounding words or echoing insults when I'm flustered. It's ridiculous to say that Olivia, who has been nothing but friendly and approachable since even before day one, considers herself too cool for anyone.

Olivia's shocked-Pikachu face shifts into a full-on scowl. "Well, I do think I'm cooler than someone who plays quidditch and won't even own up to it."

I am determined to defend myself better this time. "Did you ever think that maybe I just didn't want to tell you about quidditch because your basic jock brain couldn't handle it?"

Literally three seconds of thought disproves this quip because I didn't tell Clarisse or Xiumiao, either, but Olivia reacts like it was a real stab. "Basic?"

"I mean, you run in a big circle." A tiny voice in my head says that maybe this isn't the way to get Olivia to fall in love with me, but the louder voice that's getting kind of heated by the whole situation—and especially Olivia's mocking—just wants to point out that she isn't as perfect as . . . I think she is.

"Yeah, I run because I'm an actual athlete. What do you do? Fly?"

Three years of humoring that same stale joke solidify into a ball of rage behind my eyes. "That is actually hilarious considering you wouldn't last two seconds on the quidditch pitch."

Olivia's eyebrows shoot up, and she smirks in Student Athlete. "I'm pretty sure I could."

"Everyone always thinks that because nobody realizes that quidditch is a truly athletic, tackle-you-to-the-ground sport."

I guess at some point I took a step (or several) closer to Olivia, because suddenly I'm looking down at her (one could even say looming) and seeing the sprinkling of freckles over her nose and the curl of her dark eyelashes over her darker eyes and the way her baby hairs halo her ears and . . . What were we talking about? I try to recover my righteous indignation, taking a quick step back. "My point is, you couldn't score one goal against me in a quidditch match, and the fact that you think you could is laughable."

Olivia takes a step forward to match mine. "Challenge accepted. When's your next practice?"

Oh shit. "Huh?"

"Y'all realize we're still here, right?" Xiumiao asks, while Clarisse *hmph*s from the couch.

I'm slow to look away from Olivia to acknowledge them.

But she's slow to break eye contact, too.

The next day, Olivia tails me to practice.

"You really do this three times a week?" she asks, watching tiny figures assemble the triple hoops in the Rec fields on the opposite side of the parking lot we're crossing. "Even on a holiday weekend?"

"Yes." My tone is short because all my brainpower is currently being used to stay focused on this challenge, instead of devolving into a puddle of primordial crush ooze and sleep deprivation. "You've seen me leave for practice."

It was a weird, tense night, at least for me. Olivia seemed fine, going about her nighttime routine perfectly casually and then climbing under her blue flowered comforter (with purple sheets and pink throw pillows—is it a bi sign or just a color palette?) while I lay under my frog-and-mushroom quilt

182

feeling like my breathing was way too loud. I would be lying if I said I hadn't daydreamed about getting Olivia to a quidditch practice, but I assumed that would happen after we were . . . I don't know, married or whatever, when she was no longer allowed to mock me or my sport. Anyway, I spent a lot of the night anxiously lying awake, trying to stay still and breathe quietly to prove that I wasn't anxiously lying awake.

But Olivia is bouncy and energetic and as full of mischief as any fae creature this morning. "I saw you leave for *soccer practice*!" She throws up her hands with exaggerated vigor. "Maybe it wasn't just a front for quidditch! Maybe it was also a front for Goth Club Swing Dancing Nights."

That . . . was oddly specific. "Is that a thing? Have you done goth swing dancing?" In my attempts to play it cool with Olivia, I may have missed out on some fascinating small talk opportunities.

Olivia ducks her head in response to my question. "Anyway, I train every single day, so I'm still going to crush you. And when I win, you have to announce at lunch that you play quidditch."

Whoa, wait, I never agreed to attach actual stakes to this challenge. Lunch announcements—usually screamed out from the top of a table in our dorm cafeteria, guaranteed to get three hundred or so hungry college students staring at you—are no laughing matter. My nose starts to turn red just thinking about it. "Is that right? What happens when you lose, then?"

Olivia shrugs and skips ahead of me. "Irrelevant. You've lost your whole intimidation factor now. But you can pick whatever you want me to do."

"Uh . . ." My brain breaks under the pressure of picking something good but not too mean but not too nice and definitely not anything involving making Olivia go on a date with me. Also, intimidation factor? What? "I . . . you can announce. That *you* play quidditch."

My brain is NOT great at this kind of thing, okay?

Olivia raises an eyebrow. "So you want to make me a liar, too? Weird flex, but it doesn't matter. I'm not going to lose."

We reach the end of the parking lot, in easy waving distance now of the rest of the quidditch team. Erin and Aaron toss bludgers back and forth while Kristal shoots a quaffle through the hoops and Paulina and Thunder mess around with two pairs of snitch shorts in something that looks a lot more flirtatious than normal seeker activity. Everyone else laces up cleats or ties headbands on the sidelines.

"Oh, there are a lot of people." Olivia takes in the scene. I take in Olivia taking in the scene. "Wait, so are the taller hoops worth more points or what?"

I stumbled into my first quidditch practice on this exact patch of grass three years ago. Already sixteen (because my parents held me and my summer birthday back to make me a tall fish in the kindergarten pond), I was prone to taking long walks around campus and feeling misunderstood. When

184

I saw the hoops and the kids running around on sticks, I had to stop to process what I was seeing. And Paulina, an over-eager freshman at the time, came running up and asked me if I wanted to play.

It's a surprise to no one that she took over as captain this year. She always was great at recruiting. And since she and Thunder started dating each other soon after I joined, my mini crushes on both of them have petered out and become a love for them as our most stable and drama-free team couple (don't even get me started on Erin and Aaron).

"Oi, new freshman!" Paulina runs straight up to Olivia and offers her hand. "Welcome! Great to have you! What's your name? I'm Paulina. What college are you at? Have you ever played before?"

I fold my arms and smile as Olivia flounders under the barrage of questions. If she's embarrassed to tell the captain of the quidditch team that she's only here to prove that quidditch is easy and pointless, that sounds like a her problem.

"Babe. Boundaries." Thunder grabs Paulina's elbow and scoots her back a bit. He's short and thin and a fellow white Latinx; his legal name is lost to the winds of time because the whole quid-mmunity just calls him by his nickname, and he calls his signature snipe-beat The Lightning (and somehow got a girlfriend in spite of that). Having been pegged in the face by his deflated dodgeball more times than I want to think about, I can't even tease him about it anymore.

Since I'm not trying to help Olivia with her cover story, I crouch and take my cleats out of my gym bag while she constructs a surprisingly convincing excuse about how she wanted to come check out the team because it seems cool and she's been looking for clubs to get involved with that will help her make friends without sacrificing her athletic training time.

I wonder if there's any truth to her lie. I would never guess that Olivia worried about making friends. I kind of assumed she was automatic friends with all the other cool athlete types. But then again, whenever I get self-conscious that Olivia will think I have no friends because I never leave the dorm . . . she's also in the dorm. Maybe, like me, she basically just leaves for classes and practice. Huh.

Or, more likely, she does have lots of cool track and field friends, and this sob story is all part of her cover.

Either way, Paulina responds with her usual enthusiasm. "Great, yeah, we do a lot of travel, but of course it's all super flexible if you're busy with track," she says. "What events do you do? Do you have to go out of town for meets? We're all very close-knit here, whether you're on the tournament team or not. I'm sure Maddi has told you."

"Oh yeah, she can't stop talking about it," Olivia says, throwing a smirk my way.

And she called *me* a liar.

"So, are you two in classes together, or . . . ?" Paulina glances between us with just enough lift in her arched eyebrows to light up my face in embarrassment. She is such a chismosa (or fofoqueira, according to her), oh my glob.

Olivia glances at me, and neither of us says anything, which is weird because I know why *I'm* tongue-tied by Paulina's implication, but I don't know why Olivia's stumbling over the very simple answer that we're roommates who never talk and aren't even friends.

Paulina's face breaks into a knowing smile.

"Anyway, let's go warm up!" I grab Olivia's elbow and tow her toward the nearest set of hoops. I realize exactly one second later that my evasive maneuvers will do absolutely nothing to dispel Paulina's suspicions, but it's too late to fix now. I slip my green headband over my bangs, grab a quaffle out of the ball bag, and take up a position about six feet in front of the hoops.

"Go ahead," I tell Olivia, tossing her the half-inflated volleyball we use to score points. "Try to get past me."

Olivia inspects the quaffle suspiciously (I even got her the good one, with rainbow stripes), and then gives it an experimental lob toward the medium hoop on my left. I catch it easily, resisting the urge to smack it into the ground instead of doing the more reasonable thing and getting full possession. I do not resist the urge to gloat.

"Come on, at least try." I throw the ball back.

Olivia shakes her head. "How is this fair? I don't even know what I'm doing yet. Plus, don't I need a broom or something?"

I stare at her. "What do you want to do, stay for the whole practice?"

Olivia grins at me and lobs the quaffle back into my hands. "Sounds good. I always wanted to try LARPing."

"We're not—!" Olivia jogs to Paulina's side and starts talking and gesturing wildly and probably asking and answering a ton of questions. Erin and Aaron, genderqueer disaster partners (beater and sometimes otherwise), sidle up to me, both pairs of eyebrows raised. "Please don't ask," I sigh.

"I had this weird idea that growing up on campus surrounded by bullshit like ours made you more mature and immune to it," Erin comments, "but I guess you're just tall, not wise." They reach up to pat my shoulder. Way up. We're a very short team other than me, which is why I've been playing keeper since I was seventeen.

Olivia has no problem with our warm-up, of course. Running laps—even while navigating a PVC pipe held between your legs like a hobby horse—is a piece of cake for a college athlete, and I catch her adding her own more rigorous flourishes to our stretches. Show-off.

"So where was the part where this was crushingly intense and athletic?" she whispers to me when we take a water break before starting drills.

I just think there should be a law that bans all hot people from whispering arrogantly into unsuspecting people's ears. Especially if they then sashay away, lips curled in a self-satisfied, heartachingly beautiful smile. It seems only fair to the unsuspecting people who might be about to die of blushing and also annoyance and also hotness.

So I wave Paulina down and ask if we can work on tackling first.

Olivia shoots me a nervous glance when Paulina calls the drill. "Not used to having to touch other people on the track, right?" I ask.

Her chin shoots up. "I've done roller derby; how different can it be?"

"You've done roller derby?" Olivia has done roller derby. Gay panic alarms sound in my head because now I'm imagining Olivia on skates, and that is just a lot to process. Also I would never in a million years have guessed it. See? This is why we should have more conversations!

"Yes, and before you start, it's not nearly as dorky as quidditch."

"No, that's not what I was going to— I've always wanted to try it. I mean, I'm a disaster on skates of any kind, but I used to watch demo games at Comicpalooza, and I was also really into that graphic novel—"

"—*Roller Girl*!" Olivia hops up and down excitedly. (Which. Unfair. Too cute. My heart can only take so much.) "I read it like twenty times in middle school."

Okay. Okay. So Olivia rereads books to infinity and beyond, behavior that literally all my past friends have side-eyed when

I did it. And she picked a brightly colored graphic novel that I happen to love, not some pretentious classic or boring adult nonfiction book, or anything that could be remotely considered cool.

Cool. This is fine. My body is definitely on fire, but this is fine.

Another big elephant in my brain—and this is not to make any assumptions about roller derby as a sport—is that *Olivia does roller derby*, and that's not a very straight thing to do. And my brain is still screaming at me not to be creepy, but this is literally the best opening I've ever had to test the waters on something I've been overanalyzing ever since Olivia put up a nearly life-sized wall sticker of Megan Rapinoe.

"And I assume you've seen *Whip It*?"

"Obviously!" Olivia laughs excitedly, and before I can launch any more probing questions, she adds, "Elliot Page pretending to be a badass Texan girl was my sexual awakening."

Okay! Now we're getting somewhere! "Yesss!" I squeal too quickly and too loud. "Well, Alia Shawkat for me, but yes! Everyone in that movie. Beautiful. Perfection. Roller skate over my face, please."

Olivia chokes on a burst of (scandalized?) laughter. Did I go too far with that?

"I just mean, my tiny bi heart could not handle." I backpedal a bit.

I feel a little better when Olivia recovers and says, "Yeah, no, same on all counts." She bites her lip. (Distracting! Habit!)

"So, uh, Clarisse is really our token straight roommate, huh?"

"I was just thinking that." Wait, does this mean Olivia didn't know I was bi until now? What have I been doing with my life, seriously?

"So you two are partners?" Paulina's voice makes me jump.

"Huh? No, we're just . . ." Paulina is looking at me really weirdly. I glance around and see that everyone else is paired up for tackling. Partners. For the drill. "Yeah, sure."

Paulina hides a laugh very badly behind a cough. "Cool. Go through it slowly with her."

Oh god. I did not think this through. Olivia blinks up at me, waiting for instructions, and her eyelashes are so long and her mouth quirks into the tiniest curious smile and why is she allowed to make such a cute expression? Seems like it shouldn't be allowed. She's looking at me like that and she's not exclusively into guys and she's . . . funny and interesting and fun to talk to? Holy shit. I was pretty sure I had a handle on being in love with Olivia, but I wasn't prepared to also like her, like, a lot.

"Right, so." I swallow. "So tackling. You want to kind of, well, the goal is to redirect the other person's momentum and impede their movement, so you want to get low and hit at or below their . . . their waist level like . . . Is it okay if I . . . ?"

It takes a couple of demonstrations, but Olivia picks up the basic motion of wrapping my hips between her head, shoulder, and arms pretty quickly. Which is just fantastic and does not cause me any heart palpitations or sweat explosions. Her torso is warm when I wrap it in turn, and I have to break for water before Paulina calls it.

"AAAAAAH, I like your sticker!" Olivia says, pointing excitedly at the plain geometric Bureau of Balance logo stuck to my water bottle, because *of course* she's the first person I've known in real life that's also into *The Adventure Zone*. Because it wasn't enough for her to be my physically perfect but unattainable roommate. "I can't believe you have that!"

"I can't believe you know *The Adventure Zone*!" I reply, and then I feel guilty because, well, based on the past twenty minutes, I shouldn't be surprised. I haven't really asked Olivia anything about herself since we moved in, or else I wouldn't be surprised by any of this. I really did anxiety-crush myself out of getting to know a super-cool person. Wow.

"Passing and shooting drills!" Paulina calls. "We need three lines for offense, and, Maddi, do you want to be on defense with Erin?"

I love defense. I mean, I like offense, too, which is why being a keeper is so much cooler than playing goalie in any other sport, because it doesn't require me to stick close to the hoopline and gives me just as much opportunity for sick dunks as a chaser, but I also form the backbone of our defense and get to smack shots out of the air or crush people's dreams of making sick dunks.

But as Olivia lines up with a quaffle under her arm and a broom between her legs, I suddenly feel defenseless.

"I, uh, I'm actually going to run to the bathroom. Sorry."

The trek from the fields to the Rec bathrooms is long enough that it can give you a five-to-ten minute break. You can even miss a whole drill. Depending on when you go and how long you spend staring at your extremely red face in the bathroom mirror, trying to regain some part of your brain that isn't stuck on the soft curves of Olivia's body, you could even miss several drills and only make it back in time for scrimmage.

Theoretically.

When I get back, Paulina breaks us into two teams, with only one beater each because we're a little short on players. Olivia asks to be on the team I'm not on.

"So if I score on you . . ." she reminds me as she passes on her way to the opposite hoops.

"Yeah, it—y-you won't." My trash talk is at an all-time low. *Get it together, Maddi. It's just quidditch.*

Kristal leads most of the other team's drives for the first five minutes after Brooms Up. Aaron and Thunder keep drawing each other into beater battles in far corners of the pitch, so my chasers and I have to use our bodies to stop the drives, which is fine with me. Dragging Kristal to the ground a few times makes me feel more like myself, and the rhythm of the game shuts down my panicked and hypercritical inner voice.

Despite my web of self-conscious lies, I do actually love this sport. I feel good when I'm playing, calm.

At least until I see Olivia whisper something to Kristal, who nods and then passes her the quaffle.

Olivia advances up the field, eyes glued to mine, and I freeze.

I am not good under pressure. I should not have accepted this challenge. I am helpless and mesmerized by the goddess flying up the field toward me.

Except, hold on a second, this goddess implied that she used to find me intimidating. She rereads graphic novels and listens to dorky brothers play D&D with their dad. She's maybe even been to a Goth Swing Dancing Club, whatever that is.

I wrench myself out of deer-in-headlights mode. Olivia is not a mystical being placed on Earth to tempt and torment me. She's not a perfect untouchable human. She's not even a too-cool college jock. She's a chaser, and she's trying to score on my hoops. I'm a keeper, and I can't let her do that.

My cleats launch me on a crash-course trajectory. Olivia hesitates, tries to juke, but I stick with her, keeping low, coming in fast with my arms ready to wrap.

I catch her right arm, keep it pinned as I spin her out and down.

But the quaffle isn't there anymore.

As we collapse in a tangle of limbs and PVC, I hear whoops and groans and Olivia's voice in my ear. "If we'd done roommate icebreakers like I *wanted*, you would've known I'm ambidextrous."

I roll my head to look at the quaffle, which Paulina is running to retrieve from behind our hoops. "You made that shot?" Left-handed and falling, ten feet away and at an angle?

Olivia sits up, breathing heavily. "Yep. Told you."

I refuse to rise with her. I may never get up from this patch of grass. This may be my life now. The universe is clearly cursing me, so maybe it's best to just let it win.

"But, uh, you were right," Olivia says. My head and shoulders pop up to see her more clearly. "This is intense." She offers me a hand up. I take it, and it's warm and sweaty and rough.

"Water break?" Paulina asks. "That was fifty points, and it's almost six, so we could also call it." Everyone glances around, probably all remembering how much homework most professors assigned over the long weekend (my parents are the worst offenders of this no matter how many times I try to appeal to their humanity), and we start a group nod.

"Oh, is practice over?" Olivia asks. There's the tiniest pout in her expression. It is extremely cute.

"You already defeated me," I tell her. "Do you need to keep going just to rub it in?"

Olivia shakes her head and rolls her eyes. "You'll get me next time, Maddi."

"Next time?"

Olivia's smile is pure mischief. "It's like you don't know me at all."

Olivia and I make it official—in the most ridiculous way possible—the Monday before Thanksgiving.

Xiumiao is driving Olivia to the airport (any excuse to avoid going home), and my driver's-license-less butt is tagging along (any excuse to spend more time with Olivia). They're complaining about how weird it's going to be back at their parents' houses, and I'm chewing on my lip wondering if a vacation is going to somehow reset Olivia's brain. Maybe she'll come back realizing that she's way too awesome to be hanging out with her clingy roommate all the time.

Sure, she *claims* to be a ball of anxiety and running endorphins who is perfectly happy to spend all of our evenings together, either conditioning, marathoning overly dramatic shows, or pretending to watch those shows while we get distracted with other endorphins. But what if she changes her mind? A lot can happen when you don't get to make out for a week!

"And I know as soon as I get in it'll be all, 'Do you have a boyfriend or a girlfriend or a theyfriend?'" Olivia sighs. "And my high school squad is going to be even worse."

There's a beat of silence. Was that a pointed example? Is she expecting me to say something?

"Well . . . what are you going to tell them?" I ask, trying to sound casual while my adrenal glands go full fight-or-flight.

"I figured I'd say that I'm talking to someone, but she's afraid of commitment." Olivia's eyes twinkle.

"Hey! That's not true!" I'm extremely pro-commitment! I'm not extremely good at broaching the topic of commitment, maybe, but I sort of thought commitment was implied by the way I hang at Olivia's side literally everywhere these days. Also all the making out.

Of course I want commitment! She's my favorite person and she lives in my room and she is unbearably cute and gives perfect hugs and perfect tackles and . . . She's sticking her tongue out at me in the rearview mirror, so I clearly have to kick the back of her seat.

"Keep it up, please." Xiumiao rolls her eyes. "You two are making living at home more appealing by the second."

It's fine. I speak Xiumiao better now, and I know she loves us as much as we love her.

"Well, what should I tell them?" Olivia asks.

My brain is never great under pressure, so it's a good thing this answer is instinct. "Tell them yes. If you want."

My heart stutters in the split-second suspense.

"Yeah. I want."

Cool. Olivia is my girlfriend *official* officially. My chest aches with relief, and suddenly the long and makeout-less stretch of Thanksgiving break seems a tiny bit less looming.

"Have y'all not been dating since literally week one?" Xiumiao groans. "Because as an enthusiastic connoisseur of the sapphic dating pool on campus, it is very obvious to *us* that y'all have been exclusive."

"I think technically it was week three," I say, nose turning red. "But thanks for noticing." Maybe I still have progress to make on accepting that people like me, but at least now I can work on progressing with my *girlfriend*.

"Okay, so that part is settled." Olivia does a mini flounce in her seat, because she is the cutest in the world. The cutest *girlfriend* in the world. "But I have a larger problem. How do I tell my parents—much less my high school squad—that I joined a quidditch team?" She clutches her head in mock horror.

"Don't," Xiumiao suggests. "Preserve the last shred of your dignity."

"Hey now," I say. "Don't worry; there's a very simple, time-honored solution for this exact problem . . ."

"What?" Xiumiao asks while Olivia groans, "Don't encourage her, please."

I smile. "Just tell them you play soccer."

THE GIRL WITH THE TEETH

Kayla Whaley

Content warning: self-harm
(biting, blood, and depersonalization)

THE GIRL WITH THE TEETH CALLS HERSELF WARNING. WHEN she woke for the first time, she saw a moldy handwritten sign on the back of the door that read *WARNING: EXTRACTION IN PROGRESS*. She thought the message was addressed to her. *Hey, Warning, be careful.* She didn't realize yet that no one had bothered to give her a name because her name was inconsequential. Her teeth were the important thing. She learned soon enough.

Warning likes her name. Rhymes with *morning*, the time of day when these corridors seem friendliest, which is to say the least like a sudden, sickly breath on the back of your neck. For a few moments, tender yellow light whispers through the porthole windows, scattering the shadows before the sun escapes this dread-drenched place. Warning takes a mean sort of comfort in knowing the sun's freedom will be short-lived. Like her, it will always return. Neither girl nor celestial body is strong enough to break the curse of code.

With this last attempt she made it as far as the spa on deck 9 before she slipped on the dewy tile and instinctively screamed as she fell. Before her head had even cracked against the marble, dozens of slimy hands had slipped their digits into her mouth and wrenched her jaw wide. She died in a blooming pool of her own blood after the last molar had been yanked out, root and all.

Now, life refreshed, she reaches up and checks her mouth. Front teeth. Canines. Incisors. She gags as she reaches the back, but she swallows the reflex and runs her fingertips hard against the rough edges of her wisdom teeth. All accounted for. She lets her face relax, loosens her jaw, rubs slow, soothing circles into the overworked hinges.

If Warning had a choice, she might stay in this room. The only safe place she's found. It's a small room: a single bed, a bite-sized TV (disconnected) on a crooked dresser, an end table, and a table lamp (no bulb). The bathroom seems spacious if you ignore the dark outlines that mark where tub and toilet and sink should be. Next to the room's door is a freestanding closet that's not quite big enough to hide in comfortably, but it would get the job done in a pinch.

She could be happy here, she thinks. Wait for the sun each

morning to shine through the cloudy circular window over the bed, and when the panic grew too heavy, curl up on the floor of the closet until she could convince herself the skittering sounds outside were nothing more than high tide brushing along the beached hull. She could survive here. Maybe this time no one will force her out.

The door cracks open and Warning's heart drops.

Someone has come. The other side is in control now.

The game begins again.

She creeps down the narrow hallway of staterooms with her jaw held as loosely as she's willing to risk. No sense cramping up this early when she's confident she can make it at least to the pool deck without too much worry. She just has to stay focused. She just has to keep her mouth closed. The big scares are always the same. Around this corner a dark, bent something dashes across the hall, just quick enough that it might be an errant peripheral shadow. As she passes room 1206, something heavy shudders against the door. Near the elevator bank, Warning closes her eyes as a lone seagull swoops frantically past her head and into the elevator's glass door, the *thwack-snap* of impact ricocheting off the wood-paneled walls.

And always the nauseating tilt of the listing ship, its great bulk sinking starboard into the sand.

If she walks slowly, noiselessly, through this first long bout of claustrophobia, she'll be rewarded with the open air of the pool deck. She failed to make it that far her first few times, back before she knew to breathe only through her nose, to never gasp no matter how startled, to stop her chattering teeth from knocking her mouth open.

She's almost halfway down the hall when she's pushed into a run. As if a hand at the nape of her neck grabbed her collar and dragged her forward at speed. She shouldn't run. It's nearly impossible to keep your mouth closed in a dead run. The strongest will in the world can't deny empty lungs demanding more air. Warning tries to pull back, slow her momentum without face-planting. The skittering gets louder. Hundreds of tiny, tiny hands pit-pattering behind, beside, above her, a mass of greedy fingers writhing ever toward her, waiting for her to break. Invisible until they attack, the hideous skittering sound of them her only clue and her constant reminder that she's not alone, never alone.

She will not scream. She won't.

She can't stop running. Her legs ignore her desperate pleas to stop, just stop. They keep pumping faster, faster, harder, and her lungs beg *more air now, more, more now, moremoremoremore*. She bites the inside of her lips, punctures them and fancies her teeth a stapler. Numbered doors speed by on either side of her—or rather, she speeds by them. The doors aren't moving. She's moving. She's running and she can't understand why. Running doesn't help the other side. So why?

Her lungs will win, she can feel that now. They'll win and she'll suck in a mouthful of air, and she doesn't let herself remember what will happen next.

But then the broken rotating door is in front of her. She slams through, both hands gripping the jagged glass, and she's out. She's made it. She can't breathe and her palms are sliced and bloody, but her mouth is still clamped firmly shut.

She stands under a smog-dulled noonday sun, trying desperately to slow her heart rate because her lungs are still burning. Once she can breathe somewhat steadily, Warning heads for the nearby bar, or what used to be a bar. The stools have all been extracted already. Like the rest of this godforsaken ship, stripped for parts and left for dead. But the granite counter is still partially intact, and she hopes at least some of the bar's tools have remained through the pillaging. A pen and a napkin. That's all she needs. She rummages around, shoving aside glasses and bottles and a thousand tiny toothpicks.

She growls, the sound trapped low in her throat, and slams her fist on the countertop. Red splatters the granite. Warning had already forgotten about her shredded hands. Hurriedly, she slides her left index finger in her bloody right palm. Pain flares all the way to her toes, but this pain is nothing. This is the regular pain of sliced flesh. She's barely even tempted to hiss from this sort of pain.

Her blood is impossible to miss against the gray granite.

Good. She's never tried this before, but she's never needed to. They were always on the same side. Make it out without losing all her teeth. That's always the goal. So why make her run? Why risk it? She wants to ask, but she supposes the why doesn't much matter right now. What matters is standing her ground, to whatever infinitesimal degree she can.

She looks to the sky when she's finished, hoping against hope that whoever's on the other side is watching. Defiance is written on Warning's face as surely as her message is on this bar:

I WILL NOT SCREAM

The girl on the other side calls herself SunnySide. She has a given name, but she hasn't heard it in . . . she doesn't know how long. Her gamer friends call her Sunny, her classmates call her freak, her teachers call her troubled. Her parents don't call her much of anything anymore.

Sunny hates her name. She chose it for her first-ever video game, a puzzler meant to teach shapes and patterns and colors. Baby stuff. The characters were all cute little cartoon foods: banana, baguette, grapes. She liked the egg. Drawn fried the same way her dad made his every morning before letting her break the yolk, an honor she took very seriously. The trick was to slash, not slam, into the thin membrane so the steaming yellow shine would spread evenly on the plate, sogging the toast just the way he liked. As is the way of things, she used her hastily chosen name for every next game and account and user ID over the years until eventually more people in this world knew her as Sunny than knew her birth name.

Sunny envies the girl with the teeth, who has no need for a name. She looks down at the hands resting on her keyboard and smirks meanly. Beneath her signature fingerless gloves, she wears a battery of bite marks. Some older and faded, some still stinging red. Most not quite deep enough to draw blood, but sometimes she misjudges. (This is a lie she tells herself. But let's leave her this last thin membrane of a shield, for now.) Maybe *she* should be called the girl with the teeth. Maybe she will be if Lisa, her onetime best friend, tells people what she saw in the locker room today. Sunny's normally so careful, but she didn't think to check the showers since she didn't hear any of them running. She should have checked.

On the screen in front of her, *I WILL NOT SCREAM* is written in bright red, the kind of red no blood in real life has ever been but always is in horror games. A way to communicate the idea of blood when you're working with early–*Silent Hill*–level graphics. Although, she has to admit that despite the cartoonish color, the grainy letters do look somehow . . . drippy in a way pixels shouldn't. The girl with the teeth stands next to the message and looks up—at the camera, as it were. Breaking the fourth wall is a nice touch Sunny wasn't expecting. By all accounts, this game was supposed to be a pretty straightforward indie horror: walk around, jump scare, jump scare, jump scare, gore. You're in, you're out. Twenty minutes tops.

But so far, the atmosphere has been more creeping dread than *Outlast* or *Five Nights at Freddy's*. She likes the skittering sounds. They pan unpredictably in her headphones, as if something really is creeping around behind her. Pretty sophisticated sound engineering, honestly. And now this meta component. Did she trigger it somehow? She was pretty sure she was about to lose earlier in the hallway. Maybe near death prompted this turn in the story. She's not sure, but the message feels like a challenge.

She cracks her knuckles and winces only slightly as the skin between the first and second splits again. Time to test this game's limits.

The hallway was a warm-up, Warning now realizes. In retrospect, the other side might only have been getting a feel for the controls earlier, assumed that speed was the best approach. But then Warning had to go and stomp her feet like a child, and now she can *feel* the other side's intent. Warning ducks behind a row of slot machines (she won't be allowed to stay here long) and wills herself not to cry.

She's never made it to the casino before. Deck 5. Across the nowhere-to-hide expanse of the pool deck, through the endless maze of toppled chairs and tables in the buffet, down to the spa, through more narrow, dim stateroom corridors leading to blocked staircases and dead ends.

All the while fighting the one controlling this nightmare. Whenever Warning tries to sneak, she's forced to run. When she heads for the next correct door, the one that will lead her ever closer to deck 0 and The End, she's turned around and shoved in every wrong direction.

Meanwhile, the walls cry a black sludgy sheen, like an oil spill in shallow water.

Meanwhile, shadows flicker in her periphery, people-shaped but wrong, limbs too long or joints too many.

Meanwhile, the feel of invisible fingers feathering over her skin.

Meanwhile, the skittering.

But she does not scream. She will not.

Warning will seal her lips together with dried saliva—

will chew her cheeks to bloody pulp—

will use her coveted teeth to tear holes in her tongue—

But she will

not

scream.

Her head is pounding, either from the hours of clenching her jaw or from the cacophony of the casino. Rows and rows of machines, all high-watt strobing neon, packed into this low-ceilinged cave of a space. And the sound. The *noise*. Volume turned to max on every damn machine, each playing clashing versions of the same tinny synthetic music. Maybe that wouldn't be so bad if it drowned out the skittering. But the skittering is still there, louder even than before. Or maybe not louder so much as closer. Under her skin. Warning claws frantically down her arms, knowing there's nothing truly there, not on her, not yet, but needing to do *something*.

The slot nearest her lets out a particularly piercing squeal. The suddenness of the noise cuts through the fatigue and overstimulation, and she realizes what's wrong here. This is a dead ship. There's never been any power. She searched so long at the start. She thought if she could turn the power back on, maybe she could call for help (she hadn't thought far enough ahead to determine *how* since talking required opening her mouth). When she finally found the main power room, she cried. Wires shredded; giant terminals ripped from the floor, leaving potholes big enough for burial. Warning took in the undeniable wasteland and let out large, gasping, open-mouthed sobs. She died gagging as much on her lost hope as on the creatures making mincemeat of her gums.

The point is, none of these machines should be on at all. Maybe they aren't. Maybe she's hallucinating, the stress of this endless loop finally breaking her. Would that be better? Easier to bear?

She makes to stand again, expecting at any moment her puppeteer will compel her out into the open anyway—might as well beat them to it—when the lingering power shuts off. Darkness. There are no windows in the casino. The sun could be hovering right outside the hull, peeking in to see where Warning's got to now, and she would never know. She blinks hard. Blurry washes of color break up the black: afterimages of all that burning neon searing her eyes.

In her ears, the echoing *ring*-ding-dong, *ring*-ding-dong of the slots. Her hands ball into useless fists. The skittering and the other side are equally bodiless, unreachable.

Let me leave, she begs wordlessly, mouth still clamped firmly closed. Her tongue is so dry it sticks to the ridged roof of her mouth. She is so tired.

Warning breathes deeply through her nose, once, twice, and she stands. On the third breath, someone screams.

Something's wrong with this game. It isn't following its own rules. Sunny has done every wrong thing there is to do. The fear meter at the bottom of the screen has been fully red almost the whole time Sunny's been playing, and still this bitch will not open her mouth. It should have been game over ages ago. The code must be broken. What's even the point if the primary game mechanic doesn't actually do anything?

She should write the dev, let them know that their game isn't gaming right and maybe also try to get her five dollars back. Somebody else probably has, though. There's likely already a patch on the way. She checks the itch.io forums and Reddit, but she can't find anything about *The Girl with the Teeth* being broken. In fact, she can't find anything about *The Girl with the Teeth* whatsoever.

She clicks through . . . No posts on any of the forums, no playthroughs on YouTube, no livestreams on Twitch. Nothing. And when she goes to the game's itch.io page, she's smacked with a message: THIS PAGE DOES NOT EXIST.

Maybe the dev found out about the problem in the code and took the whole game down instead of patching it? Doesn't explain why everything else would have been scrubbed from the internet though. Sunny swears she remembers seeing people talk about it. How else would she have found it in the first place?

How *did* she find it? She can't remember now.

She closes her browser and full-screens the game again. The girl with the teeth is crouched behind a slot machine. It's weird. The earlier levels of the game were much more retro in style. Blocky animation, mostly gray scale, jerky transitions. But this casino setting is different. Technicolor. And the rendering is leagues above what came before. This doesn't look like an indie game made by one guy on Unreal Engine in his downtime. How did they even manage this level of graphics? Why wasn't the whole game animated like this?

Maybe this is another meta thing. A commentary on the

state of the indie horror genre and gamers' expectations for them or something. Who knows. And honestly, who cares, because Sunny did not come here for stellar graphics. She came here for jump scares and gore and maybe making herself feel fucking anything.

Her phone vibrates on the desk. Are you okay? the text reads. Lisa. Sunny didn't realize she still had Lisa's number saved. She sets the phone back down without responding.

"Why won't she scream?" Sunny mutters to the screen. "Why are you broken?"

Another buzz. I don't think you're okay.

Buzz. I think you need help.

Buzz. You need to talk to someone.

Buzz. I know it's been a while but if—Sunny shuts off her phone before finishing the message.

On-screen, the casino goes dark.

The girl with the teeth stands, even though Sunny isn't touching her keyboard. Sunny didn't tell her to move yet. She shouldn't be moving. The warning meter is still full—overfull even, red beating past the limits of the gauge and flooding the right side of the screen. The girl with the teeth should be screaming—not moving. Why doesn't this bitch do anything she's told to do?

Sunny leans forward and shouts, "Why won't you scream?"

The girl with the teeth startles. Turns. She looks up and behind her at the ceiling of the casino.

No, not the ceiling.

She looks at Sunny.

Warning runs. She's free.

The other side is . . . missing. There was the voice rippling through the darkness, then a strange rush in Warning's ears, then control slipping back as fully as when she's in the room at the start before someone comes. As soon as she realized, she ran as hard as she could bear, and then a little harder.

She barrels through the promenade, avoiding the mannequins in beach hats and bathing suits, their plastic arms extended toward her. She doesn't fear them. They are set dressing. They have no use for teeth because they don't have mouths. They don't follow her.

She pauses to check the giant ship's map hanging in the main atrium on deck 3. The last thing she needs is to get lost when she's this close to the way out. Three more decks, that's all. She's seen the atrium before, but only ever from above. Decks 4 through 10 overlook the marble-encrusted cavern. She had considered jumping from deck 5 once, a shortcut, but she didn't think she'd be able to keep her mouth shut through the impact. To her right a wall of liquor glimmers behind the bar, somehow still intact, as if waiting for happy hour to call the passengers to their shot glasses and highballs. To her left, darkness. The map points her away from the shadows, and she runs.

The ship's small art gallery next, deck 2. It's hung with dozens and dozens of the same picture, different sizes, different frames, but all the same image: bite marks. She tries not to look, but her eyes drag across them almost without her permission. Not like before, when the other side told her where and when and how to be. This is simply an unconscious choice, the desire to look at what we do not want to see. The images are all extreme close-ups. Deep red rivets captured in such detail they could instead be craters on some fleshy moon, not the memory of angry teeth. She absently rubs her knuckles. These aren't the same image, she realizes. They're the same *teeth* but not the same bites. Different depths, different angles. One's redder than the others, fresher. Blood leaks out of the ridged punctures. She's never felt the impression that teeth leave on skin. Her teeth are never used, only stolen. She reaches toward the image. Behind her, the sound of shattering glass. *Focus, Warning.*

She runs. The skittering follows.

Sunny is frozen. She hasn't moved, maybe hasn't even blinked, in five minutes? Ten?

Her monitor is still on, the game is still running—and the girl with the teeth is booking it. She heard Sunny scream. Sunny *knows* she heard even though that's impossible. Right, impossible. It was probably just coincidental timing.

Something in the game triggered the character's motion right when Sunny shouted. That's all. That's all.

The girl with the teeth is in some sort of museum. She keeps looking behind her as if she's being chased. She probably is. Why is she running, though? Or rather, *how*, since Sunny hasn't pressed a single W, A, S, or D since the casino? Is this just one super-long cutscene?

Sunny reaches for her keyboard, and blood trickles out from under her glove. *Dammit.* The clot broke again. She clenches her fist hard, feels the skin pull more. A bright stinging sensation, and she can focus again.

On-screen, the girl with the teeth slows, stops running. She's staring at one of the pieces on the wall. The graphics are even more lifelike than before. Sunny's seen AAA releases with shittier animation than this. The textures are so vivid she'd swear she could reach out and—

Sunny finally sees what the girl with the teeth is staring at: Sunny's hand. All of them, every one of the pictures currently in frame, are of Sunny's bitten hands. This isn't a coincidence. Those are *her* hands. She recognizes them. And this one—the one the girl with the teeth has stopped in front of, is reaching for—it's today's.

She was in class when the feeling hit. The swarm, as she's come to think of it. She doesn't know how else to describe it. Most of the time, she is a void. All her feelings and wants and intention scooped out of her like a pulpy mass of pumpkin seeds. But sometimes, for no reason she's been able to discern, she suddenly . . . isn't a person anymore, not even a void person like usual. She's a swarming mass of bees. Not literally, of course, but nothing else comes close to capturing the tangible *wrongness*. She can feel the swarm roiling in her gut, buzzing in the meat of her every limb, into her throat and bloating her skull. Sometimes she can ride it out, wait for the swarm to recede on its own, but not today. This time, she rushed to the locker room (safer than the bathroom when gym's not in session), ripped her gloves off, and sank her teeth as hard into her hand as she could. She doesn't know why but it's the only thing that can stop the swarm. Like turning a pressure valve. She doesn't do it because she likes to hurt or wants to bleed. She just wants to stop the swarming.

This time she bled. And this time, Lisa saw. Not just the biting or the blood, but the history of both marked across the expanse of her hands. Lisa, essentially a stranger ever since Sunny cut her off—along with all her other old friends—last year, for no particular reason except that being around people reminded Sunny how often she felt like Not A People anymore. Lisa, who kept texting Sunny for months after, asking why, why couldn't they just talk whatever it was through, who still sometimes looked at Sunny with confused pain in her eyes.

Lisa saw, and Sunny ran.

The girl with the teeth is going to touch the picture of Sunny's hands. She's inches away. She can't. She *can't*. Sunny can't let her. The very idea of it makes bile rise up in the back of her throat. She panics, picks up her turned-off phone and hurls it toward the computer screen. The glass spiderwebs outward from the point of impact. The girl with the teeth hears. She runs.

It's getting closer. The skittering. Warning's legs burn and her lungs are ready to give up entirely, too long with too little air being asked to pump too hard, but she's on deck 0 now. The final level. She just has to find the door. Her mouth hurts so badly. It's hardly even a mouth anymore. It's the vault where she keeps her teeth, and her body is the prison where she keeps the vault. She would give up her teeth, she thinks. She would give every last one if it meant she could be free of this pain and this perpetual terror. But they won't take them cleanly, and even if they did, she would have to just start over again. Those are the rules.

Fuck the rules.

Warning keeps on down the narrow corridor. The exit shouldn't be far now. Just keep moving and do not scream.

She pushes through one of the heavy emergency doors that separate each section of this deck—and sees light. Sunlight. It must be. Coming in through an open door just around the next corner, her ending finally in sight.

Warning almost smiles in relief, but her lip stings at the

216

unexpected movement after so long frozen in place, and she stops herself. She will not lose now, not after everything.

She takes a step, and—

The other side yanks her backward so hard she flies ten feet and lands hard on her ass. She only barely manages to hold in a yelp. She tries to stand again, to head toward the light just a little ways down this hallway, just *right there*. But the other side won't let her. She can't move.

All this, and now she's trapped. Held down by invisible hands, while the sound of the other invisible hands grows ever louder, the ones that will descend upon her like a flock of starving crows if given the chance. Warning thinks of the images in the art gallery and imagines herself biting the other side, leaving welts like in those pictures. She wants to hurt the other side. Badly. Why should she be the only one who hurts? Why should she be flung around like a paper doll, at the whim of some anonymous master? She might think she's being punished, but she's done nothing worth punishing. She couldn't have. She was born already in this prison. Not born. Designed. *Developed* to perform this nightmare loop over and over until—what? Until she dies? That's funny. She'd laugh, truly, if she could. She cannot die, not for good. Her code won't allow it. All she can do is thrash hopelessly against the other side's will and *not scream*.

• • •

Sunny doesn't know what to do. Everything is wrong. Everything. This game and her broken screen and Lisa and there's blood dripping down on the carpet now and her head is swimming, no—swarming, no—skimming along that yolk-thin membrane of a shield, the final lie. Because she wants so badly to bite. She *wants* to bleed. She needs to feel her teeth break the skin again, right now, *right now* to stop the swarming, and harder is better, harder means blood and blood means the swarming stops sooner.

She's got her hand halfway to her mouth when she hears something. A buzzing.

No, a skittering.

The same sound that so impressed her in the game earlier. Except her headphones are lying forgotten on the desk. The skittering isn't coming from the game. It's closer than that. She whips around, half wild, but the sound moves just as quickly, now above her, now behind again, now tangled in her frizzed-out curls. It's everywhere and nowhere. It feels a cousin to the swarming, each rising to match the other, and it's all too much, too loud, she's too *full*.

Sunny grabs her mouse and keyboard. She has to end this, and she knows with uncanny certainty that there's only one way to be sure: the girl with the teeth has to scream.

Warning likes her name. Rhymes with *morning*. Rhymes with *mourning*, too, and that's also fitting. She is nothing if not the perfect manifestation of death and dawn, forever looped one into the other.

The skittering is a warning, too, she thinks deliriously as she holds her knees to her chest, eyes shut tight, mouth shut tighter, on the dingy lowest floor of this dead ship. *Monsters,* the skittering says in its own skin-crawling way. *Monsters are near, Warning.* The sound is on top of her now. And not just the sound but the *things* making the sound. Hundreds of grubby, groping fingers, scrambling over each other in waves trying to find purchase, to find the door to the vault where she keeps her teeth. She can't remember now what a mouth tastes like free of blood and bile. Maybe she should give up. Why fight? Why bother when she will never, ever be free anyway?

Warning hates her name in that moment. A warning is the prelude to something dangerous, something powerful. She's neither. She's not even really a girl when it gets right down to it. She is a binary-built doll, a programmer's puppet—and that is all she'll ever be. Those are the rules. Not even the sun can break this cursed code.

A digit finds the seam of her lips and the whole mass ripples in recognition. She gags, bile puddling on the back of her tongue. Here they come. She can't hold them off any longer. Fingertips slick over her mouth, nails scratching her chapped lips. Others ball into fists and batter her jaw. Meaty palms plaster themselves over her nose. She can't breathe. She can't win.

But she refuses to lose.

Warning does the only thing left to her.

She screams.

Lisa finds Sunny curled up on the bedroom floor heaving loud, gasping sobs. She rushes over, brushes the tear-matted hair off Sunny's face, whispers soothing nothings, not even words, just soft hums of sound. She had debated for hours whether or not to even come over. Sunny wanted nothing to do with her, that much was clear, but Lisa hadn't been able to shake the sight of Sunny in the locker room today. The panic in her eyes. The fear. How long had she held all that all by herself? How much must it weigh?

"She did it," Sunny finally manages to say. "She won."

"Who won?" Lisa asks gently. She doesn't know if Sunny will respond, or if she's even fully aware that Lisa is here, but maybe talking will slow the crying, steady her breath some. That seems like the first thing.

"She *screamed*. I wanted her to scream, but then she did and it . . ." Sunny gestures in front of her, as if at a painting. "The screen was just this bright, bright orange, like looking into the sun. And then it faded and she was alone. She sent them away somehow. She screamed and the skittering *vanished*."

Lisa hums some more. It feels important not to interrupt even though none of this makes any sense. *Doesn't make sense to* me, she corrects herself. *It makes perfect sense to her.*

"I don't think she believed it, either," Sunny continues. "She stood up and her mouth was . . . was open and she still had all her teeth. She looked at me then. Right at me. Right directly *at me,* not like before when she got startled but as if she could actually see me. She ran for the door but I couldn't have stopped her if I wanted to, and I didn't. I didn't want to anymore."

"Okay, okay," Lisa says. Sunny's getting worked up again, differently now though. Animated, almost close to hyperventilating. "Hey, let me go call your mom for you, okay?"

Sunny grips Lisa's wrist to stop her getting up. Finally looks at her. "She broke every single rule, Lisa. All of them. She broke her entire fucking *existence* to be free of that hell. I don't— I didn't . . ." Sunny takes a long, slow breath. In through the nose, out through the mouth. "I didn't even know I was in hell, Lisa. I thought this was just how it was. I thought I just had to live like this."

Sunny looks down at her hands; the gloves are gone. Sunny's bleeding again, like earlier that day at school, when Lisa realized exactly how not okay her friend really was. Lisa reaches for Sunny's hands slowly, leaving plenty of time for Sunny to say no. She doesn't, and Lisa takes her bitten-up, bloody hands.

"You don't have to live with this. I don't know what you're going through, but I promise you don't have to do it alone, Sunny."

A pause, contemplative this time, not pained. Sunny speaks again. "She smiled at me when she stepped off the boat. She has a beautiful smile. I think she knew the connection, whatever it was, was dying. She shouted up at me, 'My name is Warning.'"

"That's an odd name."

Sunny smiles. "She's an odd girl."

They sit in silence for a few long minutes. Lisa continues to hold Sunny's hand.

"Lisa," Sunny says, voice quiet but steady. "I think I need help."

SPITE AND MALICE

Shaun David Hutchinson

THE ELEVATOR DIDN'T WORK, FORCING ME TO CARRY BOXES filled with dishes and books up five flights of stairs to the new apartment my mom and I had moved into. My arms and legs were jelly. I was thinking I should file a child labor complaint, but I'd probably still have to finish unpacking the truck, and I was barely halfway done.

Each time I passed the elevator, I pushed the button, hoping it might work. It was like standing in front of the fridge, opening and closing the door and hoping there might be something other than out-of-date lunch meat and a thousand condiments inside.

"It's out of order," a voice behind me said.

A guy my age was walking toward me carrying a couple of cloth bags heavy with groceries. He was tall, with the kind of deep tan not common in Seattle, and a smile that shook my jelly legs.

"What about folks who can't use the stairs? My mom's got a busted back, and stairs are killer for her."

The guy frowned sympathetically. "There's a freight elevator on the other side of the building, but it's really slow and feels like the cables could snap at any moment and drop you to your death."

"Oh."

"I'm sure it's totally safe, though."

He didn't sound like he thought it was totally safe, so I figured I'd stick with the stairs. A wave of embarrassment hit me as I realized how I must look *and* smell. I'd put on deodorant that morning, but I doubted anything could mask the stench clinging to me from unloading the truck in the summer heat.

"I'm Dan," he said.

"Benji—"

"Like the dog?"

"I mean, that's not where most folks go with it, but sure."

"Cool." Dan lifted the bags a little. "I should get these inside."

"Right. Yeah. And I should finish hauling these boxes up five flights of stairs. In the heat. Because the elevator's busted."

"Good luck with that, Benji." Dan turned and headed down the hallway.

I'd kind of been hoping he would offer to help, preferably shirtless, but I hadn't expected him to. There weren't many people who would've willingly dropped what they were doing to help a stranger carry moving boxes. Still, I didn't totally mind watching him go.

A few more trips and I was nearly done. But as I was lifting a box of Mom's cast-iron cookware off the sidewalk, a sharp pain lanced through my leg. I stumbled. The box slipped from my hands.

"Got it!" Someone helped me ease the box to the ground. When I looked up, I was staring into the face of a guy with ruddy cheeks and a shaved head who was smiling like he'd been waiting for a chance to swoop in and save the day.

"You all right?" He had a soft accent I couldn't quite place. East Coast, maybe.

"Uh, yeah. Charley horse."

"Moving in?"

I nodded. "Fifth floor, and the elevator doesn't work." I hadn't been impressed with this place when Mom had first shown it to me, but the building seemed to spawn cute boys my age like they were Pokémon, so maybe it wasn't all bad.

"You know, there's a freight elevator way down on the other side of the building. It rattles like the cables are gonna snap, but it's probably mostly safe."

"Thanks, but I'm almost done." I cleared my throat. "So, you live in the building?"

"Nah. My boyfriend does." He held out his hand. "I'm Andy, by the way."

"Benji."

Andy's eyebrows rose. "Like the—"

Please don't say dog. *Please don't say* dog. *Please don't say* dog.

"—rugby player?"

I couldn't help smiling. "Neither of my parents watch rugby, so probably not."

Andy gave an "aww shucks" snap of his fingers. Then he motioned at the boxes. "Need some help?" Before I could answer, he grabbed the nearest box. His biceps bulged against his sleeves.

"Did I mention I'm on the fifth floor?"

"You did, but I skipped leg day at the gym yesterday." He winked, and I melted.

Andy was cute and I was too exhausted to turn down the offer, so I hefted a box and led him inside.

"You going to Lincoln High?" Andy asked as we climbed the stairs.

"Yeah. Eleventh grade."

"Me too! Maybe we'll have some classes together. It's gotta be tough starting a new school without knowing anyone. Now you'll know me." His cheerful optimism was endearing.

We dropped off the boxes and then went down for more. Andy kept up a light chatter, telling me about his favorite parks and where the best takeout Chinese was. "You're gonna love it around here. I mean, sure, the rain's a lot sometimes, but it's really chill." He glanced over his shoulder at me. "Where're you from anyway?"

"Um . . . Northgate."

Andy furrowed his brow. "Like, Northgate, New Mexico, or Northgate, a ten-minute drive from here?"

"The second one."

Andy's cheeks turned red. "You probably grew up around here, didn't you?" When I nodded, he said, "I moved from Baltimore five years ago, and here I'm acting like I know everything there is to know about the city."

He hadn't given me much opportunity to get a word in, not that I'd minded. "No worries. Anyway, I figured you weren't from Seattle."

"How?"

"It was the accent. Also, people around here are polite, but they wouldn't have offered to help carry boxes." I smiled wearily. "I'm glad you did though."

Despite knowing Andy had a boyfriend, I felt like we were having a moment. I imagined him telling me he was glad, too, and then giving me his number so we could spend hours trading flirty messages back and forth. But that didn't happen.

As we approached the third floor, the door to the stairwell popped open and Dan poked his head in. "There you are!" He bounded down the stairs to the landing and kissed Andy.

"Sorry," Andy said. "Benji just moved in, and he needed some help. I lost track of time."

Dan rolled his eyes playfully. "That's because you're the sweetest person I know."

Right. It figured the two cute guys I just met were already a couple.

Andy shifted the box he was carrying and knocked his shoulder into Dan. His smile lit his eyes. "Dan, Benji. Benji, this is my boyfriend, Dan."

"We met," I said.

Dan scooted out of the way so Andy and I could pass. "Come on. Drop those off. I don't want to miss the previews."

"We're going to a movie," Andy said. "You should come."

"He's probably still got a lot to do," Dan said.

"But he's new around here, babe. He probably hasn't got friends—"

"Northgate," I said. "Remember? Ten minutes away? I've got friends." Of course, *they* weren't helping me carry boxes, but I could read Dan's signals loud and clear.

"See?" Dan said.

"Besides, I'm tired. And I stink."

"I mean, I didn't want to say it." Andy immediately broke into a laugh. "Kidding. Another time?"

"Definitely."

After we dropped off the last boxes and I waved Andy and Dan goodbye, I went to grab some water. My mom was hiding in the kitchen—just as I walked in she jumped out, scaring me so badly I would've wet my pants if I hadn't been so dehydrated.

"What the hell, Ma?"

My mom was an imposing woman with a wide nose and a nest of blond curls. She tousled my hair like I was six instead of sixteen. "Making friends already?"

"Just some guy who lives in the building—"

"Is he cute?"

"Yeah, but—"

My mom broke into a grin. "Tell me everything."

"He has a boyfriend." I poured a glass of water and chugged it, dribbling some down my chin.

"Oh." Mom's enthusiasm evaporated. "Well, I'm glad you're making friends anyway. I know you can see Rachel and the others whenever you want, but you should have friends nearby, too."

I leaned against the counter and folded my arms over my chest. "It's not fair. Dad should've been the one who had to move and get new furniture and make new friends."

Mom stood beside me and rested her head against mine. "Life deals the hand, Benji. How we play is up to us."

"I guess. It's just too bad Dad cheated to win."

I spent the next couple days unpacking boxes and building furniture. Mom really *could* have kept the house and the furniture if she'd wanted to—Dad *was* the one who'd slept with someone else—but she wanted a fresh start free of anything Dad had tainted. I doubted Dad had tainted any of the furniture in my bedroom—at least I sincerely hoped he hadn't. Anyway, that's how I ended up building flatpack furniture in an apartment one-third the size of our old place. Slowly, the tiny apartment began to look like a home. Not *our* home, but the home of someone who'd stolen all our shit.

A few days after moving in, I was trying to watch a movie in the living room, but Mom was on a video call with clients and kept motioning at me to turn it down. Without AC, my bedroom was an oven, so I grabbed a book and went upstairs to the roof. I hadn't expected to run into anyone, so I was surprised when I heard my name as soon as I exited the stairwell.

"Hey! Benji!" Andy's baritone was already familiar, and I turned to look for him. He was waving at me from a corner near the grills where he was sitting with Dan and three other people.

I wandered over and offered up a shy wave. "Hey."

"Everyone," Andy said, "this is Benji, like the rugby player."

"I thought it was like the dog," Dan said.

"That's because you're a prick," said a girl with violet lips, warm eyes, and box braids that hung to her shoulders. She saluted me. "Jasmine."

The guy across from her nodded. "Casper." He was thin and gangly with long, curly hair held off his face by a headband.

At the end of the table, across from Andy, a person with short, straight hair and a smile that toed the line between innocent and devious said, "I'm Jia. I use they pronouns. Cool?"

"Totally." Knowing everyone's names made me feel less

awkward, but I wasn't sure whether Andy called me over just to say hi or if he wanted me to stick around. I held up my book. "Well, I'll let you get back to whatever you're doing."

"Have fun," Dan said.

"We're playing Spite and Malice." Jasmine kicked out a chair with her foot.

Dan frowned. "We're in the middle of a game and—"

Andy yanked the cards from Dan's hand and tossed them in the middle of the table. "We can start over. You were losing anyway."

"I was not!"

Jia threw Dan a sympathetic smile. "You kinda were."

Dan shoved his chair back and stood. "I need a drink."

"Bring some chips back with you?" Casper asked at the same time as Jia said, "I'll take some water."

Dan's nostrils flared. "Anyone else?" When no one replied, he stalked off.

"Are you sure it's okay?" I hiked my thumb in Dan's direction. "He doesn't seem like he wants me here."

Andy started to speak up, but Jasmine cut him off. "Dan's got the personality of a grumpy cat. He'll demand belly rubs and then scratch you if you stop."

"Or if you don't stop," Jia said.

"Or if you don't scratch exactly the way he wants," Casper added.

"Just my luck," I said. "I'm a dog person."

Andy busted up laughing as he gathered the cards. He handed some to Jasmine, and they each began shuffling.

Jia said, "Dan's kind of a prick, but he's the friend you'd call if you needed help burying a body."

Casper nodded. "True."

"And he's a good kisser," Andy said.

Dan still seemed like a jerk, but my best friend, Rachel, could come off prickly at first, too, so I decided to withhold judgment for now. I motioned at the cards. "How do you play this game?"

"It's super easy," Andy said. "Everyone gets a stack with the first card turned faceup. That's your stockpile. Then there are four decks in the middle. You'll also get five cards to hold. The goal is to be the first to get rid of the cards in your stockpile."

It was difficult to follow Andy's instructions because I was busy watching his lips and the way his whole face moved when he spoke, but I tried my best.

Andy continued shuffling as he spoke. "You build the decks in the middle in a sequence starting with aces and ending with queens."

"What about kings?" I asked.

"They're wild."

Jasmine traded stacks with Andy. "Think of it like solitaire."

"Except you don't play alone?" I said.

"Exactly." Andy's smile was distracting. He had a slightly crooked tooth I found inexplicably cute. "During your turn, you can play cards from your hand or from your stockpile."

"Don't forget your discard piles," Jia said.

Andy smacked his forehead. "Right. Shit. You end your turn by discarding into one of four piles in front of you. You can play from them, but you have to play the top card first."

Casper, without looking up from his phone, said, "You're confusing him, dude. We should just play."

Dan returned then, carrying two bags, the first filled with a selection of chips, the second with bottles of soda and water. The others descended on the food like they hadn't eaten in months. I was always a little hungry, but I felt weird eating Dan's food until he leaned over and offered me an open bag of cheese puffs.

"Thanks."

Dan nodded perfunctorily.

"So what's the deal with the name?" I asked. "Spite and Malice?"

Maybe they didn't mean to, but everyone subtly—or in Jasmine's case, not so subtly—looked in Dan's direction.

"You'll find out," Dan said.

He wasn't wrong. The game was confusing at first, but I figured out the rules and settled into a rhythm. The spite and malice came into play because, since others could see what card you needed to get rid of from your stock deck, they could block you. Jasmine played aggressively, Jia was an opportunist, Casper's strategy was to not have one, and Andy was careful but clever. Dan, however, was utterly ruthless. If there was a chance to wreck someone's game, even if it didn't immediately benefit him, Dan took it.

Dan held out his hands and shrugged. "Sorry, Benji, but I play to win."

Jasmine rolled her eyes and hissed like a cat.

I tossed my cards on the table. "I can handle losing."

Dan held my eye a moment. "Good to know."

His intensity caught me off guard, and I was too flustered to respond. Thankfully, Andy nudged Dan in the side and said, "He's a bad loser and a worse winner. He's lucky he's cute."

We played a few more hands. I managed to lose less badly each time, but only slightly. Andy won one game, Jia won another. Eventually, my phone buzzed. It was my mom looking for me.

"Thanks for the game," I said. "Gotta run."

"Hope we'll see you again," Jasmine said.

I was surprised when Dan added, "We play up here pretty often—it's free and it's better than Netflix."

"Good to know."

It wasn't exactly an invitation, but it was more than I'd expected from Dan. And, despite my initial impression, the thought of seeing him again made me smile.

• • •

Over the next couple weeks, I settled into a routine. During the day, I helped Mom decorate the new apartment or met up with my friends from my old neighborhood. But in the evenings, with the lazy summer sun loitering in the sky, I played Spite and Malice on the roof until long after dark. Hanging out with Andy, Dan, and the others made me feel more at home than the pictures I'd hung on the walls or the new towels Mom had bought for the bathroom.

One night at dinner, before I went to the roof, I was telling Mom about my afternoon hanging out with Rachel.

"You can visit your father when you see your friends," she said. "You don't have to avoid him for me."

"I know." My father was the last person I wanted to talk about.

"He's still your dad." Mom twirled spaghetti noodles around her fork.

"Dad cheated on you. He's the reason I had to leave my school and my friends—"

Mom set down her fork. "I said you could stay with him. You still can."

I carried my plate into the kitchen, scraping the spaghetti into the compost pail by the sink. I wanted to shout at my mom for suggesting I live with Dad, but I pushed it down because she didn't deserve my anger any more than Dad deserved my forgiveness.

"I'm going to the roof to see if Dan and Andy are there."

I took off before Mom realized I'd stuck her cleaning up. I found the boys exactly where I'd expected. Dan was sitting with his legs propped on the firepit, Andy was beside him. They weren't one of those couples who held on to each other like they were terrified one of them would become unmoored by gravity and fly into the atmosphere if they let go for even one second. Yet there was still an intimacy between them that spanned the distance.

"Where's everyone else?" I flopped onto the seat opposite them. I'd gotten over the awkward feeling that I was constantly intruding. If they wanted to be alone, Dan had no problem saying so.

Andy ticked them off on his fingers. "Casper's on a date. My guess is with one of the guys from his D&D group."

Dan rolled his eyes. "You think everyone's gay."

"I caught him looking at your ass!"

"He doesn't have to be sexually attracted to me to admire my butt. It's a primo quality butt." Dan stood and struck a pose. "I'm right, aren't I? It's okay, you can say it."

I glanced at Andy for help, figuring he wouldn't want me checking out his boyfriend's behind, but he was also waiting for my answer. "I mean, sure, it's a good ass. I wish I had a backside like that." The rest of Dan was pretty good, too—long, lean, and muscular.

"All you have to do is go back in time and start dancing when you were five years old." Dan sat again.

"You're a dancer?" It wasn't exactly how I saw Dan

spending his free time. He seemed like the type who probably had a notebook in which he collected the names of people
who annoyed him.

"Ballet."

"Anyway," Andy said. "Your butt aside, Casper could still
be on a date with a guy."

"What about Jasmine and Jia?" I asked.

"Jasmine's at a family thing, and Jia's grounded for missing
curfew last night," Dan said.

I couldn't hide my disappointment. "Guess that means
no game."

"We can play with three." Andy was smiling, like always.
He reminded me of a puppy that way.

Dan stretched his arms over his head and yawned. "Why
not? Kicking your flat asses will put me in a better mood."

We moved to a nearby table. Andy shuffled and dealt the
cards. It was the first time I'd been alone with them since
the day I'd moved into the building. The conversation began
slowly, beginning with safe topics—favorite TV shows, books,
how Dan got into ballet, what classes they were taking in the
fall—before moving into more personal areas.

"So, how long have you guys been together?"

"Since eighth grade," Andy said at the same time as Dan
said, "We got together freshman year."

I waited for one of them to clarify, but neither seemed willing. "Which is it?"

Dan glanced at Andy's stockpile, which had the four of

spades faceup, and threw the four of hearts onto the build stack that had a three of clubs showing.

"Baby," Andy whined. "Why?"

Dan shrugged. He played ruthlessly, even against his boyfriend.

Andy sighed and set his cards facedown on the table. "So the story is that I had a crush on Dan for all of eighth grade. I was in love with this kid even though he barely knew I existed."

"I knew you existed," Dan said.

"Anyway," Andy went on, "Valentine's Day rolled around, and I decided it was time to let him know how I felt. I gave him a card and some candy and asked him to be my boyfriend."

I smiled imagining Andy and Dan as awkward eighth graders. "That's sweet."

Dan wore a sardonic frown. "It was a generic card and a pack of those nasty Necco Wafers."

"It's the thought that counts," Andy said.

"No, it's not."

"Well, I must've done something right, because Dan looked at the card and said, 'Sure, whatever.' We've been together since."

"I only said yes because Andy had a PlayStation. We didn't even have our first kiss until the Halloween carnival in ninth grade."

It wasn't exactly the heartwarming story of first love I'd expected. I turned to Andy. "So you thought were you dating for nine months before Dan did?"

"Basically."

"Dan!"

"What?" Dan looked at me, surprised. "Andy wanted a boyfriend, and I wanted to play *Spider-Man*."

"And you were okay with that arrangement?" I asked, trying not to sound too judgmental, especially since I'd never even had a boyfriend.

"Dan's stubborn. He does things on his terms or not at all." Andy's phone rang. He looked at the screen and then stepped away from the table to take a call.

When Andy was out of earshot, Dan leaned in and said, "I knew I was into Andy from the moment we met. But, you see how he is, right? He thinks the best of everyone. He didn't have a crush on me; he had a crush on some weird idea of me. I wanted to make sure he knew who I really was."

It was such a weird and complex way to begin a relationship, and I had a ton of questions. Unfortunately, I didn't get the chance to ask them before Andy returned.

"I have to run. Anna's having a meltdown because it's too hot, and Dad wants me to help him install a window unit at her place." He kissed Dan's cheek and waved goodbye to me before taking off.

"Anna's his sister. I swear she's twenty months pregnant." Dan collected Andy's cards and shuffled them into the pile.

Without Andy as a buffer, I felt awkward around Dan. "I guess I should get going."

"Why? It's still early, and my little brother's having a slumber party. The apartment's filled with shrieking eight-year-olds."

"Yikes. Glad I'm an only child."

"I don't mind Rory most of the time, but there are days I'd definitely trade him for some magic beans." Dan had a dry, deadpan way of speaking that made it difficult to tell when he was joking.

The only things waiting at home for *me* were a few back issues of *Ascender* and the dishes, because there was no way my mom didn't leave them in the sink for me, and my desire to put off going home outweighed any weirdness I felt being alone with Dan. "Sure, let's play."

We didn't talk for most of the first game, but it wasn't uncomfortable. Dan didn't seem like the type of person to fill the silence with unnecessary chatter, and I appreciated that it allowed me to focus on playing, though Dan still beat me easily.

"Almost had me that time, Benji. You're not so bad at this."

It was as close to a compliment as Dan had ever given me. "Can I ask you a question?"

"Sure."

"When I first moved in, it seemed like you kind of hated me."

"I didn't hate you."

"Good—"

"I didn't like you, either. You showed up one day, got my boyfriend moving boxes for you, and invited yourself into my group of friends." Dan's blunt honesty was unnerving.

"Andy invited me."

"Andy would invite Thanos to Thanksgiving." Dan pursed his lips and dared me to contradict him.

I lowered my head. "Sorry."

"I'm not. You turned out all right."

I gathered the cards to shuffle, and when I looked up, I caught Dan smiling at me with his soft lips and amber eyes and this dimple in his left cheek. A warmth blossomed in my chest, a wisp of a flame that I hadn't felt in forever.

I coughed and returned my attention to shuffling and dealing the cards for a new game.

If the conversation had made Dan uncomfortable, he didn't show it. "Why'd you move here, anyway?"

Grateful to talk about something different, I said, "My parents are getting divorced."

"Oh."

I didn't mean to dump my problems on Dan, but talking to him was easy in a way I hadn't expected. "My dad cheated on my mom, and she didn't want to live in the house where he'd been with another woman, so here we are."

"That sucks, Benji. I'm really sorry."

I arranged my hand while waiting for Dan to play a card. "I don't get it. How could my dad just fall in love with someone else?"

Dan tossed a card on his discard pile. "It happens. I'm sorry it happened to your parents, but it's not uncommon."

241

He was right, but that didn't make it less awful. "He didn't have to cheat. He could've told my mom the truth."

"Maybe he was scared."

"That's no excuse." I played a card from my stockpile, discarded, and fell back into my seat.

Dan's eyes softened, and he looked at me sympathetically. "I'm not saying what your dad did was right. Just, I don't know, relationships are messy."

I hung my head. "I wouldn't know. I've never had a boyfriend or even kissed anyone." I couldn't look Dan in the eye.

"Oh. Well, that's no big deal."

"Easy for you to say. You and Andy have been together for a while, so you've probably done everything."

Dan's rich, deep laugh filled the night. "God, no. We've never had sex."

"That's . . . surprising."

"Is it?" Dan cocked his head. "I suppose TV shows make it seem like gay teens are screwing everyone we meet, but I'm not ready. Neither is Andy, though he thinks he is."

Dan's honesty and openness were refreshing. "Only one of my friends has done it, and she said she just wanted to get it out of the way so she could focus on school."

"That's both strange and admirable," Dan said. "I think I'd like her."

"Or hate her. I'm not sure how you two would get along . . . You *can* be kind of a jerk."

"I know."

I frowned at him. "Then why are you? Why not be nicer?"

Dan leaned back in his chair, holding his cards close to his chest. "I'm plenty nice."

"You didn't offer to help me move boxes when I ran into you."

"What kind of person drops what they're doing to help a stranger move?"

"Andy."

Dan played a card and then set his hand facedown on the table. "Look, if you've got a thing for him, I get it. He's cute, everyone loves him."

As I'd gotten to know Andy more, the crush I'd had on him the first day had waned. He was cute and funny and nice, but I didn't have the kinds of feelings for him Dan was implying. "I don't have a thing for him!"

Dan went on like he hadn't heard me. "Andy's the kind of guy who'll ditch his friends to help his dad install an air conditioner in his pregnant sister's apartment. But Andy's solar powered, Benji. When life's good, Andy's there. But when the sun sets and life gets tough, he shuts down."

There was a sadness in Dan that tugged at my heart. "Are you guys okay? I don't know much about relationships, but yours seems so solid."

Dan sighed. "I love Andy, I do, but it won't last. One day he'll float off to a sky with a brighter sun."

"C'mon. I've seen the way he looks at you."

"And I see the way he looks at *you*." The statement wasn't accusatory, but it still felt like a punch.

"I swear I'm not interested in Andy." Andy didn't make my stomach flutter or my palms sweat.

"It doesn't matter. It'll be someone else then. I won't ever be enough for him." There was no self-pity in Dan's voice, only the acceptance of the inevitable.

I didn't know what to say to comfort Dan, or if I even could. Instead, I asked, "What would you have done if I *had* been interested in Andy?"

"Let him go."

"Really?"

Dan nodded, and I finally understood what Jasmine and the others had meant about Dan. He might complain, and he might be cold and distant and rude, but he would do anything for the people he cared about, even if it hurt him to do so.

"You seem surprised," Dan said.

"The way you play Spite and Malice, I figured you'd do anything to win."

"This is cards, that's life. The rules may be the same, but in life, *how* you play matters."

The warmth in my chest spread through my entire body. I wiped my sweaty palms on my shorts. "I really should go."

Dan glanced at the cards. "We're in the middle of a game."

I flipped over my cards. "You won this round." I stood and

took off. When I reached the door to the stairwell, I turned around for one last look at Dan. He was watching me, too.

It was nearly two weeks before I saw Dan alone again, but that didn't stop me from thinking about him. He was the foot-tapping rhythm of a song I couldn't stop singing. I'd hoped the first swells of the crush I'd developed would fizzle and fade the way they had for Khalil after he'd told me his favorite musical was *Cats*, but they didn't. Some days, when I was with the group playing Spite and Malice, I thought I might suffocate if I couldn't touch Dan.

I should've stayed away—it might've been better if I had—but I didn't.

I was getting dressed to meet the gang on the roof for Spite and Malice when my mom walked into my room holding her phone in front of her like it was a rabid rat.

"Here." She shoved the phone at me and left.

I didn't know who would be calling me on my mom's phone, but I wasn't expecting the voice that came out of the speaker.

"Hey, champ."

"Fuck off, Dad." I disconnected the call and marched into the dining room where Mom was working. "What the hell, Ma?"

The phone buzzed a couple of times. I tossed it on the table.

"He's your father, Benji. You have to talk to him eventually."

"No, I really don't." I stormed out of the apartment without giving her a chance to respond.

I won my first hand of Spite and Malice that night. I was focused and vicious, driven by my anger. Every card I played hurt someone, and while I might've joked around and said I was sorry, I wasn't.

Eventually, Andy left because he had to get up early in the morning. The others peeled away one by one as the night went on. Even Dan left. When I was alone, I sprawled out on top of the table with my hands under my head and stared at the sky. I couldn't see anything through the clouds, but it wouldn't have mattered. The sky could've been full of stars, and it still would've felt empty to me.

"Heya, Benji."

I looked behind me and saw Dan walking toward me, carrying a plate of chocolate chip cookies.

"Dan?" I sat up. "I thought you left."

Without asking, Dan plopped down on the table beside me. "You looked like you needed cookies." He held the plate out to me.

The cookies were still soft and warm. "Did you go downstairs and bake cookies for me?"

"Don't make it more than it is. I scooped some dough out of a tub and stuck it in the oven."

I nibbled at a cookie and then, unable to stop myself, shoved the rest in my mouth.

Dan leaned back on his hands. He was wearing a tank top that rode up and showed off his flat stomach. "You played some good games tonight. Congrats on your first win."

"Thanks."

"You don't sound happy about it."

I looked at the plate, and Dan nodded that I could take another cookie. "I guess I've just got a lot on my mind."

"Your parents?"

"Yeah." I told him about the call with my dad.

Dan grimaced. "Yikes. I'd be pissed, too."

My thoughts felt like a swarm of hornets buzzing in my brain. I got up and paced in front of the table. "Before this, I actually got along with my dad. He was more than my dad, he was my friend. All he had to do was *not* cheat on my mom. I don't . . ."

I choked up. Tears welled in my eyes, and I tried to stop them. "I hate this so much! I hate him! I just want things to go back to the way they were." I sat again, falling heavily onto the table. Unable to hold them back any longer, tears ran down my cheeks.

Dan reached into his pocket and produced a napkin. "You are a seriously ugly crier, Benji."

I laughed through the tears and shoved him.

"No joke. Maybe whatever guy you hook shouldn't see you cry until after you've reeled him in. Just saying."

"It doesn't matter," I said. "No one's biting anyway."

Dan rolled his eyes. "Self-pity's an even worse look on you."

"It's not pity. Just, I always fall for the wrong guys."

"Like?"

"There was Arjun last year. Football player, debate team captain. Straight. Broke my heart without ever knowing it."

"Falling for a straight jock is a rite of passage." Dan stretched, lengthening his body in a long, graceful line. Most of the time, I had trouble imagining that Dan danced ballet, but moments like these, I could see how beautiful he must be when he danced.

I took another cookie to cover my awkwardness. "Then there was Lucas, who definitely had a crush on me until I got the role he wanted in the spring play. There was a boy at the bookstore I spilled coffee on while trying to get his number."

"I'm not laughing at you." Dan was definitely laughing at me. "But you either have bad taste or bad luck."

"Both."

Dan caught my eye. He reached up and wiped my chin. "Chocolate." He showed me the brown smudge on his thumb. "Anyone else?"

Maybe I imagined it. I almost definitely probably imagined it. But it seemed like Dan was daring me to tell him I liked him. I held the cards, I just couldn't play them. Not without hurting someone. "I don't know. It doesn't matter."

"Sure it does."

"Dan, I—"

Dan leaned in and kissed me gently, and then pulled back. "Is this okay?"

Dazed, I nodded and possibly grunted something that sounded like positive consent before Dan kissed me again. His lips were a storm that drifted in gently to tease before being followed by a gale that whipped the rain and tore the leaves from the trees. Ferocious and violent and beautiful. He rolled toward me, the weight of him pressing me back against the table.

I didn't think, I just stood in the middle of the storm with my face tilted toward the chaotic sky, and this time I could see the beautiful everything.

And then Dan pulled away. He was still leaning over me, smiling, and god, it was a handsome, *dangerous* smile. "How was your first kiss?"

"I . . . Dan . . . I . . ." My brain was short-circuiting. The kiss was everything I'd wanted, but it didn't belong to me. I tried to put my feelings into words but failed. Instead, I scrambled off the table and ran inside.

I didn't go to the roof for a week. I avoided Dan by spending as much time in my old neighborhood as possible. When I told Rachel what had happened with Dan, her advice was to not get involved with people I lived in the same building with. It was good advice, and might've been helpful *before* Dan had kissed me. Before I'd kissed him back.

I was walking to the bus stop on my way home from Rachel's when a familiar car pulled up to the sidewalk. My dad rolled down the passenger-side window.

"Benji? What're you doing?"

I gave him the finger.

"C'mon, Benji. Can we just talk?" Dad leaned across the center console to open the passenger door. He looked like a dog at a shelter desperate for someone to give him a forever home.

"No."

"Then how about lunch? We'll grab some burgers."

My stomach rumbled, reminding me I hadn't eaten since breakfast. "Dick's?"

Dad nodded.

"And a milkshake?"

"Whatever you want."

It went against my better judgment, but lunch was the absolute least Dad owed me after what he put me and Mom through, and I wasn't going to pass up a chance to collect. Dad didn't try to talk to me until we were in the parking lot, sitting on the trunk, stuffing our faces.

"I've been trying to reach you to—"

"Tell me why you did it, Dad. Why'd you cheat on Mom?"

Dad set his half-eaten burger aside. It'd only been a few weeks since I'd seen him last, but he looked thinner. Gaunt. And he had more gray in his hair than I remembered. "Look, Benji, relationships are complicated—"

"Stop bullshitting me, Dad."

His Adam's apple bobbed. He was quiet for a moment. "When I was your age, I assumed I'd have it all figured out when I was an adult, but I don't. The only thing I know for sure is that my biggest regrets in life are the chances I didn't take."

"Do you love her?"

Dad paused and then nodded once. "I do. And if you give her a chance, you might find you have a lot in common. Allison—"

"I meant Mom."

"Oh." Dad looked like I'd kicked him in the crotch with steel-toed boots. "I'll always love your mom, Benji."

"But you still left her."

"I—"

"What if it doesn't work out with you and your new girlfriend?"

Dad returned to his burger, though he seemed less interested in eating it than in having something to do with his hands. "Then I'll have to live with the consequences. That's how life works. You take risks or you don't, but you'll always have to live with the consequences."

"Was it worth it?"

"I don't know yet, Benji. At least, for me, knowing and being wrong is better than always wondering."

I wished my dad had told me all of this before. I still would've been angry, but I might have understood. And what he said made me think of my own situation. If I never spoke to Dan again, would I wind up an old man thinking about the chance I didn't take? Would I spend the rest of my life regretting the cards I didn't play?

"I don't forgive you, Dad."

"I don't expect you to."

"Good."

Dad cleared his throat. "But, maybe, you could stop cussing me out when I call?"

"I'll try."

We finished our burgers, and Dad offered to drive me home. As we neared Mom's place, Dad asked me how I'd been spending the summer, so I told him about my new friends and the rooftop and our games of Spite and Malice.

"I used to play that in college," Dad said. "But we called it by a different name."

"You did? What was it?"

"Screw Your Neighbor."

When I got home, I sent Dan a message to meet me on the roof. He showed up ten minutes later looking cute with his hair combed back in this perfect swoop. His smile as he approached made my bones ache. I sat balanced on the railing at the edge of the building with my back to the city.

"Hey."

I nodded. "Hey."

Dan tried to squeeze between my knees and wrap his arms around me. I almost let him. My defenses nearly crumbled, but I held the line, though it cost me.

"Oh."

"I can't, Dan."

"Okay." He shoved his hands in his pockets. "Why?"

"Because you have a boyfriend. Unless things have changed between you and Andy."

"They haven't."

"And they won't, will they?"

Dan's shoulders slumped and he bowed his head, refusing to look me in the eye. "I love him."

"Even though you know he'll get bored and leave you?"

"I don't want to hurt him." Dan's voice was soft but sincere.

"So instead you'll wait around for him to hurt you?" I blew out a sigh. "Sounds like a great plan."

Dan's eyes flicked up, and there was anger there, but it quickly dissolved and he buried his face in his hands. "I don't know what to do, Benji." He moved toward me again, and I let him in to lean his head against my chest. "This would've been easier if you'd liked Andy."

I wanted to kiss Dan and convince him to choose me. I wanted to make the case for myself, list the reasons Dan and I would be good together, but I didn't. I just held Dan and burned the memory of how he felt pressed against me into my brain in case this was the last time.

After a moment, I gently pushed Dan back, creating a

space between us. "You have to do what you think is right. You know what I want, but while you're with Andy, we can't be together." I wanted to win, but I refused to cheat to do it.

Dan shut his eyes and clenched his jaw. "This sucks."

I ran my thumb along Dan's cheek. "It really does, but you were right. This is life, and how we play matters."

We stayed on the roof because the others were coming over for a barbecue, but we didn't talk much. I had no idea what Dan was going to do. I don't think he knew, either.

Jasmine showed up first and got some music going, Jia brought food to grill—most of it vegan. Casper arrived on the arm of a young woman who introduced herself as Scarlett. Andy arrived last. I wish I could say I was happy to see him, but watching him kiss Dan was a knife between my ribs.

As the evening wore on, Andy regaled us with horror stories about the customers at the coffee shop where he worked. When a good song came on, Jasmine tried to make us dance. I gave it a shot, but my moves were as flat as my behind. Dan, on the other hand, showed off what he could do, seriously testing my resolve. Scarlett told us how she and Casper had met in a VR game and had played together for hundreds of hours before realizing they lived three blocks from each other. Dinner came out burned, but no one complained.

Eventually we gathered for Spite and Malice. Jasmine, Jia, and Casper were explaining the rules to Scarlett. Instead of joining them, I stood off to the side.

"Come on, Benji," Andy said. "What's the holdup?"

Dan nudged the chair across from Andy with his foot. "You gonna play or what?"

"I don't know. Maybe I should call it a night."

Andy grinned. "What's wrong? You're not scared to lose, are you?"

"Maybe," I said. "Or maybe I'll win."

Dan pushed the chair out farther. "Can't do either if you don't play."

If I walked away, if I didn't make Dan choose, then I wouldn't have to risk him choosing Andy and breaking my heart. But then I'd never find out if he chose me, either. I might miss out on something great. If I left now, I'd never know what might've been, and despite the potential for pain, I needed to know.

I grabbed the chair, took my place, and said, "All right, one game."

GAME OF THE GODS

Francesca Zappia

LAWRENCE HIGH'S FOOTBALL STADIUM IS A SHRINE TO THEIR god, and we are marauding pagans. This is not a comment on the fact that they're a Catholic school, though they are; it's an observation based on the size of the bleachers. The home side is a towering crenellated wall of stone and brick, carved with a motif of lightning bolts, the gothic lettering LAWRENCE LIGHTNING in relief on the outer face. It's a holy monument, a grand temple to Zeus.

The visitor stands are a pipework of aluminum, fenced in with chain link and cold on the butt.

I sit at the top of the visitor stands, my back to the fencing, chewing a piece of my hair while I count fans filling the stadium. I have the rough numbers Boots gave me earlier on how many people we could expect from our school, but I don't need them. This is homecoming. Well, it's Lawrence High's homecoming, and they're our eternal rivals. My little sister is one of the first-string wide receivers, and our school, Elmwood, loves my little sister.

For all these reasons, the Elmwood side will be full, and it'll be my job to make sure the Furies notice. We always play Lawrence at their homecoming—they think we're weak and easy—and it's been half a decade since we last beat them. This year's different. I won't let them win while Nicky's playing, despite what she said to me earlier today, despite the cold unease churning in my gut. If I waver, the Furies won't grant us the help we need.

If we are to be pagan marauders on this foreign field, then let us raise our pagan god.

It's chilly this mid-October evening, so Boots has their entire body stuffed inside an array of thick knitted garments. Sweater, mittens, leggings. Their knitted Uggs slide across the bleachers as they hurry toward me. Short, bristly straw hair pokes wildly out from under their cap.

"Breezy," Boots wheezes, "the Rowleys forgot their signs. Again. The third quarter sign flip is going to have gaps."

"We still have the layout of the design, don't we?" I ask, surprised to find I feel only about half of Boots's urgency. Boots nods, hands on hips, sucking air into their round pink cheeks. "Then tell Poole we need them remade. It's only three signs, and they're all solid colors. It shouldn't take more than half an hour, and we have the supplies already."

Boots nods, already typing away on their phone. I'm surprised their phone doesn't have a knit case.

"How're the radio staff?" I ask.

"Already setting up in the box."

"And the cheerleaders?"

"About to take the field," Boots says. "This is the third time you've asked me since we got here. Are you for sure going to launch Hail the Queen, then?"

"We don't talk about that until we have to do it," I say. Boots knows better. Hail the Queen is a last-ditch effort, only ever to be used in fourth quarter, and only when the game is so close you can feel the hairs on your head splitting in two from the stress. The Furies love it. If we decide to do it, it'll generate so much energy on our side of the field I'd be surprised if the Lawrence players can even focus. But you can only do it once per game—rarely do even minor deities reward you for repetition—so you have to save it for when it counts.

The marching bands line up outside opposite ends of the field, readying for their entrance. Normally this is the part where I feel my blood start to pump harder. Tonight, though, I feel only hollowness in my chest, and hear Nicky's words rattling around in my head.

I play. You cheer.

She's harsh sometimes because she's got a big ego. I know that. I have a big ego, too. I know she'll be sorry for saying it later. But that doesn't mean it didn't hurt at the time. It's not as if I have a lot outside of the game. I get okay grades, but I don't like school. I don't make friends easily. Boots and the squad are more like colleagues. My parents know Nicky is the successful one in our family. If I could play the game forever, I would. But I'm not even playing it *now*. I'm tangential. I'm an accessory.

Boots nods and goes back to their phone. "If we need it, the other side has an ambassador."

My lip curls. The other side—not the Lawrence High team, but their Favor Squad. Favor Squads, like us, aren't just the cheerleaders on the field, they're a whole network of fans whose job it is to rile the crowd in a display for their god. Running a Favor Squad is a full-on career in most college and professional sports leagues, but it's more like a club at the high school level. Completely student run. The high school sports board says it encourages a more level playing field between schools, but Elmwood would never have the money or prestige to curry favor with a god like Zeus.

Greek deities are popular because they pay good attention to any kind of competition, but others will reward favor, too. Lawrence has the money to put up stadiums to Zeus. Elmwood only has Furies money—the Greek Furies, the sisters Alecto, Megaera, and Tisiphone—but if you ask me, the Furies like us better for our fighting spirit. In myth, they're underworld deities older than most other gods, and they bring eternal wrath and punishment. Pretty hardcore, yet they aren't well-known, so they tend to end up with smaller teams.

Favor teams are the closest anyone gets to communing with gods. There's no direct interaction, no talking with them, only this exchange of energy: our prayers in the forms of cheers and action, their favor granting us more exciting games and temporary abilities beyond the norm.

I've been scanning the Lawrence bleachers for the last twenty minutes trying to pinpoint their Favor Squad in the crowd. "The Eagle isn't coming out, I suppose?" I say the name with all the sarcasm I can muster.

"No. Cando's still acting as ambassador."

"Fine." So Will won't come talk to me himself. It's been two years. I think he knows he's outmatched. Money can only get you so far in the favor game, at least with most deities.

"Oh, there he is," Boots says. "Sitting against the wall of the announcer's box, far right."

I take the binoculars and scan the other side. There he is. Will Elkin, also known as the Eagle, a lanky kid with nicely trimmed hair, a thick pair of glasses, and a Carhartt jacket like the farm kids wear. He's led the Lawrence Favor Squad for two years. Last year they pulled off a flash mob in the bleachers during halftime and made headlines across the state. We like to glare at each other across the stadium.

His head turns. I know he sees me. I know he sees me because he points with two fingers at his own eyes, then at mine. I remove one hand from the binoculars to flip him the bird. He smiles. So do I. With teeth.

"Cando says he's a cool guy," Boots says, settling down next to me, rearranging their knits.

"You're talking to Cando now?"

Boots shrugs. "He's not so bad. And he says Will has a brother on the Lawrence team. You two have more in common than you thought."

"Goody. Can I keep the binoculars for the game?"

"Sure. They're Poole's. If she asks where you got them, you found them lying around."

"Got anything else hidden in all that knitting?"

"Don't worry about it," Boots says.

Boots is obviously not their real name. Mine's not Breezy. But these are the names we've called each other ever since we banded together to pursue this thing called *winning*. We've been the head of the Elmwood Favor Squad for three years, since Nicky joined the football team. I decided I was going to do whatever I could to support her. I wasn't going to let anyone give her a hard time because she's a girl playing football in a small conservative town. She's pretty self-assured—we both are—but if I can back her up, I will. Boots and everyone else who assists in the crew gets something out of it, whether it's a chance to use their skills, a temporary thrill that the gods are favoring us, or the knowledge that they helped the team.

There's plenty to keep us busy. Planning after school to

make sure we're all on the same page and we can get the word out to the network. Late-night craft sessions to make posters, jerseys, and all the other paraphernalia we'll need for each scheme. Meetings with the coaches and athletic directors to get an idea of when we should push for favor.

I'm good at leading a Favor Squad, but there are a lot of times I'd rather be good at the sport itself. Taller, leaner, less in my own head. I'd rather receive that favor. Soar across a field on a god's wings, stop my opponents with a god's strength. I'd rather look up at the bright lights from the turf and know that in those crowded stands there was someone watching me, cheering for me. But that's not going to happen. So I deal.

The Lawrence High band starts to play. They come onto the field in a snaking line of red, white, and silver, instruments flashing in the stadium lights, feet marching in time. The marching bands are excellent for spurring that initial hit of favor, and the home team marching band usually gets the spotlight, so we're already at a disadvantage. I raise my binoculars again and find Will Elkin in the opposing stands. He's forgotten me and is watching the band play and talking with Cando, a scraggly haired kid who can't stay sitting for more than a couple minutes at a time. Will looks too calm for this. He should have something planned for when the players come out onto the field. Zeus is notoriously needy. Will should know this by now. He could be pretending to be calm, I suppose . . .

This is what I hate about him: I can never tell if he's bluffing.

But nothing happens. No sooner does Lawrence finish their fight song—I tune it out because it's Satan's noise—than the Elmwood Marching Raiders spear in from the other end of the fence, lining up along our side of the field and blasting the Lawrence fans with a lively rendition of "The Lasting Fury."

All of the Elmwood fans rise to their feet at the same time and belt out the song. This is old hat for us now. I don't even have to convince people to do it anymore. Hairs raise all along my body, the feeling of being watched from all directions, though no one is looking. The Furies' eyes are on us now.

When the song is done, I ask Boots, "Everyone knows the order?"

"Two stomps, yell the name," they say.

"Good."

Our team is announced into the stadium first. The Lawrence announcer has a roster he reads off of, so of course that means plenty of the names get mispronounced. I've planned for that. As each name is called, our fans stomp twice and then yell the name back, pronouncing it properly.

Then they get to Nicky.

"Number eighty-two," the announcer calls, "Nicoletta Cala-brace!"

Our stomps are furious. We yell back, "CALA-BRAY-SAY."

She runs onto the field. Swift and solid, as tall and lean as I'd like to be, her dark hair hidden beneath her helmet. A bright 82 on her back below the name CALABRESE. Nicky's one of only three girls on football teams in the county, and she's better than most players, regardless of gender. She's always wanted to play football. It's a certainty for her, a thing she knew she was supposed to do.

Her voice replays in my head, over and over again. Her short glance. Her teasing tone. She had meant it to be something cute. "It's not like you can't do *anything*," she'd said earlier today. "I play, you cheer. You know the Furies love what you give them. You're way better at that than you were at playing, anyway."

I was sure she'd meant it to be reassuring, too.

As I watch her run, that heavy weariness returns. It's not a surprise, though this is the first time the feeling has been so strong. I want her to do well, I want her to succeed, and it's not about me.

The Lawrence High team is announced to the marching band playing in the background. They jump through a huge archway hung with red sparkling streamers and decorated with lightning bolts around the outside. All of their names are pronounced correctly. Their fans cheer each player, but not unified, like we did. I scan our friend Will Elkin for any sign of life. He's checking his phone.

"Now he's overdoing it," I say. I offer Boots the binoculars so they can take a look.

"Looks like he's not doing anything," Boots says.

"Exactly. What's his plan here?"

But even as Boots shakes their head, I see it. The Lawrence players have lined up along their side of the field. They clasp arms, then twist themselves in one long snaking pattern. There's something attached to their sleeves, some kind of thin tube. Before I can get the binoculars back from Boots, the stadium lights slam off, throwing us into darkness.

A purple lightning bolt runs down the other side of the field, along the light strips attached to the players' arms, accompanied by a thunderclap over the stadium speakers.

The Lawrence side erupts. The entire stadium crackles with energy, the favor of Zeus flowing to the other team before the game has even started.

I press my lips together. The lights come back up; the Lawrence players, hyped, are ripping the strips from their arms and tossing them behind their bench. In the stands, Will Elkin beams.

"Nice theatrics," I say. "Let's go, Boots. We've got work to do."

Nicky is only a year younger than me. Growing up, we operated in the same social circles, each of us making up for what the other lacked. Nicky was the bright, outgoing one, always game for a contest or a dare, quick to make friends. I was happier letting her talk while I analyzed situations and decided our next plan of attack. How would we win that contest, or that dare? Were the friends we made good people, did we mesh well together?

We both loved playing sports. But around middle school, skill and ability suddenly counted for more than passion, and Nicky had a lot more of those than I did. She was a starter. I got cut. I told her not to worry about it, that I was fine, that she should keep playing because she was beyond good, and I would cheer for her. But I wasn't really fine. It's like being the weak deer in the herd, and the coach is telling you, *Stay behind to die, the rest of us will be better off without you.*

Nicky and I don't have so many overlapping friends anymore. We're not complete strangers, nothing that serious, but she spends so much time in practice and training that we've lost a lot of the common language we used to share. I'm sure when I go to college next year, and when she gets a scholarship and goes off the year after that, we'll change for good. She'll keep playing, but I won't have anyone to cheer for anymore. There are college Favor Squads I could join, even run, but what would be the point?

At the end of the first quarter, without the help of the Furies and while I'm focused on the future, Nicky runs in a touchdown and a roar goes up from our stands. It takes me a moment to cheer with them.

"You okay?" Boots asks when the noise dies down. "What's wrong? Did Elkin make a move?"

"No," I say, "just momentary existential dread. It's all good. Let's check on those signs."

Boots and I climb the stands to the small metal booth where our school radio hosts sit. They're on a commercial break between quarters. In the corner is one of the three costumes for our mascot, the wild-haired Tisiphone, Fury of vengeful destruction. Lavender skin, green mohawk, piercing eyes. It's here because there's a big rip up the side of the foam head that needs to be fixed. Poole and a few other squad members scribble blue marker wildly over sheets of white paper.

"I thought we were using colored paper for the sign flip, not *coloring* the paper," I say.

"We were," Boots says. "But *someone* spilled coffee all over the extra blue sheets, so we had to improvise."

Poole, looking smaller and daintier than normal in an oversize Elmwood sweatshirt, looks up from her work. Shrugs sheepishly.

I glance out the booth windows. The stadium is bright, the teams like flocks of milling birds. Why am I here? Lawrence is going to flatten us, and Nicky doesn't need my help. She just scored a touchdown against a Zeus-empowered team without any help at all from the Furies. She's so good she's rendering me useless. She doesn't need me.

But my chest tightens when I think that. What if she looks up into the stands and I'm not there? It's so easy to forget the other half of what she said to me earlier.

I play. You cheer.

But I wouldn't play nearly so well if I wasn't trying to impress you.

Impress me. She was being nice. She meant trying to impress the gods through me.

"Really, Breezy, you aren't getting sick, are you?" Boots steps up beside me.

I roll my shoulders, trying to get my sweatshirt back into the right position. It doesn't feel like it fits anymore, choking and scratchy. "I'm thinking about Nicky, that's all."

"Is she okay?" Boots asks.

"She's fine," I say. "Just . . . never mind. We need to go spread the word about the second quarter chants." I could tell them what's up, I'm sure they would understand, but I don't feel like explaining right now. How do you explain feeling loved and used at the same time? Being both useful and worthless?

Boots's phone pings. They check the screen and scoff. "Connor Lowrey and Jake Lin found a couple of the Eagle's crew sneaking around the south side of our bleachers. Had a handful of what they think might be stink bombs."

Another ping.

". . . what were *definitely* stink bombs," Boots said, rolling their eyes. "Jake took one outside the fence and broke it."

"Stink bombs, now?" I rub my forehead. "Text Cando. I want to talk with Will. *Not* Cando, I'm not wasting time talking to Cando. Interfering with the opponent fans is against the rules."

There's no doubt I'm a stickler for the rules, but the rules aren't why I need to talk to Will.

Cando doesn't send back Will's confirmation of the meeting until halfway through the second quarter, so we have to spend the time patrolling the stands, making sure no other Lawrence saboteurs show their faces. The score is 7–7 at halftime. The bands are back with Lawrence's homecoming floats, themed after board games. The buzz of favor fades around the stadium—I don't think Zeus is super into board games. Bad choice on their part.

It's customary to hold meetings at the visitor stands so as to limit the home crew's ability to interfere with the visiting crew. Boots and I wander under the southeast corner of the stands and watch the curve of the fence until Cando and Will come around the track. Cando's bouncing on the balls of his feet, every inch of him wiry and alert, looking like he stuck his finger in an electrical socket; Will lopes along with his hands in his pockets and an easy smile on his face.

I have my sunglasses on—yes, it is nighttime, and yes, this is entirely so he can't read my face—and I keep my gaze on Will as they stroll up.

"Breezy," he says. "Boots."

"You're resorting to stink bombs now?" I ask.

Will's smile falters. "What?"

"Stink bombs in our stands," Boots says, all authority. "We caught some of your boys doing it." They take from their pocket one of the stink bombs, a little capsule that can be broken on the ground.

Will stares at it in bewilderment. "We didn't plan this."

"Interfering with the opponent's fans is illegal and punishable by school contract," Boots continues. "I'm sure the Lawrence High administration would love to hear that some of their students were setting off stink bombs at the homecoming game."

"Hey, we didn't—" Cando begins, starting forward, but Will holds an arm out to stop him.

"We didn't do this," Will says. "If you can tell me who you saw, I'll make sure they know their place." He looks at me. I keep my face as unreadable as I can. "I don't play dirty like this. You know that."

He never has before, anyway. And I knew that when I asked Boots to get him over here. I turn to them. "Boots, Cando, can I have a moment alone with Will?"

"The Eagle should be addressed by his proper—" Cando starts, but is again cut off by Will. Will motions to the fence line, away from the bleachers. With a sour look, Cando jogs off, followed by a dagger-eyed Boots.

Up close, Will is a few inches taller than me, clear-eyed

and clean-cut. He radiates an aura of calm that I don't get much in school or at home, where everyone is always going going going and everything has to be done perfectly and on time. I will always be locked in a deep and abiding grudge match with him, but I do have to admit that it's nice to hang out with someone who doesn't make me feel like I'm lagging behind.

"I don't know why they all call me that," Will says once Boots and Cando are out of earshot. "I've tried to get them to stop."

"Zeus's messenger eagle, Aquila," I say. "Names are important. Look, I know you didn't order the stink bombs."

"You do?"

"You're too smart to screw up your senior year with a stunt like that."

He frowns. "Then why did you call me over here?"

"Why are you doing this, Will?" I ask.

He doesn't answer. The frown deepens.

"Favor Squad?" I go on. "Calling to Zeus? Getting everyone pumped? Is it a power thing? Or for fun?"

"You feel okay, Breezy?" he asks.

I finger my sunglasses, sliding them slightly up and down my nose. "I need people to stop asking me that."

He shrugs. "For Jacob, I guess. My brother. I was never into playing football, but when I'm in the stands I still feel like I'm helping him."

I thought he'd say that. "Didn't you ever want to play yourself?"

"No," he says simply.

"And you don't feel like you're . . . you're being used? Like the only reason you're here is because your brother is?"

He squinted at me. "Are we talking about me, or you?"

"Shut up and answer the question."

"I don't get that hung up on things," he says, eyes sparkling with good humor. "I like watching football, and cheering for football, and cheering for my brother. If I didn't like it, I wouldn't do it. You don't do this just for Nicky, right?"

My nostrils flare. He cocks his head. "It's just a game," he says. "Currying favor. It's a game as much as football is. It's been you and me against each other for two years. It'd be a bummer to find out my archrival only thought of it as a job."

Archrival. I mean, yes, he's the worst, and I want to beat him at all costs—I want *my team* to beat *his team* at all costs, but . . .

I fix my sunglasses firmly back in front of my eyes, suddenly afraid he can read all my thoughts. "Never mind. Keep your goons on your side of the field. If I see anyone messing around on our side again, the call is being made."

Will watches me for another moment, then shakes his head and strides off. Cando breaks away from the fence line to join him. Boots hurries back to me.

"What did you say?" Boots asks. "What did he say?"

"I made him swear to me they weren't his boys. Figured

he'd be more likely to spill the truth if Cando wasn't around, and I needed you to watch Cando."

"Yeah, of course." Boots nods. Looks at their phone. "The signs are ready. First time Nicky gets the ball. The Furies should give her all the speed she needs."

Sweet Boots. So dedicated, so focused, so trusting of me. Are they here just for the game, too? When did I *stop* being here for the game?

"Thanks, Boots," I say. "Let's get back up top."

The double-sided signs have been distributed throughout our stands by the beginning of the third quarter. High school games can't generate as much favor as college teams, much less pro teams, but when you have the entire visitors' bleachers holding up massive segmented signs, they're visible by passing airplanes.

The first catch Nicky makes in the third quarter is at the fifty-five-yard line, and when she jukes past the first defender, I yell, "UP AND OUT!" The cry is echoed down the bleachers. All at once, signs are raised. The first side is the blue, which displays the word RUN. Nicky reaches the thirty-five. I yell, "FLIP," my words drowned out by the growing roar of our crowd, but signs flip to the white side, bearing her name in bold. The twenty. Flip, drowned, obeyed.

RUN NICKY RUN

She runs. The stadium crackles with favor, so much I feel the hairs lifting on my head. There is no physical evidence of the Furies besides this atmosphere and the inhuman speed with which Nicky moves, but it's enough to know what's happening. The Furies give wings to her already fleet feet. She's beautiful, uncatchable, tailed by six boys who fall farther behind with each step. I worry about her whenever she gets tackled, even though I know she can take it, but there's no chance of her being tackled on this play. There are recruiters who will see this and drool. She is great, and she is doing what she loves.

She floats into the end zone and flips the ball to the referee, hardly pausing to celebrate. Making up for it are several of her teammates, who crash into her, jostling her into momentary frivolity. When she breaks away from them, she looks up and sees our sign flip one last time between RUN and NICKY. When I think she might be angled toward my end of the stands, I stretch both my arms high over my head and hold all my fingers out. She throws her arms up, too, fingers splayed, and bounces on the balls of her feet before she trots back to her team.

I smile. I love her, despite everything.

We make our field goal. 14–7. In the other stands, Cando's pointed face is twisted as he yells something toward the field, but Will sits undisturbed. That means something's up. The favor buzz on the field skews toward the Furies.

The fourth quarter rolls around with us still in the lead. The night has grown darker and the stadium lights brighter. I lean against the chain-link fencing and rub my eyes. Never has there been a time when I'd rather be sleeping than at a game, but my bed sounds pretty good right now. I want to be alone. I want to be away from all of this, from the buzz, so I can think. How did I feel when I loved this for what it was: not a chance to support Nicky, but a game I could play? A game just for me?

"Breezy. BREEZY." Boots shakes my arm, looking panicked, eyes following the players on the field. Lawrence High is taking up a formation I haven't seen them use before. Will is on his feet, making some signal with his hands to the other side of their crowd. The crowd rises. Begins stomping feet in a constant roll of thunder.

The snap. The ball disappears in a flurry of Lawrence players, in our pushing defensive line. The buzz intensifies, Zeus easily taking over.

All at once, the Lawrence fans clap their hands together in an echoing *boom*. The thunder continues to roll under their feet. The buzz spikes like lightning in the sky.

One player streaks out of the fray, jagging through Elmwood players before they see him there. It's like the Elmwood players are disoriented, unable to react. Zeus's hands tightening over them.

Another clap. Another spike. Their player runs too fast, ours too slow. He's past them all. Twenty. Fifteen. Ten. Clap. Clap. Clap. Touchdown. The Lawrence fans go wild. Boots curses so loudly I can almost hear them over the boos of the Elmwood side.

"What the hell was that?" Boots yells. "Who pulls out a completely new play in the fourth quarter of the homecoming game?"

"A team that thinks they're going to lose otherwise," I say. "They're scared. They won't do it again."

"It doesn't matter, it doesn't matter." Boots flaps their hands. "They're going for the two-point conversion, we'll stop them, our defense hasn't been *that* bad this whole—"

We don't stop them. The score flips to 14–15. Boots drops about thirty f-bombs. In my earbud, our commentary drops off for a moment, then comes back in disappointment. I take it out of my ear.

"Why aren't you more upset?" Boots asks, throwing a hand out toward the field. "There's four minutes left and they've got the lead."

I hesitate. For too long. Boots snaps, "Breezy!"

"Get out of my face, Boots," I say. "I see the score."

"It's *homecoming*. What's the plan? What are we doing?"

Boots's impatience comes from fear, not anger, even though it looks like the opposite. The squad relies on me. Nicky relies on me. *I play, you cheer.* I have to have the plan. I have to be ready to rumble, always.

"Go big or go home, right?" I say. Boots's eyes widen. I clap them on the shoulder. "Tell the cheerleaders to send the signal."

"Hail the Queen?" Boots says.

I nod. "Hail the Queen."

Boots is off like a shot, teetering along the bleachers while they type furiously into their phone. Hail the Queen is never hard to get going. It's the one setup everyone knows, even if they haven't been briefed. But everyone has to do it. Everyone has to be on board. The effect has to be overwhelming, enough to really spur the Furies to help us this late in the game, otherwise it's just more noise in the stadium.

I have to do it, too. One more cheer. I bounce on the balls of my feet to get the blood flowing.

By the time Boots gets back, the clock is running low. Our Red Raiders are still in the game, but they're lagging, the wind taken out of their sails by the last touchdown. Nicky claps her hands over her head, trying to rally them.

One more cheer won't kill me. One more cheer, to help the team win. This is the way I can help.

"They're ready when you are, Breezy," Boots says, nervous but wired.

The latest play ends. Raiders in possession on the sixty. Two downs left. I can feel my hairs splitting.

I motion to the cheerleaders, who are watching me, waiting for the signal. They face the stands, and together, we stomp both feet, one after the other. Clap. Stomp-stomp-clap. Stomp-stomp-clap.

Boots joins in. Then the people closest to us. Then the people past them. With the cheerleaders projecting to the crowd, it spreads faster than Will's thunderclap, and grows louder. The rhythm has taken over our entire side by the time the teams re-form their lines on the field, and when I feel that rush of favor over my skin and the collective racing of the crowd's blood, I yell out:

"WE WILL—WE WILL—ROCK YOU."

That takes even less time to catch on. Our entire fanbase yells it into the night air, drowning out the Lawrence side in their coliseum stands, the referee's whistle, the noise of the game. Red Raiders glance our way. Some throw their hands up. We are here for them, with them on the field. Nicky looks up my way, blows me a kiss. I know she loves me, too, even if she doesn't realize that what she said earlier hurt me. I stomp harder, my feet numb, my thoughts, temporarily, locked away.

We keep chanting and stomping after the play starts. We can't afford to lose momentum, because if we do, so will the players, and the Furies' favor will wane. The snap. The quarterback backpedals, looks around. Nicky's there, in an opening between defenders. The ball goes up. Nicky catches it. She's going to do it, she's going to get through—

An overwhelming thunderclap of a stomp issues from the Lawrence stands. The blowback of favor is like a physical wall of air slamming into our stands. A defender appears out of nowhere, clobbering Nicky to the ground. The Furies' favor fizzles beneath the onslaught of Zeus.

Boots drops their arms. "It didn't . . . it didn't work."

I stare, shocked. How? With Hail the Queen *and* Nicky's skills, we couldn't even get a first down? I scan up and down the stands, looking for the people who didn't participate, the ones who left a gap in our cheer and weakened it. But everyone's standing. Everyone is yelling at the field, furious.

Everyone except me. I cheered, but only because I was supposed to. It was my job.

I look down at the field. Nicky is up and isn't hurt, but her head is raised, scanning the stands. She finds me and holds up a single finger.

One more down. I know. The clock is too low.

I look across to the Lawrence stands. Will is in his spot, watching me. He gives me a knowing smile. Holds up his hand, flicks his fingers. *Bring it on.*

A fire sparks, catches, and flares in my chest. This is my game. Not the one Nicky's playing on the field; *that's* tangential. My game is the one between me and Will. I know how to play this game. I'm good at it.

"What are we going to do now?" Boots asks, looking lost. "We're still at the sixty and there's no time left, and without Hail the Queen—"

I think fast. I was the problem. The Furies withheld favor because of me.

They're waiting for *me*.

"Stay here," I tell Boots. "I have an idea."

I run back up to the radio booth. Ignoring questions and cries of dismay over the game, I grab the Tisiphone mascot costume. Alecto is on the track with the cheerleaders, Megaera in the stands. I hurry outside, toss the costume up onto the roof of the radio booth, and then use the fence to climb up myself.

I get the costume on just as the next play starts. Shove the ripped foam head on, its wild green hair flying around me. I'm impossible to miss up here. A cry rises from our stands as people notice me, as I stand on the edge of the booth and raise my hands, holding Tisiphone's fake-metal spear over my head. The third Fury has appeared above them all, ready to rain hell on the field. There's a spike in energy from the fans, but there's another, bigger one from the Furies. They didn't expect this, either.

"*RED RAIDERS!*" I yell with vicious pride. I yell it at Will, at the players below, at the Furies, wherever they are. This is *my* game, and *I will win*. "FIGHT FIGHT FIGHT."

The Elmwood crowd picks up my chant.

The snap. Our quarterback looks for an opening, looks, looks, but there isn't one, there's no one out there. We yell louder. I hold up the spear and turn my scream on Zeus. Daring him directly. *Come at me.* The air grows heavier, but instead of weighing on me, I am held securely in place. The

Furies are here. Now. Screaming with me. Screaming with everyone in the stands.

Nicky loops around behind the quarterback; he laterals the ball back to her. She tucks it under her arm and continues her same pace as if nothing happened, moving to the other side of the field. We keep chanting. The Lawrence crowd shoots to their feet, having seen what many of their players haven't. The air crackles with the gods' favor, both the Furies' and Zeus's, the press between the two so strong some of the stadium lights start to flicker.

Nicky slips between two linemen and cranks the gas. Lawrence players catch on to her like flies. She jukes one, then weaves past another who lunges for her legs. The Furies aren't as powerful as Zeus, but they're tricky and smart, and they love a challenge. Nicky runs on her toes, so fast it's like she's not touching the ground. She leaps over a defender who mysteriously trips, and then it's just her, tailed by one last Lawrence player alive with god-favor. The name on his jersey is ELKIN.

I'm the first to break from the chant.

"RUN, NICKY!"

Will Elkin's brother makes a final desperate leap before Nicky reaches the end zone. His arms tangle around her legs, hooking one foot before she can escape him. My breath catches. The chanting stops, suddenly and all at once, as the crowd watches Nicky fall. She has both hands on the ball, her arms stretched out in front of her, her whole body extending forward as far as she can reach.

She hits the ground hard.

The ball breaks the plane of the goal line, still clutched firmly in her hands. There's no god-favor in that hold, just good old-fashioned grit.

The referee calls a touchdown with four seconds to spare. The Elmwood stands erupt in celebration. Below me, Boots bursts into tears. I can't feel my hands or my feet, but I'm screaming, too, and my sunglasses have fallen off inside Tisiphone's head, and I don't think I'll be able to hear tomorrow.

I tear the head off and squint to see if Nicky's okay. Will Elkin's brother offers her a hand, which she takes to pop back to her feet. She disappears under the swarming mass of her teammates' bodies.

I breathe hard for several seconds. The tension in the air lifts, the Furies fading away. They've left me, but the blood still pounds in my veins. At least for a little while. The feeling won't last forever, but what does? Might as well enjoy it while it's here.

I throw Tisiphone's spear to the radio booth roof at my feet and yell, *"FUCK YEAH."*

Later, when the teams have left the field and the stands are empty, I sit with my back against the broadcasting booth and my legs stretched onto the bleacher row below me. The field is a beautiful uninterrupted plane of green and white. Quiet except for the rush of cars on the distant street. Not a hint of gods here, now that all the worshippers have gone.

I told Boots to go to the party without me. It's been twenty minutes. I might give it another thirty minutes. Or an hour. Or two.

Footsteps ring out. A lanky form climbs the right-hand staircase onto the bleachers.

"I thought it was you," Will says. "Saw you from the parking lot. Not many people at the game wearing sunglasses at night. Mind if I come up?"

I pat the seat next to me. With a few long-legged strides, Will climbs the stairs and slides into the spot.

"Sucks to suck," I say.

"Yeah, yeah," he replies, waving his hand. "If you're so pumped about winning, why are you sitting here looking bummed instead of heading to what I'm sure is a very fun post-win homecoming party?"

"I will. Trying to get my head in order first. I've had some revelations tonight."

"Oh?"

"I don't like giving you credit for literally anything, but you were right. It's just a different game I'm playing now, and I don't have to play it for Nicky. I can do it for myself."

He smiles. "Glad you came around. I'll try not to rub it in

too much. But, uh, speaking of all this, the Favor Squads, I wanted to ask you something. You going to college?"

"Yeah. I got into SU for sports management."

"Just management? Not particularly Favor Squad management?"

"That's what I've been sitting here thinking about. I wasn't sure, for a while, if I even wanted to keep doing this. But I think I'm coming back around to it."

His smile widens. "Good, cause I'm also going to SU," he says. "You're not leaving me behind, sorry. What are you going to do when we're on a squad together?"

I hadn't seriously considered what it would be like to be on a college-level Favor Squad. It's a lot of work, but the rewards are huge. Especially if you're good at it. I press my lips together to keep from smiling too widely.

I can start somewhere new. Play my game the way I want.

"How good are you at taking orders?" I ask.

He throws his head back and laughs. It echoes across the field. "Looks like we're gonna have to compete for squad captain, too."

I smile. I didn't expect anything less.

Will stands, offers me a hand. "Let's go. My ears are freezing."

I take the hand. We descend the bleachers and leave the field. The night is cold and getting colder, but there's a warm party not too far away where my sister is waiting for me. I'll spend time with her while I have it, because I love her. Nicky will always be my sister, no matter where we are or what we're doing, but I no longer have to play this game for her.

This is *my* game. It always has been.

DO YOU SEE IT NOW?

Laura Silverman

"I'M EXCITED TO FINALLY CHECK THIS PLACE OUT," I TELL THEO as we walk up to the brick-exterior storefront. A large picture window allows sunlight to flood inside.

The Magic Bean is a gaming and coffee shop. It's nestled in a nearby college town, a bit east of my Atlanta suburb, and it offers everything the heart could desire—a dizzying array of games, in-person tournaments, and, according to Yelp reviews, the best chocolate chip muffins in the state.

It's a Saturday afternoon, and Theo and I are here to pick out something new for the game night we're hosting this evening.

"Baked good first?" Theo asks as he opens the door for us. He's wearing a thermal shirt, blue sleeves pushed up to his elbows. His golden-brown hair glints in the sun as a little bell chimes over our heads.

I grin at him. My boyfriend knows me well. "Yes, please."

We walk inside. Immediately, all of my expectations are

met and even exceeded. The midsized space is crammed with shelves of games and glass displays of cards and collectibles. The scent of roast coffee and cinnamon infuses the store with warmth. Plants are set up hodgepodge near the window, ivy trailing along the sill, pinks and purples blooming. A few customers browse the stacked shelves, while others sit in mismatched chairs playing various tile and card games. It's the definition of cozy perfection.

I blink up at Theo. "I love it here."

He smiles and wraps an arm around my shoulder. "Me too, Alexis. Me too."

Theo and I bonded over our love of games. As sophomores, we were in the same friend group, a tangle of twelve people who always sat together during lunch. I thought he was cute, with his blue crinkly eyes and a left dimple that only appeared when he thought something was *really* funny. But we never talked much, positioned at opposite ends of the table. That is, until I brought Sushi Go! to school.

Lunch usually passed by slowly for me. I had trouble focusing on the five conversations happening at once but also too much energy to passively scroll my phone. The solution: play a game.

Only a few people agreed to play at first. Theo was one of them, practically jumping out of his seat (and therefore almost tripping over his gangly limbs) the second I put the deck on the table, shouting, "I love that game!"

I wondered if he could see my blush.

It didn't take much time after that for gaming to become a core component of every lunch period. The nerd ice was broken. Our tablemates, especially my best friend, Nisha, became just as enthusiastic as Theo and me. We brought in new games to try each week and garnered the attention of our fellow students, their necks craning to see what was going on, some even asking to join us. We started bracket tournaments, and once even livestreamed for fun: "Troy Creek Tigers Play Catan in the Cafeteria."

Theo and I were in charge of the stream. We had twenty-seven viewers and one singular comment that read *this is weird*.

As the rest of our friends departed the lunchroom that day, Theo and I stayed behind to reply to the comment. I noticed when Theo scooched a bit closer to me on the bench. His soap smelled like pine and spearmint. My cheeks grew warm as I typed out, *Thank you for your important feedback! We will take this under consideration and be back with you within three to five business days.*

Theo laughed. *Hard*. So hard he snorted, which of course made me laugh as well.

Our eyes connected, and suddenly there were a hundred swarming butterflies in my stomach. I barely had time to stop giggling before he asked me out. I said yes, of course.

Now it's four months later, two of which were long-distance since Theo spends the summer in Florida visiting his grandparents. We're juniors, and I still can't believe I have a boyfriend, my *first* boyfriend. And not only do I have a boyfriend, but I have a boyfriend whose ideal weekend activity is hosting a game night for our friends. I feel like I've won the high school romance lottery.

I'm smiling as we walk over to the bakery section. A barista stands behind the counter. He's wearing a grey beanie and a black T-shirt with a dragon on it. "What can I get y'all?" he asks.

"She'll have one of the chocolate chip muffins," Theo says, pulling out his wallet.

"Toasted?" the guy asks.

"No thank—" I start to say, but my voice is too quiet.

"Sure," Theo responds.

I'm kind of worried about the warm chocolate chips melting all over my fingers, but the barista has already turned around, and I'm too shy to stop him.

"Thank you," I tell Theo, since it's clear he's paying. He's done this a few times now, ordering for me and buying. It makes me feel a little awkward, but I know he means it as a sweet gesture. "You don't want anything?" I ask.

"Nah." He pats his stomach. "Dad cooked up his signature waffles and sausage this morning."

I make a face. I'm Jewish, and even though my family doesn't keep strict kosher, pork always sounds gross to me.

Theo laughs. "If you're ever over for breakfast, I'll make sure we have turkey sausage, too."

"Now, *why* would I ever be over for breakfast?"

Theo's cheeks flush. "Good point, good point."

A minute later, I have my chocolate chip muffin in hand, which is as delicious as the Yelp reviews promised. I grab a napkin to make sure I don't leave a trail of gooey chocolate all over the store.

"Where to first?" Theo asks.

"Let's check out the multiplayer games," I say as we begin to roam the shelves. I already have a big collection at home—most of my birthday and Hanukkah presents go toward the cause—but hosting a game night is an excellent excuse to get *just one more.*

"I've heard Azul is fun," I say, pointing to a pretty box. "I think that's what they're playing over there. Ooh! Or 7 Wonders!"

"Can I help you guys?" someone asks.

We turn to find another employee behind us. He's tall and lanky, wearing a flannel shirt and square-rim glasses.

"Sure!" I reply. "We're hosting a game night at my house. I have a ton of choices, but I'd love to find another party game."

"Tired of Apples to Apples, huh?" he asks, his eyebrow arching.

The comment bristles me. Not that there's anything wrong with Apples to Apples. It's a perfectly fine game. But, well, it is kind of bottom tier. Basic.

"Here," he says, turning around and walking us over to

another section. "These are some new releases. Super fun and under the radar." He glances back at Theo. "What kind of stuff do you like? Strategy? Drafting? Social deduction?"

"Uh." Theo runs a hand through his curls. I wait for him to turn to me and consult, but he doesn't. "Strategy, definitely."

"Awesome," the guy says, clearly only talking to Theo, like I've disappeared from the face of the planet. "You should check out these two. This one has great replay value, and this one is great for groups of four or more. How many at the party tonight?"

"Six, I think." Theo finally looks over at me for confirmation of this number. "Right?"

I give a tight nod.

Frustration claws at me. The employee is talking to Theo like I don't exist even though *I'm* the one hosting the party tonight *and* the one better versed in games. Theo loves playing, more than most people, but he's not quite the fanatic I am, with thirty games stacked high in my closet. My friend Kelsey told me this happens to her all the time when she goes to the comic book store with her dad. The employees only talk to her dad and never give her the time of day, like she, *a girl*, couldn't possibly have an interest in comics.

"Awesome!" The employee pulls the box out carefully. "I'd definitely go with this one, then. You won't regret it."

"Great, thanks, man," Theo says, taking the game with a smile, while I stand by like I'm invisible.

"Just let me know if you need anything else! My name is Jack, by the way. You can find me over at the card counter."

Jack waves goodbye and leaves us alone.

Theo hands me the box: it's a game I already own.

"What?" Theo asks, brow creased with concern.

I must be making quite the face. "I'll tell you in the car," I say, putting the box back on the shelf.

A few minutes later, we're driving back toward my house. Our friends will be arriving in a couple of hours. 7 Wonders sits on my lap. I picked it out in a rush, eager to leave, embarrassed after that incident to hand the store my hard-earned pet-sitting money but even more embarrassed to leave with nothing.

The light turns green, and Theo presses lightly on the gas. I've always liked that Theo is a good driver, calm, steady, both hands on the wheel. He's never once pulled out his phone while driving, not even to skip a song or see who texted him.

"So what's up?" he asks me.

Honestly, I thought it was kind of obvious what happened back there. But I guess Theo is a boy. He's not used to seeing that stuff like girls are.

"That guy in the shop was only talking to you," I tell him. "Like I wasn't even there. It was kind of sexist."

"Oh," Theo says. "I didn't notice. Sorry."

I go to automatically accept his apology, but my brain snags on a thought. "Wait." I pause. "You're sorry you didn't notice or you're sorry it happened?"

"Um." Theo laughs. "Why does this feel like a trap?"

Irritation pricks my skin. A *trap*? Seriously?

"It's not a trap," I say, voice threatening to wobble. "I just want to talk about this with you."

"Right, right, no worries."

Uncomfortable silence beats through the car. Theo clicks on his signal before turning left. We'll be at my house soon.

I should leave it alone, but my anxiety is building. His apology rings hollow in my ears, and he's acting so blasé about the whole thing. I want him to care about this more. There's a hard lump in my throat when I speak. "Um, so, like—what was the answer then? You're sorry it happened, right? You agree the guy was being sexist?"

Theo is quiet a beat too long. "Totally, Alexis. If you think he's sexist, then I'm sure you're right."

I bite the inside of my cheek. Somehow that answer doesn't really feel like a yes.

"Mozzarella, cheddar, or four-cheese mix?" Theo asks, holding up the bags of shredded cheese.

"All," I reply.

"Good call," he agrees. "Olives?"

I wrinkle my nose. "Maybe on half?"

"Fair, fair."

He pushes his head farther into my fridge, collecting an array of jars and pouches before dumping them all on my kitchen counter. We're making nachos for game night and going *way* over the top. I'm pretty sure 90 percent of our ingredient choices are highly questionable.

But I love food experimenting with Theo. We might have bonded over games, but we quickly found other things we both liked—tennis, botanical gardens, and the Food Network. Last month, we spent an entire weekend binging *Chopped* and then convinced his parents to create us mystery baskets so we could battle it out against each other. It was a delightful disaster, the kitchen coated in coconut cake batter and corn-flake tempeh breading. Theo's little sister declared us both the losers, and then we ordered pizza for dinner.

Hopefully the nachos turn out a bit better. The good news is that our friends will eat just about anything.

"Jalapeño?" I ask. "Cilantro? Lime?"

I'm rooting around the vegetable basket, pulling out the ingredients.

"Blech," Theo says. "Cilantro tastes like soap."

I turn and gasp. "You're one of those people!"

He sighs. "A genetic blip. Ruining quality guacamole for all my years."

"You sure you don't want to try some?" I ask, holding the bunch up to his nose.

He laughs and backs away. "Definitely not. But you can add it to half the platter. I'm sure other people like it."

"The olive half or non-olive half?" I ask.

"Good question." He nods. "Maybe we should split the platter into thirds . . ."

I laugh as we continue to work. It doesn't take us long. We line a baking sheet with foil and then spread out a pile of tortilla chips. We alternate layers of cheese and toppings so everything is sure to be coated in ooey-gooey cheesy perfection.

"It's a masterpiece," I declare as I examine our work of art.

"It's almost the prettiest thing I've ever seen," Theo says, smiling at the nachos and then at me.

My cheeks tinge red. "Thank you."

He leans over and presses a kiss against my temple, his lips soft and warm. Butterflies flutter in my stomach. I do a quick listen to make sure my parents are still upstairs watching TV, and then I stand up on my toes and kiss Theo on the lips. He smiles against my mouth before wrapping his arms around my shoulders and pulling me close.

"Hi," he says, grinning down at me.

"Hi," I say, grinning up.

My first kiss with Theo was perfectly unexpected. We had just finished playing a trick-taking game called The Fox in the Forest. I had beat him by a narrow margin, slapping my cards on the table in victory, smiling widely.

"Good game," Theo said. And then he scooted his chair closer to mine. And then he laced his fingers through mine. And then he kissed me, soft and sweet. "Rematch?"

I laughed, kissed him quickly again, skin flushing at my boldness, and replied, "Absolutely."

He's looking at me now with the same affection. And I want to be just as happy as I was that day. But the incident at the Magic Bean is still there at the back of my mind, slowly irritating me like sand stuck in your sock.

"Hey, Theo?" I ask, backing up a step but taking his hand in mine. "Can we talk again? About what happened earlier?"

"What do you mean?" he asks, truly unaware.

"The game store." I try to pick my words carefully. "The sexism, and . . ."

The oven beeps, letting us know it's preheated.

"Lemme get these nachos in," Theo says. "Friends will be here soon."

I watch as he picks up the tray and slides them carefully into the oven. I like the precision he uses for everything. Steady. Capable. It would be easy to imagine him as a real chef.

After he closes the oven door, I wait for him to respond. A real response. Continuing the conversation I started. But he just nods and asks, "What drinks should we take out?"

Everyone is downstairs now, digging into the snacks and drinks in the living room. Theo never brought back up the conversation, and I hate that I felt worried to. That I'd be a nag if I mentioned it again. My stomach felt too knotted to speak, so I put on a D&D podcast to fill the silence until our friends arrived. The doorbell rang, and I quickly greeted everyone before escaping up to my room with the excuse of grabbing a couple more games.

Except, when I got upstairs, I just sat on my bed and shoved a pillow in my lap. I needed a minute alone to collect myself, to understand why I feel so awful, *uncomfortable*.

What happened wasn't a big deal. A guy at a game store was kind of sexist. It happens all the time.

But I guess I'm not worried about the guy at the game store.

I'm worried about my boyfriend.

"Okay, what's wrong?"

I look up to find Nisha in my doorway, nosing into my room with observant eyes. Her dark hair is tied back in a glossy braid. She's wearing her favorite pair of overalls with a cropped white shirt underneath. Nisha rocks the hot girl next door look with complete ease. We've been friends since elementary school, all thanks to an alphabetical seating chart that put Alexis Kaufmann and Nisha Kapoor next to each other. We split our school snacks every day, combining fruit gummies, pretzel sticks, and apple slices for variety.

"Alexis." Nisha crawls onto the bed next to me and stuffs a pillow in her own lap. He scent is more familiar to me than my own, almond soap and lavender lotion. "What's up?"

Suddenly, I want to cry. Which is *ridiculous*. I'm spiraling out over nothing.

"Alexis," Nisha prods.

"Um."

I hesitate. I've never talked badly about Theo before. I've never had a reason to before. And now it feels wrong, like some sort of betrayal, even though Nisha is my best friend, and I'm much closer to her than my boyfriend of four months. The thought makes my stomach twist a little. How well do I really know Theo? We've spent half of our relationship apart, the distance filled in with texts and online gaming. What if I read him wrong and—

No. I like Theo. I like that he holds my hand during the scary movies I make us watch. I like that he drives his little sister to swim practice twice a week and takes her to Chipotle after. I like that he's really funny and will easily crack a joke that makes the entire lunch table laugh.

It was just one little thing. I'm sure if I talk about it with Nisha, then it will be all right.

I take a short breath and meet my friend's eyes. "If I say something kind of bad about Theo, do you promise that it won't impact your opinion of him forever? You know what I mean?"

Nisha nods. "Totally get it. I promise to have an opinion on this particular situation but not let it impact all further opinions of said boyfriend."

I smile. "You sound like your mom."

Nisha's mom is a lawyer. "Oh, shut up," she says. "Now spill."

I tell her about what happened at the game shop and in the car after. She nods along, occasionally adding in exclamations like "argh" and "fuck that sexist shit."

"See?" I ask when I'm done. "It was out of line, and then Theo was kind of dismissive about it, like he didn't really believe me. I know it's not a big deal, but—"

"It *is* a big deal," Nisha interrupts. "One, the boy needs to open his eyes. He should be able to catch something that obvious without you needing to tell him. And *two*, even if he was oblivious, you, a girl, are the authority on sexism in this situation. He should have believed you and validated that shit without a second thought. I'm sorry you had to deal with that, Alexis."

Nisha's words make my chest tight. It's all the affirmation I wanted to hear, but it also means this is real. This is something I have to deal with. Sexism is everywhere, but I never thought it'd show up in my own relationship. I trust Theo. He's a good guy. But he messed up, and I think I deserve a real apology.

I sigh and look down at my pillow. Nisha reaches out for my hand and threads her fingers through mine. "I don't know what to do," I say, voice hitching.

Nisha gives my hand a small squeeze. Her voice is calm, reassuring. "You don't have to do anything right now. You can wait and see. Maybe it was a blip. No one is perfect. Or, maybe it wasn't. Give yourself a little space, decide if it's worth talking to him about or not. Sound good?"

"Yeah." I nod. "Sounds good."

My head swims with unsure thoughts.

Nisha helps me gather a few more games, and we head downstairs together.

"Longest road!" Caleb screams. He pumps his fist in the air like he just won the Super Bowl, almost knocking over a bowl of Chex Mix in the process.

As is predictable, we all ended up playing Catan with my expansion pack. Every game night I have vast and shiny expectations of trying out something new, but inevitably we settle on the classic fan favorite. And to be fair, I do love Catan.

"Longest road by *one link*," Iz clarifies. They push their blond hair behind their ears before taking a sip of Sprite. "It'll be snatched out of your hands in a few turns."

"Remember that time Caleb spent all game building longest road instead of focusing on anything else, so he only had four points at the end?" Theo asks.

We all laugh. I smile at Theo. I like it when he makes everyone laugh.

That really was a memorable game. Iz played an *any trade goes* strategy where they accepted any trade someone offered them and tried to make progress with their mess of resources.

And Kelsey went hardcore on the developmental cards and had half the deck in her hand by the end of the game.

"It was a very nice road though," Theo tells Caleb.

"Yeah, yeah, thanks," Caleb replies, grinning. "Your roll, Kelsey."

Kelsey picks up the dice, blows on them for luck, and then rolls a five. Nisha shouts, "Heck yes! My herd!"

We all laugh again. Nisha's strategy this game is a total sheep monopoly with a sheep port. She puts a stack of sheep into her hand, smiling at her good fortune.

"Hey, hey," Theo says, leaning forward. "You took five sheep. You were only supposed to take four."

My first thought is to assume Theo is right.

My first thought is wrong.

Nisha's eyes flash toward me. And I catch it—judgment. I feel it like a pit in my stomach. She clears her throat and keeps her voice friendly but firm. "Count again, Theo," she says, pointing to the board. "Two cities and one settlement. Five sheep."

"Oh," Theo says, leaning back in his chair. He glances at his phone with a yawn, clearly unaware of the tension. "Cool."

"Sorry works, too," Iz says, raising their eyebrows.

My emotions are all whirled up and tangled. There's an instinct there to protect Theo—he's my boyfriend and being put on the outs. But Theo was wrong, acting like he knew better. And he's not even apologizing for it.

My muscles tense, thoughts messy as I look down at my cards. I asked Nisha not to judge Theo off of one incident, but am I doing that? Am I letting the incident at the Magic Bean poison my view of my boyfriend?

Or . . .

Is Theo kind of sexist?

I slump down in my chair, arms crossed tight over my stomach.

"Anyone have wood?" Kelsey asks. "I can trade wheat or ore."

"Yeah, I can do that," Caleb says. "Wheat, please."

They make the trade while I look at my shoes. I can feel Nisha staring at me. I can feel Theo's obliviousness to my confused feelings. I can feel my chest knot tighter with anxiety.

Kelsey passes the dice to me, and I roll.

Nisha wins the game, her sheep monopoly destroying all of us.

"At least I kept longest road," Caleb says, and we all laugh.

"What's next?" Iz says, checking their phone. "I can stay out until ten thirty."

"I got a new game," I say, trying to put enthusiasm in my voice. "It's called 7 Wonders, and I've heard it's really fun. Y'all want to try it out?"

Nisha nods. "I'm down!"

"Hmm," Kelsey says. "Is it hard?"

"No worries," Theo says, packing up Catan. He's careful with all of the pieces, sorting everything into their correct bags and slotting the cards into their holder without bending any corners. "We can play something easy. Cards Against Humanity, or Exploding Kittens, that's always fun!"

I bite the inside of my cheek. He's probably only trying to be agreeable with Kelsey. But I spent fifty dollars on 7 Wonders today and want to try it out. I feel like he should be aware of that.

I try to catch his eye, but he's focused on Catan. For a moment, I feel as invisible as I did inside the game shop.

"I want to try the new game," Nisha says, a bit forcefully. "Come on, we're smart kids. Honor roll and all that shit. We can figure it out."

"Yes, please put some respect on my 4.0 GPA," Iz says.

Caleb laughs and gives them a high five. "You go, friend!"

Kelsey surrenders with a smile. "Okay, okay, I'm in."

Theo shrugs, putting the lid on Catan. "Cool. Sounds good."

"Cool," I echo, my voice a bit weak. *Be happy,* I tell myself. *Be happy. We're going to play the game you want. Everything is fine.*

But . . . everything doesn't feel fine.

I again try to catch Theo's eye. This time he looks at me and smiles.

His obliviousness feels like a gut punch.

"Um," I say. "I left the game in Theo's car. I'll go grab it."

Tears brim in the corners of my eyes as I escape from the

room. I'm embarrassed by them. And I'm overwhelmed by a sudden thought, sharp and clear and painful—

I'm not sure how much I like my boyfriend anymore.

The thought feels like a complete overreaction, but I can't get rid of it. Each incident today, no matter how small, was another pinprick of hurt. I want a boyfriend who believes me. *Hears me.* I want a boyfriend who doesn't accuse my friend, a *girl*, of counting her own cards wrong and can't even apologize after.

I rub at my eyes, overwhelmed with confusion. I like Theo. Of course I do. I like how he smiles at me. I like cooking terrible food with him and pressing onto my tiptoes to kiss him. Nothing bad has even happened. I'm being too picky. Too sensitive.

But there's a choked feeling in my throat that won't leave.

Theo's car is parked right before our mailbox. I walk up to the passenger door and pull the handle only to find it's locked. "Great," I mumble.

Then I hear a *beep beep*. It startles me, and I jump back from the car, turning to find Theo walking up with his keys in hand.

He smiles, unaware I've been crying.

"Thought you'd have trouble getting in," he says, blue eyes crinkling.

"Right, thanks," I say, voice muffled.

I turn back to the car, yanking open the door and grabbing the 7 Wonders box. I clutch it tight to my chest before turning back to Theo.

It's quiet out here, only a few chirping bugs, the faded sound of a TV from someone's cracked window. Theo watches me in the moonlight, concern suddenly etched across his face.

Finally, he's noticed.

"Everything okay, Alexis?"

There's a knot in my throat, so hard I feel like I can barely breathe. I dislike confrontation. I like to be agreeable. But being agreeable in a man's world often means getting walked over.

It's not fair. I'm stuck with no good options: ignore my feelings or confront Theo and be seen as overbearing and dramatic. I wish he could see this stuff on his own. But he doesn't. And if I bite my tongue again, I might draw blood.

"I think . . ." I say. I want to frame the words right, pick them carefully, make it easy, digestible. I want to make us work. I like Theo, I really do, and if I phrase this in the right way, I'm sure this is something we can fix. "Theo," I say. "I know this might sound a bit out of nowhere, and I don't mean it as an attack. It's just, well, I think you're a little sexist." I take a steadying breath as my pulse races. "And I'd like to talk about it. Is that okay?"

His brow crinkles.

And then—

And then he laughs.

That's his first response: he laughs.

His second response is "Alexis, I have a *sister*. I'm not sexist."

I want to be angry. I feel like I deserve to be angry. But instead I just feel sad, deflated, because how can I be with someone who reacts like this, who laughs when I'm trying to be honest with him?

I don't want my voice to sound weak and wobbly, because that can be used against me. Women are deemed *irrational* if they dare to show emotion. The weight from our words is stolen.

"You can have a sister and still be sexist," I say, picking my words carefully again. "You can be a woman and still be sexist, actually. That's not my point, but—" I falter. "Um. I feel like you don't— I mean, you *don't* listen to me. Sometimes. And that hurts my feelings. And you think you know better than me. Like, you just laughed when I tried to tell you something serious. Like the idea I might see something you don't is funny."

I glance down at the driveway, clutching the 7 Wonders box, then back up to Theo. He's as cute as ever—soft lips and soft hair—but the defensive expression in his eyes makes my attraction evaporate.

"Theo," I say. "I think we should break up."

His expression changes into shock.

To be fair, the words surprise me as well. But as they settle in the air, I know they're right.

He steps forward, just a bit, but it feels like an invasion of the space I just created. "Alexis, come on," he says. "You're being a little dramatic. Look, I'm sorry I laughed. It was just a reaction, not something I can control. I'm not sexist."

"I think you are," I say. "And your opinion on it is kind of irrelevant."

Something flashes in his eyes, something I've never seen before in easygoing Theo—anger.

"Wow," he breathes. "You're kind of being a—"

I raise an eyebrow. "I'm being *a what*?"

He freezes, the insult on the tip of his tongue. But then he shakes his head and says, "Never mind, whatever."

My heart breaks a little then. I thought I had won the lottery with Theo, and the disappointment aches. Already I'm questioning myself.

Theo shakes his keys, then moves toward his car, barely glancing at me. "Bye, Alexis. I suppose you'll make up a good story for what happened. Doesn't seem like my point of view matters here."

My muscles tense as he gets into the car. My hands shake, and tears threaten once more. I stand as still as possible until he drives away, then, finally alone, let out a shaky breath.

The doubts swarm.

Was I wrong?

Did I break up with Theo over nothing?

Am I a bitch?

The front door cracks open. I look up and see Nisha standing there, hip leaning against the doorframe. She gives me a small wave, a gentle smile.

My panic eases the slightest bit.

No, I'm not a bitch. My boyfriend wasn't listening to me. And I don't have to stay with someone who doesn't listen to me. I'm capable of making my own decisions. Of making *good* decisions.

Nisha's voice calls out across the yard. "You gonna teach us that game or what?"

"Yeah." I steady my breath. The house is warm, lights glowing in the windows. I roll my shoulders and walk toward my best friend. "Let's play."

PLUM GIRLS

Kathleen Glasgow

Content warning: death, violence, and alcoholism

WHEN YOU SIT IN A MOVIE THEATER, DO YOU EVER WONDER, has someone died here? In this very seat? Do you look at your teacher, patiently explaining linear equations in front of the whiteboard, and think: Has Mr. Filson ever killed someone? Wrapped those fingers, perhaps still stained with marker, around a trembling neck and squeezed until the thrashing stopped? Do you let yourself drift into darkness, or do you hold it at bay?

What I'm saying is, death is all around you. All the time, whether you choose to see it or not. The sidewalk you travel from bus stop to home may be invisibly littered with people whose stuttering hearts simply gave out, right there, near that empty soda can, where your sneaker is about to land. Someone died there. Do you travel through their death? Does it touch you? Does some remnant of them still exist in that space where their last breath eked out into the atmosphere? For instance, when I'm particularly quiet, I can still feel the warmth of Hannah's hand in mine, just before she was pushed from the bridge's railing, her head splitting on the rocks beneath the river's surface as neatly as an egg cracked against a bowl.

I'm asking you to believe that many years ago two young men pulled up to an old farmhouse on the edge of town, just as a family was settling down to a dinner of mashed potatoes, meatloaf, peas, and milk, and rang the doorbell. Asking to use the phone, for they were lost. Those were the days that a phone lived on the wall of your house and not in your pocket, days when doors were answered and strangers in need were allowed inside. Those were different times. The strangers were supposed to wipe their feet, say hello, enter, use the phone, and leave, not slide machetes from their rumpled coats. There was no way you could know the mashed potatoes you were looking forward to would soon be dampened with your blood.

The young men finished their business and ate the dinners, rivulets of blood dripping from their faces to the meatloaf to the peas. They ate it all, and then they left.

When they were caught three states and four days later and asked why they did what they did, one said, "We felt like it, is all. We wanted to see what would happen."

Sometimes the explanation for horror is the most frightening thing of all.

Of course, you'll find the fact that I went to the house at all to be ridiculous, and I agree with you. An anonymous note in my locker, the words penciled neatly: *Tick-tock, run out the clock / If you can survive from one to three / You will get a lot of money.* Not a solid rhyme, but I'm not one to criticize. It wasn't the first note I'd received. The others had been full of questions, spare and tinged with possibility.

> *Did you really do it?*
> *I think about her all the time, and you. And them. Do you?*
> *How many more years do you think you can carry this?*
> *What would you do if you could change everything?*

I thought about that last note more than I cared to imagine. I didn't know if whoever left the notes slipped them through the slats in my locker, or if they knew the combination. I'm sure there were plenty of kids at Hedgewood High who knew how to find out such things.

That last note, I wrote back. *I would do whatever it took, of course.* Scrawled that at the bottom of the note, taped the note to the outside of my locker. Whoever was writing the notes: they would get it. I knew that much.

I stood in the hallway, looking at the address at the bottom of the new, rhyming note. Of course I knew the address; everyone in Hedgewood did. We'd grown up with the rhymes, the rumors. *Whack whack, forty jabs in the back / They did their crime at dinnertime.* The machete and mashed potato house had never been torn down or put on the market. It simply stood, a weathering wood tombstone in a copse of trees at the end of a dirt road.

I read the rhyming note again. Was it a joke? A prank? Something extra cruel from my classmates, who, by and large, had ignored me for the past year?

Dr. Lamprey had warned me there might be trouble when I returned to Hedgewood. "People believe what they want to believe," he said, his voice warm and deep. "And there is nothing you can do about that."

A few kids spit in my direction in the hallway; in gym, my locker was filled with used tampons. And every once in a while, I would hear it, the merest murmur, hushed, floating behind me as I walked the path from chem to calc. *Murderer.*

But those things don't frighten me, because I'm the one with the power. One small step from me, in the direction of the whisperer, the spitter, the tampon toter, one look from my dark eyes, and they shrink away. The stink of death surrounds me. They don't want it to touch them.

Maybe that's why no one tore the murder house down. Perhaps no one wanted to get close to it.

But the notes to me, they were different. Whoever was writing them was not afraid of me, and perhaps that's why I chose to go along with it.

Why didn't I question it further? Because I just didn't,

that's all. I'm seventeen. I guess I just wanted to see what would happen.

I stood alone at the start of the dirt road leading to the Mulvaney house, my gloved hands gripping the handlebars of my bike. It wasn't hard to leave my house at 12:30 a.m. on a Friday night. My parents had long been lost in a fog of misery and alcohol, no doubt silently pining for the day I turned eighteen and left. I love them, and they love me, but as Dr. Lamprey told me, twining his wrinkled hands together, "They will always wonder. They will always have a whiff of doubt." We travel around the rooms of our house like ghosts, feeding and washing and clothing ourselves. We don't speak of Hannah. I'm careful not to get too close to them; they flinch.

I wished I'd brought my knit cap. My ears stung from the bitter cold.

I was about to climb back on my bicycle when I heard the rumbling of a car and the distinctive keen of feminine laughter behind me. The headlights of their car blocked my vision.

"Hot damn, Plain Jane! You too? Well, get it going, girl! We don't have all night!"

The laughter of the girls pealed, high and cruel, from the car's windows. Then the car took off toward the house, spraying dirt in my direction.

My heart sank.

They were waiting for me outside the house. Mercy, Gibby, and Lou. I leaned my bike against Lou's car. Mercy grinned at me, white teeth flashing. Her mother was a dentist. I never liked opening my mouth around Mercy's mother, ashamed of my crooked teeth. Mercy is a girl with good teeth, good clothes, an outward shine of health and wealth. Wide shouldered from swimming, she always carries the scent of chlorine.

Gibby just stared at the ground, fingering the zipper on her hoodie. I willed Gibby to look at me, but it didn't happen. Once, we'd all been friends. It hurt the most not having Gibby anymore. Gibby was the first to run away that day, after Hannah fell, her dark braids churning against her back as she ran screaming into the forest. Gibby comes from awful people, really. They often forget her. As bright as Mercy's well-kept teeth are, Gibby's are the opposite: dull-looking and thick.

"It's like old times, all of us together," I said softly.

No one answered me.

Lou patrolled the front of the house, touching the windows, peering inside. Lou always takes charge. She turned around.

She'd become so beautiful, it took my breath away, really, seeing her up close after all these years. A sharp kind of beauty, one that glistens, even in the dark night. Some girls are like that: they switch, almost overnight, from small, plain things to something electric. You can't take your eyes from them.

"What's your note say, Plain Jane?"

"Is this a trick?" I asked. "Are you pranking me?"

My voice didn't waver. Once, all those years ago, it would have. Lou had that effect on you. She was the type of person you despise, yet you desire. You want them to love you, maybe because then you hope they'll stop hurting you.

Lou held up her hands. "Whoa, whoa. Why would I do that? You wanna see my note?"

She reached in the pocket of her jeans and withdrew a piece of paper, tossing it on the ground in front of me.

I picked it up and unfolded it.

Who will be alive
Who will survive
The slaughterhouse
One hour or three
Will it be you, Lou?
$10,000 to the winner of the game
If you are still standing after blood and shame

"Interesting," I said, and crumpled the note, letting it fall on the ground.

Lou snorted.

"I think it's a Plum Girl haze," said Mercy, snapping her gum. "We'll be seniors next year. Two hours in the house. If we pass, we can be Plum Girls."

I frowned. The Plum Girls. Every year, a group of junior girls at Hedgewood High were initiated into the Plums. If they made it through copious drinking, shoplifting, mailbox bashing, and gross things with senior boys, they got to be a Plum. A Plum meant popularity, parties, a clasp of safety in a school that often feels like hell.

Gibby's voice shook. "This seems a little extreme for the Plums. And why would they have ten thousand dollars? That's ridiculous."

It was ridiculous. Our town had suffered the closure of a factory years ago and never bounced back. You can walk, as I often did, the streets of downtown, surrounded by boarded-up storefronts for block after block. My parents were lucky; they had jobs at the hospital in the next town over, scrubbing floors and sending enormous medical bills. Gibby's parents did odd jobs: raking leaves, shoveling snow. For as long as I'd known her, her life was bare.

Gibby was still looking at the ground.

"Last year they took a group of girls out to Pigeon Lake and had them take off all their clothes, swim out to the middle, and tread water in the dark for three hours," Mercy said. "But that doesn't explain *you*."

She glanced in my direction but wouldn't meet my eyes.

Lou shrugged. "Who knows? Jane here's done her time, maybe all is forgiven. Or maybe *she's* the haze. Worst-case scenario, somebody dies."

Mercy and Gibby looked uncomfortable. I studied their faces. They were remembering Hannah, and what had happened, I'm sure. I wondered if they wanted to ask me how it was where I went.

Lou laughed. It sounded flinty, like two thin stones being rubbed together.

Mercy said, "I would rather not die in this house, thank you."

"But what about the girls?" Gibby whispered. "The ones who disappeared after coming here?"

It was true. What teenager doesn't, on occasion, visit a death house for kicks? Scores of kids had probably been out here over the years.

Lou punched Gibby in the shoulder. "How stupid *are* you? Can you not google? Lindy March is working over in Kramerville at the Piggly Wiggly. Eloise France is currently at some keg party at Goofy-Goofy-U in Bumstock, Weirdland, getting bombed and groped. Okay? They're *fine*."

She sighed heavily, inspecting her bright pink nails. There was the faintest sheen of silver glitter on her eyelids.

"Let's just *go* already."

She turned and marched up the porch steps to the front door. She reached out a hand, somewhat tentatively, and tried the doorknob.

The door opened as smoothly as if it had been buttered.

We followed her, one by one, just as we did when we were girls and went into the woods on one of Lou and Hannah's adventures.

I wasn't going along with them out of curiosity anymore. I

just slipped into my old way of being with them. We all went along with what Lou did. We were the Wildflowers once and did everything together.

Mercy turned on the flashlight on her phone and held it up. Gibby squinted.

Lou said, "Well, all darkness is going to be creepy, for sure."

I listened to them breathe, the light from Mercy's phone traveling through the room, offering glimpses of framed photographs on the papered walls, a couch in the corner, a bookcase still filled with books.

And then the room exploded with light. Gibby cried out, shielding her eyes.

For just a moment, I thought I heard something, far off in the house. Upstairs, maybe. The sound of muffled laughter. But I couldn't be sure. Sometimes my mind tricks me.

"The hell!" Lou held her arms out as though protecting herself from a mad animal. "Who did that?"

Every light in the house, at least on the first floor, was on. The light fixture hanging from the ceiling in the front room, the tall lamp in the corner. In the kitchen, the ceiling light buzzed and crackled.

"Okay, who *did* that?" Lou demanded. Her eyebrows were creased. I could see the slightest bit of sweat beginning to shine on her forehead. She looked at me.

I shrugged. "Plum Girl prank?"

Lou frowned. "I don't know how they could do *that*."

"People do all sorts of things you think they aren't capable of," Mercy said quietly.

I looked at Mercy curiously. She wouldn't look at me.

"That was weird," Gibby whispered. She wrapped her arms around herself. She must have been cold in her thin, worn hoodie. Her parents were never the best at taking care of her.

Lou flicked the light switch by the front door. The ceiling light stayed on. She pulled the cord on the tall corner lamp. It never darkened.

"This is *definitely* a Plum prank," Lou said. She marched over to what appeared to be a closet and yanked the door open.

"Come out!" she yelled. No one did.

There were still coats hanging in the closet, and boots and shoes lined up neatly on the floor.

Lou closed the door softly.

"Don't you think that's weird," Mercy said, "that, like, stuff is still . . . here?"

"Yes," said Gibby. "But, no? I mean, maybe I'd be too afraid to come here and, like, clean it out? After what happened."

Lou was checking her phone. "Why?" she said, not looking at Gibby. "That's ridiculous. Come and pack up the stuff, sell it, burn it, whatever, and get rid of the house. It's just a *house*. It's not like that dead family is still here. Dead people are *dead*."

"Are they, though?" I asked softly. I took off my gloves and slid them into my coat pocket. "Sometimes I think I can still feel Hannah's hand in mine, you know? I've always wondered if the last touch of a dead person stays on you. Or on things. Like perfume."

I don't know what made me say that so suddenly, and out loud. Something about the house, and Lou's discomfort, made me bold.

I could feel Mercy and Gibby freeze. It was palpable, the heaviness that settled over the four of us at that moment.

Lou's eyes flashed at me. She wasn't afraid of me. She wasn't one to look away. The thing she did at school when I came back was to simply pretend I didn't exist. Her eyes slid over me like silk but never landed, and thus, she remained safe.

"I guess you would know then, wouldn't you." Her voice was hard.

I smiled.

Lou shoved her phone in her back pocket. "None of the Plums are answering me. It's one oh five a.m. We have until three a.m. I say we case the house, make sure they aren't hiding somewhere. It's only two goddamn hours and then we get our money."

She held out a hand, palm down.

It was an old gesture. One we used all the time when we called ourselves the Wildflowers and set off into the forest on a weekend afternoon. One for all, all for one, that sort of thing.

Gibby and Mercy piled their hands on Lou's. Some sort

of muscle memory forced my hand out and in the direction of theirs, but they yanked their hands away before I could make contact.

Lou and Mercy clomped up the stairs, Lou calling out, "Hello, we know you're here! I'm not afraid of you, Plums!"

Beside me, Gibby whispered, "Are you afraid? I'm kind of afraid. I don't like this."

I gazed at her. Gibby was always the type of kid who shook during lightning storms and quivered at a scrum of ants. She never liked our treks to the forest, but she came, looking behind her at the disappearing world as we walked deeper and deeper, Lou and Hannah leading the pack. Hannah loved the forest. The way pine sap stuck to her palms. The satisfying crunch of leaves and twigs under her shoes. I liked the forest, too, especially when you looked up and the sky was just fragments of pale color between the branches of trees. The branches always seemed like fingers to me, spreading over us, protecting us. We were eleven. The forest was dreamy and magical and just a little bit frightening, but we liked that, too.

Gibby's eyes met mine suddenly.

"You don't look any different," she said softly. "That's weird to say, but you don't. Your face is still the same, your hair. You're not really even that much taller. It's like you . . ."

She trailed off. I knew exactly what she was talking about. I think about it a lot. These girls had changed and grown and morphed into the girls they were meant to look like, and I, stuck in an airless place of desolation and constant pain, had stayed the same. It's like I stopped. The only thing that grew were my thoughts. And perhaps my rage.

"Let's look around," I said gently, to distract her.

That day with Hannah, Gibby hadn't wanted to go so far, but I held her hand. We'd never made it as far as the river, and Lou and Hannah wanted to get there before dark.

I walked from the front room, Gibby slowly following me, to the kitchen.

The Formica countertops were cracked. Some of the cupboard doors sloped from their hinges. I tugged at the refrigerator door. It stuck, and I pulled. It opened with a sucking sound.

"Look," I said, trying to make a joke. "No one in *here*."

The refrigerator was bare. Someone had taken the trouble to remove the food. I guess you'd have to, after all. What would cheese and milk look like, or smell like, after thirty years?

Something skittered in the cupboard beneath the sink. A scrabble, like tiny fingernails.

Gibby jumped.

"Probably a raccoon," I said. "Or mice. This house has been empty a long time. Things move in."

Although I didn't say it aloud, I did wonder why the house was so tidy. If this was the Plums' doing, they must have done an awful lot of cleaning. There was no dust or grime or rust on the faucet, and the refrigerator was clean, as though someone had recently scrubbed it deeply.

Above us, shoes clattered over floorboards, the sound of Lou and Mercy moving and talking.

My eyes roved the walls of the kitchen and landed on the phone.

Did the father even have time to hand the receiver over to them? Was he caught by surprise by the first pain of the machete, dropping the phone, letting it dangle? Did the killers replace the receiver? There were two of them, enough to handle the chaos of the mother and the two children, who must have screamed and tried to get away. Children are surprisingly slippery when panicked.

The archway in the kitchen led to the dining room. Gibby made a small sound in her throat.

"We have to go in," I told her firmly. "What if they're watching us right now? The Plums?" I gestured to the ceiling, the walls. "Maybe there's a hidden camera. The note said money. Maybe that's true. Don't you want your money? Don't you want to be a Plum?"

I was silent my first year at the hospital, and when I did finally speak, Dr. Lamprey was overjoyed, clapping those weathered hands together. He said, "I want to hear all about all the things you've been keeping inside. Tell me everything."

And I did. I told him about Hannah, and Lou, and Mercy, and Gibby. That Lou was very mean and smart, and always fighting with Hannah, because Hannah was mean and smart,

323

too, and that Mercy was somewhere in between, her moods switching between sweet and cruel, but that Gibby was always kind, a shy, timid girl who just wanted to be loved. Who would do anything to be loved.

"Yes," Gibby said softly now. "I do want to be a Plum."

"Well, then, come, Plum Girl." I motioned to the dining room.

I've often thought how spectacularly creepy and perfect it would have been if the dining table had been set with plates and napkins and silverware. A jug for milk in the middle and clean glasses at each setting. Just like it was the night of the murder. I was disappointed that this wasn't the case, that the table was simply empty, with scratches and grooves like any other old table in any other old farmhouse dining room. A painting of a river at dusk on the wall. There was an ironing board set up the corner, with the iron still upright on it, plugged in. A nice, if unsettling, touch.

"This is the room." Gibby's voice was strangled. Was she having a panic attack? I remember that happening to her sometimes. Sometimes she would even faint.

I'd spent a long time on the internet after receiving the rhyming note, researching the Mulvaney murders. Looking around the dining room, with its faded flowered paper beginning to peel away from the ceiling, I knew exactly where each family member was found because I looked at the crime scene photos. Everything is out there for you to peruse, if you want to. A whole blood-soaked world.

I reached out and touched the wallpaper. A slight heat ran through my fingers.

Someone spent a long time cleaning the blood from the wallpaper, but there were faint outlines. I looked down. The slats of the wood floor were separating a bit from age. The blood would have soaked into the wood, and if not sopped up right away, the wood would absorb it. The two men had taken time to eat dinner after the massacre, the blood thickening around them.

We were standing on blood.

I made the mistake of saying that out loud.

Actually, thinking about it now, I may have said *all* of that out loud. It's hard to remember, but I do remember Gibby screaming.

And I remember the tumult of shoes on the stairs and Lou and Mercy running into the room, faces startled. Mercy wrapped Gibby against her chest.

"What did you do?" she said fiercely. "What did you do to her?"

"Nothing," I said. "I did nothing."

That was exactly what I told Dr. Lamprey, after I'd warmed up to him.

"I did nothing," I'd said. "And that is why it's my fault."

We had our sessions in the sunlit room on the second floor of the hospital. From the large windows, you could see the well-tended lawn, the pond where ducks fluttered and bobbled, clusters of oak trees in a ring around the grounds. Beyond that, for miles, the world.

It had taken me a long time to speak after they came for me on the bridge, an array of adults with sour and sad faces saying things with complicated words I didn't understand. And when I reached for my mother, she stepped away, my father holding her by the shoulders. And then it was like a dream, for months, years, a dream of silence, where I went from room to room in the hospital, eating, cleaning myself, washing myself, playing with the toys Dr. Lamprey spread before me: a windup bird, a small truck, a thin rubbery doll with long hair, all the while thinking that someone would come for me, and I would go home, until one day I realized no one was coming, and that the hospital would be my home.

To tell you the truth, I wish I'd never been released. I felt safe there, inside, in a way I'd never felt in the world. I felt protected.

But Dr. Lamprey left one afternoon to go home and he simply never returned. He died. They actually didn't tell me that; I found out later when I returned home. I looked him up, and there was his obituary. But his replacement came to the hospital and sat with me in the sunlit room, paging through my file while I brushed the doll's hair, even though I was fifteen at that point, and far too old to be attached to a doll.

"What on earth are you still doing here?" she exclaimed. "This is ridiculous. You have been here for *four years*."

"Because," I told her gently. "I'm a monster."

In the dining room, Lou stepped closer to me. "You never should have come back. How dare you? This was supposed to be fun, and you ruined it. I don't even know why they let you out."

"I didn't do anything. To Gibby, just now." I paused. "Or even back then. To Hannah."

I stepped away from her. The ironing board wobbled against my back. "That's why they let me out. Because I didn't murder Hannah Williams."

Lou's eyes glittered.

She smiled.

We'd made it to the bridge over the river. It was the farthest we'd ever gone, and Lou and Hannah had been sniping at each other all day. It was exhausting being with them sometimes, honestly. Hannah was a strong-willed girl with straight dark hair, soft as velvet. Lou wasn't as pretty then as she would become. Her hair was often stubbornly tangled and her face had a habit of breaking out in pimples which she would pick at. She'd been picking at them all day.

"You look like a pincushion," Hannah said. She tested the railing with her hands and carefully pulled herself so she was sitting on it, facing us, her jeaned legs dangling. Her hands were tight on the railing, knuckles white with effort.

Lou stopped touching her face.

"Shut up," she said.

"Make me," Hannah laughed.

"I want to go," Gibby whined. "It's so cold, and I'll miss dinner."

"Don't be such a baby," Mercy said. She'd watched Hannah carefully and hoisted herself onto the railing, too. She glanced back and down, at the wide river below, and teetered.

"Be careful," I said, touching her knee.

She pushed my hand away but jumped down.

"Come up, Lou," Hannah said. Her cheeks were pink from the cold. Her lips shook. "Don't be a chicken."

"I'm not a chicken," Lou said. "I just don't want to."

Her fingers crept at her face.

"*Stop* it," Hannah said harshly. "Or you'll be the ugliest girl in class."

Lou's hands left her face and grabbed for Hannah's legs, pulling them up. Hannah tilted backward.

"Jerkface."

But her voice shook. She was gripping the rail tightly, her back arched uncomfortably. Lou was holding on to her ankles, forcing her back, back.

Now Hannah looked afraid. "Stop," she said. "Stop, now."

"Lou," Mercy whined. "Let's go. I don't want to get in trouble, and I don't want to walk home after dark. You're scaring me."

Lou pulled up on Hannah's ankles again. Hannah cried out, her neck swiveling in the air. The veins beneath the skin stood out, tense and blue.

The air then became sharp and warm. I could feel the atmosphere changing around us. Everything slowed, became dreamlike.

Stop, Hannah said.

"Lou," Mercy whispered.

Lou yanked Hannah's ankles as high as she could. Hannah tipped backward, her hands loosening off the rails, flailing in the air. I caught one of her hands just as Lou let go of Hannah's legs, and Hannah's eyes, round and filled with a fear I can't describe, met mine as I was yanked closer to her, my chest slamming against the railing, her weight crushing me against it. I felt as though my arm was going to pull from its socket.

Her body was dangling downward into the air. She twisted in fear, her nails digging into my wrists.

The heels of my shoes were leaving the ground, my body being forced up and over the railing. Hannah's screams sliced my ears and I closed my eyes.

I loosened my fingers and let go of her hand.

Gibby was the first to run. Then Mercy. But Lou stayed, just for an instant, before she ran down the bridge and into the forest, too.

The water was like a fierce howl in my ears. I couldn't feel myself, not my heart beating, not my thoughts. I stepped in and out of myself at the same time and I stayed that way.

When the adults came, I was sitting on the bridge, frozen with cold.

Lou was holding her mother's hand.

"It was her," she said. "She did it."

You know one thing I didn't miss? School. I mean, Dr. Lamprey took care of that. He had lessons for me and books to read and things to talk about.

"You didn't push that girl," he said to me once. "I don't think that's true. I think that you let go of her hand because you were afraid she would pull you over. What do you think of that?"

I didn't answer. Honestly, I didn't like thinking about it all that much, because when I did, the hand that had held Hannah's started to prickle, like she'd never truly left me.

"You were very young," he told me.

"I let go," I said finally. "Therefore, it's my fault, isn't it?"

"Excellent use of 'therefore.' But honestly, Jane, how long could you have held on without help? If a person next to me at

330

a cliffside slipped and I grabbed their hand, how long should I hold that weight before I let go or die as well? It's a very nuanced question. But I'm more interested in another question."

I didn't answer Dr. Lamprey then, because who would have believed me? Mercy and Gibby lived in fear of Lou, or perhaps the fear and adrenaline had clouded their memory.

But I said it then, in the dining room of a murder house.

"It was you," I said to Lou. She was so close to me I could smell the remnants of her mint toothpaste.

"You're deluded," she whispered. "You pushed her."

I looked over Lou's shoulder at Mercy, still holding Gibby in her arms.

"And you," I said.

Mercy's face flattened.

"You were standing right there," I said. "And you didn't help."

Mercy's eyes filled. "I was scared. I . . . she said . . ."

Lou glared at her. "Careful," she warned.

I looked back at Lou. "But mostly you. She was falling and I tried to help her, but it was too late. But you were the one who started it. You meant for her to die. I tried to save her."

I reached out and grabbed the scruff of her coat. She struggled, her breath hot on my face. With the other hand, I reached behind myself and took the iron into my hand.

I felt strong inside. Burnished clean. Proper and righteous.

You will think it's impossible, you'll think I'm lying, or that this is too strange to be true, but it is true.

I did not have to let go of Lou with the hand that held her to turn on the iron because it had already turned itself on and was glowing.

I knocked the iron gently on its side and took hold of Lou with both hands. Her voice caught in her throat, like a thousand wet stones had been lodged there.

Nononononono.

I forced her face, once a field of angry red sores and now as smooth and beautiful as unbroken water, closer to the iron. She closed her eyes against the heat.

"Say it," I said.

"Jesus Christ," Mercy said. "Jesus Christ, stop."

"Do you want to save her?" I barked. "Because you didn't do that for Hannah, did you?"

I leaned down to Lou, the tears steaming on her face from the iron's heat.

"Say it."

Do you want me to say what I would have done? How far I'd take it? How far I was willing to go? I'm not vengeful. Like I told you, I liked the hospital. It was peaceful and the people there were not liars. Some of them were very bad and had done very bad things, which they would happily admit to you. Some of them were as filmy as a bride's veil, and their stories came out sweetly and gently, as horrific as they were. But they were not liars.

Only out here, in the world, do liars live and prosper.

I could smell the minuscule, downy hairs on Lou's cheek beginning to singe.

"I did it. It was me. I did. I wanted her to die. I did. She was horrible, and awful."

I let her go.

At this moment, ask yourself, did you want me to press Lou's cheek to the iron? Did you put someone else's face in place of Lou's in your mind, someone who has wronged you? Stolen your lunch? Mocked your clothes? Beaten you?

I don't judge you for that. Because sometimes in life you do what you need to make sure you survive. You let someone's hand slip from yours. You follow the directions of a note because you think it will bring you some kind of peace, no matter how far you have to go.

And you have to live with that.

Lou fell to the floor, hugging the wall, her hot cheek in her hand.

Gibby eased away from Mercy. She pulled her phone from her pocket and looked at me.

She pressed her phone.

Lou's voice echoed through the dining room. "I did it. It was me. I did. I wanted her to die."

I looked at Gibby. "Congratulations," I said to her. "You pass. What a Plum you'll be."

There was a clatter in the front of the house, the door opening. Four girls appeared in the doorway of the dining room. The Plums. Only one of them smiled. The rest looked wary, and frightened.

From the floor, Lou choked out, "What the fuck?"

The smiling Plum was a girl with luxurious red hair that in another time, someone would write a whole poem about. Gibby handed her the phone.

"I'm in?" Gibby said.

"You bet. Welcome, Plum."

The red-haired girl looked at Lou. "I always thought it was you. Something never sat right with me, all these years. I couldn't put my finger on it. But I've been watching you."

"You were a little bit our class project," one of the other Plums said.

Lou's face, fiery on one side from the heat of the iron, blossomed on the other. "What . . . even are you going to do? We were *eleven*."

The red-haired girl shrugged. "I'll figure something out. Hannah was my cousin. I have a lot of blood in this fight."

Lou tried to rise, but one of the Plums put a pretty sneaker on her leg and pressed down.

The red-haired Plum turned to me. She drew an envelope out of her pocket and held it out.

I took it.

"Sorry," she said. "This was the only way. You want to be a Plum?"

I looked at Lou on the floor, pinned by a sneaker; at Mercy, weeping; at Gibby, her face now gleeful and content, because she was going to belong to something again. From Wildflower to Plum.

"God, no," I said. "I'd rather die."

Mercy shook her head at me, tears creasing her cheeks. "I didn't know what to do. She told me to say it was you. She said, she said . . ."

"I don't care anything about you," I said.

And then I left the house.

Outside, I kicked up the stand to my bicycle. Opened the envelope.

It was not ten thousand dollars, of course. Not even close. But there was money, and I put it in my pocket.

I rode away, sounds of terrified sobs in the house gradually quieting behind me.

I didn't question it. None of it, any of it, made sense, anyway. An angry girl pushes another girl from a railing, and another girl tries to save her and can't. A car with two strangers pulls up to a farmhouse and eats the dead's food with blood on their hands and faces.

I rode my bicycle into town, and I bought a ticket at the bus station for a city on the ocean so I could have some peace. I live here now, reading books on my days off and serving people like you plates of overcooked food on my other days.

I don't feel better or worse for what happened in that house. The worst thing in the world has already happened to me.

It wouldn't have made sense for me to stay in Hedgewood, anyway. I was already tainted in my parents' eyes. How could I live with them when the very presence of me frightened them? I could tell them: *I didn't push her, I know now, I had to let her go to save myself,* but they wouldn't believe me. I know they loved me, still, but it was a love that had been spoiled. They would never forgive themselves for that. I was letting them go to save them.

There are many unexplained things in the world that swirl and dip around us every day, without us knowing. Hannah got up and brushed her teeth and ate breakfast and went into the forest with us and died. It was a game she didn't even know she was playing.

Sometimes things just happen, is all.

WORLD OF WONDER

Kimberly Jones and Gilly Segal

MORNING HAS ALWAYS BEEN URSULA'S FAVORITE TIME AT World of Wonder. It's not just because the amusement park her family owns has been her second home since she was a toddler. Or because Frank at the funnel cake stand always makes her an extra special funnel cake and egg sandwich. Or because the guy who runs the bumper boats spritzes her before the sun gets too high. Or because only the people who work this early know the throwback WoW greeting the newbies don't use anymore—"It's a wonderful day at World of Wonder!"

It's because when she's alone in the park, it feels like it belongs to her.

Mostly alone. They're only an hour away from opening on the official first day of summer. Renee stands by the midway carnival games across from the go-kart attraction that Ursula manages. Her hair is twirled into a neat bun with curly tendrils hanging down. Under her collared navy-blue WoW logo shirt, a metal necklace with a pink ceramic bow glints against her tawny skin. Renee's trademark is putting a unique touch on her uniform. Ursula has always been a little jealous that Renee has the energy for it before coming to work.

Ursula's family owns WoW, while Renee's family keeps it running. The girls grew up together. Maybe it's inevitable you become best friends when you've spent all your after-school hours living that small-town amusement park life. But this summer at the park will be their last together. In just a few months, Renee will head up north for design school, while Ursula stays behind, managing the park with her dads. Even though Renee will visit WoW on her breaks, things will never be the same.

"See you at the meeting?" Ursula calls, slamming the go-kart gate extra hard. No matter how many times they've replaced the latch, the door sticks. The metal needs replacing, but the park's budget won't allow for that.

Renee falls in step beside her. "Any heads-up on this summer kickoff meeting?" She asks because Ursula always knows everything about WoW. "Are they finally taking Wallace's walkie-talkie away?"

Wallace the security guard is everybody's nemesis. He harasses employees for wearing their name badges in the wrong location, among other infractions. And after Renee rerouted the lines for Skee-Ball right through the area he preferred to use for his smoke breaks, he declared her persona non grata. Lucky that move created space for a brand-new seven-foot-tall gumball tower that even David, the Serious Businessman Owner, loved.

"They couldn't pull that walkie from his cold, dead hands." Ursula grins as they walk through RetroWorld—their domain.

The carnival atmosphere makes Renee feel like she's on the set of a charming black-and-white movie. At WoW these days, kids run to line up for laser tag and the high tech games first, but families end the day in RetroWorld, having laughter-filled races on the go-karts and competing over which sibling can rack up the highest Skee-Ball score. That's how Renee and Ursula spent most of their own weekends from elementary school to the present.

As Ursula looks around at the quiet early morning park, the thought hits her again. "What am I going to do without you, once you run off to Parsons?" Ursula says quietly.

Renee also hates thinking about the fact that the timer is running out for them. Ursula's future is here, managing WoW. Renee's future, she hopes, is behind the scenes at runway shows in Milan and Paris. Not that she won't miss her friend.

Renee sees Ursula's smile droop. "We still have this summer. Even if we do have a million more meetings to get through first."

• • •

The summer kickoff meeting takes place on the second floor of the administration building, in the party room that has a new chalkboard wall but also a poorly patched spot they drywalled over after finding asbestos years ago.

Ursula's dads, Greg and David, stand at the front of the room before the little crowd. It's not like WoW is Six Flags. So the gathered staff includes the old-school employees hired by Ursula's grandparents, before her dads inherited the park. Namely, Wallace, Betsy the ticket taker, and Frank the concession manager. Greg dubbed them the Customer Care Crew, though unofficially, everyone else calls them the Counter Crabs.

Renee and Ursula are there representing RetroWorld, since the rest of their staff is a rotating assortment of part-timers. And finally, there's Ethan and his ever-expanding band of Shut-Ins. They work the indoor games—video games, PS4 stations, the laser tag room, and *Dance Dance Revolution*.

Today, instead of his normal pleasant grin, Greg wears the giddy looks of a parent about to announce they're taking their kid to Disney World. Renee regrets her snarky thought immediately. She loves WoW, even though the park is not as shiny as it used to be. Her earliest memories are running through the cobblestone courtyard of RetroWorld. She even got to take the inaugural sail on Bumper Boat Lagoon. Neither she nor Ursula had been tall enough to go on their own. Ursula had ridden with Greg, while Renee sat on her father's lap, steering into more walls than other boats.

Greg clears his throat. "It's an exciting day, WoWers! Not only is it the first day of summer, but the Phantasm I launches this morning!"

"As you know, WoW is one of a select few locations in America to debut Phantasm System's new AI platform," David adds. "And its first game, *Artifact Hunters*!"

An actual cheer goes up from the corner of the room where the Shut-Ins sit. Ethan rocks back in his chair with his feet propped on a party table, where the littles have to eat their pizza and cake slices. Typical Ethan, though Renee smiles anyway. When he first started working there, Renee couldn't help but notice the angle of his jawline and his brilliant head of brown curls and golden highlights. At first, he gave off seriously distant vibes, but after he worked up the courage to ask her out, she realized that was more his painful shyness than an attitude problem. Two months later, they're still in the disgusting-cute phase of dating where they're totally enamored with each other.

It's sweet how excited he is by the news about a new virtual reality system.

After the cheer dies down, Ursula raises her hand, which makes Renee smile wider. She might be the owners' daughter, but she treats them like they're her bosses. Ursula does polite professionalism better than anyone else their age. "And we're still convinced that having this thing in the middle of the main courtyard makes sense?"

"Yeah," Renee adds. "Isn't having people running around wearing space-age helmets kind of contrary to the old-school charm of RetroWorld?"

Wallace—who might be ninety-four or forty-four, but who's been around their whole lives—pipes up from the front of the room. "No running in the park." He's already wearing his full security guard uniform—the official black pants and WoW collared shirt along with a black hat with SECURITY written above the brim and his precious walkie-talkie. He's also got unofficial gear he's added on—a utility belt with keys, a heavy-duty flashlight, a measuring tape no one has ever seen him pull out, and an American flag pin.

"Yes, we know," Greg adds. "But we are all excited about this new rollout."

"It's about time the outdoor eyesore got a digital upgrade," Ethan says.

Renee quivers. "Eyesore? I know you don't mean our vitamin D wonderland. Retro doesn't need an upgrade to be fun, unlike your machines, which are always going out of date."

"It's the throwback aesthetic that people are drawn to," Ursula says, sounding superior. Ethan politely hides his grin. Everyone can hear Renee talking out of Ursula's mouth whenever she starts mentioning the aesthetic.

Zoe, the Shut-In's unofficial second-in-command, barks

a laugh and pushes back. "The park revenue report proves otherwise. The digital arcade is busier than your rotting theme park these days."

"Come on, now," Ursula says. "Those rides have been around forever, and they'll *be* around forever. You'll probably come back here and take your kids on the bumper boats someday."

"Most of us are only seventeen," Logan, another Shut-In, says. He swirls his long locs up into the neat man-bun he wears during the summer. "Can we please not talk about future hypothetical children? I'm getting hives just thinking about it."

"The hives are from all this people-ing you're doing," Renee says. "Aren't you normally limited to just rebooting the system every time *Dino Dance* glitches?"

At that, David jumps in to lower the temperature of the debate. "Folks, we're all one WoWerful family. Let's not let this become a battle."

Greg puts his arm around David and smiles. "Yeah, everyone, this is a good thing!"

"I just think they're overestimating how cool people think the indoor games are," Renee says. While she normally appreciates Greg's extreme positivity, she has to stick up for her and Ursula's side of the park. "Guests take a whirl through the arcade because they have to get to RetroWorld. But everyone knows we're their ultimate destination."

Ursula slaps her a high five. "Yes!"

"You wish," Ethan says.

"We don't wish," Renee says. "And you'd know that if you ever bothered to come out and try the rides yourself, Vampire Boy."

"Wanna bet?"

Renee crosses her arms over her chest. "You're on."

"You know what? That's a great idea," Greg says, clapping his hands together, trying to regain control of the runaway meeting. "One day only—analog versus digital—for ultimate supremacy."

"What's the get?" Zoe asks. "You want us to go all out, it better be for more than bragging rights."

"Hmmmm, what is everyone's least favorite park chore?" David asks.

In unison, the crew says, "Cleanup!"

"Okay. Losing team has to clean up the winning team's stations for a week," David says.

Betsy the ticket taker stands, her orthopedic shoes squeaking on the sticky linoleum floor. "I am sixty-two years old. What kind of tomfoolery is this?"

"Sounds like chaos," Wallace says. "We don't need the potential liability of a clandestine employee competition while guests are on location."

Renee smiles her most winning smile. "We won't let it get out of control. Greg can even monitor Team Retro."

"We claim David," Ethan says quickly.

"Sure, I can keep an eye on digital," David says, a little glint in his eye. Everyone thinks he's the serious one, with his Harvard MBA, and his focus on the financials. But every once in a while, David emerges from the office—which everyone calls the Crow's Nest—and dominates at laser tag. He laughingly says that he fell in love with WoW even before he fell in love with Greg. Ursula sometimes thinks that might not be a joke. "And Customer Care doesn't have to participate in the competition. Maybe it's best if you three are the judges."

Frank, the concessions manager, looks perturbed. "But what are the parameters?" Of course Frank wants a rule book. He's read every WoW policy manual from cover to cover.

"How about this," Greg says. "The winning team will be the one that earns the most money in ticket revenue."

Ethan confers with his Shut-Ins—they're in. Renee and Ursula exchange a look. Are they willing to let their beloved RetroWorld go up against the more modern games? Renee can tell by the look in her best friend's eyes that she'll never back down. She nods at Greg, officially throwing Team Retro's hat in the race.

They're ready to win.

The meeting breaks, and with just fifteen minutes left before the park opens, Ursula and Renee retreat to their bunker in the staff-only basement to strategize. The staff-only basement is actually an old fallout shelter Ursula's grandparents constructed in the 1960s after President Kennedy announced everybody needed one.

The space is full of boxes of cheap prizes, containers of soda syrup, WoW-branded paper goods, and the shells of games and attractions that no longer work. There's even a huge fiberglass horse from the carousel that fell into such disrepair it had to be scrapped entirely. Renee knows this space well. She spent most of her weekends here with her father while he repaired broken games, just like he had done with his own father before him. Her great-grandfather and Ursula's served as GIs together in the Pacific during World War II. The Phillips patriarch built WoW when he came back, and the Broward patriarch opened up a maintenance shop to service the park. The families have been intertwined ever since.

The musty smell of the staff-only basement bothers the other managers when they have to come down here, but it feels like home to Renee.

"We need a plan," Ursula says.

"We do," Renee agrees. "I am not about to lose to Ethan and the Shut-Ins." From their first date—playing video games at Ethan's house—everything between them has had a competitive edge. Ursula finds their back and forth exhausting, but it seems to make the two of them glow.

Ursula sits down on the carousel horse hard enough that it sways. The faded paint and rusty metal contrast sharply with her crisp WoW logo shirt, the sleek chignon she fixes her ginger hair into, and her pressed khaki cargo shorts. "It's more than that, though. We're fighting for RetroWorld's honor."

Renee smiles gently. "I get it. We both know it's the best part of the park. But we have to be strategic about this. We can't come across as desperate."

"The problem is, how do we know how to win when we know next to nothing about Phantasm?"

"We need to conduct a little espionage," Renee says, pulling out her phone. With a quick text, she summons Ethan, who saunters into the basement.

"You beckoned the gaming king?" he says, softening the brag with a silly smile.

Ethan thinks highly of himself but only when it comes to gaming. And it's not totally unwarranted. He's placed in a few local gamer competitions, and he's a tech whiz who went straight into an IT certification program after he graduated from their high school last year.

"Details, right now, Game King," Renee says.

"Isn't this cheating? Or nepotism or something?" Ethan tugs at the hem of his perpetually rumpled WoW shirt. "You're just trying to get close to me to scope out the competition."

Ursula snorts. Ethan's crush on Renee was WoW legend long before he asked her out. That she's chasing him for a change is proof of how much she wants to win. Ursula wonders suddenly if Renee doesn't feel a little jealous of Ethan sometimes and the attention he gets from her dad when they work together on maintaining the digital games. She feels something similar about her own dads and how focused they've been on the arcade. Most of their profit these days goes into new games instead of repairing the old rides.

"Come on, honey bear," Renee says. Ethan grimaces. He doesn't usually mind that nickname in private, but he hates when she pulls it out at WoW. "Just tell us."

"Phantasm is the most sophisticated AR ever invented. It's a free-form multiplayer boundaryless coliseum that enables players wearing state-of-the-art wireless helmets to fully immerse in a virtual world experience."

Renee and Ursula stare at Ethan, trying to compute the description he rattled off. His enthusiasm is impressive. This is his Super Bowl.

"Did you swallow a press release or something?" Renee asks. "You sound like a hologram spokesperson."

He blushes. "It's a VR game—but a really unique one. The way it works, the more you move around, the more game there is to explore. Doesn't really seem like you have a chance against it—or against me."

Ouch. That does not bode well. It sounds like a never-ending gaming experience, which Renee knows will be hard to beat with Retro rides like a single-loop kiddie roller coaster. She narrows her eyes and stares at the muscle jumping in Ethan's jaw. Normally, he's dialed up to an eleven on a scale of ten when he's talking about new games. He's too casual right now.

"No more secrets," Ethan says, heading for the door. "You'll see the rest for yourself when you try it out later, when you and your Retro games are living in the Loser Zone."

Before either of them can snipe back, he's gone.

"Huh," Ursula says. "He ran out of here like his butt was on fire."

"He knew, in another minute, I'd have pried all the intel from his sneaky little brain." Renee glances at her Apple Watch, which she's attached to a band hand-painted with musical notes. "It's WoW time. Park is opening. We need to get out there. As for how we prove RetroWorld is the real MVP, we're just going to have to wing it."

When they emerge onto the arcade floor, there are no lines at *Dino Dance* or laser tag. The indoor area is unusually empty for the first thirty minutes of the day. Then they notice Logan, a Shut-In at the far end of the building, close to the doors to the RetroWorld exit and far from his normal domain of laser tag, his slender form surrounded by a group of tweens.

"You gotta come check Phantasm out," he says.

"But what exactly is it?" asks one of the girls, a little dark-haired pixie of a thing who clutches her token card tightly and gives a furtive glance at the *Dino Dance* gaming center.

With a line shorter than she's ever seen, she's probably desperate to get over there and play, but Logan's enthusiasm is convincing.

"It's the most badass VR simulator," he says. "There's no limit—the algorithm adapts and grows the more you explore. Every step you take opens up new areas, new adventures, and new challenges, and the pattern in which you explore changes the game. You could play a thousand rounds, and it would be different every time."

Renee and Ursula share a panicked look. Endless options and infinite space? Phantasm's a game changer. They have to do something—fast.

"You know, every Skee-Ball game you play is different from the last, too," Renee blurts.

Logan's little crowd turns to stare, the tweens whispering among themselves. Ursula thinks she detects a rolled eye or two. Then, horrifyingly, one of the moms chimes in. "I used to love playing Skee-Ball," she trills. "It was the most fun game in the Atlantic City arcade my family used to visit when I was a kid."

Logan can't hold back his laughter. The tweens edge away from their nosy mom and her old-school story and toward him. Renee flails. She has to bring this conversation back into the current century. "Look, you can stand in the line for that new game with a hundred other people and do nothing while you wait, or you can come challenge me to a Skee-Ball match. I'll give the first three people to beat my high score a free fifty-token game card."

"Bribe the customers much?" Logan hollers as his rapt audience drifts toward Renee. She fans the token cards in her hands like a professional poker player and waves them around.

"All's fair," Ursula says. "Why don't you come check out how the Retros get things done? Maybe you'll even have a little IRL fun for a change."

Renee grins and bumps her hip against Ursula's. "Nice one," she says.

The changes to WoW's courtyard might not stand out to the casual observer, but they hit both Renee and Ursula hard every time they walk by. To make room for the Phantasm kiosk, RetroWorld has been gutted. Or at least, that's how it feels to them. The game kiosk isn't large, but it requires power. Electrical wires crisscross the courtyard, held down by ugly orange safety tape, hooked up to the kiosk to charge rows of VR helmets and gloves. As Ursula looks around, her lower lip trembles. She could make her peace with some changes, but this feels like a whole new park. Ursula takes a deep breath as Renee turns and gives her a side-hug and steers her away from the offending sight.

The carnival midway is housed in striped yellow-and-red

tents holding a menagerie of old-school games, like the water-cannon-operated horse race and the ring toss, balloon darts, and high striker. Cotton-candy-colored stuffed animals are strung along the tent tops on a wire. Renee pulls a token card from her pocket. She has a manager version with unlimited swipes that she is supposed to use to give away a free game when the machines jam, but that she also uses when a kid runs out of swipes and their sibling taunts them because they still have enough to play more games.

With the flock of tween ducks bobbing along behind her, she runs down the row of Skee-Ball machines, swiping like a wild woman. With every flick of her wrist, another Skee-Ball machine sends a cascade of balls rocketing down the chute. Ursula flies along behind her, shoving kids forward. "Step right up," she yells, sounding like a carnival barker in a movie, as the kids start playing.

"Heard the Retros are over here playing dirty," a voice says, just loud enough to be heard over the crowd.

Renee flinches and spins to see the sun glimmering in Ethan's golden highlights. Beside him stand Noor and Logan. "Snitch," she says.

"I had to bust up this cheating ring," Logan says. "Free games? That was not part of the deal. These swipes don't count toward your ticket sales!"

"I'm not worried. Everyone knows once you start playing Skee-Ball, you can't stop!" Renee grabs a set of balls from the nearest machine and hands them to the boys. She picks up another and gets into perfect form. "Now this takes some real skill. It's not just handling a joystick."

Ethan chokes on his own saliva. He fumbles the ball, and it lands on a toe exposed by his Nike slides. While he hollers and hops around, Renee grins and rolls a fifty-point shot. "Whew," she says, rotating her throwing arm. "That was just a warm-up."

With her next throw, she sinks the ball into the tiny hundred-point ring. Ethan, meanwhile, steps up to the machine beside her and throws the Skee-Ball equivalent of a gutter ball, earning a measly ten points.

"Hey," cries the little pixie, who, like Ethan, is rolling mostly low-value shots. "How are you doing that? What's the trick?"

"No tricks," says Renee, the reigning queen of Skee-Ball. "All skill."

She walks over to demonstrate, using another manager swipe to restart the girl's game. Within a few more rounds, the tweens have picked up enough to sink higher-value balls. It spurs them into a raucous competition of their own—and as Renee suspected, they start swiping their own cards to keep playing. Ursula glances toward the entrance to the tent and sees Frank standing in the doorway, wearing his apron and hairnet from the funnel cake booth. He's waving to a large group of kids out in the courtyard. She nudges Renee and tips her head toward him.

"Is he directing traffic our way?" Renee asks.

"Shhh, just let him do what he does! Team Retro needs all the help it can get," Ursula replies. Just then, the walkie-talkie clipped to Ursula's belt crackles.

"Go for go-karts." It's Wallace. He's the only one that consistently uses the walkies. Everyone else chats in the group text.

Ursula sighs and lifts the walkie. "Loud and clear, Officer Jackson."

"We have a Code Green at the Kiddie Koaster."

Logan, Ethan, Renee, and Ursula groan. Noor gags and holds a hand to her mouth. Wallace loves the walkies and the codes. He requires every manager to sign out a device at the top of their shift, and he makes them all memorize the lingo. A Code Blue is a water spill. A Code Red is a lost child. Code Yellow is machine down. But Code Green is every manager's worst nightmare. Puke.

"Mic check," Wallace repeats. "Do you read? Code Green at the Kiddie Koaster."

The Kiddie Koaster is adjacent to the go-karts, which makes this Ursula's problem. Greg's rule is minimum-wage employees aren't paid enough for vomit, so the manager has to truck down to the basement for sanitizing supplies and handle cleanup themselves. Besides, the Kiddie Koaster will remain closed until it's scrubbed down. Pre-lunch is prime toddler roller coaster hour; they can't miss out on those swipes. She sighs again, depresses the button on her walkie, and says, "Wilco. Over and out."

"Grooooooss," she adds, making a face and heading toward her section.

"Don't worry. I've got this covered," Renee calls after her. Another tween has stepped up to take over the empty Skee-Ball machine. "I'll make sure we hold on to this clear lead."

"And I'll make sure we're playing fair," Ethan says. He grabs for her manager swipe card to prevent her from giving away another free game. She holds it in the air and tries to twirl away, but he throws his arms around her. It ought to be a slick move, but Ethan's no Hemsworth brother, and they're clearly in the *com* half of the rom-com. Instead of catching her in a gentle hug, Ethan's momentum propels them into the machines. They fall backward on a Skee-Ball ramp in a tangle of limbs. Ethan's torso presses against her. His laughter reveals a row of sparkling white teeth, with one adorably crooked incisor.

"Admit it. We're beating the socks off of you," Renee says. She means it to sound snarky, but it comes out a little bit breathless. She forgets how adorable Ethan is, when he's locked away in his digital cocoon. They stare at one another for ten seconds. Twenty. Ethan's face dips toward hers. Renee raises her mouth and lowers her eyelids, waiting for his lips to touch her, forgetting they're in the middle of the midway until Ethan's fingertip gently boops her nose instead.

"We have an audience," he whispers. She eyes the tweens who are watching and giggling and—oh man, is one of them filming? She shoves Ethan to his feet and follows him up, while the crowd cheers.

"Yeah, well, don't get too excited," Ethan says. "Phantasm is up next. Meet me there in an hour."

By the time Ursula finishes her cleanup on aisle nine and Renee shepherds her Skee-Ball crew through rounds of whack-a-mole and ring toss and water-cannon horse races, the clock hands have drifted toward the steamy afternoon hours. Normally, the guests escape indoors at this time of day to cool down with a drink and lunch, but the courtyard bubbles with people waiting for a turn at the new VR game. Zoe and Logan are on duty, hooking each player up with helmets and gloves. Ethan ushers Ursula and Renee to the front of the line. Noor trails along behind him, his designated partner for this round.

"You ready for an upgrade, Team Retro?" Ethan teases.

While Logan fusses about helping Ursula get her equipment on, Renee taunts him back. "Scared because we're off to such a strong start?"

Ethan scoffs. "Not even a little. Wait'll you try this masterpiece of a game. We don't even need any other attractions. Look at the line. No one queues for your games like this."

Renee flinches. The line winds around and around the courtyard. It's even longer than the one they had when they first opened the bumper boat ride. "Yeah, but how fun is it to stand here and gaze at your phone while you're in line all day? Winning requires a team, not a single star game."

Despite her protests, Renee is curious to see how this game works. She wonders if it's as revolutionary as Ethan says.

Noor smoothly slides a helmet over her hijab and settles into her controller gloves with ease. Renee and Ursula watch with envy. Of course the Shut-Ins have experience; they've been training on it for weeks. Renee tries to follow Logan's rapid-fire instructions but she quickly gets lost. She'll be lucky if she manages to make the game work at all.

When everyone is suited up, Logan activates the game and instantly they are dropped into a lush forest that's just slightly off from reality—plants hang upside down with their roots exposed, trees grow candied mushrooms with gooey centers. Neon-colored animals run and fly past. They're surrounded by forest sounds—running water, birdcalls, even a distant roar that might be a bear. Or a dragon. Vaguely, Ursula is aware of the stifling summer afternoon and the murmuring of the WoW crowd around her, but she's otherwise immersed in the game.

When she looks down, she sees the VR has overlaid them with elaborate digital cosplay. Ursula appears to be clothed in a brown cotton suit and a long beige cloak. She's holding a walking staff. "Surprisingly good uniform!"

"Where are we?" Renee gasps.

"In the realm of Zenoir." Noor's voice breaks through the illusion. Renee turns in her direction and finds her wearing a royal purple ball gown with gold trim and a black velvet cloak.

She also wears a purple hijab that matches her gown. "Our task is to collect the kingdom's artifacts. They've been stolen by bandits. If we return them all, we inherit the kingdom's greatest treasure."

Practical Ursula can't help but ask, "Which is what?"

The sound of a smile is thick in Ethan's voice. "You only find out when you beat the game."

"Hard to get excited when you don't know the prize," Ursula mutters.

"You can customize your appearance, if you want," Noor says. "Open your palm faceup to retrieve your menu."

Renee adorns herself in a sleek black bodysuit with kick-ass high-heeled boots and glittery silver fairy wings that give the illusion that she's floating a few inches above the ground. She hates to admit this is pretty cool.

Ethan, in game, wears a pair of leather pants with a jeweled dagger strapped to his thigh and looks like a high-fashion woodsman. He looks hot. Their elaborate costumes make Renee flash back to Wicked WoW Week, the park's Halloween festivities. WoW doesn't do zombie jump scares because their niche is more "family" fun. But they go all out with decorations, covering the park with cobwebs and mummifying the dancing bear statue in the courtyard fountain. For just a minute, Renee wishes they could experience one last Wicked WoW Week together, but in the fall she'll be gone.

"Let's go," Ethan says, shaking Renee from her reverie. She

follows him and Ursula into the digital forest, dimly aware that in the real world, she has to narrowly avoid the edge of the fountain or trip face-first into the water. Her eyes blur a little, trying to keep track of both the digital and the physical. It reminds her of *Pokémon Go* and other games that overlay game play onto reality, but leveled all the way up.

"The game controls are super straightforward. You'll figure them out as you play," Ethan says. They step into the cordoned-off area of the courtyard set aside for people in the VR helmets to roam around freely and get lost exploring and solving puzzles to recover artifacts. Some require them to manipulate virtual objects. The sophisticated, adaptive software makes it easy for Renee to imagine she's really opening treasure chests and breaking into locked towers. And Ursula's left-brain logic lets her ace the clue-based challenges. Ethan and Noor are annoyingly good at both. To Renee's surprise, Noor sets aside their Team Digital versus Team Retro rivalry to reassure her that it's just because she's played similar games in the past.

Eventually an electronic chime sounds, and the digital world fades. Time's up. Renee already misses her jumpsuit and glittery wings.

"So," Noor asks. "How was it?"

"I admit," Renee says, a little sheepishly. "That was fun." She feels a flicker of worry. If she, as the team co-captain, loved the game so much, Retro might be headed for an upset.

"Fun?" Ethan yanks off his helmet. "That was EPIC! Have you ever seen such clean graphics in a VR environment?" He vibrates with excitement. His hair is sweaty and plastered to his forehead. He even has a red indentation in his skin. He unselfconsciously goes about powering down his gear without fixing his hair.

"We must've had a thousand NPC interactions," Ursula adds, removing her own helmet. She also doesn't bother to fix her hair.

Ethan raises an eyebrow. "What do you know about non-player characters?"

"I've played video games before, Ethan," she says. She smirks at Renee. She's been the third wheel on enough of their dates that he knows this. It's just that no one rises to the level of Ethan's commitment to gaming.

They hand their gear in for sanitizing and find Betsy the ticket taker sitting on the edge of the courtyard fountain, her lunch box beside her. "I can't say it was all that much fun watching you four bumbling around in Jetsons helmets."

"Who?" Ursula asks.

"A really old cartoon," Noor explains. "About a weird futuristic family."

"Anyway," Betsy says, stuffing her leftovers in a nearby trash can. "I wasted my lunch break here watching you all play imaginary games. You sure spent a lot of time in Tron."

This time it's Renee's turn to look confused. "Where?"

"Another retro reference," Noor says. "Eighties movie."

"How do you know this?" Ursula asks, sounding more surprised than she should.

"I respect the throwbacks." Noor laughs. "I even like a good game of *PAC-MAN*. But I want to play it on my Xbox and not an old arcade machine. It doesn't have to be all or nothing, you know. Old school or new school . . . how about both?"

Renee shrugs. "It's a competition. I came to win."

But she can admit to herself how much fun Phantasm was. She never imagined a game would let her indulge her wildest cosplay fantasy so realistically. A world where she could test limitless design options without spending money on fabric? Ethan was right; it was epic.

And by the crowd around the VR kiosk, it seemed like a lot of other people knew it. Maybe Team Digital is in the lead. Renee shoots a glance at Ursula. They're going to have to get their focus back if they want to win.

But then there's a shout from across the courtyard. David strides out of the administration building, hurtling their way so fast you can almost see the wind stream behind him. His coiffed silver-fox hair is ruffled, and he holds his cell phone to his ear—a WoW no-no that Wallace normally enforces strictly. No exceptions for the owners.

"What is going on here?"

"David," Ethan cries, holding up his hand for a fist bump that David does not return. "Pretty sure Team Digital just took the lead. One of my people just messaged me that the arcade is packed. They're crushing it! Wait till you see all those ticket swipes."

"Meanwhile, the crowds are crushing WoW," David says sternly. "You're playing instead of gearing people up for Phantasm. Rafael is waiting for Betsy to sub him out at the ticket counter. I'm getting complaints we're out of TP in the women's room—has anyone performed restroom maintenance in a while?"

Ursula blushes red as a poppy. David sends a disappointed glare her way. She'll hear about this on the car ride home. Her dads expect her to be a model employee. They've made clear that if she wants to step into the management role she's been asking for, she has to prove she can handle the responsibility.

She squares her shoulders and says, in as calm a voice as she can muster, "You're right, Dad. I'm sorry. We were neglecting our stations, and we won't let it happen again."

The others mumble their own apologies. David nods. "I get it, guys. The competition is fun. But we have jobs to do. We can't leave the park unattended to goof around."

As David heads back to the Crow's Nest, the crew checks out their stations. Leaving the park to run itself took a toll. Lines are backed up. Games are glitching. Customers are complaining. The manager crew runs around trying to restore order. Despite their desire to win, none of them wants the park to fall apart so they can prove a point about their favorite games. They all take pride in having well-run workstations and making guests happy. They've all worked overtime more than once, without complaining, to keep games up and running or birthday parties staffed.

By 3:45, there are only fifteen minutes to go before the shift change, and Ursula's nerves bubble to the surface. She flits between the rides in her section, sweat beading in her hairline, monitoring the length of the lines and the number of guests. Getting waylaid by Phantasm earlier not only put her on her dads' bad side, but it disrupted their efforts to bring more guests to RetroWorld games, though Renee had given away funnel cakes tastes to entice people into the midway and Ursula had given away all her "skip the line" passes that they normally reserve for when a ride breaks and they need to calm an angry customer. But was it enough? There's not much time left to prove once and for all that retro is better. She doesn't want to disappoint David by sneaking off again. Maybe the responsible grown-up thing—the park management thing—to do is let it go. Her shoulders sag.

Renee steps close to her and squeezes Ursula's hand. "We got this."

And then David's voice replaces the cheery background Muzak playing over the PA system. "I'd like to invite all guests and managers to gather by the go-karts for a special event."

The end, Ursula thinks, and looks back at Renee. "RetroWorld forever."

Renee nods. They'd have this—even as everything changes over the next few months.

Renee and Ursula are the first to arrive at the go-karts station. "Do you think he's going to announce who won?" Renee asks.

Ursula slams the gate as a round of riders files out. "I'm surprised, given how angry he was earlier."

David and Greg both come down from the Crow's Nest. David's earlier grouchiness is gone. He must be happy they all got the park under control. They high-five guests and encourage them to follow along to the go-kart track.

Renee hops from foot to foot as Greg jumps up on a bench. "So this is it, right? The big reveal? Who's the champion, Greg?"

He smiles down at the assembled crowd. "I'm going to let our official ticket taker do the honors." He gives Betsy a hand and she climbs onto the bench, wobbling a bit in her black Crocs and holding on to her boss to stay steady. Renee sneaks a peek around for Wallace. If he sees this, he'll write up a safety violation, even against the park owner.

Betsy clears her throat. "I've tallied all ticket swipes from opening until ten minutes ago. Counting the carnival midway games plus RetroWorld rides against the digital arcade and

Phantasm and . . . it's too close to call! Ticket sales were within a few dozen of each other. In my expert opinion, it's officially a tie."

A disgruntled cry goes up. Ethan and his Shut-Ins moan in disbelief. "No way!" Logan cries. "I demand a recount!"

Ursula turns to Renee and frowns. A tie? They had not counted on it being a draw.

"Are you questioning my integrity, young man?" Betsy demands.

"You old-timers have been Team Retro all along!" he says.

Frank pushes his way to the front of the crowd and crosses his arms. "Sides were not taken. The old-timers kept this park running today while you youngsters messed around."

Logan holds up his hands in defeat. "Okay, that's fair."

"Are we just going to live with a tie?" Ethan asks. "Feels like a boring conclusion to an epic battle."

An idea shimmers in Renee's mind. It's a bit devious, but everyone will enjoy it anyway. "How about a tiebreaker? One go-kart race, Team Retro versus Team Digital. First to have all members cross the finish line is the champion."

"This tiebreaker seems very pro-Retro to me," Ethan says, narrowing his eyes.

"But it would be a crowd-pleaser," Renee says, waving her hand at the large group that has assembled in the courtyard. "It would be more fun for the guests than watching us walk around in VR helmets."

"But there's four of us and only two of Team Retro," Noor says.

"Actually, I can fix that. Team Retro's other two drivers are right here," David says, swinging his arm around his husband's shoulder.

"Hey, no way!" Ethan cries.

"Sorry, kid." David puts his other arm around Ursula, who links elbows with Renee. "This part feels like a family affair."

"Wait," Noor says. "Who's going to run the ride? After Ursula, Greg's the only other qualified operator."

There's a moment of silence, and then Greg says, "Why don't I run it?"

"Then who'll be the fourth?" Ethan asks.

Renee and Ursula look at each other, mirrored smiles spreading over their mouths.

"You know who we need?" Renee says.

Ursula nods. She lifts her walkie-talkie. "Go for Wallace 'the Lightning Bolt' Jackson."

There's a pause, then a crackle, then a booming reply. "I've been waiting for this call."

Wallace parts the crowd of guests. By this time of day, he's always too hot in his uniform, and sweat beads on his bald head. But he walks with as much energy as the little kids on their way to ride the karts for the first time.

"Wallace," Renee says. "We need a driver."

Wallace unclips his utility belt and hands it to Greg. "Hold this."

Ursula bustles around, arranging eight single-seater racers for the two crews. Noor, Logan, Zoe, and Ethan wait as Ursula checks gas tanks and gauges. While David and Renee settle into their own cars, Wallace circles his purple racer, toe-tapping the tires and testing the tension in the wheel before he climbs in and revs the engine. From her bright yellow racer, Ursula launches into the safety spiel, because of course she does. Renee has heard it so many times she could give the speech herself, but the others listen carefully and check their seat belts when directed. They give the "got it" thumbs-up Ursula asks for, too. Renee smiles. A lot of people that come through this line are jerks about the safety speech. Ursula's a little earnest, sure, but it's important. Go-kart accidents are some of the worst that happen at the park. It makes Ursula puff with pride that Wallace and her competitors take her seriously. Everyone really knows it'll be her park someday.

Finally, Greg changes the light from red to green, and the racers stomp on their gas pedals.

Renee quickly shoots into the lead in her metallic black car. She loves the go-karts. Her favorite memories of WoW are doing test rides with her father. After he'd fix a racer, he'd always have to test it before introducing it back into the fleet. When he was certain it was safe, he'd never fail to take Renee along for the ride. She knows the curves and turns of this course like she knows her own neighborhood, and she hugs them tightly all the way around the track.

Ethan starts out close behind, but soon he's eating her dust. He makes the rookie mistake of assuming anyone can pilot a go-kart, but it's harder than it looks. He has to slow before the turns or risk spinning out. Despite that, he's screaming with laughter and grinning with his whole face.

They all make three full laps around the track, fighting for the lead. At the sidelines, a massive crowd gathers, and the racers can hear them cheering. Greg even uses the PA to announce the race like a NASCAR commentator. Betsy and Frank are both lined up at the fence, Frank equipped with pencil and notepad.

Wallace and Renee trade the lead—inching forward then back until the last lap, when it looks like Zoe might catch up. She whoops with joy. But then, in that last fifty yards before the finish line, Renee and Wallace burst forward, stomping on the pedals, flying ahead as if their racers came equipped with booster buttons the others don't have. With a holler, Renee screeches across the finish line an instant before Wallace.

She jumps out of the racer, pumping her fist. Greg, from behind the operator's podium, high-fives her. Renee spins and celebrates, while the crowd cheers. After Wallace climbs from his racer, smiling like he won an Olympic medal, he leans over to catch his breath, with just enough energy to fist-bump Renee. When the Team Digital competitors finally cross the finish line and emerge from their racers, they file past, accepting their defeat graciously. Ursula catches Renee's eye, beaming. Ethan even pats Wallace on the back.

"Didn't know you had it in you, dude."

Wallace straightens. "That's *sir* to you, young man."

Ursula turns and cups a hand around her ear, ostentatiously signaling how loud the cheering from the guests assembled along the fence has become. Ethan, Logan, Zoe, and Noor boo and hiss, but without venom. They can sense what's coming.

"The winner is . . ." Frank booms over the sound of Ethan mimicking a drumroll on the side of the operator podium. "Team Retro!"

Ursula and Renee throw their arms around each other triumphantly. "Retro rules!"

After a moment, Renee whirls and hugs Ethan, too. "No hard feelings? But listen, for cleanup duty—no copping out with Lysol wipes. Nothing but a good old-fashioned rag and spray bottle will do for the carnival midway, okay?"

"That's what I have a staff for, right?" Ethan winks. "But seriously. Rematch soon. We'll get *Dino Dance* in on the action next time. There's no way we can lose."

"Wait, wait, wait," David says, holding up his hands. "Any rematches have to take place after-hours. I can't handle another day of chaos like this."

"Fair enough," Ethan says. And then he leads the Shut-Ins

in a handshake line, saving a special congratulatory kiss for Renee.

Ursula gives Renee another tight squeeze. "You're on for a rematch—but only if Renee and I are always partners."

"Oh, Urs, you shouldn't make that condition." Renee pats at the corner of her watery eyes. "What happens when I'm not around anymore?" She hates to put a painful reminder in her friend's face during such a happy moment, but when the summer comes to an end, she's moving on.

To her surprise, Ursula smiles. "WoW will be here when you come back to visit. It will always be a wonderful day at World of Wonder."

WEEPING ANGELS

Yamile Saied Méndez

Content warning: drowning

THE LIGHT CAME ON AND ELLIE FLUNG HER ARM OVER HER face. "Turn the light off! What are you doing, Maisy? Get out of my room!"

It was the most she'd said to her little sister in months. But she'd been expecting her. It was the last night of summer, and even though Ellie had lost track of time, trapped in her room, something in the marrow of her bones pulsated as it counted down the days to late August.

"It's Last Night," Maisy said. Her voice sounded younger than twelve.

Had Ellie sounded that little just three years ago when she'd been on the verge of starting seventh grade, too?

Maybe it was disappointment that made Maisy sound so little. Over the years, their family's traditions and celebrations had come and gone, merged and morphed. But the last day of summer celebrations remained sacred.

Ever since Ellie could remember, the night before the first day of school, the neighborhood kids from seventh to twelfth grade had gone out to play games until bedtime.

But Colin had died in June.

His death had knocked the axis of the world off-center.

How could there be a Last Night without him leading the games? Without his infectious laughter when he threw his head back and clutched his stomach over a silly joke?

He included everyone—he was the glue that kept them together.

Colin had been the leader of their group of neighborhood kids since preschool. More than that, he was everyone's best friend. At least that's what everyone posted on social media after his death, what everyone said at the funeral, even people Ellie had never seen him with.

He was kind and happy and full of life.

He *was* life. The sun. Now that he was gone, everything was dark.

Maisy stomped through the room and opened the curtains. The stars winked over Timpanogos. Ellie and Colin had climbed to the top last year in ninth grade. Everywhere Ellie looked, there was a memory of him.

"Get out!" Ellie bellowed again, and threw a pillow at her sister.

Maisy dodged her easily and clicked her tongue. She was twelve going on twenty-one but fiercely proud about being a seventh grader. Finally. "It's my room, too."

"What do you want?"

"I just need a light jacket." She paused, and then she sighed, her shoulders falling dramatically. "They're all here, you know? Only you are missing."

He's missing, too.

Somehow, it was easy to imagine him downstairs with the rest of their families.

The Fav Five's group had been born at a first-time-parent hospital tour when Cindy, Finn, Oscar, Colin, and Ellie had been chilling in their respective cocoons in their mothers' bellies. Their families were from Venezuela, South Africa, Korea, Brazil, and Argentina. The things they had in common were being immigrants in tiny American Fork, Utah, and having a baby on the way.

After a night of board games and ginger ale, the parents had become friends for life. Their friendship had carried the Croxford, Thomas, Walsh, Santos, and Turner families through many highs like birthdays, sport events, dance recitals, and holidays, and all the lows. Like Mrs. Croxford's scare with breast cancer three years ago, the worry about Finn's sick grandma who refused to move from South Africa, and now the worst one of all: Colin's accident.

The kids hadn't been back together since that night, the

one Ellie wanted to blot out of the space-time continuum.

If her mom's outlandish new age ideas were real, somewhere in a parallel universe there was another Ellie who was still mad at Colin, and another one who hadn't made a big deal out of a misunderstanding. Another one would have kissed him the night before instead of just flirting and wasting time. But there would be thousands of others going through the horror of seeing him die a thousand deaths, including the one that had actually happened in her timeline.

Colin had drowned. Drowned. Him. The swim team captain. Colin Santos, the best of them all.

The star that kept their families united even in death.

Yet another Ellie would be heartbroken and destroyed, but she wouldn't feel so much guilt and regret. Had she gone with him that night, bridge jumping into the river like they'd done hundreds of times, maybe she wouldn't have been able to change anything. But she could have done something to look for him. She could've found him faster than the useless search and rescue people who looked in the wrong place. Anything but being asleep while her whole world came crashing down.

Ever since that night, she'd been sleeping. Anything was better than waking up to a world that kept on going even though Colin was gone. He was gone.

Maisy rummaged in the mess of their room while in the nest she'd made in her bed, Ellie spiraled.

Her lungs couldn't expand for her to take a breath. Or ask for help. Or even cry.

Ellie remembered that time she'd been babysitting the Walshes' youngest, Oscar's sister Navy. It was award night for his debate team, and at eighteen months, Navy was already a hellion. They couldn't bring her along. Navy had been asleep when Ellie showed up. It was all fine until Navy woke up and realized her parents were gone without her. She started crying.

She let out a wail so protracted that at first Ellie thought it was funny, how long a little tiny thing could exhale. And then Navy's face turned bluish. Then a dark purple. Navy had looked at her with terrified eyes, asking for help before her little body crumpled like a withered flower and she fainted.

All of Ellie's babysitting training went out the window.

Unable to think, she'd screamed, clutching Navy and running in circles. She was about to call her mom when she felt the baby squirming in her arms again. Ellie looked into her dark brown eyes, so much like Oscar's. Navy tried to smile and then snuggled up to Ellie. She was okay.

That day the tears had come so easily. She had cried and cried for the two of them, thanking God and every deity she could think of for the miracle of breath in Navy's lungs. Even after coming back from her faint, for a few minutes, Navy had been so subdued. It was eerie.

Finally, Ellie called her mom in hysterics, and then the

ambulance had come, and the Walshes with Oscar's trophy in hand. But they were so grateful to find their baby alive.

Her parents later told her that sometimes young children did that. Let out all the air in their lungs. The lungs are like balloons, and when all the air comes out, the interior walls cling together and cramp up. The body's defense mechanism is to faint to do a hard reset.

Usually there are no other incidents after the first one.

And for Navy there hadn't been. She'd cry and let out a long wail, and all those around her would wait until she finally inhaled again and continued crying to her heart's content.

After that day, Ellie had taken CPR lessons.

Maybe that night at the bridge if she'd been there with her friends, she would have found Colin and saved him.

"Hey," Maisy said again, and clutched her hand.

Ellie's senses came back to her in a rush.

Ellie stared at her little sister like she was a miracle. Because she was. She wasn't that little anymore. Maisy was so warm. So full of life. This summer she'd shot up and gotten some curves that hadn't been there before, had they? She had spaghetti strap tan lines on her shoulders, and her braces had come off. With her creamy skin and light brown hair, she looked so much like their dad. Ellie had taken after their mom, tawny skin, hair like mahogany. But now, spending months in the darkness of her room, her skin had a greenish tint. She imagined her face didn't look much better than a zombie's.

"Please, will you come down to say hi?" her sister asked.

Maisy looked at her with such love and concern, Ellie's armor almost crumbled. But when she saw her little sister's eyes fill with tears, Ellie made the walls around her heart come up real fast. Taller and thicker than ever. She couldn't let it go past here or she doubted she'd be able to get up ever again. Much less go back to school tomorrow, where everyone would be talking about him with those strained voices and faces, everyone pretending they'd loved him the most. But it wasn't true. She had loved him most. That's why she'd been so mad at him that night. Not because she was an unfeeling bitch.

Which was what she was being now, with her sister. Ellie rolled her eyes dramatically because she knew it would hurt Maisy and get her out of her hair. "Hell no. There's no way I'll go down there and see them and cry."

"It'll be good for you, Flávia said."

Ellie didn't feel like she deserved anything good. Much less the compassion of Colin's mother. Colin was an only child. How could Flávia keep going without him?

Maisy rummaged in her jeans back pocket. A piece of paper. No, a photo, judging by the gloss. She looked at it for a second and then stretched out her hand toward Ellie. "Flávia brought this. She thought you might want it. It was in a family time capsule they opened yesterday."

Ellie didn't move. She couldn't move. Her mind was

screaming that Colin would've loved the time capsule. Why did they open it without him?

Maisy, apparently confusing the lack of reaction for indifference, sighed. Her shoulders slumped. She dropped the paper and it glided to the carpet without a sound. Ellie wished she could explain to her sister why she froze, why her words evaporated from her parched lips, but she couldn't.

Before walking out of the room, Maisy asked, not even looking over her shoulder, "Should I turn off the light?"

There was so much hope in her voice for Ellie to say no. That eagerness. That desire for Ellie to fix the world.

But Ellie couldn't fix anything.

Wrenching herself out of the spell, she covered her head with the comforter that smelled rancid, like old sweat, and managed to yell, "Turn it off and don't come bothering me again."

Maisy left.

From downstairs came the sound of voices. Pleasant, friendly voices. Ellie could *almost* pretend this was happening at any other point in her life.

She could fully imagine the conversation downstairs. The five pairs of parents looking at Maisy with hope and then her disappointed expression as she shook her head no. All of them feeling bad for poor old Ellie.

It was torture to imagine their expressions, but anything was better than seeing Colin in his dad's eyes. His mom's smile. She knew she wouldn't be able to look at them without crumpling.

Her eyes flitted to the paper on the carpet.

Slowly, her body unused to moving, Ellie rolled out of her cocoon. She grabbed the paper and opened it. The memories flooded her.

It was a picture of their first Last Night, right before seventh grade, three years ago. Colin stood between Oscar and Finn. That year the boys had buzzed their hair after a botched hair-dye experiment had scorched their hair. The girls flanked the boys in what they called "the coolness sandwich" pose, sticking their tongues out. That day they wore matching orange bikini tops and jean shorts.

The kids they had been could've never imagined being apart.

Ellie plopped on the bed, staring at the photo that was like a little window she wished she could crawl through to be with them one more time.

One last time together.

The Fav Five had all lost Colin, and that had taken a little bit of each one's heart.

A voice that sounded like Maisy told her that her friends were waiting for her in the yard.

She couldn't stand not seeing them. Even if when she did, she'd realize everything had changed.

Slowly, she got dressed in the semi-darkness, her heart pumping hard in her ears for what she was about to do, who she was about to see.

She had shut the others out of her life, too. She missed

them. Even if she wasn't going to walk down to see their parents or anyone else on Last Night, she had to see them and she had to show them the picture.

Ellie opened the glass of her window to climb down like she'd done millions of times before.

Grabbing her trusted tree branch, she swung her body out. Somehow, her muscles still remembered the gymnastics moves she'd learned from the time she was three and that Colin could do naturally just because.

She landed in the grass, almost giddy with the surprise of having pulled off that kind of stunt after weeks in bed.

Her face wasn't used to smiling, but she could still do it after all.

That was, until she lifted her eyes and saw the blue Jeep.

She gasped with outrage.

How dare they drive his car? Why did they do that? Why had no one told her?

All her excuses of not wanting to go out so she wouldn't be reminded of him immediately proved right. What if one day she was driving back from school or work, or minding her own business, and she saw his car?

She swallowed all the words that crowded in her mouth and headed to the backyard.

The rest of the Fav Five were standing around the old wooden swing set, as she'd known they would be. Cindy wearing a tank top and cut-off shorts. Her long hair was pulled up in a high pony, her skin perfectly tanned. But her supermodel look had a sharp edge that hadn't been there before.

Finn and Oscar were in matching jeans and soccer jerseys, Barcelona and Tottenham Spurs.

Cindy saw her first, nodding in acknowledgment. Finn and Oscar turned around. Oscar's dark eyes widened in such an expression of joy that Ellie's throat tightened. Finn ruffled his red hair. He looked paler than usual, and then Ellie remembered his parents had taken him to South Africa; it had been winter there. Finn never tanned well, while Colin had always looked golden, kissed by the sun.

"We were waiting for you," Finn said unnecessarily. "We figured we could do a game for Last Night, but not in the neighborhood."

"Everyone will be watching us," Cindy said. Her voice sounded deeper. Ellie almost didn't recognize it.

They all looked and sounded different. They hadn't been together since the funeral in June. The boys were taller. Cindy was thinner. How would Colin have been different with three extra months of life?

Oscar bit his lip and then said, "His mom gave me the Jeep keys, but—"

"I can't do that," Ellie said, recoiling inside.

Even if that was the only way to exorcise him, she wouldn't do it. She couldn't even imagine getting back into his car. Smelling the scent of pineapple air freshener. Feeling the softness of the seats on the back of her legs. Seeing someone else driving the Jeep he'd put together and worked on since he was fourteen would be a crime.

He took that car on his inaugural drive to get his license. He'd passed his test on the first try, of course. Just two weeks before the accident.

"I know," Oscar said, making a calming gesture with his hands. "Let's go in mine."

"Where?" Ellie asked.

"We'll see," Finn said in the kind of voice Colin used to take them to the most amazing adventures. Most likely, he'd said it that night, too.

Oscar's new car wasn't flashy or memorable like Colin's had been. It was very Oscar though. A silver nondescript Honda Civic. Solid. Dependable.

No one had called it, so Ellie said, "Shotgun."

There was a moment of tension in which the boys exchanged a cryptic look, but no one protested. Quietly, they all shuffled into the car, as if they'd done this countless times before.

Maybe the rest of them had. She wouldn't know as she'd missed three months of summer with them.

The heat made the silence in the car feel even more oppressive. Ellie rolled the window down. She pulled at the seat belt that constricted her, but it didn't help.

"Are you okay?" Oscar asked softly, and Ellie felt like a jerk for making them all so uncomfortable.

In the back seat, Finn and Cindy sat looking out their windows, both crossed-armed, shiny eyed.

"I heard you started going to church with your mom," Ellie said to Cindy because she didn't know what to tell Oscar. She tried to make her voice as nonjudgmental as possible, but considering Cindy's reaction, she failed.

"Why? Do you care?" Cindy said, all sharp and loud.

Oscar held on to the wheel, looking ahead. Finn bit his lip.

Cindy's reaction hurt, but Ellie saw her point. She had avoided them for months, but not because she didn't care. She didn't know how they could function again without Colin.

"I care that you're okay," Ellie said, stretching out her hand to Cindy.

She meant all of them. That they'd survived on their own somehow.

Cindy took her hand. The boys seemed to exhale in relief. Maybe it helped they were together.

In the park, kids played, rode their bikes, waited in line at the shaved-ice place. Oscar drove around town like they were looking for Colin and couldn't find him.

Ellie felt his absence in every cell of her body. She knew the others felt the same, too.

"I have flashlights in the trunk," Oscar finally said, turning toward the mountains.

Something jerked inside Ellie.

"Weeping Angels?" Cindy asked, echoing the questions swirling inside Ellie. "We don't have enough players, do we?"

They'd usually played with other kids from their grade. But tonight, it had to be just the four of them. Ellie didn't know if the others had already agreed on this, but she felt like before they could rejoin the rest of the world, they had to figure out how they'd function without him.

"We have enough players if we go to the maze," Finn said, shrugging one shoulder. "We need a contained place."

The maze was a corn plot by the old slaughterhouse. It all sounded ominous, but the truth was that three years ago the land had been developed to serve the ultra-high demand of people moving to Silicon Slopes from California. The grain fields had been filled with cookie-cutter houses that cost more than a million dollars. But the developers had left the corn maze and the old, abandoned slaughterhouse for character.

How many times had they played Weeping Angels here? Especially during Halloween when Colin had pretended to moo in their ears when he snuck up on them moments before they could shine the flashlight in his face.

He was always pulling pranks. Stupid, stupid boy.

If they were going to exorcise the ache of his absence, there was no more perfect place or time.

The last day of this summer that had been eternal and ephemeral, like life.

"Who's the angel?" Finn asked.

Oscar shrugged.

They all turned to look at Ellie. She sighed, hoping they'd understand that she wanted anything but to be in charge of making decisions. That had been Colin's job.

And then she realized something that she'd always known—after Colin, it was her in the ladder of leadership.

She didn't want to lose them, either.

"We'll draw straws," she said. "The long one is the angel."

Without complaint, they all looked around for a little stick.

Weeping Angels was a game they had inherited from the older kids in the neighborhood. It was a form of tag inspired by *Doctor Who*. Ellie had never seen the show, but she knew by now that the Weeping Angels were possessed sculptures that came closer to you when you weren't looking. In their game, one of them would play the angel going after all the other players, and when you got tagged by an angel, you became one, too.

The flashlight was your only defense. Shine your light, and the angel must freeze for ten seconds, giving you time to seek another hiding place.

She picked a stick from the ground and waited for the others to return with theirs. Oscar measured them, and then gave them back to Ellie.

Her hand was sweaty.

They all looked at each other, nervously.

"One, two, three," Finn said, and they all pulled their straw.

"Ah!" Oscar said. "I'm the angel."

"Of course," Ellie said, and it came out sounding sarcastic.

She'd have preferred to be the angel, the one searching, anything but hiding alone, waiting to be found. But hadn't she done that all summer? Wait in the dark while her friends and family flashed a light to her once in a while?

Maybe she'd been practicing for tonight.

They all placed their backs to each other in a circle.

Ellie got the countdown.

"One, two . . ." Ellie counted.

At "three!" Cindy and Finn took off toward the cornstalks that surrounded them.

Oscar ran to the slaughterhouse to give them time to hide.

Ellie stood in place for a couple of seconds, and then she, too, ran toward the corn. The withering stalks scratched her arms and legs. Something tangled in her hair and pulled her back. But she kept running and running until she reached the edge. Gasping for air, she crouched, eyeing the purple thistles that grew among the rubble.

The darkness shrouded her. Timpanogos was still blocking the moonlight, and the stars weren't bright enough to do more than blink yet.

She realized Oscar had been counting only when he said, "Ready or not, here I come!"

In spite of everything, she smiled, thinking of how Colin

had always made the most horrific Weeping Angel because like with everything else, he gave his all to a performance.

He'd growl and run with his arms wide open to scare the shit out of the kids hiding, who were so panicked that their flashlights trembled in their hands and they couldn't even think of using them to stop him.

How many times had Ellie almost cried in fear as she waited to be tickled to even more tears? Sometimes she'd laughed so hard watching how terrified Finn and Oscar were. Their expressions had been the funniest thing in the world. Then, lured by the sounds of her laughter, Colin would change course to get her instead. Ellie never had the strength to stop laughing or even freeze him with a light beam to give herself a few seconds to run.

But the night Finn and Oscar had shown up at her house, the fear on their faces didn't make her laugh. It took the air out of her lungs. She hadn't taken another breath since, it seemed, judging by how much her chest hurt. How dimmed all the lights were. How everyone looked at her, as if waiting for the moment she'd draw breath again. Counting the seconds. How long had it been?

It happened during that first week of summer break. All the families always vacationed together in July, and the rest of the time there was one tournament or another, mainly for Colin because he did every kind of sport.

That first week was pretty much the only time the Fav Five had to do whatever they wanted. Ellie wanted to go bridge jumping in the river. They'd waited all their lives to be old enough. But the night before they'd planned to go, she'd found Colin smoking a joint on the roof of his house. She'd been so furious. She'd called him horrible names. The noise alerted their parents, and they both got grounded.

Ellie's parents didn't believe that she hadn't been smoking, too, so they took her phone away. Colin had been too scared to admit in front of their parents that it hadn't been his first time, either.

And she was furious at Colin for not clarifying things with her parents. Ellie's uncle Río had been in and out of rehab in Argentina, and Colin knew how his addiction had affected her family even though they were thousands of miles apart from him. Ellie knew pot wasn't the same as the drugs that had ruined her uncle's life. But she'd always promised her parents she wouldn't try it. And Colin knew that, too. He let her get grounded to save face with his parents.

The morning after their grounding, Maisy had whispered at her that her friends were still getting together by the river.

"But Colin's grounded," Ellie had said.

Maisy had smirked like a know-it-all and said, "He's sneaking out, duh . . ."

Ellie clenched her teeth and decided that she'd show her parents that she was to be trusted.

She didn't go. She waited for Maisy to bring back another message that they were coming to get her. Or that they had changed their minds. But the hours went on and there was no message.

And then Finn and Oscar had come to tell her in person. That they had all jumped together. Holding hands like dorks. They lost each other as a head collided with an elbow. Kicking feet. Cindy gagging because she'd swallowed water.

Ellie's hands pressed against her ears to block the sounds of the night.

Colin never came back up for air.

Back in the cornfield, Ellie couldn't breathe.

She didn't really remember what had happened after her parents drove her to the Jordan River. She just recalled flashes of the water rippling and the searchlights shining and then the sun coming up. And his parents crying. And four of the Fav Five standing on the edge of the river, holding hands, calling him, "Colin, Colin, Colin," but he was gone gone gone.

The search and rescue team found him later that day not too far from the bridge. His leg was tangled in some bramble. When they cut off the weeds, they also cut off the anklet—a red thread for good luck—that he'd worn since seventh grade.

Ellie didn't remember the funeral. She relived it in her skin.

Her mind had shut it out, but here crouched in the dark of the cornfield, it came back to her in flashes. His cousins singing his favorite song, "Lean on Me," because he'd been so dorky and cheesy. The table with all his achievements, medals, and trophies, his Eagle Scout shirt full of patches. The countless photos with the Fav Five.

And the whole time, Ellie wasn't breathing.

The moon finally peeked up over Timpanogos, and the silver light fell on the whole corn maze. Ellie could see the corn leaves were starting to darken and curl in the edges.

Summer was almost over.

She heard Cindy laughing, and the sound was so beautiful Ellie almost laughed, too, but she couldn't. She felt she was falling even though she was crouching on the ground.

She clasped her shirt as if she was holding on to something. She saw the flashing lights and heard her friends' voices.

The whole time, she imagined Colin was next to her showing her all the beauty around her. "Look at that worm!"

"Ew," she'd say.

And then he'd point out the perfection of the worm's body and make her laugh and give them away.

Now, months later in a world without Colin, Ellie grabbed the earth, needing to feel something solid between her hands.

Two beams of light swept through the corn. Oscar must have found someone.

Ellie had lost the thread of the game.

"I'm sorry," she said, her voice barely a whisper.

She imagined Colin sat next to her, his face soft and honest. "I'm okay," he said. "You're okay, Ellie. I love you I love you I love you."

"I'm sorry." The ties around her heart broke slowly. It hurt so much.

"Ellie, look at the light." He pointed ahead, puckering his lips.

"Ellie!" Cindy called, her voice trembling. The boys echoed her, "Ellie! Ellie!"

She had been okay, and now she was spiraling again.

The flashlight beams illuminated her friends, but this time, instead of turning away from them, she kept her eyes fixed on them. She wouldn't lose sight of them.

Their voices had switched from happy to frantic.

"We shouldn't have come!" Finn said, on the verge of crying.

"I should've stayed close to her," Cindy said.

"We shouldn't have come!" Oscar roared.

She wanted to ask for help. She wanted to tell them where she was, but she couldn't draw enough air to make a sound. She'd left her phone in the car because those were the rules of the game, but now she couldn't call for help.

Was this what Colin felt in the river?

She wished she could faint and wake up in her room, wrapped in her sweaty, stinky comforter.

But the moon was so pretty. She'd never imagined how perfect the sky looked from the edge of the cornfield.

And she loved her friends so much.

Next to her, Colin smirked. "You're undefeated, Ellie. Undefeated for always."

The expression of mischief on his face made her laugh. And when she took that one breath, her chest expanded to let her heart grow and take over the sorrow.

"I'm here! I'm here!" she gasped, making her legs hold her steadily.

They ran toward her, crashing through the drying corn leaves. Cindy stumbled, but she scrambled back up on her feet and kept running toward Ellie, who held the photo of them high in the air.

Oscar hugged her, and Finn patted her head as if he was trying to make sure she was okay.

"Are you okay, Ellie?" Oscar asked, his voice breaking through the roar the blood made in her ears.

Her friends surrounded her. Together they made a circle.

"What's that?" Cindy asked.

"From the time capsule," Ellie said. "Remember that day?"

"Our first Last Night," Oscar replied.

"The Fav Five forever," Finn said.

In each other's arms, they remembered and wept.

For Colin. For the last true summer night, the first one without him. For how beautiful everything was in the moonlight.

And when they had no more tears to cry, they laughed.

Because they were alive and together. But Colin wasn't, and it all felt wrong.

And then together they got back in the car, knowing that never again would they come here to play this game.

"Ice cones?" Ellie asked when Oscar turned the car on.

They all looked at each other and nodded.

Cindy smiled. "We'll never be too old for shaved ice."

When Oscar parked at her curb, their parents' cars long gone, he said, "Pick you up for school? Seven twenty?"

Ellie shrugged. "At least we'll be on time for once in our lives."

They smiled and Oscar drove off.

Ellie went through the back door. She expected everyone knew she'd left the house but didn't want to speak to her parents just yet.

She was startled when she saw Maisy sitting on the back-porch swing.

"Maise?" she said.

Her sister whipped her head around to look at her, and Ellie's breath caught in her throat again. But this time it wasn't because of shock or pain too big to process. Maisy was so beautiful.

"You went out after all," she said, her voice a little smug, as if she knew the part she'd played.

Ellie sat next to her sister on the swing and took her hand.

"Are you nervous about school tomorrow?"

Maisy shrugged. "Yes and no. I mean, it's school." Her words were dry, but her face was lit up with excitement for the future.

Ellie couldn't ignore that light inside her sister anymore. It had pulled her out of the darkness after all. It had brought her back to her friends.

"What's wrong?" Maisy asked, her cheeks flushing under Ellie's intense gaze.

"Everyone says middle school sucks, but it's not always true."

Maisy rolled her eyes, unbelieving.

"Seriously," Ellie said, shoving her playfully with her elbow. "That's when Cindy and I really became friends."

"Really?"

"Really."

"And Colin and Oscar and Finn?"

Ellie imagined talking about Colin would never be easy. But such a life had to be remembered. Celebrated. So she promised herself she'd tell Maisy about the Fav Five's most famous adventures even if it hurt.

Ellie laughed through her grief. She was happy she could still laugh.

She had tried to keep the darkness and shadows around her like a cloak. But the light always found its way in. And in the light, she saw so much beauty even in the things that would only live in her memories. Especially those things. Those memories.

Like Last Night with her friends.

Maisy had so many questions and opinions, about school, and life, and friends, and a lot of things Ellie didn't have an answer to. But it was good to wonder aloud, together.

NIGHT FALLS

Kika Hatzopoulou

YOU'RE SITTING ON THE FLOOR, YOUR TULLE SKIRT BLOOMING around you like a black dahlia, your bangs curling at your cheekbones like Medusa's baby snakes, and I'm pretty sure you're the murderer, but you look so cute I'm going to burst.

I tear my eyes away from you as Jamie clears his throat. The liquid light of the fireplace borders his figure, veiling his face in shadows. I can only see the white of his eyes and the flash of teeth as he speaks. He put on his most charming grin the moment Martina's cousin Fernanda walked in a couple of minutes ago—tall and long-necked, just his type. She's now sitting down with her drink, which is Jamie's cue to enter, center stage.

"I see there are newcomers, so I will rewind and set the scene one more time for you," Jamie says, winking at Fernanda, and then shamelessly goes on to mimic rewinding, arms flailing backward like a wind-up toy going berserk or a broken-down robot or a very bad slow-motion Zack Snyder film.

Pretty much everyone in the room is rolling their eyes, and a couple even take out their phones for doomscrolling, because we've all heard it before: when the game actually started an hour ago, or every Friday the past year, for us regulars.

"The game is called Mafia, the setting is this lovely town, the players the lovely youth around me." Jamie spreads his arms wide to show off his enormous living room and the twenty or so friends and classmates gathered in it. "In this game, we are each cast randomly in a role. Except myself, as you can probably tell. I serve as the game's narrator."

There's a scatter of applause, and Jamie bends at the waist. Fernanda is four years older than us, a college senior majoring in sociology, which is probably why she looks thoroughly unimpressed.

"Wow," you whisper, tilting your face up to me. "You weren't joking. It's the same speech as earlier, word for word. He really has the whole thing scripted."

"Oh, y-yes," I whisper back, momentarily distracted by your arm strewn across my legs. I'm in the armchair, you're on the floor next to me, and I never knew something as casual as *sitting* could make a person giddy. I vowed to be all chill and laid-back tonight ("No hyper shit," Sasha made me promise), and I was doing a good job at it until you slung that arm over my knees. Now I'm a puddle of nerves, a toneless earworm in my head: *Is that a move? Are you making a move? Are we here on a DATE?*

Be cool, Mara. I can do this. I can . . . (*big exhale*) . . . flirt.

I tilt my head and my hair cascades like a curtain between us and the rest of the room. Jamie's living room is gargantuan, compartmentalized into smaller sections by off-white sofas and a sleek matte-metal ceiling-hanging fireplace in the center of the space. The whole room looks straight out of a sci-fi movie, but it offers no privacy, which means I have to resort to creating my own by the classic hair-curtain technique.

"You don't understand," I whisper. "I know it by heart. Here, I'll show you. *This town used to be full of life.*"

"This town," Jamie says a few seconds later, "used to be full of life."

Your mouth drops open in delight.

My stomach lurches—that smile!—and now I must lean hard into the joke. I mouth Jamie's speech in tandem with him, exaggerating his expressions: "There were twenty-one of us. Each had a role in this town of ours: a sheriff, a mayor, a traitor, a doctor, several innocent townies, and, of course, the two murderers. We had our houses, our cars, our jobs. Our little slice of perfection. But evil struck. Two murderers have infiltrated our town and killed half its citizens." The dead players all around the room give Fernanda solemn waves or nods of the head. "Every Night round, the murderers sneak into our houses and kill one of us in their sleep. Every Day round, the survivors gather in city hall and vote to execute whoever they think is the murderer."

At that, Fernanda pauses her cup inches from her lips. "Who wins?"

I stop mouthing as Jamie steps away from the fireplace in the middle of the room. We can finally see his face clearly. His cheeks have gone red as Santa's. "Well," he answers, "the murderers win if all the townies die. And the town wins if the two murderers die."

"So who I am going to be?" Fernanda asks, eyeing Jamie over her tiny, tinted glasses. I've seen these new trendy glasses in ads, but never in real life. It feels like she's stepped straight out of the future.

You and I lock eyes, and your lips turn down into a *sheesh!* And you're absolutely right. This is absolutely a *sheesh* moment: the game is almost over. He can't add new players now. It's about to be deliciously awkward. I might not know if you're into me or if this is a date, but I do know you and I both enjoy a good, harmless piece of hot goss.

(That's how it all started: film buff busybodying. You saw me and Troy doing the *How-many-Spielberg-movies-can-you-name* challenge on my Stories and immediately DM'ed me wanting to know the winner [me]. You asked if anyone remembered *Hook* [we had not] because, as you wisely pointed out, everyone catalogues *Hook* as a Robin Williams movie and not a Spielberg movie. We stayed up way after midnight discussing which Spielberg movie our teachers would star in, which was delightful, and in the next few days, we moved on to anime suggestions and later to anime co-streaming.)

Jamie makes a valiant effort to save face: "Ah, this game is almost done. But you're welcome to join our, erm, next one."

Okay, time to save the poor guy. I inch forward on the armchair, very conscious of my bare stomach pressing onto the skin on your arm, and tell Fernanda, "There's only six players left now. The gist of it is: there are two townies, completely innocent little does, three other characters with questionable motives, and one murderer. We killed the other murderer a few rounds ago."

At this point, hands reach out to thump Tavin on the back, Jamie's unfortunate new friend from drama club who was the first murderer. In Mafia, the sheriff knows the identity of the first murderer before the game begins, which means the first murderer is pretty much guaranteed to die early. Poor Tavin got to play only three rounds before the town banded up against them. Tavin—newcomer, sophomore, wonderful tenor—was so intimidated that they kept rubbing their hands and sniffling their nose during the Night rounds. I've never seen a person embody Ball of Anxiety better than Tavin.

Fernanda responds to all these rules with a single matter-of-fact nod.

That's probably all we're getting from her, so I carry on. "We were just coming out of a Night round when you came in, where the murderer chooses their next victim while everyone else has their eyes closed. Now that it's 'Day'"—I air-quote it—"Jamie's about to announce who is dead. All good? There's always other games," I add, nodding toward the pool table.

She takes a slow sip of her drink, while her eyes seem to be cataloging the room: the remaining players on the sofa and armchairs, the basketball team standing by the kitchen counter, the drama club playing pool at the other end of the living room, Chen's boyfriend and their debate club friends sitting on the floor pillows by the glass porch doors, Sasha's dance group gals squashed on the sofa between Christopher and Troy. "Nah. I wanna see who dies."

It sounds incredibly ominous; you and I exchange an alarmed glance before I say, "Cool, cool. Stage is yours, Jamie."

He gives me a quick, scowling look and turns to address the room in his best mysterious narrator voice, acting out the scene in subtle but precise movements. "The night has felt endless to the residents of the town, but the dawn breaks over the horizon, dewing everything in pinks and oranges. Tentatively, the townies tiptoe to their front yards and look at each other. One is missing."

There is a collective super-long inhale from the crowd gathered around us. It's one of Jamie's superpowers: he knows how to put on a show. We're all sitting in a semicircle facing him, an amphitheater to his Greek tragedy. The coffee table at the center is strewn with red cups, bowls of snacks, and a black-and-gold deck of cards. They've got a horned figure on the back, all dark and menacing, which is just how Jamie likes it.

I got that deck for him in the beginning of the school year, when we opened up these gatherings to the public, so to speak. Jamie wanted to bond with his drama club mates, Sasha and Chen wanted to meet guys, Christopher and Troy wanted to meet girls, I wanted to play, and Martina just goes along with everything. We had been playing Mafia for a few years at that point (after randomly discovering it when googling "games to play with a deck of cards" during a blackout), and our old deck was a completely uninspired checkered pattern. When we opened the game up, Jamie had demanded *something with pizazz*, so pizazz I provided.

Jamie lowers his voice to a reverential lament. "His cold body is slumped in his favorite gaming chair, controller in his hands, earphones around his slit neck . . . Christopher Jameson is dead."

Christopher, all six feet seven of him, sprawls on the sofa in dramatic sputters of death. The girls from Sasha's dance group that he is squashing squeal in agitation. His girlfriend, Lili, sobs equally dramatically, reaching for him over the coffee table. A bowl of popcorn topples over, but it's all part of the show and we're so deep into this game that no one even cares. After four years of friendship—broken by a brief and ill-advised two months of dating last summer—I've learned this much is true about Jamie: drama is infectious. When you receive a much-coveted invitation to his Mafia parties, for example, you're expected to act accordingly.

I was so into that, you don't even know. The game, the atmosphere, the *murrrderrr.* If I got killed early in the game, you wouldn't catch me playing pool or fiddling with the Spotify playlist like others do. I stayed at the scene of the crime, watching players get eliminated, guessing at the murderer until the bloody end.

I always got it right.

(Listen, it's not boasting if it's factual truth.)

But now I'm not Jamie's girlfriend. Now I'm here with you, and this is supposed to be a date, and I'm not sure you know that.

I'm not even sure you know I'm bi.

This was a giant mistake, for which I've only got myself to blame, because what kind of fool invites the first girl she's ever dated—correction, is *trying* to date—to her ex-boyfriend's Mafia party?

At least it looks like you're having fun. Aside from the whole arm-dangling-over-my-legs thing (and let's put that way, way aside because I might *implode*), you've been chuckling all night, getting thoroughly invested in the game, and you haven't rolled your eyes once at Jamie's over-the-top storytelling choices.

You even ask, more than eagerly, "Who *was* he?"

Jamie gives you a thumbs-up and turns to Christopher. "There are six characters left in the game: the murderer, two townies, the sheriff, the mayor, and the traitor. Who did the murderer kill on this bloody, bloody night? Christopher, bro, show us your card."

Christopher obediently folds up from the asphyxiated dancers on the sofa and palms his card on the table, faceup. I can't help it, I lean in for a better look: king of spades.

The sheriff.

Uh-oh.

The two dozen people in the living room go into panic mode. On the arm of the sofa, Martina is squealing, both fists in her mouth. Over at the kitchen counter, the entirety of the basketball team (they died so early it's like the murderers had a vendetta) push each other around, drinks sloshing all over. Even Jamie looks mournful, brows tilted comically. Fernanda is bewildered at the chaos around her, like a lunch lady during a kindergarten food fight.

But I'm only watching you.

Your bottom lip is between your teeth and you're suppressing a smile so hard that your dimples look like they're being tortured. Can you sprain a face muscle? Because that's what's happening to your face right now and I need everyone to notice so I can convince them all you're the Murderer Capital M, but of course they're all busy lamenting the loss of our precious sheriff.

To hell with the sheriff!

Anyone who really knows how to play Mafia knows that the sheriff is only valuable until the first murderer is killed, and that was *eleven rounds ago*. Christopher didn't even need to convince the rest of the town that Tavin was the murderer—they shook like leaves every time there was a town vote.

The real danger here is you. Tavin was your lackey; you're the actual mastermind. Unlike most Mafia newbies, which you claim to be, you didn't waste your time figuring out the characters with "special" abilities, like the sheriff and the mayor. You focused entirely on the townies, which, granted, are easy to spot—look for the most bored, least invested players in the room—and nearly annihilated them in less than an hour. The only thing stopping you from winning the game is the last two remaining townies, poor souls!

And no one suspects you but me. I can't even blame them: as far as we know you've never played Mafia before; you've just moved back from Tokyo and you dress like it—girly and colorful "but make it fashion,"—you're unapologetically into *The Sims*, *Riverdale*, and girls, and your smile can outsparkle a unicorn.

And you've been playing the game so well. *Sooo weeell!* I swear I'm like 200 percent more attracted to you than before the night started.

"Let's vote!" I call out over the racket of twenty people talking murder, which is not the right move. Looking too eager to vote makes you a prime target to the murderer on the next Night. But to hell with it. There's not going to be another Night, because I'm going to convince them you're the murderer and I'm going to win.

(Why am I like this, you might wonder? I honestly don't know.)

A room of friends and classmates looks at me expectantly. Even Sasha, my best friend, who was killed off like an eon ago—smart move on your part, she was the life-saving doctor—glances up from her phone and gives me a look. A *go-girl* look. I am *really* good at this game and everyone here knows it.

"I'll go first," I say.

Christopher whispers, "Avenge me, Mara."

"I think Christopher was murdered by none other than Jiah Matthews over here." For good measure, I pat you lightly on the head.

You have the audacity to wear a very believable face of surprise, all arced brows and round (extremely kissable) lips. "*Me?* I've been lucky to survive this long, now you want to vote me out?"

"You realized Christopher was the sheriff after we voted out Tavin and he boasted, 'We get things done in this town.'"

"Everyone realized!" you argue.

"True," Christopher interjects, putting up his twists in a high bun. "That's on me."

("Shush," says Martina. "Haven't you heard, *dead men tell no tales*?")

"*But*," I stress, "you didn't kill him for several rounds, because he was convinced poor Amirah was the second murderer and kept trying to get the town to vote for her. The moment he succeeded—"

("Sorry, Amirah.")

("For god's sake, stop talking, Christopher.")

"—you threw him out of the game."

You furrow your brows—thick, spectacular things—up at me and remove your arm from my legs. (*Noooo.*) "Maybe you're the murderer, Mara Angelakis. Maybe you want *me* out of the game, because there's only *two* things, *two* players, stopping you from winning." With each stressed word, you stick your finger in my face.

Your strained dimples are still there, and—*oh my god, you're such a good liar!*

I love it.

Honestly, I'm fighting hard against the urge to grab your face and kiss you right on the lips, here in front of everyone. Accusing your accuser is a classic Mafia move, but implying you're the precious, innocent townie whose death would mean everyone else loses, too? That's *chef's kiss*.

I want to glance at Sasha, who's no doubt wearing an *oh-she-got-you* face, but everyone's watching and I can't let them see the master player befuddled.

Thank god, Chen, who's one of the five players left alive, snorts and says, "For your information, new girl: Mara's brutal." (He pronounces it: BROO-TAL.) "If she was the murderer, this game would be done ages ago. Nah, I think Troy is the murderer. I heard him moving during the Night round."

I heard him moving is the weakest, puniest, most pathetic of Mafia arguments, because yes, if you hear someone moving during the Night round, it might mean they're the murderer pointing out their next victim to the narrator, but it might also mean someone's fidgety. A no-movement, no-sound mandate will do that to the calmest person. But I keep my mouth shut. Who am I to complain when the attention of the whole room has been blessedly steered away from me?

Georgia is nodding emphatically. She's not supposed to do that, none of the dead players can influence the game in any way, but this is such a high-stakes round that people *can't* not interfere.

"Guys, I *have* to move," Troy says, "I've got allergies." He points at the tissues gathered like a mountain of snowballs in his lap.

Georgia and Chen, sitting at either side of him, groan "Dude!" and lean away.

"But I vote for Mara, too," says Troy. "She's looking anxious tonight."

That's a low blow and he knows it. Of course I'm nervous,

I'm here on a date with a girl who's out of my league ("Only a little," Sasha said, because god forbid she minces her words) and who probably doesn't even know I'm bi. Besides Sasha, Troy's the only one in our friend group who I texted about bringing you to tonight's game night.

And now he's smirking knowingly at me, the doofus.

"Martina?" asks Jamie.

Martina, the turncoat, gives me a little look before saying, "Mara."

"Three votes for Mara, one for Troy, one for Jiah," Jamie says.

Well, dang!

"Wait," you say. "I didn't vote for Mara. I said it *might* be Mara."

I tuck my legs under me to stop them from bouncing. What are you doing? With me out, you've won the game. These guys are going to vote out Troy next round, who I'm pretty sure is the mayor (a good role, you can make your vote count for two during one round in the game), and you're going to sail to victory as smoothly as a bar of soap in a wet bathtub.

Jamie seems puzzled. "Who are you voting for, then?"

"Troy," you say nonchalantly, like you're naming a capital of Europe in a trivia quiz and not upending this entire round.

The whole room turns to me. I have to change my vote and break the tie, and of course I'm voting: "Troy. Sorry, dude."

Drama ensues, right on cue. Troy clenches his heart in betrayal and slips off the sofa, taking his gross snowballs down with him. Some of our audience cheer, others shake their heads. Someone yells, "Card!" and from his deathbed behind the coffee table, Troy lifts his card in the air.

Ace of cups. The traitor.

Ha! Bad move, Jiah! Very bad. The traitor knows who the murderers are and tries to assist them in the voting during Day rounds—a win for them means a win for him. But the murderer doesn't know the identity of the traitor, which can often result in these unfortunate killings, boohoo for him, but yay for me. I'm in the clear, and that's all that matters!

Okay, that didn't sound nice. I need to calm myself down.

I can't let this unravel into another Paintball Incident.

I very carefully show no reaction, lest these fools think I'm the murderer.

Hmm, I've got to recalibrate. I was sure Troy was the mayor. He played with his phone during this whole game and looked up only when we started counting votes. I assumed his solitary interest in voting was because he was trying to figure out when to use his double vote, but maybe he was just basking in the glory of the murderer's killing spree?

If Troy is the traitor, that means that we've got two townies, the mayor, and the murderer left. I'm 99.9 percent sure you're the murderer, and I know what *I* am. But which character is Chen? Which is Martina? Who are you going to kill next? And, more importantly, why did you let me live?

Wish me luck, because I'm going to try to fish it out of you.

"Why didn't you vote for me?" I blurt. It comes out way too loud.

Thank god, everyone else is discussing Troy's identity, and no one witnesses the small humiliation of you jerking wildly at my whispered scream. Still, you regain your stealthy smirk quickly and say, "Should I have?"

"You tell me. I'm supposed to be the murderer, right? Why let me live?"

You shrug and pucker your lips—playfully, I think—while your fingers are running over the plumes of your skirt, like an avant-garde Marie Antoinette.

I scowl down at you. "What are you planning, you evil, devious, plotting . . . plotter?"

("Nice one," Sasha deadpans from the sofa, without raising her eyes from her phone.)

You laugh at Sasha's sarcasm and mimic sealing your lips to me.

A horrific exasperated groan escapes my lips.

It only makes you laugh harder. You smack my knees (you do a lot of smacking, which is weird but also weirdly cute) and say, "Oh my god, this is *Animal Crossing* all over again. Why can't you just take the victory? Why do you need to know the why behind it all?"

Sasha lowers her phone. "How on earth did you manage to make *Animal Crossing* competitive, Mara?"

I open my mouth to answer—probably something

humdrum along the lines of *You're not part of this conversation, Sasha* or *Mind your business, Sasha*—but you're faster.

"It was actually pretty fun," you say. "We set a time limit and we had to—"

Sasha lets out a nasal *Nah-uh*, cutting you off.

As if on cue, Jamie calls out to us, "Hey, less talking, more dying over there."

You scrunch up your lips to the side and whisper comically: "Your friends are intimidating."

It isn't the first time you've said this. Instantly, I am hyperventilating, and a pure vomit of words comes out of my mouth, with no coherence whatsoever. "Do you wanna go— We can go if you want— I don't even like them that much— Let's get out of here."

I'm not kidding in the least, because right now it feels like bringing you here was the worst mistake of my life, but your grin is wide and mischievous.

"Absolutely not," you reply. Your eyes are narrowed and you jab a ring-clad finger in my face. "You're not tricking me into quitting, Mara Angelakis. Who's the plotting plotter now?"

Sasha butts in to offer you a high five.

It is decided: Sasha is no longer my best friend.

Jamie throws us all a glare and says, "Only four citizens left in our town: Mara, Jiah, Chen, and Martina. One of them is the killer, the other three need to root them out to win. Brace yourselves, sweetest friends, because . . . NIGHT FALLS."

Night falls is Jamie's biggest move, the reason he is King of Mafia and his house is the Town of Doom. He claps his hands, and boom, all lights in the living room go out. The hanging fireplace blazes in the center, outlining Jamie like a god of flames. Our silhouettes elongate on the walls, birthing many-armed leviathans. Light catches on the bangles on my arm, and I suddenly realize how close our hands are where they're chilling on the arm of my chair. Our fingers are almost touching—

Oh, to hell with it.

I muster up all the courage in my brash, willy-nilly heart and graze my thumb across the skin at your wrist. You don't snatch your hand back (*phew*), but you do look up at me. The fire leaves rosebud kisses on your cheekbones and neck. Flames reflect in the black of your eyes, and your dimples have disappeared.

Are you nervous? You look nervous, or maybe . . . uncomfortable? God, am *I* making you uncomfortable? I've gone and done it now. It's the Paintball Incident all over again: I overzealously try to flirt in my typical tactic of *crushing this game*, with disastrous consequences. My first girl crush ends up with thirteen bruises and never talks to me again, and I end up crying the whole car ride home with Dad, which leads to a surprisingly-tender-but-still-utterly-humiliating coming-out-to-my-parents moment. Scarred for life is an understatement.

"Players, close your eyes," Jamie commands. "The time of judgment has come."

It takes you and me a moment longer than the others to obey.

Shadows coil across my closed eyelids. I listen for your movements, for any clue that you're as nervous as I am, but all I can hear is my own heartbeat. *Thud, thud, thud.* Have I made a mistake? Did you think this was a friendly get-together? But even if you did, friends touch each other, don't they? Sasha plays with my hair absentmindedly *all* the time. I can play this off as a friendly touch, I tell myself. I will *not* let this escalate to Paintball Incident levels. I will *CHILL* and I will be your normal, absolutely not crushing friend.

"Got it," Jamie says to whoever is the murderer. He claps his hands twice and the lights come on. "Day arrives. It's a bleak morning, cloudy and cold. The citizens of the town rush to the street. One of them is missing. During the Night, the murderer visited their newest victim and—"

Jamie's phone buzzes loudly in his pocket.

He looks at the name on the screen, his face splitting into a grin. He's moving before the rest of us even realize what's happening, and gives us a simple, glib "Martina's dead" over his shoulder before he slides out the doors to the back porch.

We all stare at each other. If this moment had a subtitle it would be *What the . . .* This is probably the first time anyone here has seen Jamie, Lord of Murder, Host King Extraordinaire, interrupt a game. Even his basketball buddies, who've known him since he was ten, are gawking at his figure through the glass, as he paces up and down the back porch.

"Wait," Martina complains. "I'm dead?"

We all nod in unison, apologetically.

"Fine." Martina flips her card over on the table and stalks out of the living room. (A sore loser, our Martina.) Her cousin, I notice, doesn't follow her. Instead, Fernanda lifts her chin to peek at the card. A simple seven of spades. A townie.

A wave of whispers vibrates through the room like a low-scale earthquake. It's one of the most suspenseful games we've ever played. First of all, it is full of twists—like the one you just pulled! Secondly, everyone is so invested, even the dead players (well, Sasha excluded) are watching. And lastly, it's still unclear who the murderer is (to everyone but me).

I can see the uncertainty, the doubt on everyone's scowling faces . . . Who is the murderer? Three players left: me, you, and Chen. Three characters left: the murderer, the mayor, and the townie. It will all come down to this Day round and the vote: If we vote out the murderer, the Town wins. If we vote out the townie, the murderers win. And if we vote out the mayor, it's a win for the murderer, because they will kill the townie on the next Night round.

This is my moment to strike—swiftly and precisely, right to their gullible hearts—but the absence of our Mafia authority (aka Jamie, out there on the porch), is making our group break up, talking in close circles, heading for the fridge or the bathroom. I need Jamie back in the room.

I catch Troy's gaze, make a quizzical phone-call-pacing-on-the-porch pantomime, and he answers with a silent *Stacey*.

"Ah, Stacey," says Sasha, who never, and I mean *ever*, misses a thing.

"Who's Stacey?" you ask, true to your gossipmonger heart.

"Jamie's first crush," I explain pointedly, glaring daggers at Sasha for bringing this to your attention. It was Sasha and Troy's favorite subject while I dated Jamie: Stacey from Philadelphia, and how often Jamie talked to her on the phone. I honestly didn't care about her, which I guess is pretty indicative of how *not* into Jamie I was. "The quintessential One That Got Away."

"Mara's archnemesis—" Sasha starts saying. Then she seems to realize who exactly her audience is. Her eyes drop to you and her jaws close with a comically audible *snap!* She chuckles uncomfortably and tries to save it with a drab "Never mind."

Too late, Sasha. Best friend card: rescinded and cut up into pieces before her very eyes.

You're peeking up at me through your feral bangs. "So, um," you mumble, "you and Jamie dated?"

"Like, for a second," I answer quickly. "We've been in the same friend group forever. Last summer we were the only two left in town and things happened, but it only lasted like two months. We just didn't work together, and it was never awkward to hang out afterward."

Oh, no. I'm getting hyper. And everything will sound like a lie, even though it isn't. Everyone knows Jamie and I dated—there's photos of us cuddling in group pics all over social media—but did I just send you the wrong message? That I'm straight and possibly not over my ex? This is such a disaster.

"It was such a conscious uncoupling even Gwyneth would be impressed," Sasha butts in, bless her soul. In a conspiratorial whisper, she adds, "There was *zero* chemistry."

(Okay, Sasha can have her card back.)

I'm nodding way too emphatically. When the loneliness variable was removed, there was absolutely nothing romantic between us. "Like, subzero," I say. "Glacial. Arctic. Siberian."

This is too much! I need to stop!

You say a simple "Okay."

I exchange a worried glance with Sasha over your head.

I've got to fix this. It's as good an opening as I'm going to get. *Yes, I dated Jamie, and yes, I'm into guys, but I'm also into girls.* Or *I'm over him and I'm into you.* Or a simple *I'm bi.* So why can't I say it? Why is it so hard, and tiring, and boring, to come out to every new person I meet? I've got my rainbow flag on my Insta profile, isn't that enough? Does it have to be actual words to actual girls I have an actual crush on?

I'm about say something when you stand up abruptly, your tulle skirt puffing out like a jellyfish in motion. You say, clipped, "Where's the bathroom?"

I blurt out, "Why? Are you making a run for it, *muuurdereeer?*"

You just look at me. I swear I can see the gears in your head swinging toward: *Nope. No, thank you.*

Sasha points up the stairs.

I watch silently as you weave through the kids in the room and disappear down the corridor. I slump back into the armchair, my cropped sweater rising almost to my bra. I wore my sexy bra and my croppiest sweater—god, I was optimistic. I cross my arms over my chest and wait for what I know is coming: a stirring Sasha lecture.

"Three months," she deadpans. "Three months we've spent, obsessing over every like and DM, analyzing every movie and book recommendation. We devise a dozen perfect asking-out plans, and *this* is what you go with? Playing Mafia at your ex's party?"

"We were streaming *Booksmart* and remember that murder mystery dinner? I mentioned Jamie's Mafia parties and she got super excited and . . . I thought . . ." I trail off under Sasha's scathing look.

"You thought trying to convince our whole class to execute her just screams romance?"

"Well—"

"Don't say it."

"—it *is* kind of sexy."

Sasha groans.

A smile pops on my lips, but it fades fast as I remember your face when I touched your wrist, when I talked about

Jamie, when I made the ill-advised running-away joke. I have messed this up, royally. Paintball Incident Number Two: Mafia Edition.

"Okay, I'm going to try to put it gently." Sasha says. "You like winning. I get it, we all do. But if you like winning more than you like playing, that's a problem. It's part of the reason why you and Jamie never took off. You had to win at everything."

(Not true: I had to win in the things I was better at, which is hardly my fault!)

"This is a moment of growth for you," Sasha continues, looking pleased with herself. "You want to have a chance with this girl? You've got to let her win."

I can't even be angry. A moment of growth? That's a good line.

I pull my hood over my head, hiding from Sasha's *you-know-I'm-right* look. I could, theoretically, let you win. I can imagine it: everyone in the room will start whistling and *stab-stab-stabbing* the air, and you will be crowned Lady of Murder for the rest of the night. I doubt you need longer than that to charm everyone's socks off, so by weekend's end you won't be the new girl anymore, but one of *us*. You'll get invited to next Friday's Mafia party, and the one after that, and I will have time to flirt with you at my own, snail-like pace.

I can let you win.

Dammit. I'm gonna have to let you win. I'm going to have

to drop my paintball gun and let you shoot me right in the face.

I barely have time to wallow for a few seconds before Jamie marches back in, a grin plastered on his face, calling everyone to attention. "Gather around, people! We've got a murderer to catch!"

As our friends waltz back from the kitchen and bathroom, Jamie sits on the arm of my chair and bumps me on the shoulder. "What's up, Angelakis?" With his chin, he gestures behind him to the corridor, where I'm guessing you're coming back from the bathroom. "Is that film buff girl?" he whispers.

"Mhm," I grind out through my nose.

(Yes, I told him about you. Yes, we're one of those disgustingly tight-knit groups of friends.)

"Good for you," he says. "Finally, a match."

It's a weird thing to say, which makes me glance up at him. But he isn't looking at me. He's looking at you. You're coming down the corridor, your skirt billowing around your calves like black wings, your combat books stomping the marble in a perfect catwalk, and your face—you're smirking. Dimples out, full blast power. One of your eyebrows is arched, and your eyes are nailed on me as you make a beeline through the room and stop in front of me. Jamie doesn't even have time to officially start the Day round before you say, "I vote for Mara Angelakis."

I say nothing. You've claimed the stage; the least I can do is let you have your moment. Besides, I am curious. You looked upset when you left, but you came back bathed in—dare I say—*homicidal* glory.

"Troy voted for you, he's dead," you say to me. "Martina voted for you, she's dead. You've taken your vengeance silently, in the Night, but now it's Day. Now the sun shines. Now it's *our* time. You're the murderer, and all this death stops today."

My mouth is open, half gaping, half smiling.

You didn't just take the stage—you *destroyed* it.

This is a top-notch performance, the kind we all aspire to when we come to these parties. This is drama of the highest quality. Everyone's impressed, and more importantly, everyone is convinced, and I'm for sure going to lose this game, but *I am so happy.*

I don't need to let you win.

I don't need to drop my gun and take a paintball bullet to the face.

I don't even need to rein it in. This, right here, legs bouncing, drinking in the gory theatrics, jumping out of my seat to look at character cards, watching every player like a hawk, delighted when I guess right, is Pure, Unrestricted Mara.

And you seem to like it.

You seem to . . . *match* it.

Your smile is an invitation. Your raised brow is a challenge.

Everyone around us is going nuts, accusations and counterarguments flying left and right. I don't break our gaze or drop my smile. I should say something to defend myself, but it feels futile, and anyway, I'm dizzy with anticipation, my chest shaking with escaped chuckles.

Distantly, I hear Jamie call for Chen's vote. He says my name. I lift my card up for them and bask in their terror: I'm the last townie, and you've just convinced everyone to kill me—you have outsmarted us all and ended the game bathed in glory. The group goes wild, half of the room showering me with condolences, the other half crowning you the new Queen of Mafia. ("BROO-TAL!" hoots Chen.)

Your smirk finally cracks into a brilliant grin. You giggle and your shoulders rise almost to your ears under everyone's scrutiny. Then in one delicious, smooth movement, you slip down into my lap, arm slung around my neck, and bury us both in the black tulle of your skirt.

"Let's go again," you say, but you're only looking at me, no one else, and I'm finally sure this is, in fact, a date.

ABOUT THE AUTHORS

Sona Charaipotra is the author of the YA rom-com *Symptoms of a Heartbreak* and co-author of the Tiny Pretty Things duology (a Netflix original TV series) and *The Rumor Game*. Her next YA contemporary, *How Maya Got Fierce*, draws on her years as an entertainment journalist at *People*, *Teen People* (RIP), and other magazines. She has profiled your favorite celebrities for publications from The *New York Times* to *Cosmopolitan* and was editor of the Barnes & Noble teen blog, where she interviewed beloved authors, too. Sona earned her master's in screenwriting from NYU and an MFA in creative writing from the New School. She is a former We Need Diverse Books board member and co-founder of CAKE Literary, a boutique book packager focused on high-concept diverse titles. If her writing makes you crave Indian food, you can find her on the web sharing recipes and talking about chai, Bollywood movies, and books.

Sona's favorite game is Monopoly because she wants to rule the world—or at least own a beach house down the Jersey shore.

Amanda Joy is an author and currently lives in Chicago. She earned her MFA in writing for children from the New School. She is the author of *A River of Royal Blood*, a Junior Library Guild Selection, and *A Queen of Gilded Horns*. You can find Amanda touring the city's best coffee shops, going on long drives with her dog, Luna, and online @amandajoywrites.

Amanda's favorite game is bid whist, which she learned by sitting under tables, listening to her family call out bids and slap down cards.

Katie Cotugno is the *New York Times* bestselling author of seven messy, complicated feminist YA love stories, including *99 Days*, *How to Love*, *Fireworks*, *Top Ten*, *9 Days & 9 Nights*, *You Say It First*, and *Liar's Beach* (coming in 2022), as well as a forthcoming adult novel, *Birds of California*. She is also the co-author, with Candace Bushnell, of *Rules for Being a Girl*. Her books have been honored by the Junior Library Guild, the Bank Street Children's Book Committee, and the Kentucky Association of School Librarians, among others, and translated into more than fifteen languages. Katie is a Pushcart Prize nominee whose work has appeared in *The Iowa Review*, *The Mississippi Review*, and *Argestes*, as well as many other literary magazines. Katie studied writing, literature, and publishing at Emerson College and received her MFA in fiction at Lesley University.

Katie lives in Boston with her family, who will tell you that she is occasionally a sore winner at Scrabble.

Gloria Chao is the critically acclaimed author of *American Panda*, *Our Wayward Fate*, and *Rent a Boyfriend*. After a brief detour as a dentist, she is now grateful to spend her days in fictional characters' heads instead of real people's mouths. Her award-winning books have been featured on the Indie Next List and the "Best of" lists of *Seventeen*, Bustle, Barnes & Noble, PopSugar, *Paste*, Chicago Public Library, and more. Visit her tea-and-book-filled world at GloriaChao.wordpress.com, and find her on Twitter and Instagram @GloriacChao.

Gloria is an avid curler, loves puzzles like the ones from Mystery Hunt, and enjoys board games like Parks, Takenoko, and Forbidden Island.

Nina Moreno's first novel, *Don't Date Rosa Santos*, is available now from Little, Brown Books for Young Readers and was a Junior Library Guild Selection, Indie Next pick for teen readers, and SIBA Okra Pick. Her next YA novel, *Our Way Back to Always*, and the illustrated middle grade *Join the Club, Maggie Diaz* will be available Spring 2022 from Scholastic.

Nina's first love is Garrus Vakarian and her entire *Mass Effect* squad, but she's been known to spend many seasons on her *Stardew Valley* farm and is still in debt to Tom Nook.

Isaac Fitzsimons is the author of *The Passing Playbook*. A lifetime dabbler in the arts, his background includes performing sketch comedy in college, learning how to play three songs on the banjo, and, of course, writing. He currently lives outside Washington, DC, and works in arts advocacy. You can connect with Isaac on Twitter @isaacfitzy, Instagram @isaacfitzbooks, and through his website IsaacFitzBooks.com.

Isaac loves soccer, but unlike the characters he writes, Isaac is more adept at watching sports than playing them.

Anna Meriano is the author of *This Is How We Fly*, *It Sounds Like This*, and the Love Sugar Magic series. Her work has received starred reviews from *Kirkus Reviews*, *School Library Journal*, and *Shelf Awareness*. She graduated from Rice University with a degree in English and earned her MFA in writing for children from the New School. Anna works as a writing tutor in her hometown of Houston, Texas. You can find her online at annameriano.com.

Anna is a player for the Houston Cosmos, a local soccer team . . . Just kidding. Anna really does play quidditch, an all-gender, full-contact sport that she joined in college and is only occasionally ashamed of.

Kayla Whaley is a fiction and nonfiction writer living outside Atlanta, Georgia. Her work has appeared in numerous anthologies including *Unbroken*, *Vampires Never Get Old*, *Up All Night*, and *Allies*, as well as in publications like Bustle, *Catapult*, and *Michigan Quarterly Review*. She holds an MFA in creative nonfiction from the University of Tampa, and is a graduate of the Clarion Writers' Workshop.

Kayla grew up on the SNES and N64, and she still loves video games of all kinds, from *Dark Souls* to *Stardew* and everything in between.

Shaun David Hutchinson is the author of numerous books for young adults, including *A Complicated Love Story Set in Space*, *The Past and Other Things That Should Stay Buried*, *The Apocalypse of Elena Mendoza*, *At the Edge of the Universe*, and *We Are the Ants*. He also edited the anthologies *Violent Ends* and *Feral Youth* and wrote the memoir *Brave Face*, which chronicles his struggles with depression and coming out during his teenage years. He currently lives in Seattle. Visit him at shaundavidhutchinson.com.

Shaun is a *Beat Saber* addict. Slicing virtual blocks with a light saber set to music is what got him through the year of isolation, no matter how silly he looks while doing it.

Francesca Zappia lives in Indiana and graduated from the University of Indianapolis with a degree in computer science and mathematics. She was chosen as the 2017 Emerging Author at the Indiana Authors Awards, and her second novel, *Eliza and Her Monsters*, was chosen as a *Kirkus Reviews* Best Teen Book of 2017, a Junior Library Guild Selection, and was among the Top 10 of the YALSA 2018 Best Fiction for Young Adults list. She is also the author of *Made You Up*, *Now Entering Addamsville*, the online serialized story *The Children of Hypnos*, and a short story in the *Up All Night* anthology. You can find her on Twitter and Instagram @ChessieZappia, and on her website, francescazappia.com.

Francesca loves sports, video games, and board games, but her favorite game of all is probably *Minesweeper*. Yes, that one on the computer, with the numbers. What a classic.

Laura Silverman is an author and freelance editor and currently lives in Brooklyn, New York. She earned her MFA in writing for children at the New School. Her books include *Girl Out of Water*, *You Asked for Perfect*, *It's a Whole Spiel*, *Recommended for You*, and *Up All Night*. *Girl Out of Water* was a Junior Library Guild Selection, and *You Asked for Perfect* was named to best teen fiction lists by YALSA, Chicago Public Library, and the Georgia Center for the Book. You can contact Laura on Twitter @LJSilverman1 or through her website LauraSilvermanWrites.com.

Laura fell in love with chess after watching *The Queen's Gambit* and hopes to be half-decent at it one day.

Kathleen Glasgow is the *New York Times* bestselling author of *Girl in Pieces*, *How to Make Friends with the Dark*, and *You'd Be Home Now*. You can contact Kathleen on Twitter @kathglasgow, on Instagram @misskathleenglasgow, and on TikTok @kathleenglasgow, or on her website kathleenglasgowbooks.com.

Kathleen's favorite game is hide-and-seek because you never know who (or what) you might find when you start looking . . .

Kimberly Jones is a young adult author known for co-authoring the books *Why We Fly* and *I'm Not Dying with You Tonight* and for the viral video "How Can We Win" published during the George Floyd protests. She also has an overall deal with Warner Bros. TV and is the proud mother of a gifted teen.

Kimberly loves *Homescapes*, which allows her to drown out the world for some much-needed peace of mind.

Gilly Segal grew up in Florida, spent her college years in Israel, and now calls Atlanta, Georgia, home. She is the chief legal officer for an advertising agency, as well as a co-author of *Why We Fly* and the *New York Times* bestselling, NAACP Image Award–nominated *I'm Not Dying with You Tonight*. When not writing, Gilly enjoys exploring Decatur with her three kids and sampling flavors of French macarons. Find her on Instagram @really.gilly.

Gilly's favorite game is hockey, and she can be found cheering on the Tampa Bay Lightning and her son's peewee team with equal fervor.

Yamile Saied Méndez is the author of many books for young readers, including *Furia*, a Reese's YA Book Club selection and the 2021 inaugural Pura Belpré Young Adult Gold Medalist. She was born and raised in Rosario, Argentina, but has lived most of her life in Utah with her family. An inaugural Walter Dean Myers Grant recipient, she is also a graduate of the Vermont College of Fine Arts. Connect with her at yamilesmendez.com.

Yamile loves soccer and playing *TENS!* with her friends.

Kika Hatzopoulou writes stories for all ages, filled with lore and whimsy. She grew up in Thessaloniki, Greece, and earned her MFA at the New School. She currently works for the Greek publishing house Patakis and is hard at work on her first novel, about murder, the Greek Fates, and the complicated bonds of sisterhood. You can find her @Kikawrites.

Kika loves Settlers of Catan and the Greek card game called Biriba.

ACKNOWLEDGMENTS

Mom and Dad, thank you for always supporting and loving me. I'm so lucky to have you both. Mom, thank you for our countless games of Scrabble (it's so exciting when I beat you) and our countless games of Boggle (it's so exciting when you beat me). Dad, thank you for begrudgingly playing games when we are with our family. You're actually pretty good at 20 Questions.

Contributors, thank you for writing these brilliant stories. From laughter to tears, you all brought magic to this collection. It was a true pleasure to work with all of you, and I'm grateful for every single word you placed on the page.

Jim McCarthy, thank you for being my anchor in publishing. I'm amazed by all of the books we've already brought into the world. Here's to many more!

Kelsey Murphy, thank you for both your kindness and your incredible insights. You've been a fantastic editor. I've genuinely enjoyed every moment of working together, and I hope to work together again one day.

Stephanie Singleton, thank you for your gorgeous cover design. Your art perfectly captures the energy of this anthology, and I always smile when I see it. Maria Fazio, thank you for your beautiful jacket design.

Penguin, thank you to everyone who has worked hard to put this book together. Thank you to Tessa Meischeid, Krista Ahlberg, Abigail Powers, Sola Akinlana, Madeline Newquist, Vivian Kirklin, Ellice Lee, Marcia Wong, and the many others who have brought *Game On* to life.

My friends and family, thank you for your love and your support. Writing a book isn't easy, and I'm thankful I don't have to do it alone. Thank you to: Bubbie, Papa Bobby, Kayla Burson, Kiki Chatzopoulou, Alison Doherty, Brittany Kane, Deborah Kim, Katie King, Alex Kuntz, Elise LaPlante, Katherine Menezes, Anna Meriano, Lauren Sandler Rose, Ariel Russ, Melissa Sandler, Amanda Saulsberry, Lauren Vassallo, and Kayla Whaley.

Readers, teachers, librarians, and booksellers, thank you for all you do to support books. You are the pillars of our community, and I'm so grateful for all of you.

Avid gamers, from video games to sports to chess, thank you for your enthusiasm and intelligence and skill. I've loved games my entire life—from Scrabble tournaments with my mom to Catan with my best friends to video games getting